Jayne Beacham has been in love with books since childhood.
Here's the Thing is her first published novel in a trilogy, all following the journey of Evie Wallace.
Jayne lives in Somerset and is now writing full time.
She is currently working on her fourth novel, set in southern Ireland.

In memory of Rupert, my very own Henry.

A huge personality, sadly missed every day.

Jayne Beacham

HERE'S THE THING

AUSTIN MACAULEY
PUBLISHERS LTD.

Copyright © Jayne Beacham (2017)

The right of Jayne Beacham to be identified as author of this work has been asserted by her in accordance with section 77 and 78 of the Copyright, Designs and Patents Act 1988.

All rights reserved. No part of this publication may be reproduced, stored in a retrieval system, or transmitted in any form or by any means, electronic, mechanical, photocopying, recording, or otherwise, without the prior permission of the publishers.

Any person who commits any unauthorized act in relation to this publication may be liable to criminal prosecution and civil claims for damages.

A CIP catalogue record for this title is available from the British Library.

ISBN 9781786125637 (Paperback)
ISBN 9781786125644 (Hardback)
ISBN 9781786125651 (eBook)

www.austinmacauley.com

First Published (2017)
Austin Macauley Publishers Ltd.
25 Canada Square
Canary Wharf
London
E14 5LQ

Acknowledgements

With thanks to Hayley Knight, Walter Stephenson and Liz McCann at Austin Macauley. Dr Tristan Elkin for all things medical, Colin Fricker and Ben Chant for fitness advice, Dean Porritt for providing information on the Armed Forces and Jack at Silverstone racetrack for an incredible driving experience.

Robin, my mother, and dear friends Rowena, Steph, Sarah and Liz.

Chapter 1

Evelyn was so mad she thought she might combust on the spot, she wanted to scream so loudly and not stop. Why were all the guys she dated utter dickheads, nutjobs and fuckwits – why? Slamming the locker door shut she stormed out through the gym reception. Luckily Stacey was busy with a client as she was in no mood to speak to anyone. Stepping outside she felt the warm sunshine on her face and broke into a slow jog to her car. She heard her name being called; but she wasn't stopping for anyone – not today. Once inside her car she realised she'd been holding her breath and sighed with relief, deliberately ignoring Jack's attempt to try and catch her attention.

Ten minutes later she manoeuvred her car into a space by the posh supermarket and went over to the ticket machine. Ticket on the windscreen, she started to walk across to the store when something caught her eye and stopped her in her tracks. My – oh – my – she was beautiful. Pausing in front, she crossed her arms, tilted her head slightly and gave it an appreciative stare. Yes she was beautiful alright, a shiny dark grey coupe with leather seats. She really missed her sports car, not all of the time but on a day like today it would have been fantastic just to drive and escape all the crap of the morning. Evie walked around it being careful not to touch; it was so beautiful, powerful and drop-dead gorgeous. She bent down to peek into the cabin. Oh yes, this was just what she remembered.

Jonathan Dempsey was on his way back to his car when he spotted her. She was dressed in workout gear so he guessed she'd probably come straight from the gym. The girl had a swinging ponytail of dark brown wavy hair which was really shiny and she had a great figure. He couldn't see her eyes as she was wearing her sunglasses; but he slowed down, curious to see what she was doing. She wasn't going to try to steal it, that much was obvious, but the way she looked at the car as if she knew it somehow, intrigued him even more. When she bent down he noticed she had a great bum, no doubt due to all that exercise and felt his thighs twitch – *Oh get a grip!* he told himself, *you're not a teenager.* He watched her sigh and turn away towards the entrance to the supermarket and without thinking or pausing he followed her inside.

Evelyn picked up a basket. Now what did she want to eat? something lovely to make up for her shitty morning. Pushing her sunnies onto the top of her head she carefully chose an avocado, squeezing and discarding any not ripe enough for today. Two oranges and a bag of salad followed, she then doubled back and chose some raspberries and blueberries. Making her way towards the back of the store she couldn't help overhearing a retired couple asking the produce boy how they could tell if a watermelon was ripe. The poor boy looked totally lost and before she could stop herself she'd joined in the conversation. Jonathan watched her take the melon and knock it with her knuckles and they all laughed. She had a great laugh and he wanted to see her eyes close up. She disappeared around the corner and he tried to follow; but was delayed by the sheer number of shoppers. The gods must have been shining on him though, for as he peered down the first aisle he saw her deep in conversation with Fiona. And that meant only one thing, that Fiona's husband David wasn't too far away probably in the wine section. This was good, he could force an introduction and his mood lifted. Striding over to the far wall he was relieved to see David peering at a bottle of wine he'd chosen.

"Hello stranger."

"Jonathan, hi; what brings you into a supermarket of all places, has the cellar run dry at Chateau Dempsey?"

"No not quite but I'm always on the lookout for something new."

"Fiona's in here somewhere. Come and say hi."

He grinned; he couldn't have planned it any better himself.

The two of them sought out Fiona and she was in exactly the same place Jonathan had last seen her.

"Hey! Look who I bumped into."

"Jonathan hello," Fiona kissed him on both cheeks, "Long time no see – still busy-busy?"

"Well you know how it is."

"Oops sorry. You don't know Evie do you, let me introduce you." It had been as simple as that.

"Evelyn Wallace, this is Jonathan Dempsey". Evelyn put out her hand. "How do you do," and smiled at him. He shook her hand, a firm but tiny hand, he didn't want to let go; but had no choice. Big brown eyes smiled up at him; a man could lose himself in eyes like that. He noticed she had great breasts too; Lycra left nothing to the imagination – thank God. She was intriguing; the combination of eyes, smile, hair, bum and well lots of other things made him very interested.

"I was just telling your wife off," Evelyn spoke to David, "She's missed more than a couple of weeks of my classes, don't think I hadn't noticed your absence missy," and she laughed whilst waggling her finger at Fiona.

Christ, all Jonathan could think about was nibbling that finger and sucking it in his mouth – he had to concentrate.

He asked her, "So how do you know each other?"

"Oh I've known Fiona for a few years now and David is my doctor. I was just telling Fiona about my crappy morning; but now I've decided to treat myself to a lovely lunch to cheer myself up."

"Your boss still being an arse?" asked David.

"Oh yes and then some," she sighed.

"Jonathan works in London during the week."

Before he could answer Evelyn responded, "Oh God how awful, I have to go up one day every month and that's more than enough for me. I don't know how you do it"

"Oh it's not so bad." He smiled at her. So she was there one day every month, interesting, wonder why?

"Well I must get on. I'm getting hungry just standing here."

"Are you looking after yourself, what's on the menu for your lunch?"

"Yes doctor," she laughed, "don't panic; it's all under control. Today it is a chicken, avocado and orange salad followed by fruit," and she pointed at her basket.

"Well I can instantly see a flaw in that plan of yours," laughed David.

"Oh yes and what's that?"

"No chicken in your basket."

She grinned. "Well, Sherlock Holmes, I already have cooked chicken at home, it just means less for Henry and he won't mind. I'm supposed to be doing some domestic drudgery this afternoon; but now I'm playing hooky instead, I thought I'd sit in the garden with Henry and re – read one of my favourite books."

I would love to sit in the garden with you; but not to read books, was going through Jonathan's mind. And who the fuck was Henry?

"Sounds perfect," said Fiona enviously. "Anything to put off domestic chores, what were you planning?"

"Well the usual things, hoover, general tidy, strip the bed." Jonathan inhaled sharply and had to force his thighs together really fast. Why did she have to mention the words strip and bed in the same sentence? He couldn't get the image of her stripping for him whilst he lay on the bed out of his mind now. Desperately he tried to refocus on the conversation.

"Tell you what, why don't you come over for supper on Wednesday and we'll have a proper catch up?"

"Oh that would be lovely; but I can't make this Wednesday. Can I be cheeky and suggest the following one instead? What shall I bring?"

"Just yourself, still the same foodie things?"

Evie smiled. "Yes no wheat and I'm also on a no sugar, salt, caffeine, alcohol and only vegan dairy plan at the moment; but don't let that bother you."

"Jesus Evie, what's left?," laughed David.

"Oh there's plenty don't worry, only wheat makes me ill, the rest is just a personal choice."

"Evie is a fabulous cook," explained Fiona to Jonathan.

"Oh really?" So she could cook too.

"Well I wouldn't say fabulous," Evie replied. She could feel her face going red – honestly how embarrassing.

"Don't listen to her, she cooks this amazing chicken dish which is to die for."

"Sounds wonderful," he looked into her eyes, she was blushing and he realised she was a bit shy, he was willing her to invite him round.

Evie hugged Fiona and David and shook Jonathan's hand. "It was lovely to meet you," she smiled at him and with that she was gone. His eyes followed her until she was out of sight and a little while later he said his goodbyes and made his way out of the store. This girl had piqued his curiosity, he couldn't quite put his finger on it; but one thing he knew for certain was that he desperately wanted to find out more about her. She was pretty and funny with a great laugh and those eyes as well as that smile and a great bum too. He scoured the car park but there was no sign of her. Feeling disappointed he unlocked his car, yes that car she had been so interested in belonged to him and he drove home, not really concentrating at all; but thinking how he find out more about Evelyn Wallace. She wasn't his usual type. He hadn't been interested in anyone for a while, well not until today that was. Smiling to himself he definitely wanted to get to know her a whole lot better. He just needed a plan.

Chapter 2

After taking a shower Evie felt human again and concentrated on making her lunch. She took the bowl out into the garden where Henry joined her in the sun. Whilst eating she realised she was a lot calmer about Jack and it dawned on her that it was never going to lead anywhere so why was she so upset. Maybe not upset just annoyed he'd lied to her and made her feel like such a fool. She only had herself to blame as she'd broken two of her own golden rules, never date anyone at work and avoid blondes at all cost, she'd ignored her own advice and look where it had got her?

Over the past year or so she'd forced herself to get back in the dating game; none of the dates had gone well, she was a lot for anyone to take on really and they'd all ended badly, so why would this have been any different? Oh he'd been so smooth and clever too. He joined the gym about a year ago as a personal trainer and their paths didn't really cross for the first six months; but then he'd been so clever reeling her in slowly like a fish on a line. It started with just the one word, hello or morning, then it had progressed to two words, nice day, hello there, good morning and so on until they were having chats on a regular basis. He seemed really nice and when he'd invited her out for a drink to celebrate his first year she hadn't hesitated to say yes. There was going to be a group of them going from the gym and it sounded like fun. And one thing was for certain she was in desperate need of some fun.

When she arrived at the pub the car park was more or less empty which was odd; but maybe she was early or had got the time wrong. Walking into the pub she saw Jack stood at the bar so knew it was the right place. Well he'd been charm itself, saying how the others would be along shortly, he bought them both a drink and they found a table together. After an hour or so he had confessed that he'd only invited her as he wanted to spend time with her on her own. She'd been flattered and they'd had a good evening. He persuaded her to drop him home and when she drew up outside he'd taken her by surprise and kissed her firmly on the lips making it crystal clear he wanted more. There was a lot more he needed to know first and Evie pulled away.

Having slept on it, the next day at the gym she had thought, well, why not? He was single, she was single, maybe she ought to try to get back into the habit of dating as it had been far too long? She hadn't seen him that morning and after her two classes were over she'd gone into the female changing rooms and then into a cubicle in the ladies' loo. Which was where she was when the main door had swung open and two girls entered, giggling and gossiping. She remained in the cubicle as she was never sure whether to make it known she was there or just to keep quiet. Well thank goodness she'd kept quiet for one of them was telling her friend about this new bloke she'd just started seeing but it was a big secret apparently and she was sworn to secrecy. The upshot was her new boyfriend was Jack; but he wanted to keep their relationship a secret as it would be unprofessional if it got out that he was dating a client etc. They sniggered together as she had told her friend how gorgeous and dreamy he was and wasn't she the luckiest girl etc.

After what seemed like an age they left; but in reality it could only have been five minutes. Evie unlocked the cubicle and went over to the sink. She washed her hands and gripped the front of the basin, trembling, with both rage and her own stupidity. What an idiot she'd been, the first pretty face to ask her out for ages and she'd fallen for it hook, line and sinker, well he could go jump now as there was no way in hell she was going down that road. Back in her garden she sighed and picked up her book, well she'd learnt a lesson and funnily enough now she had had time to think it through it would never have worked. He was just too immature and self-centred to take her on – he'd have failed at the first hurdle. She opened her book and began to read.

Back home Jonathan Dempsey switched on his laptop, he needed to find out more about Evelyn Wallace, it couldn't be that hard could it? Why hadn't he met her before he wondered? David and Fiona had never mentioned her to him, mind you he was rarely in town and he never went to the gym. He thought back to their meeting only an hour or so ago, she was all smiles and big eyes; but a bit shy and he liked that about her. Not a scary ball breaker like the women he usually met, no she was different, really different to his usual type, maybe that was where he'd been going wrong? He wasn't sure if she was just shy with him or with everyone, still he'd love to find out.

Sat in his kitchen he leant back and rested his head in his hands, closed his eyes and tried to remember everything about her.
Huge brown eyes – hopefully they would get him into a whole heap of trouble.

Great smile – soft lips – he groaned, how would they feel on his lips, on his skin, on his penis?

Fantastic bum – he imagined her lying on top of him with his hands squeezing her bum onto his erection

Lovely breasts – what he could see of them anyway, he'd need to see more.

Tiny soft hands – soft hands all over his skin, this made him shiver.

Firm handshake – would her hand be firm stroking his penis too? Christ he bloody hoped so.

Long, shiny, wavy hair – was it soft? He imagined his hands running through it as it cascaded down her back and over her breasts.

Pale soft skin – what was the rest of her skin like?

Laughter – would they share a lot of laughs together?

Shy – would she be shy in the bedroom, he didn't know; but was desperate to find out.

His mind continued to drift imagining the two of them in bed. Shaking himself, he returned to his laptop. First he searched for local gyms and checked out their websites for staff pictures. Sure enough he found her photo, she looked exactly as he'd remembered, all smiles and big brown eyes. There was a short resume about what she taught etc.; but nothing else. He tried typing her name into the search engine; but it returned nothing about her. Then he had a stroke of genius and grabbing the computer he strode over to the main house. What he needed now was his little brother, Jamie. He found Jamie in the kitchen leaning on the open fridge door swigging orange juice straight from the carton.

"Morning Jon."

"I think you'll find it's the afternoon J," Jonathan replied sardonically.

"Whatever – don't see you over here very often what's up?"

"I need your help with something."

"Bloody hell that's a first, you must be desperate to ask me."

"Well will you help me or not?"

"Maybe, it depends, what do you need?"

Jonathan paused, "How would I go about finding someone on say Facebook?"

Jamie spat orange juice all over his T-shirt, "Christ I never thought I would hear you say that, what gives?"

"Well I met someone today and I want to find out more about her; but I'm struggling to find out anything to be honest."

"Maybe there's nothing to find?"

"Hmm, maybe but could you at least take a look?"

"Okay what's her name?"

Jamie spent the next ten minutes trying various social media websites, all to no avail. He could count the things that his brother knew about social media on the fingers of one hand and still have fingers left, honestly he was hopeless. There was simply nothing there about Evelyn Wallace to be found.

"Isn't that a bit odd?" asked Jonathan

"Well sometimes people don't want their private life put out there for all and sundry to see, you'll have to think of something else. Is she someone important?"

"Possibly J, yes possibly." He left and walked back across the yard to the converted stables where he lived. Jonathan was getting frustrated now, he could recite what he knew about her in 10 seconds and that simply wasn't enough, not by a long way. Running his fingers through his hair, he had to try to think of something, he was a bright chap for crying out loud, switching the kettle on he racked his brain for an answer.

Jonathan spent the week in London as usual and although every day was a busy day for him, when he had an idle moment his thoughts returned again and again to Evelyn. On Thursday night he pushed his fork around a bowl of rather unappetising spaghetti Bolognese. He'd failed miserably to come up with any sort of plan and felt frustrated. Sighing loudly he didn't want to just phone Fiona and ask her, no that was far too obvious. He still didn't know who Henry was and he felt depressed at the thought of her sharing her bed with some other bloke. But surely he was being irrational as if Henry was her boyfriend then he would have been invited over to supper too. No that couldn't be right and with that thought it gave him some hope that maybe he was in with a chance. Sighing again he decided he would look for her in town this Saturday and the next one if needed, make it look like a purely random meeting and if both days resulted in failure, then and only then would he call David.

Evie's week passed in a blur, she always went up to London on the train on the first Wednesday of every month. She had a regular appointment in the morning at 10.00 and another at 3.00. Most times she met her friend Alice for lunch if Alice was free and then she was home by 7.00pm. Goodness knows how people managed to commute every week, even for a day she found it tiring. She ran a bath as was her usual ritual as she always felt so grubby on her return and soaked in the hot water, her body relaxing, happy to be home. Her thoughts idly drifted onto Jonathan Dempsey. He seemed very nice; but probably wasn't going to be interested in someone like her, once they found out everything guys never were.

On Friday Evie met up with her best friend Rowan for some girly gossip and she could forget for just a few hours how lonely she had become. Rowan was a scream at the best of times and always seemed to have more guys on the go than Evie had eaten hot dinners, but she loved her all the same. Saturday morning was work as per usual and she managed to avoid Jack even though he had been constantly plaguing her with text messages. Finally she'd replied and asked him to leave her alone, for didn't he already have his hands full seducing at least one other gym client than to waste time pestering her. Abruptly his messages stopped and for that she was thankful.

Evelyn taught her Saturday morning classes as usual. She needed to go to the florists afterwards and run some errands but she was in no particular hurry. Parking her car she made her way up the High Street to the florists. Unbeknown to her Jonathan had spotted her five minutes ago and had practically punched the air right this was his chance and he wasn't about to let it slip through his fingers. He watched her enter the florists and casually walked slowly past, he could see Evelyn chatting to the assistant and they were both laughing together. What was it about her, everyone she met always seemed to be smiling or laughing when she was around? He smiled just thinking about this.

Evelyn ordered a bouquet to be delivered for Alice's birthday next week. Alice was engaged to Harvey and she was very happy for her, well happy for both of them in fact. She was nearly out the door when she spotted some very early season peonies, they must have been grown in a hothouse abroad but they were her absolute favourites and she couldn't resist buying a bunch of them. On leaving the shop she turned and headed for the market stalls that set up every Saturday until 2.00pm. She wasn't really paying much attention and so when a voice said hello she was startled back into reality.

Stood before her was Jonathan Dempsey and she had to admit he was looking very fine today, oh yes very fine indeed.
"Hello again, fancy bumping into you, what lovely flowers."
"Oh hello, how are you? Yes, aren't they lovely, they're my absolute favourites and I couldn't resist," Honestly could she think of anything more idiotic to say, she stared at the ground, maybe it would just swallow her up before she made a complete and utter fool of herself.

He noticed again she seemed shy and a bit nervous around him, he didn't know if this was a good or bad sign? "I was going to grab a coffee would you like to join me?"

She smiled back, on safer territory now, a busy coffee shop was fine. "Umm yes, that would be lovely."

MUSIC:-HOLD MY HAND – JESS GLYNNE.

They walked along together side by side, he was desperate to grab her hand in his; but was trying to play it cool whatever the fuck that was these days. They reached a point where they had to cross the road and he placed his hand in the small of her back. Oh sweet Jesus his hand was hot or was it just her reaction to his hand being there at all. Feeling her reaction to his hand he wondered what her reaction would be to both his hands running over her naked body, Christ alive, what a thought. He was desperate to touch her hair; but that was off limits for now. They waited for a gap in the traffic and when the road was clear he moved his hand from her back and took her small hand in his. It seemed the most natural thing in the world and she didn't pull her hand away when they reached the other side. He was very happy to be holding her hand, this day just kept getting better and better. Opening the door of the coffee shop he allowed her to go first; but he still didn't release her hand.

"What would you like to drink?"

"Oh a fruit tea would be lovely, maybe raspberry or lemon please."

"Anything to eat?"

"No just tea will be fine thank you, I'll find a table." And with that he had no choice but to let her hand go.

THE MAN couldn't believe his luck, both of them in the same place at the same time, well it made his job a lot easier. He'd hang about for a bit and then send the photos over to HIM. HE'D be very pleased, very pleased as it looked as if Dempsey and HER might be together.

Evie found a spare table, it was very low with three comfy chairs around it. Well this was unexpected, very unexpected indeed. When he'd put his hand on her back she thought it would burst into flames, she had to calm down she didn't want him to think she was some kind of idiot. Jonathan was about 5'10" or 11," tall at a guess, with short thick light brown wavy hair, green eyes, glasses and a good build – very nice, yes very nice indeed she mused.

He was back in less than five minutes; but no sooner had he placed the cups down on the table than a large chap wearing a mustard coloured jumper and bright red trousers proceeded to plonk himself down in the empty chair. Oh fuck, not now, Jonathan sighed to himself this just could not be happening.

"I thought it was you old chap, don't mind if I sit with you it's very busy in here today." Jonathan had no choice but to murmur his consent and then introduce Evie to Jacob. They'd been at school together but the truth was he barely remembered him.

Jacob was that rare thing, an ex – public schoolboy with no social boundaries whatsoever. He proceeded to bombard Evie with question after question until she felt like she was in some sort of Spanish inquisition or being interrogated in a court of law by some slick and sleazy lawyer. It was endless, on and on and on and on he didn't stop once, it was relentless like rapid machine gun fire:-

So Evelyn –
What do you do?
Where?
How long for?
Pay well?
Funny job?
Like it?
Go to London?
When?
What for?
What does your father do?
When was that?
How?
Mother-lives where?
Sisters?
Brothers?
Lives where?
Does what?
You Uni?
Study what?
Left when?
Do what?

Left why?
Like to travel?
Hobbies?
No wheat, why?
Where do you live?
Own it?
How long lived there?

She hardly had time to answer a question before he'd moved on to the next one. On and on and on and on it went, Evie's head was pounding and it felt like it was going to explode. Evie felt breathless, her chest and head hurt and Jonathan was no help just sitting, smiling and drinking coffee. She figured out that Jacob was a lawyer and was quite used to cross examining people without taking no for an answer. Her mind flitted back to her previous interrogations firstly in hospital, her propped up in bed unable to see anything; but she could hear the endless questions repeated on a loop. And then at the police station, questions and then more questions over and over asking the same things again and again until she actually thought she might be going slightly mad. She hadn't thought of that time for ages, in fact she'd hoped to erase it all from her memory at some point; but it had proved impossible.

Tears pricked her eyes, she wasn't going to start crying here, not now anyway. Surely Jonathan would step in, make him stop? Jonathan meanwhile was sat quietly, finding out everything he'd wanted to know about her without even asking her one question –which was pure bloody genius as far as he was concerned.

Well she'd had enough of this, she needed to leave, so her answers became monosyllabic and her voice was quieter too. She began to be evasive and only telling half-truths.

"Do you live on your own?"
"No I live with Henry."
"Oh how long have you known him?"
"About four years."
"What does he do?"
"He's a part-time hunter."
"What does he do for the other half?" Jacob laughed as if he had made a joke. Jonathan meanwhile had been bolted out of complacency and was

hanging on her every word, so she lived with Henry-what the fuck? She'd held his hand crossing the road, did she now suddenly have a boyfriend?

"Oh as little as possible, he's probably still asleep in bed right now."

Jonathan thought, 'Shit – that wasn't what he wanted to hear'.

Two could play at this game, she was so angry now and was past caring. Her privacy was extremely important to her after everything that had happened and this oaf was violating that bigtime, she was extremely uncomfortable and this had gone on for long enough. Just as Jonathan took a big sip of coffee she planned her escape. Suddenly she stood up to leave. Jonathan was caught out, where was she going now, she was running away and he'd barely had time to speak to her, he could thump Jacob.

"Well this has been lovely; but I think my car park ticket is about to run out so I must dash." She hated lying but to be honest this had rapidly turned into a bloody nightmare. Shaking hands with Jacob she muttered lovely to meet you, not really meaning a single word of it. Jonathan struggled to stand up from the low chair; but her hand pushed hard against his shoulder and she said firmly, "no need for you to desert your friend. Stay and chat for a while. Thank you for the tea," and with that she was gone. Then she was out the door, taking a huge gulp of fresh air she bolted for the other side of the market square. Running now as fast as she could without bumping into anyone she wanted to be back in her car and gone. Her flowers were all but forgotten lying on the floor by her chair and Jonathan picked them up. He tried to follow her but coming through the doors of the café was a mother with a double buggy and it had taken quite some time before she was safely through and he was outside. Now where was she? He scanned the marketplace but couldn't see her at all. Shit, shit it had started out so well; but had quickly disintegrated before his very eyes. Then he spotted her on the far side but she was running, really fast, no longer strolling or jogging, she looked purposeful and he realized he'd blown it bigtime.

THE MAN watched this play out, oh so there was trouble in paradise already, with Dempsey and HER, well HE would be thrilled whatever the outcome. Time for him to go home.

Jonathan walked back to where his car was parked. Now he was in a really bad fucking mood. True he knew a bit more about her now; but at what expense? He hadn't stopped Jacob at all as he was so keen for information about her. Looking back, that had been a huge mistake on his part. Jonathan had hardly spoken to her, so much for wanting to spend time with her, suddenly it had rapidly gone from bad to worse. He still didn't have her phone number, e-mail or address, fuck – in fact he hadn't even arranged to see her again, shit, shit what was he going to do now? She'd bolted unexpectedly and quickly, making her escape in record time and had left her flowers behind too. Feeling like such an idiot he reached his car and couldn't believe his bloody eyes, for pushed under the wiper blade was a parking ticket. That had to be the most expensive cup of coffee ever! But was probably deserved, none the less.

Evelyn made it back to her car and drove away, she was trembling and shaking with rage, how bloody dare he just sit there whilst she was interrogated and cross examined like that? She'd foolishly thought he'd wanted to spend time with her, get to know her, talk to her – what a fool she'd been – again! Jacob and his interrogation had really got under her skin and after a few miles she realized that crying and driving were a bad combination as she couldn't actually see where she was going. She pulled off the road into the first layby she found and continued to cry. First Jack and then seven days later Jonathan, why couldn't she find a good decent man, there must be one out there somewhere. She took her mobile out of her bag and rang Fiona.

Fiona picked up almost straight away. It took her a while to get any sense out of Evie as all she could hear was crying and words like interrogation and endless questions, just like before. Forgot my flowers too. Fiona let her cry until she was all cried out and then quietly asked her to tell her what was going on. Fiona listened, gently encouraging Evie to explain. She was horrified at the tale that unfolded, how could he just sit there and do nothing this was just too much. When she told her she was in a layby Fiona almost yelled at her, "You have locked yourself in the car haven't you?" She hadn't; but she pressed the button immediately, Fiona heard the noise and relaxed slightly. Fiona soothed Evie and after a while she persuaded her to dry her eyes, drive home carefully and to text her when she was in the front door. Sure enough 15 minutes later Evie's text arrived. Right Fiona thought now it's my turn.

Fiona pressed Jonathan's number and waited for him to pick up. He'd barely got in the door when his mobile started to ring. His heart leapt. Maybe it was Evie. He quickly realized that was impossible as they hadn't even swopped numbers. He laid her flowers on the kitchen table and answered his mobile.

"Hello."

"Jonathan it's Fiona, I just thought you ought to know I've had a call from Evie, she's parked in some shitty layby, God knows where, crying her eyes out, what the fuck have you done to her?"

"Um well."

"Don't even speak to me I'm talking now," she spat out at him. He nodded silently and sat down at the kitchen table, he'd never heard Fiona talk this way before, this was bad, very bad.

"I always thought you were a bit of an arse and it looks like I was right all along." This was news to him but she was in full flow now with no sign of stopping. "So I gather you invited her for coffee and that your old school chum joined you and then he proceeded to launch his own bloody version of the Spanish Inquisition or courtroom cross examination, apparently he didn't even draw breath asking her every sort of personal and private question whilst you just sat there and let it happen. (Her voice was getting louder and angrier by the second). She's been through this crap before and she sure as hell doesn't need a repeat performance from the likes of you. (What did that mean? he wondered).

You rich city boys are all the same, well this might be acceptable behaviour in the boardroom, throw someone to the lions in a gladiatorial arena for sport and watch them get mauled. But this is Evie for heaven's sake she's a very shy, private person who hardly reveals her true feelings and thoughts to me and I'm her best friend, now she feels violated, utterly betrayed and humiliated beyond belief. Last week it was some dickhead at the gym who fucked her over and now a week later you've gone and done exactly the same thing, well I hope you're proud of yourself? How could you Jonathan?

If you knew what she's been through, she is the loveliest, most decent person I know, in fact she is ten times the person you'll ever be, what were you thinking letting this happen right in front of your eyes? You're not some Roman emperor for goodness sake. As for ending up in some shitty layby because she can't cry and drive at the same time – it's dangerous, anything could have happened. I even had to remind her to lock herself in so she would be safe that's how upset she is."

Jonathan had never heard Fiona shout and swear before, this was much, much worse than he could ever have imagined. "I just wanted to find out more about her – ".

"She has done NOTHING to deserve this treatment from you, this was shameful just SHAMEFUL, you behaved appallingly. I hope you're proud of yourself after today's little performance? Jesus she doesn't even know you and after this she probably never will. In fact scratch that if you ever go near her again I will rip your bloody head off-understood?" Fiona hung up.

Jonathan continued to stare at his mobile, shit, this was quite possibly the worst thing he had ever done. Fiona was right in every respect he'd behaved appallingly and God knows how he was going to make amends. He couldn't call her as they hadn't swopped numbers, he still didn't know her address. Yes, he knew all sorts of other things like where she went to Uni; but nothing that would help him now. Running his hands through his hair, he knew this had got way out of hand and he wouldn't blame her if she never spoke to him again; but he was going to have to try and put this right. She hadn't deserved such treatment and Fiona was right, he was ashamed of his behaviour.

Yes she was shy and he really liked that about her; but he'd just sat back and let Jacob interrogate her and still he'd done nothing to stop it, even after sensing her discomfort. No wonder she was upset. He'd behaved like a moron. Her flowers lay on his kitchen table silently tutting their disapproval at him. He had to come up with something he just couldn't let this chance slip through his fingers, he wouldn't.

Chapter 3

Although it wasn't even 4 o'clock Jonathan opened a bottle of red wine, poured himself a large glass, drank a mouthful and tried to decide what to do. He knew that alcohol never solved anything; but he was all out of answers. Wandering through to his study he took out a large piece of paper and began to write down everything he knew about her, this was a start and to be honest at the present moment he had nowhere else to go.

Name: Evelyn Wallace – pretty with a great smile and laugh.

Age: 20 something. Maybe 24/ 25?

Height: roughly 5' 3/5'4?

Eyes: brown, very big and mesmerising

Hair: Long, brown, shiny and hopefully soft too?

Home: Somewhere local 30 minutes away?

Occupation: fitness instructor. (Great bum. gorgeous breasts).

Work: Town Gym.

Status: Lives with Henry. (Who is this guy? Fiona hadn't invited Henry to supper and she'd held his hand whilst crossing the road – it didn't make any sense).

Family: Mother lives 2 hours away. Father died when she was 16 in a plane crash, Brother Thomas married lives in Montreal with wife and children works in shipping.

Uni: Bristol: studied English and Business studies.

Likes: friends, books, Henry, cooking, running, flowers especially peonies.

Dislikes: wheat, crying and being fucked over in general.

He drank some more wine and stared at the list and thought bloody hell was that all? It was a very short list and to be honest a lot of the things needed clarification; but it was a start. Racking his brains he knew there had to more than this, there just had to be. He sure as hell couldn't ask Fiona now or even

David for that matter. Oh why hadn't he invited her out for dinner, just the two of them, somewhere intimate where they could get to know one another? A nice restaurant, somewhere romantic, soft lights, soft music, just the two of them holding hands, he would have kissed her and then hopefully there would have been another date. He was a bloody idiot that's why. Hell he hadn't even kissed her, yet he wanted to so badly he physically ached. He would have walked her to her door, wrapped his arms around her grasping her bum and squeezing it onto his hips whilst he kissed her goodnight – God he had to stop thinking like that, it was getting him nowhere fast. What else did he know? And then it popped into his head, one thing he knew for a certainty is that she'd be eating supper with Fiona and David on Wednesday. Now this could be the opportunity he'd been searching for.

Evie ran a bath. She'd texted Fiona once she got home; but now she'd lost her appetite. She was still upset, with Jonathan and she'd forgotten her flowers too. Her head was pounding and she rarely got headaches except when she was dehydrated or overtired – or completely wrung out from all that crying just now. How embarrassing for Fiona, she really should call her tomorrow and apologise. Sinking into the hot bath water she closed her eyes, so she had been royally fucked over twice in seven days, even for her that must be some kind of record. True she wasn't bothered about Jack; but Jonathan was something different entirely. She'd hoped that going for a coffee with him would be a first date that would have led to a second one; he'd seemed so nice with light brown wavy hair and green eyes, yes very nice indeed; but perhaps it just wasn't meant to be. Maybe she was well out of it, she wanted to just empty her head and relax; but it wasn't proving to be very easy.

After goodness knows how long she realised her hands were all wrinkly and she used a foaming mousse to wash away the grime and get out of the bath. Now what? It was barely 5 o'clock, too early for pyjamas; although if she was poorly she reasoned with herself then pyjamas would be acceptable and this was a type of illness wasn't it? She chose a clean pair out of her pyjama drawer, she had a lot to choose from as they were one of her favourite items of clothing. Wrapping a blue jersey robe around her she padded downstairs. Food was next on the agenda but she had never felt less like eating. Still she had to work tomorrow and needed to eat something. She took a frozen gluten free macaroni and cheese meal from the freezer and put it into the microwave for 2 minutes. That would have to do. Whilst she waited for it to cook she thought this was exactly the same feeling you had when you had just broken up with your boyfriend, the only difference was they hadn't even started to go out together and it was over.

Staring at the pasta in front of her she idly twisted a fork in her hands, she hadn't even bothered to remove it from the carton it had been cooked in – she was so disinterested in it. Ten minutes later she was curled up on the sofa with her soft faux fur throw wrapped loosely around her. She picked up her mobile and called Alice, she would know what to do. Alice picked up straight away and they Face-timed each other. Alice knew something was wrong as Evie was in her pyjamas and it was only a bit after 5.30.in the afternoon. She listened whilst her friend explained the situation, not mentioning Jonathan by name and felt better for her friend agreeing that she'd done exactly the right thing by walking away and that yes she shouldn't have anything more to do with this creep. Evie asked Alice, "I don't suppose you know what happened to Paul do you?"

Alice was confused, "Um Paul who, sweetie?"

"You remember Paul from our office – it's just, well, I was wondering, I always liked him...."

"Oh Evie I didn't know you liked him, why didn't you tell me ages ago?"

"Why?"

"He got married last year and they're expecting their first baby any day now." Alice felt bad. Why did everyone always shoot the messenger?

"Oh! I didn't realise. Still, with everything that happened to me, he probably wouldn't have been interested in me anyway. It was just a thought you know one of those what-if kind of things." Evie wound the conversation up. Just her bloody luck, the only person she'd been really interested in was already well and truly taken – typical, could this day get any worse?

David walked through his front door a little after six, with any luck Fiona would have the children bathed and in bed ready for him to read them a story before the two of them ate supper together. Finding her in the kitchen stirring a saucepan of something that smelt delicious, he put his arms around her and kissed her cheek.

"Happy to see me?" And then she promptly burst into tears. He kept his arms where they were and let her cry. Over supper Fiona told David what had happened with Evie and Jonathan. David could hardly believe his ears but he kept quiet and let his wife talk.

He'd known Evie for quite a few years now. David had been the doctor in the A and E department when she'd been brought in. She was a complete mess, black and blue, barely breathing. He'd seen his fair share of trauma over the years but this had shocked him to his core. David had only been married to Fiona for a short time and they were expecting their first child together. He kept imagining if it had been Fiona lying there on the trolley – it just didn't bear thinking about. David treated Evie with the utmost care and respect that he could, she would need x rays, scans and at least one operation; but she was alive – just.

When she was well enough to be transferred out of the ICU, her mother had arranged for her to be moved into a private room a few floors up and David had regularly checked on her progress. Medically she was responding well, mentally though that was a whole other story. He'd asked Fiona to visit her and sit and read to her. His wife was a wonderful woman and she'd agreed without hesitation. David continued to be Evie's medical practitioner and when he'd left the hospital and joined a GP surgery, Evie had signed on as a patient under his care. He'd also arranged for her to see a counsellor every week, he knew Ian was a good man and God knows she needed all the help she could get.

His mind retuned into what his wife was saying, he was proud of her coming to Evie's defence. Fiona must have been a fearsome sight to behold when in full battle mode. He'd only seen it once before and it had slightly terrified him to be honest. Agreeing she'd done exactly the right thing he knew he'd be having his very own conversation with Jonathan once his wife was enjoying a relaxing bath. She didn't need to hear what he was going to say; although by the sounds of it she had already said most of the right things.

Just before ten, Jonathan's phone rang. He'd stopped drinking after three quarters of the bottle of red was empty and after making a plan of action was sat staring into space remonstrating with himself. The phone had jolted him back to reality and he answered immediately.

"Jonathan, it's David." Oh shit, this was going to be even worse than Fiona. He liked David and they'd never had a falling out before, so he braced himself for the tongue lashing that was coming his way.

David being a doctor always seemed the epitome of calm, it was just his way and he was a good doctor all the more for it. So there was no shouting or swearing, but this was quite possibly worse if Jonathan was honest.

Yes, everything Fiona had told him was accurate, he'd behaved appallingly and was racked with guilt and remorse.

"I just don't understand how you could just sit there, light the fuse and watch this bomb explode in front of you. She may seem tough on the outside but you have no idea what she's been through."

"Fiona mentioned something similar too, what do you mean exactly?"

"Look you know I can't tell you anything. I'm her doctor."

"You mean you can't or you won't?"

"Well as her doctor I can't and as her friend I won't."

"But this doesn't help me to understand?"

"It's not all about you, you know. You seem to have escaped pretty much unscathed from where I'm sitting. The only person who can tell you is Evie and after today's little stunt I doubt she will ever speak to you again. I'm just so disappointed in you, Jonathan. I never took you for an idiot and now you are an idiot of the biggest kind, too. Fiona is as mad as hell with you and quite rightly so, in fact we both are. I think it would be for the best if you just left Evie alone."

"But I can't, I need to put this right, I don't want to leave things as they stand."

"I really don't think you have a lot of choice in the matter do you? Now I'm going to make a cup of tea for my angel of a wife who has had an even more trying day than usual thanks to you. Goodnight Jonathan." And he was gone.

No, no, no, this wasn't going to end here, it couldn't. He wouldn't allow it. First thing Monday when he was back in London he would start to try to salvage his relationship with Evie. Well maybe relationship was pushing it but that was what he wanted, now he just had to persuade her that was what she wanted too.

Later that night Evie felt like she hadn't slept at all. Her mind when asleep kept flashing back – she couldn't breathe couldn't move, she hurt everywhere, it was just a blur and the pain was too much, HIS hands on her neck, HIS foot kicking her, sharp pains on her back, on her tummy. She woke herself up shouting and panting at 3.30am. Oh well wasn't his just peachy? As if the past 24 hours hadn't been shitty enough, now her anxiety dreams had returned. After fetching a glass of water she got back into bed and tried again. She had to get some sleep if she was to function at all at work. Closing her eyes, in desperation she started to count sheep.

Chapter 4

The rest of the weekend dragged by agonisingly slowly. Evie was in no mood for music which for her was unheard of, in fact she couldn't concentrate on the newspaper, the TV or even her book. Eventually she went for a run to clear her head. It helped a bit but not as much as she would have liked. She sighed. Roll on tomorrow, when work would fill her mind.

Monday morning, 5.30 am, Jonathan's driver Alan was driving him into the office. Normally he would read through his papers for the day ahead but he just couldn't face them this morning, and stared out of the car window as they drove steadily towards the motorway. On the journey to London he gave Alan the details of a delivery he needed him to make. That done, he couldn't do any more until he was in the office and even then would have to wait until after 10.00am; but at least he'd made a decision and that was half the battle.

All the gym staff had been summoned to Steve's office for 8.30am on Monday for a team meeting. This didn't happen very often but it meant getting up before 7.00am and Evie found that to be a struggle, especially when she'd hardly slept for the past two nights. Avoiding Jack she sat at the back whilst Steve droned on and on. She looked idly out of the window. Evie would have loved to have been outside just to go for a run and get some fresh air. She was jolted back to reality on hearing her name. "Thank you for volunteering for that, Evelyn. If you could remain here afterwards, I'll go through the details with you." Shit, she had no idea what was going on. That was the price she paid for staring out of the window and not paying attention.

It turned out the gym was getting an American P.E. student for 12 months on a break from his university. This was apparently part of his course, they were expected to take a year out and experience the world of work. She was going to be responsible for his induction and general wellbeing. He arrived on Thursday and she would be expected to have drawn up a programme for him to follow for the first month. Normally this wouldn't have been a problem; but she really wasn't in the mood which was precisely why Steve had volunteered her for this. Still, it would give her something to do to keep her mind from Jonathan bloody Dempsey, which wouldn't be a bad thing in the circumstances.

She spent Wednesday preparing the induction for the new student, a Miles Brady. Evie hoped he would be a nice guy as she had had her fill of arrogant arseholes. She laughed. Maybe she would ask him straight out if he was: Option A – a nice guy or Option B an arsehole, and take it from there. It was now after 6.00pm and she wriggled into her best jeans and pulled a soft pink top over her head. She would need to leave in half an hour to get to David and Fiona's for 7.00 and she still needed to put on some light makeup, if only to disguise the dark shadows under her eyes.

Fiona was just putting the finishing touches to the salmon when the doorbell rang. It was a little after 6.00 and it couldn't be David as he had his keys. Surely it wasn't Evie already? No it couldn't be. She dried her hands and went to open the door. A man stood on the doorstep with a large brown cardboard box.

"I have a delivery for you." Funny time to be making a delivery, she thought.

"Oh thank you; although I'm not expecting anything."

"You are Fiona Carter?"

"Yes."

"Good, then I have the correct address."

He passed her the box and left. Fiona closed the front door and placed the box on the floor. She read the label on the top and it all became clear.

FAO. Ms Evelyn Wallace c/o Dr and Mrs David Carter.

Fiona knew exactly who had sent this and now what was she going to do? She was desperate to see what was inside and thought she would ask David what they ought to do with it before Evie arrived. Well, best laid plans and all that. Evie arrived just before 7.00 and two minutes later David opened the front door. He'd been delayed, not too much but he knew the girls would just be chatting away waiting for him. They sat down to eat and talked about anything and everything except the elephant in the room, namely Jonathan Dempsey. Fiona had no chance to get David on his own until Evie went to the cloakroom after they'd finished their main course.

"A parcel arrived this evening for Evie."

"That's odd."

"I think it's from Jonathan. What should I do with it?"

David looked at his wife. "Well give it to her of course."

"Really?"

He sighed, "Yes, we can't keep it so of course you have to give it to her."

Evie reappeared. "What's with all the whispering?" she laughed.

Fiona went and retrieved the box. "This came for you this afternoon."

Evie just stared at the box. This didn't make any sense. "What is it?"

"We don't know. Why don't you open it and see?"

Fiona passed Evie some scissors and she opened the top of the box and peered inside. She gasped, for inside was the most gorgeous arrangement of pale pink peonies and creamy Avalanche roses with eucalyptus leaves intertwined. She removed them from the box and set them down onto the table. It wasn't her birthday. Then she noticed an envelope with a card inside and tore it open.

Fiona and David were holding their breath, the flowers were so beautiful and they were in no doubt as to the sender. The question was, what was Evie going to do from here?

On the card were written the words,

To Evelyn, I'm so very sorry, forgive me, Jonathan x

Turning the card over she found he'd written his mobile number on the reverse. Evie sat down abruptly and just stared at the flowers. She couldn't breathe or speak. Finally she said, "what should I do?"

"Well maybe have some dessert and think about things?" Trust David to be thinking of pudding, she smiled, the blooms were gorgeous. But his behaviour had been of the very worst kind and she wasn't sure if sending flowers was going to be enough for her to forgive him. "Do you think I was too hard on him, after all he wasn't to know about, about things in the past?"

"Not for a second," said Fiona firmly.

The opening of the box had brought the evening to a rather abrupt end and she made her farewells. She needed to think this through.

Once Evie was home she placed the flowers on the kitchen table, sat down and just stared at them, she read and re-read the card a dozen times and still she was no clearer on what to do. Maybe not do anything too hasty she thought as she climbed the stairs and got into bed. Her clock said 11.45 and she turned off the lamp.

Jonathan was pacing the floor of his London apartment. He'd been doing this for the best part of three hours now and was getting more and more anxious. There was no doubt Alan was 100% reliable so the flowers would have been delivered on time. What he didn't know was what her reaction had been, if she would take them home or leave them with Fiona, even throw them in the bin? No, surely not, she loved flowers, especially peonies. He just couldn't imagine her not taking them home with her. Question was, what would she do now, would she even call him?

Chapter 5

Evie tossed and turned, it was no use she just couldn't sleep. Eventually she switched the lamp on and looked at the clock. It was after 1.30am. This was ridiculous she needed to be in good form to spend the day with Miles and not having any sleep was hardly going to help. Getting out of bed she wrapped a robe around her and padded downstairs. She didn't really want a cup of tea so had a glass of water instead. The flowers stared at her, willing her to do something. Anything. Her mobile was on the table and before she could think about it anymore she sent a text message to Jonathan. It simply read.

Thank you for the flowers, they are beautiful.
Evelyn. – SEND

Jonathan was awake too, he heard his phone ping and couldn't believe his eyes. She'd replied and she loved them. Quick as a flash he typed:

I'm so glad you like them. Why are you awake at this hour of the morning? – SEND.

Evie looked at the text. Oh no! Now what? She had thought he wouldn't get the message until the morning. It had never occurred to her that he would be awake too.

Can't sleep – how about u? – SEND

Me neither – SEND.

He waited, there was nothing more, he typed

If I call you now will you pick up and talk to me? – SEND.

She typed. Not sure why I would? – SEND.

Fair point, I behaved appallingly but I do want to make it up to you. – SEND.

I think it might take more than a bunch of flowers don't U? – SEND.

You're right, whatever you want I'll do it. – SEND.

Do U text spk? – SEND

Um no I don't. How about we e-mail live chat? – SEND

She smiled so he didn't do texting. She was intrigued by what he had to say though.
OMG how old r u? – SEND

HE laughed, she was a bit cheeky.
Not that old! How old are you? Can I text you my email? -SEND

Oh dear. –SEND

He waited and waited, nothing
Evelyn are you still there? – SEND. Fuck what was it now?

Evelyn talk to me, please. –SEND

Eventually Evie typed,
You do realise that a true gentlemen would never have asked me my age. So what does this make you? I think this conversation is over. – SEND

He groaned, he was an idiot.
Sorry, being an idiot, see what you do to me? Please can we live chat? Please? I promise to be on my best behaviour. – SEND

She made him wait and then typed.

Okay live chat it is. – SEND

Immediately her phone pinged with his e-mail.

Need to tell you I'm sorry, in the coffee shop it got way out of hand. Whatever you want I'll do it – I'm serious – SEND

Evie picked up her iPad and began to type.

I think you are confusing me with someone who cares! So now you want me to give you all the answers, AGAIN – seems pretty lazy to me and I think your friend Jacob has more than covered that course of action, which if memory serves me right didn't turn out very well! – SEND

Oh no! She sounded mad and he'd said the wrong thing.

Please don't be mad. Fiona and David made it pretty clear I was to leave you alone, but I had to try. – SEND

What do Fiona and David have to do with this, this is between you and me. –SEND.

They both called me and told me exactly what they thought of me, didn't they tell you? – SEND.

No they didn't. – SEND.

Well amongst other things, Fiona told me I'd made you cry and I'm so sorry I never meant for that to happen – you have no idea how bad I felt.- SEND

Oh poor you, so ME crying made YOU feel bad, well Mr Dempsey, firstly – funnily enough it isn't all about you and secondly I wasn't feeling too great either. – SEND.

God she was still mad, even after the flowers. Other girls would have forgiven him by now; but he was quickly learning she wasn't like other girls and this only made him more determined.

Please Evelyn you have to try to forgive me, I've been going crazy, I didn't even have your mobile number to call you I felt so helpless. –SEND.

Well me sat in a layby somewhere sobbing as I can't drive and cry at the same time wasn't exactly how I thought the date might end, surely you can understand that? – SEND

So it was a date then? – SEND.

SERIOUSLY – THAT'S WHAT YOU GOT FROM THAT? – UN BLOODY BELIEVABLE – SEND.

Sorry I can't seem to say the right thing, I was desperate for your call and now it's all going wrong. – SEND

Well this is what comes of behaving like a fuckwit and expecting to get away with it just by sending flowers. This isn't the movies, this is real life with real feelings, feelings I might add that have been trampled on by a herd of bloody elephants. Look, it's late. I have a full day tomorrow I think this conversation is over, don't you? – SEND

But I don't want it to end. –SEND He was pleading with her now.

Tough luck sunshine, as I said before it's not all about you. –SEND

She made her way upstairs and got back into bed.

Please Evie, I'm so sorry. Will you give me another chance? – SEND

He waited and waited, just when he thought she'd gone a reply arrived.

Firstly it's Evelyn, I don't LET just anyone call me Evie, and certainly not someone who has royally fucked me over. Secondly I'm an extremely private person who doesn't overshare at the best of times even with my friends who have known me for years, let alone having my personal and private life ripped apart in public by a total stranger. This isn't exactly my idea of a good time. I felt humiliated, violated and appalled – you just sat and watched the show like some modern day Julius Cesar. How could you, Jonathan, how could you? – SEND

She didn't wait for his reply but immediately fired off-

You admit that what you did was unforgivable and yet here you are asking for my forgiveness – quite a contradiction wouldn't you say? – SEND

Oh my God she was right, how the fuck was he ever going to rectify this, he just knew he needed to try.

Every word you wrote is true, I never stopped for one moment to ask myself how you were feeling, I was just so desperate to find out more about you. Please Evelyn I want us to start over, try again, I really, really like you. You must know that? You must. I've been going out of my mind since Saturday afternoon. I've been a bloody idiot and a fool; but I don't want this to end before it's even begun. Let me take you out to dinner, just the two of us, so I can apologise. Please Evelyn, please. – SEND.

She sighed as she read his e-mail, well he certainly sounded contrite, mind you so he bloody well should. Other people would have told Jacob to fuck off and mind his own business; but she'd been completely caught unawares and she was angry having been made to lay bare intimate details of her life for idle pleasure.

I don't know, I can't think straight anymore, it's late or early depending on your viewpoint and I have to be in top form tomorrow to spend the day with Miles – SEND.

There, let him stew on that.

Who the fuck was Miles, Miles who? He groaned. He didn't even know who Henry was, now there was Miles too. He wasn't prepared for her to be someone else's girlfriend, he wanted her to be his.

I know it's late, I don't really know what more to say. But I do want to see you again, properly, more than anything. You have to let me try Evelyn please? – SEND

He sounded desperate, well let's see how hard he was willing to try.

I'm going back to bed now to get some sleep, Henry will be getting anxious wondering where I've got to. –SEND

Who's Henry, is he your boyfriend? – SEND. God, he was as jealous as hell now.

Oh he'd taken the bait, now for a bit of fun on her terms. She was fed up of being pushed around by guys.

Do you seriously think if I had a boyfriend I would be having this conversation with you? What type of girl do you think I am and, more to the point, what does that make you? – SEND

No, of course not. You held my hand crossing the road so I'm hoping there's still a chance for me? Look I know you're a pretty, smart, funny, smiley girl who would only date one guy at a time – hopefully me, but I need to ask who Henry and Miles are? – SEND

Oh, she had him all intrigued now, so he was saying all the right things; but now he wanted more answers from her again.

More questions from you, haven't we been down this lazy road before? – SEND

Please, Evelyn, I need to know if I have a chance.-SEND

Well maybe she would put him out of his misery, although she was having fun with this.

Okay, don't get your knickers in a knot Julius, take a guess who Henry is. You're supposed to be a bright chap, although from my perspective the jury is still out on that.-SEND

She was laughing at him now. This was a good sign. She'd stopped being mad at him and was now in a much more playful mood. God he wanted to be in the same room as her when she was in a playful mood, who knew where it would end up – in bed hopefully. He shook his head. Concentrate, think!

You're going to have to give me a clue.-SEND

Really already? You've come up with nothing? I hope your business doesn't catch on to the fact that you're not as bright as they think you are?-SEND.

Yes, that's true, not a day goes by without me thinking I will be found out. – SEND

She laughed. Oh, so he did have a sense of humour in there somewhere – that was good to know.

Come on stop prevaricating, you want to know who Henry and Miles are so think harder. – SEND

Okay Henry first, is he your child? – SEND

No, I don't have any children. Do you? – SEND

No I don't. Well he's not your boyfriend or your child. Is he your husband? – SEND

Priceless! You think nothing of me sitting here e-mailing you when my boyfriend might be upstairs in my bed waiting for me, so now you think I'm MARRIED. Again – UN BLOODY BELIEVABLE.-SEND

Okay, okay I'm running out of options here. –SEND

Well I've decided to take pity on you as it's now after 2.00am and some of us need our beauty sleep – I mean you of course! The conundrum that is Miles will keep for another day. – SEND

So who's Henry? – SEND

He waited, nothing, still nothing.

Are you still there? – SEND

Patience, patience! We all know it's a virtue, but maybe you don't have many of those? – SEND

Just tell me please, you are toying with me now. – SEND

Yes I am aren't I, not very nice is it? – SEND

Touché. I deserved that. – SEND

So here's the thing, Henry is my cat, so called after Henry 8th as they both like hunting and torturing things, namely furry, squeaky, flappy, beaky type things here and they both have ginger fur/hair. Am disappointed that you didn't guess correctly. Goodnight Jonathan. – SEND

Her cat. Henry was her bloody cat, hell he'd been panicking like mad, it never occurred to him that she had a cat. He smiled. So Evelyn had named her cat after Henry 8th, one of the most brutal of all the English kings with a liking for torture.

Don't go. – SEND

I need to get some sleep. – SEND

I want to talk some more. – SEND

Surely your mother told you – we can't always have what we want now can we? – SEND.

When can I see you again? – SEND

I haven't agreed that you can. – SEND

Evelyn please I want to see you, I need to see you. –SEND

Want and need are two very different things, young man, don't you have a dictionary? – SEND

This is so frustrating. You are such a contradictory woman. – SEND

Have you met many women, I'm not so sure you have? And your point is? – SEND

If I knew where you lived I'd be over there right now and, believe me, we wouldn't still be talking about this. – SEND

She laughed. Well how did it feel being given a taste of your own medicine Mr Dempsey? This was fun. She didn't have to be in the same room as him, e-mailing had made her much braver than she would have ever dared to be in person.

Now, don't go getting all high and mighty Julius, think of your blood pressure. You don't know where I live so that's ridiculous and secondly if we weren't talking what would we be doing? – SEND

You want me to explain it to you? – SEND

It's late and I'm tired so I think you might have to. – SEND

Okay don't say I didn't warn you. – SEND

Oh promises, promises .-SEND

He smiled. This was going to be okay after all. She was making fun of him and for once he was happy to let her, he'd been mean and he needed her to get to know him properly. Now for some fun.

Well to start with you would let me in the door. – SEND

Oh and why would I do a silly thing like that? – SEND

Because we wouldn't be able to have any fun if you didn't. – SEND

What sort of fun did you have in mind? – SEND

Well for starters the sort where I wrap my arms around you and hold you very tight, squeeze your bum and kiss you senseless until you forgive me, type of fun. – SEND

Blimey, he didn't give up did he?

Sounds quite nice. – SEND

QUITE NICE, – NICE – IS THAT ALL? – SEND

Well as this is just a fantasy it might never happen and how do I know you're a good kisser, because if you're a lousy kisser then it wouldn't be very nice for me at all. Yuk, I hadn't thought of that until now, maybe this fantasy isn't such a good idea. I might need to take a rain check on the whole idea? – SEND

I've never had any complaints so far. – SEND

Well maybe your previous girlfriends were just being polite. – SEND

POLITE!! ARE YOU KIDDING ME? – SEND

No, not kidding, just stating what might indeed be a fact. You need to calm down. Gosh! You modern day emperors do get all overexcited, don't you? – SEND

Well, for all I know you could be a lousy kisser too. – SEND

Oh dear Jonathan, more ungentlemanly behaviour from you, haven't you learnt your lesson? Also it's a bit rude of you, it's possible I'm lousy at kissing I suppose, extremely unlikely but possible.
Oh deary, deary me it's such a shame that you'll never get to find out isn't it? – SEND

If you would just tell me where you live we could put this theory to the test right now and then I could show you just how overexcited I can be? – SEND

Ah well if you can't even guess that Henry is my cat I'm not sure you could ever find my house. Aren't you in London anyway? – SEND

It's less than two hours away. Think about it, I could be with you before 4.00am. You are driving me crazy – SEND

I aim to please. Now go to bed-SEND

Once again are you kidding me, I am all excited now – how am I going to sleep thinking of you and what I would like to be doing with you.-SEND

Okay, she thought, time to go. She hadn't agreed to see him again, so let's see what his next move would be.

Well, I'm going to sleep now. Big day tomorrow with Miles. Goodnight Jonathan. – SEND.

Seriously are you going to leave me just hanging? – SEND

He waited and waited, no response. She'd gone to bed, he would have loved to have gone with her. This wasn't over, in fact it was only just beginning. The flowers, well, they were predictable but something told him she would have nice manners and thank him for sending them. The rest of tonight was like winning the lottery, they were back on track he was sure of it, although which track remained to be seen, so now for his next move.

Chapter 6

Evelyn arrived at the gym just before 9.00 am. She didn't want Steve to bawl her out for being late and besides she was going to spend the day with Miles Brady. She hoped he would be a nice guy and not some ego maniac only interested in himself. Stacey called her over to reception.

"Hi Evelyn, do you know who that is in with Steve?"

"Well I'm supposed to be looking after an American student today who's going to be with us for a year so I'd guess it's him."

"You will to introduce him to me won't you?" Stacey asked eagerly.

Evelyn knocked on the office door and went inside. Well Miles Brady was a delight, pure and simple. Tall, about 6' 2," at a guess, African American from Chicago, lovely smile that lit up his whole face, quietly spoken with nice manners. He stood up when she entered the office and shook her hand when Steve introduced them. This was going to be a good day. She showed Miles around. He was smart and asked good thoughtful questions. She introduced him to all the staff who were in that day, especially Stacey who she thought looked as if she'd died and gone to heaven.

They went for lunch together and she found out more about him. Yes, they were going to be very lucky to have him with them for the next 12 months, client numbers would definitely increase once word got out that he was a new personal trainer. Jack would have a run for his money up against Miles and she would bet anything that Miles would come out on top. She taught her two usual Thursday night classes 6.00 till 7.00 and then 7.00 till 8.00, today had flown by and she was in a much better mood especially after her late night text chat with the modern day Julius Cesar. Stacey called out to her as she was leaving for the night.

"Hold on, Evelyn, you have a parcel, it arrived whilst you were teaching."

"Thanks, Stacey." This could only be from one person, he still didn't have her home address so he'd sent whatever it was to her place of work. She put the box in the car and drove home. Shower first, eat supper then open the box, she decided. Well, she showered but couldn't resist opening the box before she sat down to eat. Sure enough it was more flowers, this time, pale cream and lilac freesias with ranunculus mixed through. Not as grand as the peonies, now they really were a big gesture, but these were more intimate and somehow more romantic. She hunted round for another vase and then stared at them whilst she ate her chicken. This meant two things, firstly he wasn't going to let the idea go of the two of them being together and secondly he knew she'd message him to thank him.

Supper over, she turned off her music and picked up her iPad. It was now just after 9.30 and whilst she wouldn't normally call someone after 9.00pm she thought it was okay to send a message. She climbed into bed and began to type.

Hi. I got your parcel today, the flowers are lovely, thank you. – SEND

He responded straight away.

I'm glad you like them.-SEND

You don't need to keep doing this, you know. How did you know I'd be at work today? – SEND

I know that but I wanted to. I called the gym and asked, Stacey was very obliging. How was your day? – SEND

Oh it was really good, I spent the whole day with dreamy Miles, such a joy. – SEND

Oh no! Just when he'd relaxed about Henry, now there was this Miles person to contend with.

Dreamy? Are you going to elaborate? – SEND

No not yet, just dreaminess personified. – SEND

Is that even a word? – SEND

Don't care any which way sir. – SEND

So she was in a good mood and was toying with him again. This he liked, in fact, he liked it a lot.

Did you get any sleep last night? – SEND

Yes eventually, Henry and I cuddled up together-SEND

Luck old Henry! –SEND. She ignored this but was silently very happy.

How about you? – SEND

Well I didn't cuddle up with anyone and did get back to sleep but quite late on, but then you already know I had other things on my mind. – SEND

What kind of things? – SEND

You know very well what things, is your memory going? – SEND

My memory is just fine and dandy thank you. – SEND

So when am I going to get the chance to find out if you are a good kisser or not? – SEND

Oh he was straight to the point and getting impatient. Evie smiled.

I'm not sure if you're ever going to, I haven't forgiven you yet. – SEND

YET, so there's a chance that you will? – SEND

He was overjoyed that she was even thinking about it.

Maybe and maybe not, it all depends on your behaviour. – SEND

Yes I rather think that it does, so what do I have to do? – SEND

Jonathan, Jonathan I've told you before it's not up to me to tell you that, you'll have to figure it out for yourself. Oh by the way did your boss discover what a total fraud you are? – SEND

So no clues? And no I am still gainfully employed – for the moment anyway. – SEND

What exactly do you do at work? – SEND

It's all rather dull to be honest. I expect your job is a lot more exciting and interesting than mine, especially since you spent it with dreamy Miles. – SEND

Ah so you are thinking about dreamy Miles and yes you're quite right he spent the day with me at work. In fact I'm going to be spending a lot more time with dreamy Miles as he's here for a whole year. – SEND

A whole year? – SEND

Yes I never lie, it's one of my pet hates in life, you're just going to have to deal with it. – SEND

Maybe I should come in and meet this Miles? – SEND

Only if you're a member and I don't think you are? – SEND

True but I could join, even if it was just to meet him. – What does he do anyway? – SEND

Oh Jonathan more questions haven't you learnt your lesson yet? – SEND

Sorry. – SEND

Well yet again I will let you out of your misery. Miles is our new scholarship student from Chicago and he's here for 12 months learning the ropes and doing personal training sessions. There, happy now? – SEND-

What kind of personal training sessions? – SEND

Oh you know, very, very personal ones, very hands on type of thing, where it's just the two of you – one on one, very physical, intense and touchy feely kind of sessions.-SEND

There that should get him all worked up, she laughed.

Jesus Christ! Would this nightmare never end, he sighed.

Seriously? – SEND

Oh, calm down. You are getting your knickers in a knot again. – SEND

You are such a frustrating woman, do you know that? – SEND

Ah so the truth is finally out. Yesterday I was – now what words did you use, oh yes pretty, funny, smart and smiley and today because you can't get your own way I'm now frustrating. Interesting viewpoint. I wonder what a psychiatrist would make of it? – SEND

Can we talk properly instead of messaging? – SEND

Um not today I'm more comfortable with this, at least until I know you're not going to fuck me over again. – SEND

That's never going to happen. You have my word. – SEND

Ah, but is that the word of a gentleman or a fuckwit? – SEND

She was being brave and reckless now but wanted to see what he was made of.

A gentleman, I'm not even sure what a fuckwit is. – SEND

Ah I can help you there, look no further than last Saturday afternoon, in a certain coffee shop in town! – SEND

Fair enough! Now can we please talk about US? – SEND

US, is there an US? – SEND

Well there is in my mind yes. – SEND

You seem to be getting rather ahead of yourself. – SEND

Have dinner with me? – SEND

Why should I? – SEND

Because I want to spend some time with you, just the two of us. – SEND

I don't know if that's a good idea. – SEND

Please Evelyn. – SEND

I'm not sure. – SEND

Just think about it, if you don't enjoy my company you can leave whenever you want and I promise not to bother you again. – SEND

She was thinking, this could be dangerous. He'd already proved to be a giant pain in the arse and surely if she gave in now he wouldn't realise the enormity of what he'd done. No this was making it far too easy for him, he was probably so used to getting his own way and he hadn't even considered she would turn his offer down. She would point out the facts to him and wait for his response.

You are obviously used to getting your own way ALL the time, which by the way is very unhealthy. You have to realise the enormity of what you've done. Any other person would have just told Jacob to fuck off – which is what you should have done by the way, not just sat back and enjoyed the show. You could see my discomfort yet you did nothing, I was very, very upset, I hate that you made me cry. You might make me cry again, so no I don't think dinner is a good idea. – SEND

Shit, this was going wrong again. He'd underestimated her, in spite of all this texting and frivolity she was still hurting.

I hate myself for making you cry too, you have to believe me? You're right I should have stopped Jacob. It was a huge mistake on my part, I know that now. – SEND

So my answer is thank you; but no thank you.? – SEND

Look, tomorrow is Friday and I'll be home in the evening. Maybe we could talk again then, once you've had time to think about things? – SEND

What things? I'm not sure there's anything else to think about. Goodnight Jonathan – SEND And she was gone again.

What had started out so well had pretty much disintegrated. So now what? He would be home tomorrow and would try again. Maybe try a more personal approach this time, not give her the chance to run away.

Chapter 7

Friday was just another day, but Jonathan couldn't wait for it to be over. He'd planned to leave early so he would be home before 4.00pm in order to shower and change before setting out again. His florists had greeted him like an old friend and he'd bought Evelyn a small bouquet of scented wild flowers, old fashioned flowers he thought she would appreciate. Alan dropped him home a little after 3.30pm.

Evie finished at 6.00 and decided to shower and change at the gym. Pulling up her jeans and tying her hair back, now it was the weekend and she was free. She pulled a pale green top over her head. It was one of her favourites and she knew it intensified the colour of her brown eyes. Evie was feeling good for a change especially after the events of the past week. Some light makeup, a dab of perfume and she was ready to leave. She worked every 2 out of 3 weekends and now this one was all hers. Miles, well he was already causing quite a stir; but he looked like he could take care of himself. She'd given him her mobile number just in case he needed her advice before Monday; but was sure he wouldn't be calling. Miles held the door open for her, "Goodnight Evelyn." She'd wished him a goodnight too. He really was a lovely chap, shame he was far too young for her, perhaps he had an older brother she thought to herself and laughed, now that would have been interesting.

Evie walked out into the late afternoon sunshine and made her way across the car park to her car. But leaning against the bonnet of her car was Jonathan Dempsey, smiling at her, holding yet another bunch of flowers. Oh bollocks! How was she going to escape this time? Jonathan watched her walk towards him. She was laughing at something, a private joke perhaps; but once she'd spotted him she looked a lot more serious. Bring it on!

"Hello there. I thought if you wouldn't come to me, then you leave me no choice but to come to you."

"Hello – this is a surprise." She was nervous just looking at him, her face was starting to colour too, oh no how embarrassing.

"These are for you, I thought you might prefer these?" He handed her the flowers and she immediately brought them up to her face to smell the scent, they were perfect, just perfect. He was delighted that she obviously liked them, yes she liked them a lot.

"Thank you they're lovely; but I now have enough to open my own florists."

"Glad you like them." Oh he was good, yes very smooth, maybe a bit too smooth for her though she thought to herself. She changed the subject.

"What are you doing here?"

"I told you, I've come to see you, we've spent too long e-mailing and texting and I needed to see you in person."

"What for?"

"Oh Evelyn, you know what for. I want you to have dinner with me, just be with me, talk to me – please?"

"When?"

"Right now."

"NOW?" She sounded panicky all of a sudden, he had caught her literally on the hop and she couldn't decide which side of the fence she should be on. "I don't know."

He looked puzzled. This wasn't confident, playful Evie e-mailing him, she was shy, nervous, jumpy even, she was a mass of contradictions.

"It's just a meal, if you're not enjoying yourself then you can leave whenever you like."

"Well that's big of you," she snapped, then immediately said, "Sorry that was mean."

"It's okay, look my car is here we can be there in 20 minutes, what do you say – it's just a meal in a pub with lots of other people around – please say yes?"

"I have a question for you."

"Okay ask away."

She tilted her head on one side and looked up at him. "Will Jacob be joining us?"

He threw his head back and laughed, "Christ I bloody hope not."

"Well okay then, but I'll follow you in my car, then I really can leave whenever I like."

"Okay," he was just relieved she had said yes. "If I lose you then I'll pull over and wait for you."

"No I won't be pulling over, if you lose me then you lose me that's just the chance you're going to have to take."

Blimey! What was that all about? But he agreed and they set off, her following his Range Rover, keeping a safe distance behind.

Less than 20 minutes later he pulled into the pub car park. It was starting to get busy, well it was a Friday night after all. He waited for her to pull in after him; but she'd slowed right down almost as if she was planning to keep on driving. Just when he thought he was finally going to spend time with her it looked as if she'd changed her mind. Then at the last second her car swung in and she parked next to him. He'd never been so relieved.

His hand sought hers and he wrapped his hand around hers. Suddenly he felt better, calm and happy. He was itching to put his arm around her waist, but decided not to frighten her off before the evening had even begun. They found a table and he went to get them a drink. This was half the battle. She'd said yes, and here she was, with him, just the two of them for the next few hours.

The time went by surprisingly quickly. They ordered food and it was very good. Evie made the waitress laugh when she asked for smaller cutlery for her small hands; but they found her a smaller set nonetheless. It turned out that they had a lot in common and talked about their families, work and avoided anything too personal. Jonathan took hold of her hand across the table, "I just wanted to say sorry again for what happened with Jacob. I never should have let him carry on like he did, I'm so relieved that you're giving me a second chance."

Evie interrupted him. "Oh, so is this what this is?" She looked at him questioningly and appeared to have wrong-footed him again.

"Well yes, isn't it? I mean, I was hoping it would be. I mean I want to see you again after this… I," He was floundering now.

"I'll have to think about it." Just when he thought it was all sorted she'd surprised him again, he couldn't keep up with her.

They continued to eat, until Evie caught him staring at her, she put her cutlery down and touched her face awkwardly, "Um do I have something on my face?"

Jonathan smiled, "No I was just thinking how lovely you are."

Evie swallowed hard, went pink, picked up her cutlery and gave her salad some serious attention. Jonathan continued to watch her, if she'd been one of his previous types she'd have had a smart comment to respond with, something like, 'well yes I'm gorgeous and you're lucky to be out with me at all, 'kind of thing; but Evie didn't say a word, just got all embarrassed and wouldn't look at him. She seemed nervy and a bit jumpy and then at 9.30pm, she suddenly announced she was leaving.

"Um you don't have to rush off, do you? I thought you had the weekend free? Can I see you tomorrow?"

"It's been a long day and I'm tired," she lied. She needed to escape and put some distance between them, she wanted to think things through. Fiona and David were going to go ballistic with her for going out with him and she would have to go and see them tomorrow morning – she wasn't looking forward to that one bit.

He realized she wasn't about to change her mind and taking her hand in his he walked her to her car.

"So tomorrow then?" he asked expectantly.

"What about it," – she was being deliberately obtuse

"Can I see you again?"

"I'll think about it."

Suddenly he caught her by surprise and hugged her to him. She couldn't move.

"Jonathan what are you doing?" It felt like he was smelling her neck and seemed to be in no hurry to let her go. This was torture of the very best kind

"Just saying goodnight." She was quite tense, he had to find a way to get her to relax around him or this was never going to work. He was quite desperate to squeeze her bum; but thought if he tried it on now she'd never see him again.

"Well you can let me go now."

"What if I don't want to, I'm very happy where I am thank you."

"Jonathan, Jonathan we've talked about this," she was laughing at him. "It's not all about you, remember?" He groaned, "But you smell so good, what is that?"

She deliberately misunderstood his question and said, "I think you'll find it's called disobedience."

Laughing he let her go. "That's not what I meant and you know it. Text me when you get home?"

"Yes I will, Thank you for the meal. I've had a lovely evening." She gave him a quick kiss on the cheek, immediately he stepped towards her and Evie stepped back and put her hand out in front of her. She said quietly, "I'm going now, don't spoil it." He stayed put and with that she was in her car and had gone.

What the fuck was that all about he wondered as he got into his car? He drove home pondering his next move. This wasn't going to be as straightforward as he'd first hoped.

Evie arrived home and switched on the hall lights. She'd surprised herself and had actually enjoyed his company. After locking the front door she went upstairs. Henry would already be out on the tiles seeking some amusing diversion to toy with so it was just her. She put her pyjamas on and started her nightly cleansing routine. This was the third time today she'd cleansed her face. Someone, somewhere was making a big profit out of her. She was smiling to herself, she had enjoyed tonight, he was good company, quite charming with a good sense of humour too, plus in her eyes he was quite good looking which never hurt, did it? She brushed her teeth and got into bed. Her phone pinged at her. Oh! She'd forgotten to text him.

"Where are you, are you at home?" – SEND

"Yes, sorry I was just getting ready for bed."-SEND

"I was worried about you."-SEND

"No need."-SEND

"I enjoyed tonight, can I see you tomorrow?"-SEND

"You don't give up do you?"-SEND

"No."-SEND

"Am going to live chat now."
"I have some errands to run in the morning; but have a few hours after lunch, what did you have in mind?"-SEND

He wasn't going to tell her that, not yet anyway and liked the fact that they were back on safer territory, whatever did people do before texting and e-mailing?

"Can your errands wait? How about you come over to mine for lunch?"-SEND

"No they can't, I don't just sit about on my free weekends just in case something or someone comes along you know. I could come over for a cup of tea though if you like?" – SEND. She was curious to see where he lived so a cup of tea was fairly innocent wasn't it?

It wasn't what he wanted; but he would have taken any morsel she threw at him right now.

"Perfect, I'll text you the address tomorrow."-SEND

He waited for a reply but none came so he typed, "What are you doing now?"-SEND

"I'm in bed e-mailing this annoying person who won't leave me alone!" – SEND

He smiled, "You're in bed already?" – SEND

"Yes, but I'm guessing you are sat at your kitchen table drinking a glass of red wine, wearing exactly the same clothes you had on an hour ago, am I right?" – SEND

"Spot on, are you psychic or something? What are you wearing?" – SEND

This was getting a bit personal now, she had to lighten the mood although she was quite safe hiding behind her texting.

"That sounds a bit pervy, you do realise that there are laws about this sort of thing?" – SEND

"Just humour me, just this once – please?" – SEND

Okay Mr smarty pants you want to go down this road then bring it on she laughed, this could be fun after all.

"Okay stop getting your knickers in a knot, speaking of which surely you are running out of knickers by now, as so many pairs have been ruined?" – SEND

"Guys don't wear knickers, you must know this?" – SEND

"Okay so what are you wearing then?" – SEND

"I thought we were talking about what you're wearing, but okay I'll go first. I wear boxers. I could come round and show you if you like?" – SEND

"No need. I do know what men's boxers look like." – SEND

"So I'll ask you again, what are you wearing?" – SEND

"Pyjamas" – SEND

"I think I may need slightly more than that to go on." – SEND

"Okay, the fabric is very soft and the pattern is pale blue flowers on a white background, the hems have lace around them and a matching cami top – there. Happy now?" – SEND. Let's see how you respond to that.

"What's a cami top?" – SEND

"Boys – don't they teach you anything at these expensive private schools? You obviously have a lot to learn; but I'll explain. It's a very small piece of flimsy soft fabric with lace across the front and décolleté with spaghetti straps." – SEND

"No am still confused. I must have missed that particular lecture at school. What are spaghetti straps? Perhaps I should pop round and see for myself?" – SEND

"Nice try, but no dice. Spaghetti straps are tiny, thin straps of fabric that hold the top in place, so it doesn't fall down." – SEND There. If that didn't get him all excited then nothing would.

Blimey he definitely wanted to see this for himself; but as she still hadn't told him her address he didn't have a lot of choice in the matter. He ran his hands through his hair, what next?

"Is it getting hot or is that just me?" – SEND

"I think it's just you, maybe it's the red wine, or maybe you need to take some exercise to calm down?" – SEND

"What sort of exercise did you have in mind?" – SEND

"Something gentle like yoga or Pilates, you know lots of stretching, and slow breathing. It's very relaxing." – SEND

"Will you teach me?" – SEND. Preferably right now?

"Maybe, but it sounds as if you might just need a cold shower instead! I think we need to change the subject now" – SEND

He laughed, yes she might be right about that.

"Okay then, is Henry with you?" – SEND

She thought she'd tell a white lie, well they didn't really count did they? "Yes he's curled up keeping my feet warm." – SEND

"If I was there, you wouldn't need Henry to keep you warm." –SEND

"Do you mean you'd make me a hot water bottle and get an extra blanket?" – SEND

He laughed, no he bloody didn't, she was toying with him now and he was so used to getting his own way that he was finding this experience exasperating.

"Not exactly, again I could come over and demonstrate." – SEND

"Nice try, sunshine" – SEND. She was beginning to wish she hadn't gone down this particular route now.

Okay she'd asked for it. He was going to take a chance and pray that the gamble paid off.

"Well for starters I wouldn't be wearing boxers and you wouldn't be wearing pyjamas. – SEND

"It sounds like you definitely need to take that cold shower we were discussing." – SEND

"Will you come and scrub my back?" – SEND

"Only if you ask me nicely." –SEND

"Oh, believe me, I would ask you very, very nicely." – SEND

She needed this to stop now. What had started out as a bit of fun was getting her into deep water.

"Another time perhaps, I need to get some sleep now and stop messaging this modern day Julius Cesar chap. Maybe you know him, he's a bit of a megalomaniac, in desperate need of a cold shower who has an unhealthy obsession with women's pyjamas?" – SEND

"You're going – NOW? But I was just getting to the good bit." – SEND

She really shouldn't ask; but couldn't stop herself.

"I know I am going to regret asking this; but what pray would that be? – SEND

He paused over the keyboard, just how far was he going to go? He started to type.

"Well the particular exercise I had in mind involves just the two of us, lying in bed together, no boxers or pyjamas in sight. No blankets or hot water bottle either. – SEND

"This is very forward of you, sir, considering we haven't even kissed and I'm concerned I'll catch hypothermia!" – SEND

Jonathan laughed, no she wouldn't catch hypothermia. His penis was getting excited just thinking about it. Please God soon they would kiss and he could take her to bed. He groaned to himself. She was driving him crazy and she wasn't even in the same room as him. But she was quite a funny little thing and he realised he'd fallen for her heavily already.

"Well we could try the kissing thing tomorrow, you know just get it out of the way and no you won't catch cold. It starts off fairly cool then gets warm and gradually gets hotter and hotter. There's a lot of touching and exploring, with hands and mouths, a lot of kissing some of which is soft and some a lot more passionate and breathless, kissing in all sorts of forbidden places. There's stroking and sighing. Pleasurable moaning and then it begins really slowly, but gets gradually faster. That's the type of exercise I had in mind." – SEND

Shit had he gone too far, reading it back it was a dangerous tack to take especially with her. He waited and no reply pinged back, he waited another five minutes, shit she was scaring him now. He'd gone too far, much too far, his own impatience had got the better of him and he'd be lucky to see her tomorrow after all.

"Evie are you still there? Talk to me." – SEND

Bloody hell! She had got herself in a right pickle with this. What had started out as some fun messaging from the privacy of her own home had just come back and royally bitten her on the bum. How the fuck was she going to respond to that? She read it three times, he had a certain turn of phrase that much was true, it wasn't coarse or vulgar, just, well, just such a bloody turn on if she was being honest with herself. Shit, now what was she going to say in reply to that?

Eventually she typed: "Yes I'm still here." – SEND He had never been so relieved.

"Sorry I went too far, didn't I?" – SEND

"It was my own fault, I asked!" – SEND

"You're still going to come tomorrow and see me aren't you?" – SEND

"I don't know." – SEND

"I promise I will be the perfect gentleman, just tea and I'll introduce you to my little brother who's on holiday from uni; although personally it sounds like one long holiday to me. He has 3 friends staying so you can meet them too. Please say you'll come over Evie, Please?" – SEND

She read his message. He sounded sorry, it had been her fault she never should have asked, what the hell was she thinking – the answer was she wasn't thinking at all.

"Text me your address in the morning and I'll see you about 2.30 – Goodnight Jonathan." – SEND

He was ecstatic. She was still coming over. Mentioning Jamie and his friends had implied safety in numbers and that was a pure stroke of genius. He'd never felt so happy. Now to take that cool shower, boy did he need it.
"Goodnight Evie." – SEND

Jonathan sat at the kitchen table for quite a while after she'd gone. She'd got right under his skin, it was baffling; but it was exciting and although he was frustrated he was enjoying this, well whatever this was. The chase? No it didn't feel like she was playing hard to get, more like she was trying to protect herself. He had to find a way to break through her defences and soon, he was desperate to see her again, hold her, kiss her and then go to bed with her. His mind drifted off imagining what that would be like. She was right he needed a cold shower now, but all he could think about was the two of them in the shower together and he happily let his imagination drift on and on.

Chapter 8

Saturday was dull and overcast. After Evie had been for a run and showered, she knew she couldn't put it off any longer she had to go and see Fiona and David. They were going to hit the roof she was sure of it, but only prolonging telling them would make it so much worse. No it had to be done and she braced herself for their response.

Arriving on their doorstep just after 11.00am she could hear the children laughing inside. She smiled to herself. They were great parents, they only had two children but she was sure Fiona would have liked at least two more. They were pleased to see her and she sat at the kitchen table whilst the kettle was switched on and the children ushered out into the playroom with the door open so Fiona could keep an eye on them.

"So what brings you round again so soon, he hasn't done anything to hurt you has he?" The person not referred to by name was of course Jonathan Dempsey.

"No he hasn't, in fact he sent me more flowers, to the gym."

"Well he can certainly afford it I suppose. Have you spoken to him?"

"Yes, well texting/messaging mostly." This was only a half – truth but she was finding it difficult to gauge Fiona's reaction.

Evie took a deep breath. "Actually we went out last night for a meal together at The Lamb Inn and it was very nice." She waited for the explosion. None came. Fiona looked shocked David, being David, kept quiet and waited for Evie to carry on talking. "I decided to give him a second chance and I'm going over to his house this afternoon for a cup of tea, I thought I ought to come and tell you."

Fiona spoke next. She wasn't angry, just concerned, "Are you sure this is what you want after last week?"

"I know, I know he behaved appallingly, and he told me that both of you had called him, which by the way was news to me. I know you're only looking out for me; but if I don't take some of these chances then I never will and I'll be all alone, HE will have won and I couldn't bear that. (the 'HE' she was referring to wasn't Jonathan but someone else they never mentioned). Surely there has to be one good guy out there, after you David of course," and she smiled at him.

David spoke next. "Well we can't tell you who you should see obviously and prior to last week I always thought he was a decent chap so maybe we ought to give him the benefit of the doubt, just this once?"

Evie stood and hugged both her friends, "I love it that you bawled him out for me. I just wish I knew what you'd said. Jonathan said you were quite terrifying, Fiona."

"Well I was so mad. I just let him have it and once I'd started I couldn't stop. Are you really sure about this?"

"I have to try, if not with him then someone else. So yes, I'm going for tea and I'll text you to let you know how it goes, okay?"

Driving home she thought it had gone a lot better than she expected, yes they were concerned; but then they probably always would be. She fixed herself some lunch and made sure Henry had some food in his bowl. She wasn't planning on being late home, as she was driving to her mother's tomorrow to spend the day with her and was really looking forward to it. Her mother was the strongest person she knew, and after her father's death she really stepped up and made sure both her children didn't go off the rails. Evie would never forget the pain and anguish on her mother's face when she eventually regained consciousness. She never wanted to put her through that again.

Evie had changed into her favourite jeans and paired them with a lilac stretchy shirt type top. She put on some flat sandals with crystals down the front and they sparkled as the light caught them, casual and not trying too hard was the look she was aiming for and this would be just fine. Jonathan had texted his address and she took out her road map to make sure she knew which route to take. She was planning to visit the car showroom on Wednesday morning and order her new car, one with sat nav this time.

Just after 2.30 she pulled into a long driveway that led up to a very imposing looking house. Crikey was this where he lived? He had said to park in front of the converted stables as he actually lived there, whilst his parents and Jamie lived in the main house itself. She hadn't even released her seat belt before he was in the courtyard and walking over to her door. He looked so pleased to see her, which in fact he was. All morning he thought that there was still a good chance that she wouldn't show up at all so to see her arrive had made his day. So far he had spent the morning trying to concentrate on reading the paper but had eventually given up. He was a bit nervous and had changed his shirt at least twice before he was happy with the plain navy blue one he now had on.

Evie got out of the car and they kissed each other on both cheeks. So far so good; they both looked very happy to see each other, he took her hand and walked her in through his front door. His home was lovely and she could see that a lot of thought and time had gone into the conversion. She said all the right things complimenting him on his taste of furnishings etc. and they went through into the kitchen where he switched the kettle on. Evie pulled out her own milk and tea from her bag.

"What's that?"

"Well I don't drink cow's milk and I'm fussy about tea too, so I thought it would be easier to bring my own."

"So I invite you for tea, but all I'm supplying is the cup and the water," he laughed.

"Yep! Pretty much," she smiled back at him. Last night's messaging was not going to be mentioned and for that she was grateful. They chatted about this and that, how she'd spent her morning. He thought she looked so pretty today, her bum looked particularly fine in her tight jeans and he couldn't stop staring at her. She told him she'd been to see Fiona and David as she had owed them that much at least. And her intention to order a new car on Wednesday.

He decided not to tell her that he'd received a text from Fiona at lunchtime, saying that she knew Evie was giving him a second chance, but that he wouldn't get a third one and if he fucked up again then she really would tear him apart.

After they'd drunk their tea they went to meet Jamie. Again he took her hand in his and they went over to the main house. She followed him into what looked like the TV room. Jamie was sat in an armchair whilst three other guys were on the sofa, all shouting at the screen. Chelsea were playing and the match obviously wasn't going very well. They looked up as Jonathan and Evie entered the room, Jamie stood up, so this was the mysterious Evelyn Wallace who wasn't on social media. Brief introductions were made but they were really more interested in the match than in her as it was a critical moment of play and Chelsea were already losing one-nil.

She walked over to the sofa, asked one of the guys to budge up and plonked herself down to watch the action. "So how come we're losing and what exactly have they been doing for the past 25 minutes?" she asked no-one in particular. They started to take notice of her now. Will replied that was exactly what they'd been asking themselves too. Jonathan leaned against the kitchen doorframe watching her being so at ease with his brother and his mates. It was like a totally different Evie, not the jumpy, nervous one he'd taken out to dinner last night. Maybe she was only nervous around him and maybe that was a good sign, perhaps she was attracted to him after all, he bloody hoped so?

There was plenty of shouting at the screen and holding their heads in their hands until the half time whistle blew and the players walked dejectedly off the pitch. "Boy their manager is going to give them a bloody good half time bollocking," she said out loud. They all laughed and the ice was well and truly broken. Jonathan had just come back into the room from the kitchen and had heard what she said. "I beg your pardon" – he was laughing at her now. "I was merely pointing out that they will be getting a rousing half time motivational pep talk from their manager complete with perfectly sliced orange segments to spur them on in the second half," she smiled sweetly at him.

The boys were more interested in her now. Jamie was intrigued by her as she was unlike any of his brothers' previous girlfriends, which in his view was a good thing as most of them had been a bloody nightmare. She made a point of re-introducing herself to them all and shaking their hands. Jamie was a younger version of Jonathan with dark hair. Will was tall and lean with a charming manner that she was sure would get him into trouble with women for a long time to come yet. George was smaller with a quieter manner and that only left Francis who wore spectacles; but seemed the most intriguing out of all of them, at least to her anyway.

Jumping up she offered to make them tea or bring them some more beers. She felt quite at home talking with Jamie and the boys, she wasn't nervous at all. "Don't wait on them Evie," Jonathan scolded, "or they'll expect this treatment every time." She laughed at him," you're only jealous, now move out of the way please I want a glass of water." Everyone followed Evie into the kitchen. They had only just met her but they liked her already, she was fun and easy to be around and more than anything she actually liked football.

They all sat around the kitchen table drinking beer and she asked them what uni they were at and what they were studying. Jamie was studying law, "Oh gosh I envy you, I would love to study law; but I'm not smart enough."

Will chipped in, "Neither is Jamie but they haven't found that out yet." This was such fun she thought, no pressure and just easy conversation, what a great afternoon. Will asked her what uni she was studying at. And she'd laughed so loudly with no hint of embarrassment. "Oh William," she mocked." You sure are a charmer, but you should know that line was never going to work on me; but you are more than welcome to keep on trying." This had brought the house down and Will tipped his beer bottle to her in respect. She grinned back at him. "Bloody hell, she's got you sussed," replied Jamie.

They watched the second half but there were no more goals. It was almost a relief when the referee blew his whistle. Evie groaned, "They played worse than girls." The boys looked at her, "Point of fact, gentlemen, she said, "I'm allowed to say that as I am in fact a girl – all of you however," she wagged her finger at them, "are not – as you are boys and that would be sexist, comprende? There was laughter all round and a discussion kicked off about a controversial off-side decision. Jonathan watched Evie and his little brother, each convinced that they were in the right. Neither of them would back down and they both had different opinions. Eventually Evie said, "Okay, why don't you put your money where your mouth is Mr Hot Shot Lawyer-to-be? We need to decide this once and for all. You obviously think that girls don't know the offside rule so we'll have a bet on it," Well this was too good to be true as far as Jamie was concerned, it would be like taking candy from a baby, bring it on.

They agreed that if Evie won then Jamie had to buy her dinner at the pub and that if Jamie won then she would cook dinner for him at her house during the week. They shook hands and then the bet was on. "Tell you what," said Evie," if you win, Jamie, I won't just cook dinner for you but will cook for all four of you, as I wouldn't want your friends to miss out." They all nodded readily. Okay now down to business. They agreed that Evie would go first explaining her version of the off-side rule, Will, George and Francis were to be the judges and if they weren't happy with her description then it would be up to Jamie to convince them that his version was indeed the correct one.

Evie stood up. "I'll need to borrow two people to demonstrate this properly," and asked George and Will to stand up in front of the television a few feet apart. She asked Will if she could touch him and he smiled lazily that she was to feel free. "Question," he said. "Why did you ask me?" "Habit I'm afraid," Evie explained that she taught fitness classes and that if a client was in the wrong position she had to ask their permission to put her hands on them, it avoided law suits of inappropriate behaviour being filed against the gym. She placed Will and George where she wanted them and quietly and simply explained the rule. The boy's faces were a picture. At the end of her speech Francis spoke with Will and George and decreed that yes that was indeed the off side rule and that Evie had won the bet. Jamie didn't look happy at all. She hugged him and told him he'd learnt two valuable lessons today. Firstly never to underestimate your opponent and secondly never place a bet that you couldn't afford to lose. Jonathan watched silently from the doorway. She had these boys eating out of the palm of her hand. He was slightly jealous that she had hugged Jamie and now it seemed they were all going down the pub to celebrate. Would he ever spend any time alone with her?

They needed two cars, so Evie drove hers and Jonathan drove the Range Rover as the boys had already drunk a few beers. They tossed a coin for who went with who and Evie took Francis and Jamie, whilst Jonathan took George and Will, who were both disappointed not to be in Evie's car. They arrived at the pub and noisily entered the bar. Jonathan got the first round in and they grabbed a large table, still talking and laughing nineteen to the dozen. Jonathan took hold of Evie's hand under the table and he was pleased she didn't pull it away; but she gave his hand a little squeeze as if to apologise for his date being railroaded.

Ten minutes later Will appeared with the pub darts and announced they were to split into teams of three for a little Saturday afternoon competition. They all agreed and then tried to work out the teams. Eventually it was decided that the best and worst players would team up followed by the next and so on. George asked Evie if she was a good player and there was stunned silence all round when she admitted that she'd never in fact played darts before. Jamie asked her if she was telling him the truth and she swore on her mother's life it was true. This meant that she was paired with Francis, Jonathan and Jamie were a team and Will and George. "Sorry Francis you're lumbered with me I'm afraid." He whispered to her, "It's fine, don't worry, we are still going to win," and smiled at her. She smiled back, he really was quite delightful. Jamie interrupted them. "What are you two whispering about?" Quick as a flash Francis replied, "Tactics," and winked at Evie.

She asked to have a few practice throws and before Jonathan had a chance Will put his arm around her waist and took her hand in his to demonstrate how to throw. Well Jonathan wasn't going to stand for this and said, "Thank you William but I think if anyone is going to show my girlfriend how to throw then it'll be me." Will moved away and Jonathan took his place. Cheeky bloody upstart, who did he think he was? Evie was secretly very pleased that, A: he'd called her his girlfriend and that B: his arms were now around her instead. He demonstrated the throwing action and after a few throws Evie's darts were at least staying in the board; but more by luck than actual skill. Jonathan was in charge of keeping score and the competition began. Francis proved to be an excellent player which made Evie feel even guiltier that he'd been saddled with her; but he was such a skilful player that before they knew it they'd taken a slight lead. "Are you sure you've never played before?" Jamie asked her again. She laughed, "It's true I've never played and after this I doubt I will ever again." It was getting increasingly tight now and there wasn't a lot dividing first and second place. The boys were all super competitive and Evie had forgotten that her brother Thomas had been just the same at their age.

They all had just one throw left, soon it was just her and Will left to throw. Francis was full of encouragement and told her to aim for the middle and keep her fingers crossed. She threw and scored a triple 15. Will would need to hit triple 20 to win now. He threw and although it was good it wasn't good enough. Evie and Francis had won.

She walked over to the bar and ordered a round of drinks complete with crisps and nuts. She had Jamie and his friends eating out of the palm of her hand, literally.

Jonathan joined her. "Having a good time?" he asked, "Yes the best," she grinned back at him. "You seem to be getting on well with Jamie etc.?" He's just like my little brother whom I miss very much," she explained. They took the drinks back to their table and she asked Jamie when he would be buying her the meal she'd won. "Whenever you like" was the reply. She felt bad for him now, he'd lost the bet and had now come last in the darts. It just wasn't his day.

"Tell you what, let's forget about that; although I'm still happy to cook for the four of you if you'd like that?"

"What about me?" Jonathan sulked. "Well you'll be in London and anyway I'm sure you'd prefer it if it was just the two of us rather than with this lot?" That cheered him up immensely. Too right, he'd like it to be just the two of them. It was agreed that the boys would come round on Wednesday evening and that Evie would cook them a meal. She'd text Jamie her address on Wednesday morning and they were to just bring themselves. She asked them about any food allergies; but apart from disliking goat's cheese they seemed happy to eat anything." What is it about goats' cheese?" she pondered out loud, "girls loved it and boys hated it, it really was very strange."

She looked at her watch. Crikey! She had to leave, it was going to be a long day tomorrow and she wanted to get a good night's sleep. "Well boys I'd love to stay and chat but I need to go." There were groans all round. "Really do you have to, we haven't played pool yet." "Would you believe me if I told you I'd never played that either," she laughed. "Well I bloody wouldn't," said Jamie, "that's for sure." She hugged them all whilst Jonathan gave the landlord some money to put Jamie and the boys in a taxi at closing time. Holding her hand he walked her out to her car. He couldn't believe that they'd hardly spent any time alone today. He loved his brother; but today had to be one of the most frustrating days ever.

"So will I see you tomorrow?"

"Um… no, afraid not."

"NO, not at all, really?"

"Sorry but I'm going to visit my mother for the day," she explained.

"Maybe I could come too?"

"No you can't, – I'm going on my own, I don't see enough of her as it is, it'll just be the two of us, no impressionable young men in the vicinity I promise!"

"So I have to wait until next weekend?" he groaned

"Yes afraid so. Look text me in the week and we'll arrange something definite for Saturday okay, I'll be free after 12.30pm" She felt bad for him now too. What was it with these Dempsey boys? She kissed him softly on the cheek and before he could kiss her again she'd stepped back and zapped her car to unlock the doors.

"Text me when you get home?" he pleaded

"Okay but no chatting tonight. I need to get some sleep. Bye, Jonathan." She drove away.

He stood staring at her car long after it had disappeared from sight. How the hell was he expected to get through the next 6 days? He'd have to think carefully about Saturday, take her somewhere special, just the two of them. He was desperate to kiss her, now more than ever. He drove himself back home. He was in a contemplative mood. As soon as he put his key in the door his phone pinged. It was Evie; she was home. But there were no flirty text chats tonight, his phone remained stubbornly silent until he couldn't bear to look at it anymore.

Chapter 9

Wednesday morning and Evie was having a lie in, well an extra hour in bed to be precise. She'd been looking forward to today ever since the weekend. Her mother had been so pleased to see her on Sunday and they'd enjoyed their day together just the two of them. Groaning she threw back the duvet. Okay, get moving you lazy so and so she told herself, get up, order your new car and get the final groceries for tonight. She was very happy at the thought of spending some fun time with Jamie and his friends and they seemed only too glad to be getting a free meal.

It was some years since she'd been into the sales part of the car dealership. She'd already done her research online at home and knew exactly what she wanted so she was out within the hour and headed towards the supermarket. The new car would arrive in about 3 months which was fine with her, she'd waited this long so it wouldn't make any difference. It being the middle of the week the supermarket was fairly quiet too so she was home for lunch just after midday.

She sent a quick text to Jamie with her address and received one from Jonathan hoping she enjoyed her evening. He was still annoyed that he couldn't be there; but since returning to London on Monday morning he'd rung down to the gym in the hotel where he had his serviced apartment and booked in an hour's daily personal training session with Mike from 6.30pm. He needed to get fitter, especially if he was to keep up with Evie. Plus it would give him something to focus on in the evenings instead of wondering what she was doing all the time. Tonight, of course, he knew exactly what she was doing and later that same evening he grimaced as Mike spared him no mercy at all.

Evie was just tweaking the cutlery she'd laid out on the table when she saw the taxi pull up outside. On opening the door she was speechless; although she'd told the boys to come as they were they'd obviously decided to ignore her and were all wearing black dinner jackets and white shirts paired with jeans. Secretly she was very pleased to see that they'd made an effort;

although she suspected they thought they looked like something from 'Reservoir Dogs' she thought that 'Reservoir Puppies' might be more apt. They'd brought her some flowers and there were hugs all round as she brought them into the kitchen and got George to open the bottle of champagne. She gave them blinis with smoked salmon and they toasted "Cheers!" with the champagne.

The boys took loads of selfies of their evening and promised to e-mail her all the photos. They all seemed very relaxed and she'd already put some background music on to help ease the mood. She needn't have worried. They ate everything that was put in front of them, drank whatever was to hand and talked non-stop. After she'd cleared away their main courses talk turned to girlfriends. She wanted to know all the details, or as much as they were going to tell her anyway. Jamie it seemed was between girls at the present, Will had more than two women dancing attendance on him at any one time, George has been going out with Sophie for the past year and that just left Francis.

"So Francis you're single, have you got your eye on anyone in particular?"

"Um no not really," – the boys all joshed with him, but he took it good-naturedly as always.

"Well I'm sure someone will come along and catch your eye probably when you least expect it," she said.

Jamie then asked her, "It's your turn now, so how did you meet my charming brother? Did you know he asked me to look you up on social media – the guy thinks he's a genius; but can't figure out anything like that."

"No I didn't know that," she smiled – well Jamie was full of surprises tonight – "and I wouldn't exactly say he was charming, at least not on our first date anyway." She was careful not to give out too much information but explained they had been introduced by mutual friends in the supermarket. This brought on a coughing, spluttering fit from Jamie who took a good few minutes to recover. "Oh my God, Jon was in a supermarket, that's priceless. I'd wish I'd been there to see him with his basket, now that would be one photo that would have been on Facebook instantly." She explained that they'd gone for a coffee the following week; but that it had been nothing short of a disaster. Not saying too much she asked Jamie if he knew this Jacob character, but he didn't. "Never heard of him, he can't be a close friend of his as I've never met him or heard Jon talking about him."

"Well he's a bloody nightmare of the most epic proportions," she laughed and vaguely alluded to an interrogation more worthy of a courtroom battle or a lamb to the slaughter. "So no you could say it didn't go very well at all," she continued, "the worst things were that I was in such a hurry to escape that

I left my lovely flowers behind and then I burst into tears on the way home and couldn't see where I was going" – she made a joke of it – "boys, just so you know for future reference, us girls cannot drive and cry at the same time, it's a big failing on our part."

"So all these bunches of flowers in your house are from Jon trying to make amends?"

"Yes pretty much, I took pity on him in the end and decided to give him a second chance and the rest you know."

She jumped up and brought out dessert, asking George to pour more wine so the subject was definitely closed. Jamie was surprised about his brother's behaviour. True, his previous girlfriends were all quite dreadful in his opinion; but making Evie cry, well that was just too much – he was amazed she'd given him a second chance. .In an instant he'd e-mailed Jon a picture of the five of them squished together all in a row grinning at the camera phone, obviously having a lot of fun without him. The message read, 'can't believe you made her cry!," There, let him look at that and feel bad, in Jamie's eyes he deserved it.

After dessert she brought out a selection of cheese and they stated to talk about their families. It was interesting and they had a small competition with whose mother was the most strict. There were the usual tales of being locked out after a late night, being drunk and not getting up in the morning which usually involved pulling the duvet away until they were so cold they had to get out of bed. Evie thought she'd saved the best till last. "You think that's bad, well my mother still won't let me eat in the street and I'm older than you are," she laughed, Jamie looked confused, "What do you mean exactly?"

"Just what I said, my brother and I aren't allowed to eat in the street,- ever! The only exceptions are an ice cream, but you have to officially be at the seaside and then it is allowed and secondly you're allowed if it's a picnic; but again it has to be a proper one." The boys were speechless. George asked, "What about a can of cola or something?"

"Oh my God George," she replied laughing, "are you quite insane, drink from a can in the street without a glass, my mother would be apoplectic!" They all agreed Evie had won that round easily.

They cleared the table and made their way into the living room. Evie put on some more upbeat music and told them all that now it was time for dancing. Their faces were a picture, "You all look as if I just told you we are going to have a competition to see who can keep their hand in a pan of boiling oil the longest. Come on, up on your feet all of you, you need to work off all that food and I'll teach you some moves." Jamie propped his mobile up on the bookcase and switched on the video function, this might be worth a laugh he thought.

"I can think of other ways to work it off," Will said rather suggestively to her.

"William behave," she scolded him mockingly, "or else we will have to throw you outside and lock the door and you'll have to view us all having fun without you with your nose pressed up against the glass like this," she made a face and they all laughed. In no time she had persuaded them to move the coffee table, roll up the rug and push the sofas back and they had the makings of a small dance floor. She had them up on their feet, trying to get them to move to the beat and follow some of her moves.

MUSIC: – I SEE YOU BABY – GROOVE ARMARDA FEAT.GRAM'MA FUNK.

They were eventually dancing to songs that had 'shake your ass' and 'rock this party' in the chorus and everyone was having such a good time. After only half an hour the boys slumped in to the sofa and chairs looking exhausted.

Evie laughed at them, "Gosh! when was the last time you lot took any exercise?" Quick as a flash she said to Will, "And I mean in the gym young man not in the bedroom!" There were various murmurings and excuses.

Will asked her if she would like to be his personal trainer. She pushed her index finger into the squishiest part of his tummy and replied, "Sorry, honey, but I just don't think you could keep up with me." Well this brought the house down and there was a lot of laughter and joshing between them all. Francis went to fetch more wine just as Evie was asking if any of them had learnt ballroom dancing when they were younger. Again they looked horrified at the prospect. Francis asked what he had missed and it turned out that, yes he knew how to waltz and maybe quickstep; but it had been a long time ago. His friends tried to give him a hard time over this new information; but when it turned out he would be dancing with Evie they all quietened down with the realisation that they'd wanted to be the ones to dance with her. Before he knew it Evie had grabbed him and declared they were going to show the others how a quickstep should be done. Francis looked a little scared but she walked him through a few moves and then changed the music. Jamie meanwhile picked up his phone. He wanted to capture this particular gem, thinking he could blackmail Francis for weeks with this.

MUSIC: – HERE IN YOUR ARMS – KARAOKE KIDS

The music changed, not to something classical as they had expected but the song playing was 'Here in your arms', a remix with a fast beat and catchy chorus. Evie and Francis took up their hold position and then they were off, moving fast across the floor diagonally to the chorus and then turning slowly into the corners, with plenty of rise and fall and dip and sway. Her silver pleated skirt billowed out making it seem as if she was gliding effortlessly over the floor. His friends sat and watched Francis take control and lead Evie round the small space with ease, making it look so easy. Secretly they envied him like mad, he was a dark horse make no mistake. The music ended and Evie and Francis took a dramatic bow and curtsey. The others whooped and clapped. Who knew ballroom dancing could be so much fun? Evie hugged Francis and kissed him on his cheek, "Francis that was amazing, thank you so much. Now gentlemen if I was a lot younger – then finding a guy like Francis who can dance like that would have been the icing on the cake for me. Do you cook as well?" Francis shook his head. "Shame, as that would have been the cherry on the top," she laughed.

Jamie instantly e-mailed the footage to his brother, he wanted Jon to see this and hopefully realise just how amazing this girl was. So far Jamie didn't think his brother had tried nearly hard enough to make amends for the coffee shop episode with a few bunches of flowers and as for making her cry too, well maybe this would spur him into action. They brought out more wine and decided that nothing could top that performance so they flicked through the sports channels and found an Italian league football match and settled down to shout at the screen in their usual fashion. All too soon it was 1.00am and the taxi had arrived to collect the boys. It had been a fantastic night and ended with promises of a repeat when they were back from uni for their summer break.

Evie closed the door and started to run some water in the sink, she would rather clear the dishes now than leave it until the morning. Unbeknown to her Jonathan had received the photos from Jamie. He was right, they were having fun, fun without him and that hurt. She'd obviously told them he'd made her cry. Was he never going to be forgiven for that? He sighed 'no probably not'. Later on his phone pinged again, hoping it was Evie he checked to see who it was from. It was a message from Jamie, saying, 'Watch this and then you'll see why she is too good for you." Jonathan was intrigued and played the video. He watched Francis take hold and then it was the most surprising revelation. After it finished he just sat and stared at the screen. Wow! he'd never expected that, he would really have to up his game for their next date on Saturday afternoon. Oh yes he was going to have to try a lot harder than a few bunches of flowers and a cup of tea, a lot bloody harder.

Chapter 10

Friday lunch time found Jonathan outside his office heading for his barber's. He wanted a haircut and then maybe some new shoes for his date tomorrow with Evie. His barber sat him down as Jonathan explained he wanted a haircut; but he didn't want it to look like he'd had his hair cut. Bob was confused but started to snip away none the less. It was a strange request but he was happy to oblige, less time for him with the same price what was not to like about that? Haircut finished, Jonathan walked up to the main shopping area and opened the door of an expensive shoe shop. He explained he was going on an important date tomorrow and wanted some shoes that said he'd tried but not too hard kind of thing. The assistant grinned, leave it with me sir and was back in less than 5 minutes with four boxes of shoes to show him. Eventually he decided on two pairs of lace up chukka boots, one in a mid – blue leather and the other in a soft pale grey suede, yes they were just perfect and he left the shop to return to his florists as he now called them. Just one more purchase and he was done.

Evie finished her classes for the night and was chatting to Miles. He'd turned out to be a huge bonus to the gym and was now everyone's favourite, none more so than Stacey on reception who was so besotted with him it was beginning to affect her work. Her phone pinged, it was a message from Jonathan.

Have you had a good day? – SEND

Yes thanks, am just chatting to dreamy Miles, How was your day? – SEND

Does that boy ever do any work? To be honest today was deathly dull, all I can think about is our date tomorrow. – SEND

Yes he works very hard. Where are we going tomorrow? – SEND

It's a surprise. – SEND

So here's the thing. Maybe now would not be such a good time to tell you that I hate surprises then? – SEND

Seriously? – SEND

Yes. – SEND

Why? –SEND

Can I call you once I'm home? I don't want to do this here in the car park, plus I need to shower etc. – SEND

Sure, do you need any help with that shower? – SEND

You are very persistent; but no thanks, I'll call you later, bye – SEND

Evie drove home. It was a shame she had to teach tomorrow as she would have liked the extra time at home to prepare for their date. She'd asked if anyone would cover her classes but there were no takers. An hour later she felt more human again after showering and eating her supper, she really should call Jonathan soon as their chats could easily take up an hour maybe more. At 9.30pm she decided to message him, maybe only for half an hour this time. She really wanted to know where they were going tomorrow and maybe prepare for the worst if it turned out to be an awful surprise – as unfortunately so many of them were.

Hi, Henry and I are sat here ready and waiting for our chat .-SEND

Not sure how much Henry will be contributing? – SEND

Fair enough; but didn't want to exclude him. Where are we going tomorrow? – SEND

My, my you are an impatient woman. All will be revealed soon enough. There are some rules, though. – SEND

Rules! – SEND

Yes, have just been checking and you need to wear flat lace up shoes – not trainers and a long sleeved top. –SEND

Really, do I have to? – SEND

Yes, just for once do as you're told – please just for me – try it – you never know you might like it? – SEND

You do know I HATE SURPRISES! – SEND

It's too late to tell me that now. Why? – SEND

Well here's the thing, everyone always says 'oh you'll love it, it's a surprise' and then all the pressure is on me to love it even if I don't. You have to make THAT FACE and say ooh how lovely even if it is the worst surprise ever as you don't want to hurt their feelings. They say oh I knew you'd love it. Your feelings don't count as they've made such a special effort to go off-piste! That's why! – SEND

She really was very funny he thought; but it was far too late to change things now, plus he knew she would love it once they were there.
Okay, didn't realise this was such a big issue for you; but can you trust me please? I tell you what, if you hate it then you can tell me and I won't surprise you ever again – deal? – SEND

Well if I hate it I may not want to go on any more dates with you. – SEND. Shit, he hadn't thought of that.

Hadn't thought of that but it's a risk I'm willing to take. I promise you really will love it. – SEND

Okay, Henry says on your head be it – get it – Henry 8th/beheading/ ha ha ha! Henry made a little joke! – SEND. Now she was laughing at him so things couldn't be too bad.

That cat of yours is quite the comedian! – SEND

Yes he's funny isn't he? Goodnight Jonathan. – SEND

You're going already? – SEND

Yes big day tomorrow – could be great or our last date. Jury's out. Will shower and change at the gym so will be at yours hopefully by 12.00 BYE.- SEND

Bye. – SEND and she was gone. He was hoping for a much longer text chat with her, he always seemed to want more time with her. Well, tomorrow she was all his from midday so that was a start.

Evie couldn't wait for her classes to be over. She hurried into the shower and then was dry and changed in a flash. She'd kept to the rules and wore flat lace up shoes, a long sleeved T-shirt in a beautiful blue colour and her second favourite pairs of jeans which were faded and soft. Her car pulled up outside of the converted stables a squeak after 12.00. Jonathan hurried out, "All set, as we need to get a move on?" They jumped into the Range Rover and set off. He still wouldn't tell her where they were going and she was a little anxious as well as intrigued. He put the radio on and she was soon singing along to the latest hits not really paying much attention until she saw a sign. No it couldn't be could it? They were getting really close to the Silverstone race track, maybe they were going to watch some racing cars? Or maybe they weren't heading there at all.

He pulled into the car park a little before 3.00pm and yes it was definitely Silverstone racetrack. He turned to her, "well this is your surprise, we're going track racing today, just the two of us, and do you know what the best bit is?" He didn't wait for her to answer, "We're racing Aston Martins." The look on her face was priceless and she let out a small squeal of delight.
"Oh this is fantastic, one of the best surprises ever."
"I thought you might change your mind on that point of view once we were here."

They got out of the car and walked over to the trackside. Apparently you had a 30-minute safety briefing and then you went out with your instructor to start your laps. Safety briefing over, the two of them walked over to the cars and the instructors. Evie was paired with Frank in the silver car and Jonathan was with Martin in the black one. They tossed a coin for who went first and Evie won but decided to go second. Frank and Evie sat and watched as Jonathan started his practise laps. "So, Frank, tell me everything he's doing wrong okay? We need to win this and win it well," she grinned at him. "Fair enough," and he proceeded to tell her what gear to be in and what top speed to take certain parts of the track.

Soon it was Evie's turn and once in the car she felt right at home. This car, or at least a very similar car, had made her heart sing; true, it hadn't ended well; but that wasn't the car's fault. She started off well and listened to everything Frank told her to do. She was gaining confidence and starting to really enjoy herself when before she knew it, it was time to pull over for Jonathan's second drive. Evie and Frank stayed in the car and she decided to confess to him that she had once owned a car very similar to this one; but not to tell her boyfriend as that would spoil things.

"I think I already guessed that," Frank grinned back at her. "So how much do you want to win by?" – this was going to be a fun afternoon, he didn't get many female drivers who were this good and she was clearly enjoying herself, shame her boyfriend was going to lose but then all was fair in love and war, he supposed. She took her turn back on the track and was doing well, a bit too well for Jonathan's liking; but it had been his idea so he would have to grin and bear the consequences; but he hated losing more than anything.

Before their final laps which would be driven and timed separately there was just time for a bathroom break. Martin and Frank sat on the fence discussing their drivers. "So what do you think of yours then?"

"He's not too bad, probably drives something similar, you know the type. Think they're better than they really are. How about yours?"

"Well you've watched her. I reckon she's going to put him through the wringer and hang him out to dry." They both laughed, question was by how much?

Jonathan's lap came in at a very respectable 3 minutes and 51 seconds. He and Martin watched as Evie and Frank took their position on the starting line. Then the car was off. She was quick, much quicker than in practice, maybe she had been toying with him all along; but she had no idea they would be racing this afternoon so if she won she won fair and square. Evie crossed the finish line in the blink of an eye and slowed the car down to a stop. They both got out and were grinning at each other, they knew it was a fast lap; but how fast? They didn't have to wait for long. Evie's lap time was flashed up on the board. 3 minutes 33 seconds – she had won and won by a big margin too. They walked over to congratulate them. She hugged Frank and told Martin she would race with him next time, if there was to be a next time, that is. Jonathan hugged her, she'd done well, really well and more importantly he had earned himself lots of brownie points which on the face of it he was in dire need of.

They walked back to his car holding hands, "So you enjoyed that then?"

"I loved it, thank you so much it was the best fun ever, just wait until Jamie hears about this he'll be so jealous," she grinned.

"So now what would you like to do, home or a meal out, you choose?"

"Well as much as I don't want this day to end, it will have to be home, I have to work tomorrow morning remember?"

He couldn't get used to the fact she had to work evenings and some weekend mornings, it was difficult enough with him working in London Monday to Friday, they would have to get themselves more organised if they were to see more of each other. Evie was quiet on the way back, he turned off the music and within a few minutes she was asleep. Pressing a button he reclined her seat and she snuggled down into the soft leather. Jonathan was thinking he could watch her for hours; although his mind then drifted on to just how far the seats could recline and what they could be doing in them.

MUSIC: – THE CARS, WHO'S GOING TO DRIVE YOU HOME?

He'd never waited this long to have sex with any of his most recent girlfriends. He loved good sex; but could hardly ask her how she was in bed, plus he hadn't even kissed her properly yet. He was going to push for that tomorrow and then who knows where it might end up? Shaking himself he tried to concentrate on the road. He took his foot off the accelerator, he didn't want to hurry as he wanted to be with her for as long as possible and it was after 8.30 before he drew up outside his house. Jonathan turned off the engine and Evie yawned and stretched out her arms, "Oh sorry, not much company was I?" It didn't matter to him one bit, he was just sorry she'd be going home soon. Evie's car was sat waiting for her, it would be at least another half an hour before she would be home. She hugged him and stepped back, "Well thank you again it was a great day, I had the best time." They had their usual double kiss; but before he could kiss her again she'd jumped in her car and was starting the engine. "Text me when you get back," he mouthed at her through the window. She gave him the thumbs up sign and was gone.

He sighed as he let himself into the house, yet again she was gone. In his disappointment at her leaving he'd forgotten to see if she was free tomorrow, yes she'd be working until 11.00 or 12.00 but maybe after that. He'd text her tonight and ask her.

Evie opened her front door to be met by a very annoyed looking Henry. 'Hello there, are you all grumpy with me as it's late and you're hungry?' She asked him whilst tickling his ears, 'yes thought so. Come on then, I'll feed you and then you can go out on the tiles with a full tummy'. Henry didn't need any second bidding, he was soon wolfing down his pouch of food as soon as it hit his bowl. She yawned, she was tired and wanted some sleep, she would text Jonathan once she was in bed. First though she had to order a little surprise gift for Jonathan and have it sent to his office. She googled his office address and then got ready for bed. Whilst cleansing her face she was idly thinking about the day, what had started out as the usual Saturday morning had turned into something so exciting she almost wished she still had her old Aston. Shaking her head she knew that wasn't an option; but today had been great, so now she knew he could be fun too and as dates went it was right up there with the best of them. Evie climbed into bed and started to text.

Hi, it's me, am home and in bed – SEND

Was getting worried – SEND

No need just feeding Henry etc. Thank you for the best day – SEND

Am glad you enjoyed it, so much for hating surprises! – SEND

Yes it made the top ten for sure – SEND

The top ten? – SEND

Yes!-SEND

What exactly am I up against then in the list of best dates? – SEND

Ahh wouldn't you like to know? It's late, am not stopping to chat tonight, you know work in the morning blah blah.-SEND

What are you doing after work tomorrow? – SEND

No plans why? – SEND

Great. This was just what he had been hoping she'd say. If he played his cards right he would still be in her good books after today so would plan something else to win her over.

Would you like to go to lunch, late lunch that is, I could pick you up around 12.30ish? – SEND

Sound lovely, I'll text you my address in the morning-SEND

Finally he would have her address!

Okay, dress code is smart casual – SEND

There's a code? Am always very confused with smart/casual, does it mean smart or casual – it doesn't make any sense to me? – SEND

I'm sure whatever you wear will be just fine. – Send

Okay goodnight then. x –SEND

That was the first time she had signed off with an x, albeit a tiny single x but an x all the same. He was ecstatic.

Night Evie. X – SEND

There that little x felt so much better. Funny how the little things meant the most. Now to call in a favour for tomorrow.

Chapter 11

The following day and Evie couldn't wait to get home, shower and change. Her classes were busy as usual, it was just she didn't want to be there, which made a change for her. She was really looking forward to seeing Jonathan again. Things were going well, yes very well, she thought, perhaps she'd misjudged him after all?

At Jonathan's things weren't going to plan at all. He'd changed his clothes and now discovered that the Range Rover was covered in mud courtesy of his little brother, so he couldn't take that and he certainly couldn't take his Aston, not after yesterday, Evie would feel set up and he didn't want that. Striding over to the main house he found Jamie coming downstairs looking the worse for wear. "Can I borrow your car, J?" "Um yeah sure – what's wrong with yours?" "It's playing up," he lied, There was no time to explain things now he needed to get going. Jamie gave him the keys and then he was gone.

He knocked on Evie's door just after 12.30. She'd changed her top three times and felt a bit nervous, silly really it was only lunch. He'd brought her yet more flowers, all lilacs/blues/white, really pretty and they smelled divine. They had their usual double cheek kiss and she ran some water in the sink to keep the flowers fresh until they were back. He looked as if he had made an effort too, smart black jeans, grey shirt and some very good looking pale grey suede boots. "Nice boots, lovely colour," she remarked. "Thanks, you look very pretty today." She was looking very pretty, yes very pretty indeed, tight dark jeans, a cream lace top, navy cardigan and some shoes with peep toes, again in grey suede. Her new sexy shoe boots had been an impulse purchase; but she was very glad she'd bought them now.

"So where are we going?" she asked him.

"Ah it's a surprise."

She groaned, "Not another one?"

"Yes I thought yesterday' was so good we could try this surprise thing again today," he grinned back at her. She sighed and put her sunnies on. It was bound to be a let-down after yesterday, why oh why did she agree to this? Because she was an idiot, that's why. She got into the black VW Golf; just how many cars did he have?

"No Range Rover today then?"

"No, Jamie took it out last night and it's covered in mud," he gave as an explanation. He realised he would have to own up to the Aston soon enough but not today. They set off and after a while he put the radio on; but the music was terrible. Evie grimaced, "Do you have any CD's or an iPod in here?" "Not sure, try the glove box." Evie opened it and started to rummage about. Yes there were some CD's, odd music choices for Jonathan she thought, her hand reached to the back and she recoiled as if she'd burnt her hand. It had come into contact with something soft, silky and unexpected. She felt braver and reached in and pulled out the item. Suddenly she couldn't breathe and felt numb. In a small voice she asked Jonathan to pull over. "Um I can't right now. Do you feel okay?"

"No not really, I need you to stop the car," she said more firmly. Jonathan was concerned. What was going on? She'd been fine, just fine, now she looked weird, maybe she was going to throw up. He saw a sign saying layby in 1 mile so he put his foot down and soon pulled in.

Her seatbelt was off and she was out of the car before the car had even stopped moving. Evie walked slowly over to the fence, her legs felt like jelly and rested her hands on her knees, she was talking to herself now, don't throw up, don't throw up.

"Evie what's wrong, are you okay?"

"No not really," she said eventually. She took a deep breath. There was only one way to find out. She'd ask the question and see what he said. She turned round to face him, she did look pale, maybe she was ill?

"Okay here's the thing, I was wondering if these belonged to your girlfriend?" Hanging off her finger was a pair of apricot silky lace knickers.

Jonathan jumped up with a start, he'd been leaning lazily against the car; but she had his attention now alright.

"Where did you find those?"

"That's not what I asked you. It's a simple question, Jonathan, are these your girlfriends knickers?"

"Um no they're not, I don't know anything about them and in any case you're my girlfriend."

"So whose are they then?"

"I honestly don't know," – God that sounded lame, he could kill Jamie.

"I think you may have to do better than that or I'm going home right this minute," she didn't raise her voice but he knew she was going to bale unless he came up with some answers quickly.

"Look this isn't my car," she interrupted him, "so these aren't your girlfriend's knickers, this isn't your car, you don't seem to know very much – don't take me for an idiot please."

He ran his hands through his hair, "Look I borrowed the car from Jamie, I was in a hurry, I didn't know the Range Rover would be out of action and I didn't tidy up inside first, I just grabbed his keys and came to fetch you and that's the truth." He was gabbling now trying to make her understand.

"Why should I believe a word you've just said?"

"Because I wouldn't lie to you," he was getting desperate now, even to his own ears his answers sounded lame. "I'll call Jamie and you can ask him yourself okay?"

"Okay but I need to speak to him first."

"Yes anything you want."

He took his mobile out of his pocket and pressed Jamie's number. Inside his head he was repeating please pick up, please pick up, just when he was about to give up Jamie answered the phone. "Hi Jon what's up?"

"I'm going to pass you over to Evie now J, she has some questions for you; really important questions okay?"

This was weird even for his brother, Jamie yawned, but he had plenty of time. "Okay then."

He heard Evie's voice, "Hi Jamie. I need to ask you some things okay?"

"Right, you sound weird Evie are you okay?"

"Just answer the questions, Jamie, please." She was practically begging him now. "What car do you drive?"

"Black Golf."

"And where is it now?"

"I lent it to Jon, why has he pranged it?"

"No it's still in one piece-for now."

"What's in the glove box?"

"Um not sure, some CD's and rubbish I should think."

"Which CD's?"

Jamie rattled off three or four all of which were in the car. So it was true, this was Jamie's car and his music, now how to ask about the other thing.

"One more thing, when did you last take your girlfriend out in the car?"

"Um last week or the week before maybe?" he sounded hesitant, just where was she going with this? "But I wouldn't exactly say she was my girlfriend."

"Here's the thing Jamie, did she leave anything behind?"

Oh shit, the penny dropped and Jamie could only imagine what Evie had found. He hurriedly said, "Look, whatever you found it has nothing to do with Jon okay, believe me Evie he never borrows my car. He has enough cars of his own. I brought the Range Rover back all covered in mud that's why he asked to borrow my car – that's the truth, honestly Evie it is."

She wanted to believe him really she did, was she going to give Jonathan yet another benefit of the doubt? She passed the phone back and walked away; what was she going to do now? Evie could hear Jonathan talking to Jamie and then silence, apart from the odd car going past on the road there was only the two of them .Neither of them spoke for so long that she began to wonder if he'd gone and left her there. She turned to face him, "So now what?"

He was back leaning against the car looking as sexy as hell, why did he have to look so damn good right this minute, she sighed and waited for him to start talking.

"Well I was hoping we could still go and have lunch together. Nothing's changed, it was just a misunderstanding, one that Jamie has hopefully cleared up and put your mind at ease? If you still don't believe me then I'm not sure there's a lot more I can say?" He didn't dare move, it was her turn now, she could decide, lunch or home there weren't really a lot of other choices. Jonathan didn't move or say anything for so long he'd convinced himself that she would want to go straight home again.

Eventually she said quietly, "Okay, but here's the thing-try to see it from my point of view. If I'd invited you out and you'd found a pair of men's boxer shorts in my glove box how would that make you feel?"

"Fair enough, I hadn't thought of it like that." God he would have been so bloody mad, she did have a point. "Please come to lunch with me, I promise to be on my best behaviour." He waited again and after what seemed like forever Evie replied

"Okay I think I'd like to go to lunch now please, if that's still alright with you?"

Alright with him – it was a bloody miracle that's what it was. "Okay then shall we get going?" he held open her car door and she climbed back in, he closed the door then gave a sigh of relief. Boy, that was a close call, too close for comfort by far. The rest of the journey was a quiet one, but they were both relieved to be going out to lunch at all.

Just after 1.30 they drove through some wrought iron gates and pulled up in front of a handsome country house. She took off her sunnies and picked up her bag, the car door was opened for her and she stepped out to be greeted by an enthusiastic Italian. It turned out this was Gino who had been running this restaurant with rooms for a number of years. He greeted Jonathan like an old friend and they were escorted inside. The restaurant was beautiful, with flowers everywhere, the room was very light with a row of French doors that led outside. The lunchtime service was clearly coming to an end; but they were shown to a table by the window with a perfect view of the garden. She accepted a menu and began to read, everything sounded delicious, maybe today wasn't going to be a disaster after all. They ordered their food and some prosecco; well she felt like a treat so one glass wasn't going to hurt her now was it?

Jonathan took hold of her hand across the table, "Are we okay now, you know from before?"

"Yes," she smiled back at him, "we're okay now."

"Told you you'd love it didn't I?"

"Well let's wait until I've eaten first then I'll let you know."

Their first courses were served, prosciutto with ripe melon. Who could wish for anything more divine?. Followed by fish for her and pasta for him. They chatted idly about this and that, giving the food most of their attention which it richly deserved. Their plates were cleared away and he took her into the gardens, which were gorgeous. Strolling leisurely hand in hand they were in no hurry to be anywhere. Jonathan stopped and took hold of her other hand, suddenly he looked very serious as if he was going to make a speech.

She was nervous about what was happening. "Jonathan what's going on?" she asked quietly. "Is everything okay?"

"Yes it is now, sorry about all that back there, but now I need to ask you something, something I've wanted to ask you for a while; but we never seem to be on our own or have any time together."

"Okay go on." Where was he going with this?

"It's hard to explain really, I, um," Gosh even to his own ears he sounded nervous. "It's just that, um, when we're out in a group with J or his friends you're very calm and relaxed, when we text and message you're so confident and brave; but when it's just the two of us you seem all jumpy and nervous and I can't seem to get close to you. It's almost as if every time I take a step towards you, then you take a step back and I need to know if there's a chance that sometime soon if I take a step forward you might actually stand still or even take a step towards me – um does that make any sense, I'm not sure it does?" He looked down at the ground already convinced that whatever they had was surely over before it had even begun.

She still had hold of his hands, whispered, "Perfect sense," and then leaned in towards him and kissed him softly on the mouth. That completely took him by surprise and he pulled away. Evie smiled back at him and one look into those huge brown eyes of hers and he was lost. Then his arms were around her and they were kissing just like a young couple in love ought to, not caring who saw or how long they stood there, it was just the two of them in the moment right then.

MUSIC: – YOU'RE ALL I NEED TO GET BY – MARVIN GAYE

Oh this was great, he was a good kisser after all and she was so happy, so happy. He couldn't believe it, finally he was holding her in his arms, kissing her and squeezing her bum and it was amazing, she was amazing. Her lips were so soft and he began to really enjoy himself. It had been worth the wait and then some – at last, at long bloody last something had gone right for them for a change.

They walked around the garden, just kissing, smiling and laughing together, each of them not quite believing their luck to have reached the same place at the same time. Eventually they went inside; but neither of them wanted dessert. They just wanted to be with each other. They drove back. Evie requested if they could stop off at Jonathan's first as she wanted to see Jamie.

The two of them could hardly keep their hands off of one another. They stumbled into the TV room to find Jamie and his friends slumped in front of the television. Jamie looked worried, as so he should.

Evie leaned against the wall. "Good lunch?" he asked nervously. "Yes thank you, the best," she couldn't stop smiling at Jonathan. "But here's the thing Jamie, I'm in a quandary, I can't decide if you have taken to wearing women's underwear or if your girlfriend's bottom, which according to these (the knickers were now dangling off of her finger) is a very perky size 8 is getting a bit chilly seeing as how she left her knickers behind in your car?"

Well there were shouts and hollering from his friends whilst Jamie held his head in his hands wishing the ground would swallow him up. She tossed the knickers towards him and went into to the kitchen which is where she and Jonathan were leaning against the kitchen table kissing again when Jamie walked in.

"Oh get a room, you two" – he mumbled.

Evie and Jonathan broke apart laughing, "Well at least it's not in a car Jamie. Honestly what were you thinking? There are laws about this kind of stuff and you of all people should know that! "She was telling him off and laughing at him at the same time; it was hard to stay cross with Jamie for very long. They said their goodbyes and headed back to her house. It had been a good day after all.

Jonathan pulled up outside her house and she smiled at him. "Would you like to come in for something to eat or perhaps coffee?"

"I'm not really hungry but coffee would be nice."

"Oh Jonathan just so you know, coffee means coffee okay?" She wagged her index finger at him, laughing. Quick as a flash he grabbed her finger and started to kiss it. She laughed. "I need my hand to open the front door, so please may I have it back now?" Reluctantly he let he finger go and got out of the car. No sooner had she closed the door after them than he had his hands either side of her face and his body pushed her back onto the door, his mouth on hers, kissing her like there was going to be no tomorrow. This caught her by surprise and after a short protest she just gave in and began to enjoy it. She hadn't been kissed like this for such a long time and she quickly realized she'd missed it so much. Her hands were in his hair and they were both getting carried away in the moment, his hands seemed to be in her hair, on her back, on her bum, he only had two hands for crying out loud so this was impossible. Eventually he leaned back, breathing heavily. "God Evie, do you have any idea what you do to me?"

"Um I'm getting a good idea," she replied breathlessly.

He kissed her again and she was happy to go with the flow. After quite a while Jonathan paused and quickly she took the chance to move towards the kitchen. She thought for one moment they were going to have sex on the hallway floor. Evie liked sex and she missed it, when it was good it was the best thing ever; but thank God he'd moved away, it was too soon for their next step. She hadn't told him things, important things which she needed to explain and he needed to listen to before their relationship went to the next level.

She busied herself filling the water tank of the Nespresso machine and switching it on. Without turning round she opened the cupboard and took out the capsules and asked, "Now would you like decaf so you can sleep tonight or full caff so you can lie awake?"

"Depends."

"On what exactly?"

"Well if I'm staying over – then full caff" – he left the sentence hanging there like it was a given.

"I really think you need to get that hearing test organized. What part of coffee means coffee didn't you hear Jonathan?"

Evie was in a playful mood; but it didn't sound like he would be staying over, at least not tonight. He stood behind her and whispered into her ear, "I don't really want coffee," and started to plant small kisses on the back of her neck. She leaned into him, "This has got to stop."

He continued to kiss her as if she hadn't spoken. "And why would that be?"

She switched the coffee machine off; but still didn't turn around to face him: "Because look here's the thing, today has been great – no, better than great, wonderful. But we're not going to bed together tonight. I need to tell you some things first, and afterwards you can decide if you still want to see me or if you want to walk away."

He suddenly stopped kissing her. This sounded very ominous.

She continued. "It's complicated, I'm complicated, there are physical things and emotional things and I, or rather we, can't ignore them, like the elephant in the room."

She had him really worried now; why would he walk away from her? "I don't understand."

"I know," she sighed, "but I don't want to have this conversation tonight, we've just had the best time and I don't want to spoil it. If you decide to leave me then at least I will have some good memories."

"Why would I leave you? Evie, turn round and look at me please." He was pleading with her now.

"I can't."

"Why not?"

"Because I'm actually trapped between you and the worktop," she laughed ironically.

He moved away and sure enough she turned around to face him. She looked serious and he didn't know what to say or do. He was so used to being completely in control; but now he was floundering like a fish out of water.

"I think you'd better go home now before I spoil things. I'm not some fast city girl, I need to take things slower, I have to psyche myself up to talk to you and now is not the time or the place for that, I just can't do this now. I'm sorry." She sounded so forlorn he wrapped his arms around her and just hugged her to him, no kissing or talking, just to let her know he was okay with whatever it was that was going on with her. They stayed like that for a long time until eventually he kissed the top of her head and said he would leave.

"You've got me all worried about you now."

"Sorry that was never my intention. Text me when you're home okay?" She'd turned the tables on him, now it was him who had to text her and not the other way round for a change. He took a chance and kissed her firmly on the mouth, silently letting her know he still wanted her.

She saw him drive away and sighed loudly. Well they were kissing which was always a good place to start; but then came the tricky bit and she needed to work out what she was going to say and when. Both these things could either be the start of something amazing or the end of them and there was no way of knowing which way it would go. Evie climbed the stairs and got ready for bed. What a week it had been, a good week with the racing and the beautiful lunch and now things were getting complicated and she was scared. Scared he would listen to her and see things that would make him realise he'd been wasting his time with her after all and he would move on with someone else. HE would have won and she would be all alone – again.

Jonathan drove away, he was so confused. He already knew she wasn't like most girls he'd dated so had figured out that she was a complicated little thing all by himself; but what he didn't know was what she needed to show and tell him. She'd given no hint as to what these things might be and now he was imaging all sorts of terrible things.

He texted her once he was home.

Hi. Am home.-SEND

Good, Thank you for a beautiful day – knickers not withstanding! – SEND

She was in a good mood after all, of course she was – she was safely hiding behind her texting.

Yes I could wring Jamie's neck sometimes, my little brother has a lot to answer for! – SEND

Have you got a busy week ahead? – SEND This sounded so formal like she was asking her aunt; but she couldn't cope with any flirty chat, not tonight.

Same old, same old – when can I see you again? – SEND He could sense there would be no sexy chatting tonight; but he needed to make plans to see her. God, it was going to be a long week without her.

I'll let you know and say goodnight then .x-SEND

Goodnight, Evie x – SEND

He sent one more text and hoped for a reply.

Miss you x – SEND and he waited and waited. Just when he thought that was it until tomorrow, his phone pinged.

Miss you more x. – SEND

She'd replied and it was exactly what he wanted to read. It was true he was used to always getting his own way; but this didn't feel the same. He'd desperately wanted her to reply with those identical words and when she had, he felt not power; but relief and that was a first for him. Lying in bed later Jonathan was thinking about them kissing. He'd had to wait but when she'd kissed him, bloody hell it had been worth it. He was kicking himself for not taking her straight to bed after the demonstration in her hallway, not given her any time for doubts. If he'd done that, he wondered where they'd be right now?

Chapter 12

Evie deliberately kept herself extra busy during the start of the week. Classes were full and she was pleased to see that Fiona had returned. Miles was as popular as ever and even the manager Steve was actually in a good mood; wonders would never cease.

Jonathan opened a small parcel in his office. It was from Evie. He laughed on seeing it in the box. It was a small replica model of an Aston Martin to remind him of their date together. He sent her a text to thank her and she'd replied 'You're welcome'.

On Wednesday morning she went for a run and then bought some groceries. She was planning to do some baking in the afternoon as it was just what she needed.

Just before lunch she sat at her kitchen table pondering whether to text Jonathan. Truth was she was missing him – more than she thought she would; so she picked up her phone and started to text.

Hi it's me, do you have time to text or e-mail? – SEND

Almost immediately he replied, Yes; what's up, are you okay? – SEND

Yes I'm fine, don't want to get you in trouble with your boss though. Do you have time for this now? – SEND

He smiled to himself; he would make time. He used the office phone and instructed his secretary to cancel everything until 2.00pm. There, that should give them plenty of time to talk.

Am all yours until 2.00pm. What are you doing? – SEND

She sighed. She was happy they were communicating again as she wasn't sure how to move forward after their last conversation; it had been intense and she'd been scared and it had left him feeling confused which made a change from her.

Will switch to e-mail, hang on a sec. Just making my lunch. – SEND

What are you having? – SEND

Hot beef salad with wild rice, how about you? – SEND

I haven't decided yet; but yours sounds delicious! – SEND

I'm psyching myself up for it actually as I'm not a big fan of red meat, but David insists that I have some from time to time. – SEND

Well I could definitely share that with you right now .-SEND

Ah well the problem is that by the time you get here it wouldn't be hot beef it would be cold and very unappetising beef and am not sure you would want to have travelled all this way for that! – SEND

If it meant I could see you then I wouldn't care too much about the food.- SEND He couldn't understand why they were talking about food. It seemed like an odd topic of conversation. She sounded very down in the dumps which wasn't like her at all, what was really going on?

I'm having a baking afternoon and wondered if there was anything in particular you'd like me to make for you, that's if we are seeing each other at the weekend? – SEND

I didn't know you baked? – SEND

Yes I find it very relaxing and it gives time to think, it's very therapeutic.- SEND

Of course we're seeing each other at the weekend, why wouldn't we? You don't sound like yourself? I'm worried. – SEND

She sighed she was going to have to be honest with him, she owed him that much at least.

Well here's the thing. I'm struggling a bit really. I realized that I may have freaked you out by only telling you ½ a story or even ¼ of a story so to speak at the weekend; but it's difficult for me. – SEND She was messaging and it was a hell of a lot easier than face to face; but she was beginning to wish she hadn't started this in the first place. She'd just wanted to hear his voice, talk to him; but now she wasn't sure what to say.

Well naturally I have questions but I don't want to force you to show/tell me things you're not ready to do. I'm not that much of an unfeeling monster am I?–SEND

Evie took a deep breath. Okay in for a penny, just spit it out and wait and see.

No of course not, you didn't push it, you just held me in your arms (which was lovely by the way) and then went home which at the time was exactly what I needed from you. It's just that I have been down this road so many times before and I'm always stuck between a rock and hard place.

Here's the thing. It's always the biggest dilemma, if I don't explain and finish the relationship then I never know what might have happened if I'd been open; but when I get to the nitty gritty; although guys in the past have said, "Oh I don't care what you tell me or show me – it's you I love," (not that we are at that stage). As soon as I start to explain they can't get out the door fast enough. It becomes very demoralizing to have to repeat this pattern over and over because I never know how it's going to go; although as I'm still single you can probably have a good guess at this! It is getting to the point when I wonder why I'm bothering at all. Is this making any sense? –SEND

Jonathan read the message. He smiled when she said she liked being held in his arms, truth was he'd have held her all night if it would have made her feel better. He read on, she mentioned the L word in a very roundabout way and then it dawned on him. It was obvious, she was scared to tell him as she'd already convinced herself he was going to leave anyway. Shit, she sounded like she was in major panic mode and this being the middle of the week he wouldn't see her until Friday night at the earliest.

Evie you sound as if you are having a panic attack and I would give anything to be holding you in my arms right now. Yes, it would be very easy for me to reassure you in the same way as other guys have; but until you tell me what's going on then no-one knows the outcome. All I can say is please don't assume you know how I'll react, I'm not going anywhere. I may be a lot of things (feel free to insert fuckwit or such like here) but I'm not a coward. – SEND

You're right I'm panicking, hence the baking; but I felt I needed to give you an option to leave before it all gets even messier for the both of us.- SEND

Firstly I don't want a "get out of jail free card", just because things might (and I stress might) get a bit tricky. That's the thing with relationships, they're tricky things at the best of times which is why up until I met you I was still single –; although Jamie will no doubt have shared his own opinion with you on this! And by the way you are not single anymore you are my GIRLFRIEND, don't know how many times I need to tell you this. Maybe I should get it printed on a T-shirt for you? – SEND

She smiled, he seemed to understand and didn't want to leave her even though she had given him the option to.
Okay, I just wanted to give you an opportunity to walk away and unless I have misunderstood it sounds as if you don't want to take it (yet anyway)? By the way, when can I have my T-shirt? – SEND

No I'm not going anywhere, maybe that ought to be on the reverse of the T-shirt – just as a reminder? So you're really more interested in my presents than anything else? – SEND

Well maybe we could exchange gifts as I am not a take, take kind of girl (hope you have realised this by yourself?). How about I bake you something and you can have it on Friday night? – SEND

He smiled. No, she definitely wasn't a take, take kind of girl, in fact compared to his previous girlfriends she was completely different in every way.
That sounds perfect; what will you bake? – SEND

How about I surprise you? – SEND

So it's okay for you to surprise me, but not the other way round? – SEND

Yep, pretty much! – SEND

He was laughing now, she'd forced herself to have the tricky conversation with him and now she'd been reassured, the old Evie was back. Roll on Friday.

Okay will take the risk; but what if I hate it? – SEND

Bloody cheek – I am a fantastic cook so there is no way you'll hate it, unless you have terrible taste! By the way, Miles loves my cooking! – SEND

Why pray tell have you have been feeding Miles? – SEND He was cross at the thought of this guy who he still hadn't met being spoon fed by Evie, in fact he was as jealous as hell.

Well he's all alone in a strange place and it seemed like a nice thing to do – as I keep telling you I am a very nice person; why are you jealous or something? – SEND

YES OF COURSE I AM BLOODY JEALOUS! – SEND

Oh he sounded mad, Evie laughed

Language, language, that's two pounds in the swear jar and at least 3 Hail Mary's for you. I think you need to calm down, we have spoken before about your over-excitable tendencies! – SEND

Just you wait until Friday and then I'll show you just how over excited I can be, Jonathan thought. Feeding Miles, they needed to move their relationship on and then there would be no more feeding Miles bloody Brady, that's for sure.

Well stop making me jealous then. Shall I come over to yours on Friday? – SEND

Okay, earliest I will be home is 9.00ish though, sorry! – SEND

Fine; although wish you could be there at 6.00 for us to have whole evening together. – SEND

Me too. Better go now, I've got things to bake for a very over-excitable chap! Think you ought to get back to work now, don't want you getting the sack otherwise you'd be under my feet all day and every day. – SEND

Oh my God, thought Jonathan. I would love to be under you all day and every day and not just your feet.

Will look forward to edible present on Friday – SEND

Bye. – SEND

Bye Evie, – SEND

Miss you .x-SEND

Miss you more x-SEND.

Well that had gone better than she was expecting, she had had part of 'The Conversation' with him and had offered him a way out and he hadn't taken it. So far so good. Now, what to bake for him.

In the evening she met up with Rowan, Claire and Viv. It was good to have some girl time talking about clothes and makeup without thinking about boys for a change. She got home after 11.00 and wondered if Jonathan would still be up. After changing into her pyjamas and finishing her nightly cleansing routine, she brushed her teeth and climbed into bed. She began to type.

Hi it's me, are you still awake? – SEND

Hello you, yes I'm still awake – am reading boring papers for a meeting tomorrow. – SEND

Do you need any help with them? After all, I take it your bosses have yet to discover what a fraud you are? – SEND She was back to laughing and joking with him; safe territory.

No thanks, not that I don't think you wouldn't be able to help – just that they are very dull and that's one thing you're not! – SEND

Have been thinking. Would you like me to cook you a meal on Saturday night? – SEND

That sounds wonderful. Do you need me to bring anything? – SEND

No need, just yourself would be fine and dandy Mr D. Anything you don't eat? – SEND

She seemed a lot happier now they were making plans to be together. Only two more days and they would see each other again. How other couples coped with long distance relationships, God only knows he thought.

Can I request the same meal you cooked for Jamie, he hasn't stopped banging on about it and I want to see what all the fuss is about? – SEND

Sure, no problem. Will see you Friday night then at mine? If you change your mind then just let me know okay? – SEND

Why would I change my mind? You don't get rid of me that easily. See you Friday – SEND

Bye x – SEND

Night Evie x – SEND

She was obviously still expecting him to bale on her; but he had no intention of doing so. Yes he was dying of curiosity about what she needed to tell him; but pressuring her wasn't the right approach, he had to let her do it in her own time and until then he wanted to carry on right where they left off. His mind flicked back to their passionate kissing in the hall, yes picking up from there would be just fine and dandy with him too.

He typed one more thing.

Miss you .xxx-SEND His phone pinged right away.

Miss you more .xxx-SEND

He grinned. He was a very lucky guy, yes very lucky indeed. Roll on Friday night.

Evie switched off her phone. He still wanted to see her, even after all that confusion last Sunday. She was glad; she'd go and buy groceries so she could do a lot of the preparation on Friday afternoon. Jonathan was only coming around for a chat on Friday night, she would need to check if she had some wine for him just in case he wanted a drink. She laughed to herself, well he was going out with her, wasn't he, so he would definitely need a drink!

Jonathan was in a good mood for the rest of the week. His secretary had noticed a change from snappy and moody to pleasant and happy. Whatever had happened on Wednesday to change his mood she was very grateful for it as it made her life an awful lot easier. Driving home on Friday afternoon he kept thinking about seeing Evie tonight. He was just going round for a short time; but he was beginning to miss her more and more during the week; even his personal training sessions with Mike couldn't make up for the fact that he was missing her dreadfully. They would have to try to work out something better than just snatching a few hours at the weekends as it just wasn't enough for him now, no not enough by far.

Chapter 13

Evie raced in to the gym showers just after 8.00pm. She'd planned for her class to finish on the dot, well actually it was a couple of minutes early; but she'd worked them quite hard and there were no complaints from anyone. She'd spent the afternoon doing prep for their meal together tomorrow and had bought a couple of bottles of wine. Her car pulled up on her driveway just after 8.45pm. Jonathan would be here soon and she was surprised at just how excited she was to see him. Well, assuming he was going to show up at all, that was.

There was a knock on the door just before 9.00 and then there he was. She invited him in and took his jacket and offered him a glass of wine. They kissed briefly; but it felt a bit weird now that they were here in the kitchen together; maybe it was the remains of the conversation from the last time they were in there together. She brought out a cake tin and gave it to him. "For you."

Jonathan smiled. It was the first time any girlfriend of his had ever baked him anything and he wondered what she'd decided upon. He took the lid off and inside was a huge pile of heavenly smelling shortbread biscuits, how did she know they were his absolute favourite? "Can I try one now?"

"Of course," she laughed, "you don't need to ask, I made them for you; although I thought you might like to take them back to London with you for during the week?"

He took a bite. God, she could bake too. He would get fat just looking at them; he decided not to tell Mike, his trainer, otherwise they would go on the banned food list and quite frankly that list was getting longer every day.

"They're delicious – just like you." He grinned

Evie hurriedly poured him some wine and suggested they took it into the living room. This was the first time he'd seen more of her home apart from the video from Jamie and he had to admit she had an eye for design, very simple but luxurious, different textures layered in a similar colour palette. Yes, she was obviously very good at this. The room was lit by three lamps which emitted a soft glow, nothing harsh for the evening and they sat together on the sofa.

"So, this is very nice," he said relaxing in to the upholstery. "Can I kick my shoes off?"

"Of course. You don't need to ask," she smiled at him. Her shoes were already off and he could see she had painted her tiny toe nails a bright pink colour. He took her free hand in his and settled into the sofa next to her. He could smell her perfume and she smelt delicious.

He sipped his wine and sighed. What a week; he was glad that it was over and now it was just the two of them. She had some music playing, nothing he recognized but then he was hardly au fait with popular music as Jamie was only too keen to point out.

"Tough week?"

"Oh you know, same old same old, what about you?" This was going to be the dullest conversation on record if he wasn't careful, he had to find a way to get her to relax with him. He noticed she wasn't drinking any wine. Maybe he could tempt her to have some of his.

"Have you tried this, it's very good?" She shook her head and he offered her his glass. "Here, have some of mine," and she took a small sip. Yes it was very nice she got up and fetched herself a glass. She needed to relax as you could cut the tension with a knife and this didn't bode well for their weekend.

They made small talk easily enough and she explained she had to cover Caroline's shifts tomorrow but that it couldn't be helped and she would be done by 11.00am.

He was more relaxed now and he put his glass down on the side table and then reached for her glass too. Then he picked up her legs and swung them over his lap and put his arms around her, not kissing her but just holding her and suddenly they both felt the tension change. He gently kissed the top of her head and then moved his body so that he was leaning over hers and then he kissed her properly on her mouth. She didn't pull away and kissed him back. He smiled at her. "So did you miss me?"

"Of course I did." He shifted position on the sofa and they were lying there together holding each other kissing each other. It was fabulous and neither of them wanted to stop. They eventually broke off and grinned at each other. This was what they had been missing all week and now they were back together it felt so right. She placed the palm of her hand against his cheek and then moved her hand up into his hair. He groaned and then was kissing her harder with more passion. They could stay here forever and he'd be a happy man.

"Do you remember when you were maybe 17 and you just kissed for hours on end with your girlfriend?" she asked him when they had taken a break. Her head was lying in the crook of his shoulder and she was very happy lying there with him, "Wasn't it the best thing ever at the time?"

"Oh I don't know. I'm enjoying this now, who needs to be 17 again?" She eventually fetched more wine and they carried on much as before. He didn't push her too hard and nuzzled her neck. God, she really did smell amazing. He imagined her just wearing perfume and had to shake his head to get a grip on his thoughts, thoughts that left unchallenged would run away with him for the second time and he didn't want to make the same mistake twice.

They lost track of time. It felt so right just to be there together in the moment. The music had stopped and their bodies were still lying together stretched out on the sofa. His arms were around her and effectively pinned her against him. What wasn't there to like about this? he thought to himself. He reached up to the back of the sofa and grabbed a soft faux fur throw. It was getting chillier now and he pulled it over the two of them. Fancy dates were all well and good but just being here together, with no need to even talk, well this had to be the best feeling in the world right now.

Evie was so happy that her mind was drifting, thinking back to his passionate display in her hallway last week. Yes, she fancied the pants off him; that much she had realized; but this was more intimate somehow and she snuggled under the blanket, closed her eyes and drifted off. Jonathan was very comfortable and was murmuring something to her; but she couldn't concentrate and within a few minutes she was fast asleep.

He realised she'd fallen asleep when he'd asked her the same question twice and received no response. Jonathan smiled. So this was how they were going to spend their first night together, on her sofa, fully clothed wrapped in each other's arms under a fur throw? It wasn't quite what he had hoped for, but after last week it was nothing short of a miracle. He moved his body to ensure she wouldn't roll off the sofa onto the floor and closed his eyes.

Evie thought she was dreaming as she was having a lovely sleep, just lovely. She had a little stretch but she was warm and there was something heavy over her. Thinking it was Henry she opened one eye and realised it was Jonathan's arm. She must have fallen asleep on the sofa with him, she smiled; how lovely it felt to be waking up in his arms after all. She blinked and caught sight of the clock on the bookcase. Shit, shit, shit, it was after 8.00am and she had to be in work at 9.00. Hurriedly she tried to move his arm, but he was a dead weight and wouldn't move.

"Jonathan wake up, wake up I'm going to be late for work." She tried to wriggle away from him, but he just held her even tighter. Oh my God, she was going to get fired for sure. She was almost shouting at him now and eventually he stirred.

"What's with all the noise, some of us are trying to sleep," he said.

"Jonathan, please! it's after 8.00 and I'm late for work and if you don't let me go now I am so going to get fired," she was practically begging him now.

"Can't you stay for a bit longer?" oh, he was so charming even when half asleep and tightened his grip around her.

"Jonathan, please! I'm begging you I need to get to work, please let me go please!"

"What's it worth?" Seriously? He was bargaining with her now? He had to be the most frustrating man ever; but she was desperate so decided to pull out the big guns.

"I promise you I will kiss you all afternoon if you just let me get to work now please!" Suddenly he released his grip and she nearly fell onto the floor.

"Well why didn't you mention that in the first place?" he smiled lazily back at her.

She ran up the stairs and he could hear water running and drawers opening and cupboards slamming. In less than five minutes she was downstairs in her gym kit tying back her hair. She grabbed her bag and was checking, money keys, phone, music and she was good to go she would make it with any luck with 5 minutes to spare. He watched this scene unfold whilst leaning lazily against the kitchen doorframe, smiling to himself.

"Help yourself to food, shower, towels whatever, and I'll see you after 11.00am. Oh you might need to feed Henry too, okay?"

He nodded at her. "Okay no problem, but you've forgotten one thing?" She looked blankly at him, no she'd checked, money, keys, phone, music.

He pulled her into his arms. "My good morning kiss," and then he proceeded to kiss her very thoroughly, yes very thoroughly indeed. She was enjoying it immensely, but when he broke off she literally flew out of the door. God he was infuriating, she really didn't want to get fired. Steve would have her guts for garters and she jumped in the car praying for a quick run to work.

Chapter 14

Jonathan watched her go and ran his hands through his hair. Okay so now he had the place to himself, what to do first? He didn't even get to make a decision as at that moment Henry came in through the cat flap and glared at him. Okay so feed the cat was the first thing, then a shower and then breakfast. Maybe he could have a good look round too, get some insight into this complicated girl he had fallen in love with. He stopped short. He'd just realised he was in love with her, utterly and completely. Evie had intrigued and entranced him from day one and all he had to do now was not to fuck things up and see if she felt the same way about him. What a great way to start the day and he hummed a tune whilst opening cupboard doors looking for cat food.

Once Henry had been fed Jonathan made his way upstairs, opening the doors one by one on the pretext of looking for the bathroom; but he was just being nosy really. Guest bedroom, twin beds in white and pale green. Next the linen cupboard then another bedroom, this time a double in natural with soft pink. Then the bathroom. Painted in sea blue and cream with a small roll top bath and separate shower. Hmm…, he thought to himself, no room for two in either the shower or the bath unfortunately. Finally there was one door remaining. This had to be Evie's room. He hesitated slightly. This was her private space; but he wasn't going to touch anything, just take a quick peek inside; where could the harm be in that? he persuaded himself, and turned the handle.

Inside it took his breath away. It was the largest of the bedrooms with two huge full length picture windows looking over the rear and side of the property. She woke up to a very nice view, he decided, and then looked more closely. The colour scheme was soft white and grey with touches of navy blue, very classy, yes very classy indeed. Bedside lamps were suspended from the ceiling instead of being placed on the bedside cabinets. Expensive looking white linen was on the bed complete with a grey fur throw across the bottom. It looked like a super king sized bed to him, yes he thought plenty of room for the two of them.

Wandering over to her dressing table he idly picked up her perfume. Ah so this was not called disobedience after all and he removed the lid and sniffed it, yes this was definitely her perfume. Only the one bottle, he noted, not 3 or 4 open at the same time. There was a separate dressing area and a door which when he opened it led to the most amazing en-suite. Inside was a huge modern bath and one of those walk in showers, a double washstand completed the room and he stood there drinking it all in. There was no doubt she had very good taste and there was plenty of room for two in both the shower and the bath

Walking back to the linen cupboard on the landing he helped himself to fresh towels and then he reasoned that as she wasn't here he would use her shower as there was a lot more room. He located shampoo and body wash and 10 minutes later was stood at one of the basins with a towel wrapped round his waist. Now he wanted to brush his teeth; question was, was there a spare toothbrush? The only one he could find was a travel sized one, but it was better than nothing and at least his mouth felt fresher afterwards. He needed a shave and picked up a tube of cleansing cream, squirted some onto his hand; yes that would do, now for a razor. Well he looked a lot more like himself afterwards, but his clothes were very creased and crumpled as he'd slept in them. He decided to wear his underwear inside out and maybe he could iron his shirt, that had to look better than what was staring back at him in the mirror.

Back in the kitchen he began opening cupboards trying to find breakfast. The fridge was fairly full and there were eggs and gluten free granola, some kind of bread and vegan yoghurt and fruit. Eventually he decided on juice with granola and fruit and maybe some yoghurt depending what it tasted like. Hearing a noise in the hallway he discovered the newspaper had been delivered. Well, this was all very civilized for a weekend at Evie's. Settling down at the kitchen table he felt right at home. Shame she wasn't here with him, but he remembered she'd promised to kiss him all afternoon. Oh yes, he thought, this was the life.

Evie squeaked into work with 6 minutes to spare, told Stacey that if Steve asked then she'd been in for at least 10 or 15 minutes. She went to the toilet and ran upstairs to the studio; phew! she'd made it. Evie didn't have time to think about what Jonathan was doing back at hers, she got straight down to work and started the music.

Her 9.00am class finished and she waited for the 10.00am clients to arrive. Well there were only 4 of them and gym rules stated that if there were less than 8 then the class wouldn't take place. She asked the girls to wait whilst she went to find Miles. He was only too happy to see her and she begged a really big favour from him. Could he do some body conditioning work with her four members just so that they hadn't had a wasted journey? Miles was more than happy to help her out; she was a nice lady, very polite and had been nothing but friendly and welcoming to him so it wasn't a problem. Evie explained to the girls what was happening and, well, she needn't have worried because as soon as they heard it was Miles they were all smiles and giggles; he really did have the most amazing effect on people. Evie realised she didn't have her towel or toiletries so she would have to shower at home. She sent a text to Jonathan saying, 'home at 10.45' and walked out of reception and over to her car.

Jonathan's phone pinged. She would be home early, that was good, he was getting bored by himself. Switching on the Nespresso machine he made himself a coffee and walked through into the living room and idly started to look through the bookcases. She obviously loved books and there was quite a choice. Then he noticed some box files and A4 folders that looked more like business correspondence. Jonathan was tempted to take a look inside, but stopped himself. Toothbrush and towels were fine, private mail, no, that wasn't right. Anyway Evie would be home soon and she was cooking for him tonight. He'd fallen in love with her and wondered how she felt about him.

Driving home Evie wondered how Jonathan was getting on. She hoped he'd fed Henry as that was the most important thing in her view. She needed a shower and was very hungry. Sometimes a vegan protein bar just wasn't enough, still she'd been grateful to find it in her bag otherwise she would have had nothing to eat and that was never a good idea before working out. Just before 10.45 her car pulled up outside. She opened the front door and found Jonathan sitting at the kitchen table reading the paper. "Hi honey I'm home," she sang to him. He grinned back. Oh good, now maybe they could pick up from where they left off. He stood up to greet her; but she held her hand up and laughed at him. "Oh no you don't. I need a shower first."

"Maybe I could help you with that?" He closed the distance between them, but she was too fast and backed out and was up the stairs in a flash. Over her shoulder she called back to him, "will be down in 15 minutes." He sighed, okay round one to Evie but bring on round two. He was more than ready for it as he'd slept surprisingly well and went back to his newspaper.

Sure enough she was back in less than 15 minutes and had changed into some pale blue soft sweat pants and a matching top. He gave her his full attention and thought she looked very pretty this morning. "Gosh I'm starving," she said to no-one in particular," did you find your breakfast okay?"

"Yes apart from one thing."

"Oh what was that?"

"My breakfast kiss" – and he grabbed her and pulled her onto his lap and kissed her soundly. Oh, so that was what he had missed this morning, well he would have to wait for more as her stomach was just about to rumble very loudly.

"Jonathan, that was lovely," she smiled back at him, "but I need to eat before I fall down."

"But you made a promise to kiss me all afternoon."

"Yes I know but it's only 11.05 so technically you have to wait another 55minutes – boy, that private education sure was a waste of money for your parents wasn't it?" she laughed.

"So you're giving me the brush off on a technicality?" His face was a picture of frustration.

"Gosh you should see your face," she was laughing at him now, but she couldn't help it, he looked just like a small boy whose ice cream had fallen on the floor and he couldn't have it any more. "Um yes it certainly looks that way." She took pity on him and kissed him again, ruffling his hair then jumped up.

Letting her go, he thought: okay, so food first and then me, all afternoon. He stretched out his hands. He wasn't used to waiting for anything; but figured he'd wait 55 minutes not a minute longer. Evie poured out some juice and then helped herself to granola, fruit and yoghurt. They were eating supper at 7.00 so she'd fix them a small snack at 2.30ish to keep them going until then. Jonathan was surprisingly quiet. What was he up to, she wondered as she ate. Oh it tasted so good and she sat in silence just enjoying her food. Mind you, her view of him across the table didn't hurt either and she smiled to herself. Breakfast finished, she went off in search of Henry and found him curled up asleep in his chair in the living room. She didn't want to disturb him but just gave his fur a small stroke with her hand to let him know she was there. He was such a good cat, as soon as she had put an old blanket on a comfy chair for him he'd jumped up straight away and now he always sat in the same place unless he was sat with her.

Evie rinsed the breakfast dishes and stacked them in the dishwasher; she filled the kettle with fresh water and made herself a cup of tea. He was very quiet this morning, maybe he wasn't a morning person or maybe something was up?

"Everything okay, you're very quiet would you like some tea?" She was gabbling now trying to figure out what was up with him.

"No tea for me and am just enjoying reading the paper," hmm..., all he was really doing was clock watching as he had another ½ hour before it was midday. Evie put on some music, sat and drank her tea, she chose a section of the paper and they sat there in companionable silence. This was freaking her out. Were guys normally like this on a Saturday morning? She'd thought he would be itching to do something or suggest going somewhere; but there was none of that here today.

She gave a small jump as her phone rang and she stood up to answer it. It was her mother calling and she wandered into the living room and stared out of the window looking at the garden whilst chatting.

All Jonathan could make out were random words such as work, Henry, Thomas, a bit, no looks like rain, London – his ears pricked up at that, what about London? He wanted to hear more but it would seem both rude and a bit odd if he just followed her and started listening to what was obviously a private conversation. She was obviously in no hurry to end the call and come back to him; which was fine. He wondered if she had told her mother about him? Neither of them had met the other's respective parents; his were still away and she had refused to take him with her to meet her mother the other week, so they both had that particular delight still to come.

He glanced at the kitchen clock, 11.55, so five more minutes and then she was all his. He left his glasses and the newspaper on the table and washed his hands at the kitchen sink. It felt like a game of hide and seek as he really wanted to shout, "Coming, ready or not." Evie realised he was now in the living room and watched him sit on the sofa, pat the seat next to him and give her one of his sexy grins; okay, time to end the call and give him what she had promised.

"Okay mum, look I've got to go, okay yes I will, love you, Bye." She hung up and put the phone down on the table.

"Now I assume you are here to collect on my promise Mr Dempsey?" She smiled lazily at him.

"Well you have kept me waiting for nearly an hour now, Miss Wallace, which may I point out is very rude and bad behaviour on your part," he replied.

"No I said midday and by my watch I have one minute left."

Jonathan had run out of patience and reached over to her and took her hand and pulled her onto the sofa next to him, he put his arms around her and began to kiss her very thoroughly. They picked up exactly where they had left off last night before she had fallen asleep. This time she was pinned against the back of the sofa and had literally nowhere to go, not that she minded for she was enjoying every minute of this and realized it had been one of the best promises she had made .

Jonathan had never wanted anyone as badly as he wanted her right now, this was going to be a fantastic, but very frustrating, afternoon. Her breasts were pushing against his chest and he really wanted to go a lot further than just kissing today. His lips moved away from her mouth and he started to kiss her softly on her neck and the top of her shoulder that was peeking out from her T-shirt. Her skin was so soft and she'd obviously used some body lotion after her shower as she smelt divine; in fact she always smelt divine, he couldn't wait until she was alone with him, in bed, naked except just for her perfume.

Quite some time later they were just lying together, with no need for small talk, each lost in their own thoughts when there was a knock at the door. Evie went to move and then realized she actually couldn't. "Um, that was the door. I have to answer it." She looked pleadingly at Jonathan.

"What's it worth?" he grinned at her whilst stroking her hair which had become lose from her hairband.

"Jonathan, seriously. I have to get the door, it might be important – please?"

He moved away so that she could get up and she ran to the front door. He heard voices and then the next thing he knew Jamie was in the living room. Seriously, he just could not catch a break with this girl; what did his little brother want now?

"Hi Jon, sorry to disturb and all that; but I've gone and locked myself out and I need your keys, I thought you might be here." Oh great. Now he had to sort this out, when all he really wanted to do was to kiss Evie senseless and then repeat the process over and over again. Maybe even take her to bed?

"Seriously J do you know where your keys are or do we have to change the locks – again?"

"Um, I think they're in my bedroom, but I just need to get in the front door, so if you wouldn't mind?"

Evie looked at Jonathan who looked distinctly cross at having his afternoon of smooching disturbed. "Tell you what, Jamie. Why don't you stay and have some lunch with us first? She caught Jonathan's eye and he looked positively apoplectic; oh he was just so used to having everything all his own way. She thought it was a nice gesture to make and hoped Jamie would say yes.

"Go on, Jamie, you don't have to rush off do you, how's uni? You can tell me all about it" Jamie grinned at her. Great, he was starving and she was going to feed him.

Jamie followed her out into the kitchen and started to chat away, leaving his brother in the living room asking God what he'd done that was so terrible that this was his punishment? He'd had to stop kissing Evie and now she'd gone and invited his little brother to lunch, who looked only too happy to be sat at her kitchen table being fed by her. He groaned in frustration – would they ever just get a whole day, no, even a whole morning or afternoon to themselves? He'd missed her so badly during the week he'd been seriously tempted to take Wednesday off and come and spend the day with her. Well she'd texted him twice and although he hadn't seen her in person at least they were talking and back on track. He ran his hands through his hair, hair that had been thoroughly tousled by Evie's small hands and sighing loudly he made his way into the kitchen.

Evie was laughing at some story Jamie was relaying about Will's escapades with his latest love interest. Jonathan sat down at the table. The sooner Jamie was fed and he'd given him his key then the sooner it would just be him and Evie again.

"What would you like for lunch? We're eating at 7.00ish so how about a focaccia roll with mozzarella/fresh tomato/basil and sundried tomatoes?" she asked him. Jonathan nodded: yes, that sounded fine and it looked as if Jamie was having at least two of these rolls for himself. Evie made the lunch and put the plates on the table. She decided to have something lighter as they were having a fairly large meal tonight so she settled on some oatcakes with goat's cheese, walnuts and an apple. The boys seemed happy enough with their food and she listened whilst Jamie and Jonathan talked about their parents. They were on a round the world trip and had open tickets so were taking as much time as they wanted in each new place, it didn't sound like she would be meeting them anytime soon.

"So how's your mum Evie, still not letting you eat in the street?" laughed Jamie. This was all news to Jonathan: how come he knew less about her mother than Jamie did? It sounded to him like Evie and Jamie were talking or texting quite regularly and he hadn't realised just how big a part of his family's life she was becoming. His parents would adore her, he had no doubts about that.

"Ooh what's in the tin?" Jamie was eying up the cake tin on the table.

"Sorry Jamie, that's off limits. I baked some special biscuits for Jonathan."

"Can I have a look or try just one?" he pleaded.

"No sorry, they are just for my boyfriend." There she had said 'boyfriend' out loud, that should cheer Jonathan up who was looking a bit pissed off by this point.

He grinned at his brother, "Blimey you've got it made – what with you baking treats for him and cooking him meals, Evie, no wonder he's over here all the time. So the tin is definitely off limits?"

"Nice try Jamie; but yes afraid so, no doubt you'd be just as happy with a chocolate bar anyway?"

"Oh do you have one of those then?"

"No but you could always buy yourself one on the way home now couldn't you?" She laughed at him. There was no way he was getting any of Jonathan's biscuits; she'd baked them especially for him and she wanted him to be the only one to enjoy them and think of her whilst he was eating them.

Lunch over, Jamie scooted out the front door with Jonathan's spare key to the main house.

"Well that was nice wasn't it?"

"Why did you invite him at all? he's always on the lookout for a free feed, you're too soft on him Evie."

"Oh come on. He was only here for an hour or so!" She realized she would need to cajole him into a better mood. She cleared the table and began to rinse the plates. Jonathan put his arms around her waist and kissed her neck: "Sorry, just feeling a bit neglected."

"I think you'll find it's called grumpy bear syndrome and I did call you my boyfriend and didn't let him steal any of your biscuits now didn't I?"

"That's very true," he said smiling

"Oh! talking of gifts, did you bring my T-shirt with you?" She wanted to see if he had kept to his side of the bargain: "As you are officially my boyfriend now?"

"Sorry no haven't had time to organize that yet; but don't worry I'll make sure you get it, now please can you stop clearing up and can we pick up where we left off this morning? If someone knocks on the door again we are ignoring it, okay?" he said testily.

In a quiet voice she said, "Okay, now then let's see what I can do to cure you of this terrible grumpy bear syndrome?" She took his hand and led him back into the living room.

This was more like it, he thought.

Chapter 15

Jonathan sat on the sofa, "So what do you suggest as a possible cure?" he smiled lazily at her. Evie didn't say anything, but bent down and removed his shoes then started to unbutton his shirt, "I think this needs a wash don't you?" then she asked him to lie face down on the sofa. Poor thing looked confused but did as she asked, then she placed a cushion for his head. "Now hands beneath your head." Jonathan lay down in his T-shirt and jeans. He still wasn't sure what she was up to but was eager to find out. She knelt on the sofa then carefully straddled him so she was sat on his bum and began to massage his shoulders and neck.

Oh now he understood, well this was an unexpected and very welcome surprise to his afternoon. Evie bent down and whispered in his ear, "Now doesn't this feel better?" He murmured his agreement, truth was he was in seventh heaven. She might have small hands, but they were definitely working some kind of magic on him and his mood. Slowly Evie started to kneed the muscles beneath his shoulders; he did feel tense, not a huge surprise as he was going out with her, she surmised, and continued to kneed away until after some time she was sure he had fallen asleep. She thought his body seemed more toned, maybe he had been taking some exercise after all. Very carefully she moved up and off of him and covered him with a blanket. There now, maybe when he woke up he would forget all about being cross with her for having invited Jamie to stay for lunch.

She put his shirt in the machine on a quick wash, she would have it ready for him when he woke up. Then she went back into the living room and curled up in an easy chair with her book and read whilst he slept. It was a lovely peaceful afternoon and she could just sit and watch him all day. His job must be pretty stressful, she thought, and coupled with the constant drama of seeing her it was no wonder he was tense and tired.

Sometime later she noticed it was raining now and quite gloomy for the time of year; but she didn't want to switch on a lamp for fear of waking him so a bit before 6.00 she made her way into the kitchen and quietly began to get their supper ready. After a while she sat at the table and drank a glass of water. She picked up her phone and texted Jamie to see if he had found his keys

Hi, did you find your keys? – SEND

Yes they were in my bedroom as I thought. Tell Jon have put his key through his letterbox. R u watching footie? – SEND

No, your brother is asleep and I am getting our supper ready, will Sky + the highlights. –SEND

R u sure I can't come over for supper? – SEND

No you can't, am hoping to have cured your brother of GBS so don't want a repeat performance-SEND

What's GBS? – SEND

Grumpy bear syndrome. Has he been working out? – SEND

Jamie laughed; boy, she was getting to know Jon very well, anything she could do to cure that would be a miracle.

Ha ha, Jon def has GBS and yes he's been going to the gym every night Mon to Thursday, didn't you know? – SEND

No he didn't say. Are you watching footie with the boys? – SEND

No just me, George is with Sophie, Will is God knows where with goodness knows who and Francis is mooning about after a girl called Helen. I've told him to text you for advice-has he? – SEND

No he hasn't, I'll text him tomorrow see if I can help smooth the path of true love –as am such an expert myself – ha ha ha!-SEND

Funny thing happened in the week-not sure if I should tell you or not? – SEND

Jamie you can't leave me in suspense. You've started so get on with it, am all intrigued –SEND

Well okay. I was studying the other eve – yes I do actually do some work – it was just before midnight when Will rocks up, he's had a bit to drink, but isn't really drunk or anything. We're just chatting about stuff when he asks me if you are still seeing Jon. I tell him of course you are, why etc. Turns out he wants me to tell him if it all goes tits up as he thinks he has a chance with you – how hilarious is that – no offence-SEND

Blimey, no offence taken, am just surprised as always thought he had more women on the go than I've had hot dinners type of thing. He probably just has a little crush on me – what can I say? I'm irresistible – ha ha ha – which by the way is A JOKE! Seriously though, I've never led him on, am just friendly and josh with all your friends – you don't think I have led him on do you? Am panicking now.-SEND

No of course not, you treat him the same as Francis and George, besides I'm your favourite right? – SEND

You know you are; although Francis is a close second . – SEND

Seriously – Francis? Is it cos he can dance, cos I cud learn? – SEND

Ha ha ha, no it's always the quiet ones who are more interesting, hidden depths etc.! Will is over confident, and he's far too young for me. Can you keep it a secret? – SEND

Shall I tell Will you're too old for him? Maybe what's in it for me? – SEND

No let sleeping dogs lie, please. As a bribe I promise to send some chocolate brownies back with your brother just for you – do we have a deal? – SEND

You made brownies and I didn't even get one when I was there? – I've a good mind to drive straight over to yours again, you are a very mean girl Evelyn Wallace. – SEND

Jamie, Jamie, am not being mean, am upset you think I am (sob sob), but if I'd showed you the tin you would have been here all afternoon and I thought Jonathan would go slightly mad about that – we don't get much time to ourselves as it is and you wouldn't want to play gooseberry would you? Secret is I am hoping we are MFEO, jury still out but I have my fingers crossed. – SEND

What's MFEO? – SEND

Have to go now, will leave you to figure it out. Bye – SEND

Bye Sis. – SEND

Evie smiled. He really was a sweet boy, not that she would tell him that as boys hated to be called sweet.

As she ironed Jonathan's shirt Evie thought about what Jamie had said. So Will had a crush on her, this was indeed news to her. She would be careful not to say anything too inappropriate as she definitely didn't want him to get the wrong idea, it was interesting though. Shirt done, she went back into the kitchen to put the chicken in the oven, and packed some brownies in a Tupperware box for Jamie that would keep him happy. She smiled. Now she really should check on Jonathan next, she didn't want him sleeping through supper too. She switched on a couple of lamps and he stirred and had a little stretch. He'd been having a fantastic dream about the two of them and he hoped it would soon become a reality. He opened his eyes to see her switching on the lamps; gosh how long had he been asleep? She wandered over to him, "Hello sleepy, feeling better now?" He grinned up at her and pulled her on top of him.

"Ooh yes very nice sleep, is there no end to your talents?" and began to kiss her. Eventually she pulled away, laughing that their supper would be ruined if she didn't attend to it right away. Reluctantly he let her go and followed her into the kitchen. Whatever it was it smelt great and he realised he was very hungry.

They sat at her kitchen table facing each other, their plates of food empty. The dinner had gone down very well, yes very well indeed. The way to get these Dempsey boys onside was definitely through their stomachs, she thought. He'd enjoyed everything especially the chicken and the chocolate brownies. Fiona was right: she was a great cook.

"Oh by the way, Jamie has put your key through your letter box."

"You've spoken to him?"

"No just a text and I promised him you'd take some of these brownies home for him too."

"Honestly Evie you spoil him. You seem to spend a lot of time spoiling and texting him, when you could be spoiling and texting me, what do you find to talk about?" Suddenly he was annoyed; but sounded petulant in her view.

Oh bollocks! he sounded a bit jealous; first it was GBS now it was GEM. "Well he told me you are working out at your gym in London. I had noticed, by the way, especially after this afternoon. Are you suffering from GEM now as well?" she laughed

"What is GEM when it is at home?"

"Green eyed monster."

He was exasperated now, "Seriously though, what do you find to talk to him about?"

Evie saw his mood had changed; oh no what now? everything had been going so well. She picked up her mobile and entered the code, "Here read it for yourself – I don't mind– you obviously don't trust me" – she snapped at him and thrust it into his hand. She sighed and cleared the table whilst Jonathan read; well tough luck if he didn't like what he was about to read, he'd asked for it, she hated jealous guys they were a right pain in the arse.

Jonathan began to scroll down the text. For fuck's sake, so Will now thought he had a chance with her too? Bloody hell, this was a nightmare. He read on and realized she had shot that down straight away. Jamie was her favourite and then Francis – he'd have to watch out for him and so finally she had persuaded Jamie not to return for brownies so they could spend more time together. What in God's name was MFEO when it was at home? He read Jamie's last text, Bye Sis. Oh no – he had overreacted big time and just looking at Evie's back he knew she was mad at him.

He ran his hands through his hair and stood up and walked over to her. She was at the sink rinsing glasses. He put his hands round her waist and pulled her against him. Evie didn't relax her body at all, she was as mad as hell with him and just cuddling up to her wasn't going to work this time. He'd spoilt their evening by behaving like a spoilt child, honestly he was so infuriating. Far too used to having everything his own way, well not tonight, no siree.

He nuzzled her neck and began to place feather light kisses on the tops of her shoulders and the nape of her neck. She didn't respond at all but continued to rinse the plates and put them to drain.

"Sorry I was being an idiot?". There, maybe that would do it he hoped, but still nothing from her. He held her tighter and whispered in her ear, "How can I make it up to you?" and waited for what seemed like hours but can only have been moments before she replied quietly.

"Well I think you should leave now as it's pretty obvious you don't trust me, not even to text your little brother."

He pulled back slightly, "Seriously, you want me to leave?"

"Yes I do."

"But what if I don't want to leave?" he was pleading with her now using that soft sexy voice of his.

It would have been so easy to turn round, forgive him and kiss him; but honestly – not trusting her to text his little brother what the fuck would it be next, as much as she was enjoying his attention he needed to cool down and get a grip.

"I'll show you out," she shrugged him off, moved quickly away from him and left him standing there.

No no no, this wasn't what he had planned at all, shit not again. He walked into the hall. She already had the front door open and thrust two tins into this hands. "One for you and one for Jamie – if that's okay with you that is?" she said sarcastically.

He looked down at the tins, she'd baked biscuits especially for him and now he felt a total idiot. "Can I see you tomorrow?"

"Not sure." Evie moved the door slightly as if to say: okay, out you go. Just at that moment Henry chose to come swanning in. He glared at Jonathan and she picked Henry up and cuddled him in her arms, kissing the top of his head – pointedly showing she had no intention of cuddling or kissing Jonathan before he left. Once outside Jonathan rested his back on the door. Well that had gone from great to shit in about one minute flat; he could hear Evie talking to Henry 'Hello you, do you want a cuddle?, it's okay sweetie he's gone now it's just you and me. Would you like some milk? yes, I thought so.'

Chapter 16

As Jonathan drove home he was thinking about what had just happened. Yes he'd been cross about her texting J but as it had turned out he had nothing to worry about, so why did he have to make such a big deal out of everything? Maybe he was jealous; but if it wasn't Jamie it was Will, he sighed. He'd text her when he got home and hoped she'd reply.

Evie hadn't planned on their evening finishing so abruptly it was only a bit after 9.00 on a Saturday night. Great! she sighed to herself. Another row; she was tired of all this nonsense from him. One minute he was fine and the next he was accusing her of goodness knows what without any foundation at all. She hadn't planned what to do tomorrow as she'd rather foolishly assumed they would be spending it together; well that obviously wasn't going to happen now. She went upstairs and got ready for bed. She would watch the football highlights in her pj's with Henry and go to sleep – wow big night!

Jonathan had hardly closed his front door when Jamie appeared. "Hi! you're back early, did you bring something from Evie for me?" he asked expectantly. Jonathan thrust the tin into his hands. "Happy now?" he asked him sarcastically.

Jamie looked at his brother; he didn't look happy at all and it was barely 9.30. What was up?

"You okay Jon?"

"Not really, no."

Jamie sat down in the kitchen and opened the tin. Oh my God, the brownies looked fab and he'd taken a big bite as Jonathan just glared at him.

"If you must know we had a fight – about you this time J."

Jamie struggled to finish his mouthful and eventually said, "All you do is upset her and what do I have to do with it?"

Did they always fight? He didn't think that was true; yes, he had upset her a few times, well quite a lot of times recently; but they'd been having a great time until he had asked her about her texts to Jamie. "Well I think I may have overreacted about her texting you actually."

"It's all nonsense really, just fun stuff, uni and advice about girls you know, nothing to worry about. Want one of these?"

"Um no thanks and yes I know that now – as she let me read them."

Jamie paused, "Seriously – you asked to read Evie's text messages, why? what did you think we were typing to each other?" Jamie was suddenly angry with his brother, "For God's sake, Jon! she's your girlfriend and it just so happens I get on great with her, we all do; well, maybe not you after tonight. Sometimes I wonder just which one of us is the more mature one? So what's next?"

"To be honest I don't really know. I asked her if I could see her tomorrow and she just said maybe; God, she was hopping mad J – said I didn't trust her. Oh and by the way you can tell Will from me if he even looks at her the wrong way he'll have me to deal with, okay?"

"Really Jon, I mean really? Will is just being Will, Evie would never take him seriously, she had him all figured out from day one if you recall?"

Yes that was true – in fact everything Jamie had said was true, he had fucked up again; God, how many chances was she going to give him – his luck was running out and fast. He would text her once Jamie had gone and take it from there.

"Okay J time to go. Oh one more thing: what the fuck is MFEO?"

"No idea, mate. Sorry," and he was gone.

Jonathan made himself a coffee and opened his tin of biscuits. Even they were staring accusingly at him; he took one out and closed the lid as he wanted to keep the rest for London. He turned his mobile round and round in his hands. He knew he had to make the first move; but was a bit scared as what her reaction would be.

Hi it's me. – SEND. He waited. Nothing, nothing at all.

Okay I'm sorry – again. I know now that I overreacted, in fact Jamie has just been here telling me exactly the same thing. Can we just talk about this and move on? – SEND. He waited again, but still nothing. Maybe he ought to go back to hers and make her listen to him; problem was, what was he going to say that she hadn't already heard a hundred times before? and he wasn't even sure she would open the door.

Evie's phone was pinging like mad. Who knew she was so popular? she thought to herself. First a text from Jonathan, which she ignored, then one from Jamie.

Hi, wanted to say thanks for brownies they're yummy – SEND

Glad you're enjoying them – SEND

Just been to Jon's, he's not happy – SEND

Well that makes two of us then! – SEND Jon was right, she was hopping mad.

Are you going to forgive him? – SEND

Sorry J am not going to discuss this with you. Am watching football highlights although highlights may be pushing it somewhat! Why don't you go and show your brother my text just to make sure he is okay with it? – SEND

Okay I get it – SEND

Bye Jamie– SEND and she was gone

Bye Sis – SEND. Jamie wondered if she was going to text Jon; it looked pretty doubtful. Oh well, it was really none of his business and he settled down to watch football and eat cake. There were worse things to be doing tonight, he supposed.

Jonathan stared at his phone: nothing, absolutely bloody nothing. His mood had gone from bad to worse; he knew he'd been in the wrong about asking to see her texts, what was he expecting to find anyway? It was ridiculous, he was being bloody ridiculous!

Rowan was texting Evie about her date with her new guy; it seemed to be going well.
How come you're replying, thought you had a big dinner date tonight with his Lordship? – SEND

Yeah didn't turn out too well in the end . – SEND

Why, what happened? – SEND

In a nutshell he doesn't trust me, had to show him my text messages to his little brother to prove they were innocent – SEND

Seriously? The man's an idiot, why are you bothering? Send him a mix CD with the first song being 'Jealous Guy by Roxy Music' see if he gets it – SEND Evie laughed; trust Rowan to get to the point.

Go away and enjoy your date – my fucked up love life can wait until tomorrow xx – SEND

Text u 2moro xx – SEND.

Well Rowan had a point, why was she bothering?. She'd nearly told him everything, too, which would have been a huge mistake if this was truly the end of them. She felt tears prick her eyes, truth was she didn't want it to be the end of them, she was hoping that this time it would be different and he would stay-who was the idiot now? she wondered. She switched her phone off. She couldn't cope with hearing it ping all night, not that she thought she would get any sleep; but she turned off her bedroom lamp and closed her eyes. She would pretend she was asleep, if nothing else.

Jonathan had realised some time ago that she wasn't going to reply, not this time. He was in the bathroom brushing his teeth whilst his mind just wandered, going over things again and again. He thought they'd be spending tomorrow together but that didn't look very likely now and then it would be a whole week before he saw her again-if they were still together by this time next week that was. Groaning, he switched off the light; he didn't want to lose her, not over something as idiotic as this. No, he didn't want to lose her at all.

Chapter 17

Sunday morning and Evie was out of bed and feeding Henry in the kitchen. What was she going to do today? She had the day off. Maybe they needed her at work? but if so they would have rung her by now. Then she realized she hadn't switched her phone back on and ran into the kitchen. Sure enough there were messages but none from the gym and none from him – she felt so deflated she didn't want breakfast. She'd go for a run, that usually helped to clear her head and she bounded upstairs to change, glad to have decided on at least one thing to pass the time today.

Rowan texted her before lunch. Did she want to meet up today? Her date with Mr Wonderful had turned out not to be so wonderful after all. Evie agreed to meet Rowan at their favourite pub, which was open all day, so they could bitch about guys and natter about how bloody useless they all were until their hearts content.

Unbeknown to her Jonathan had decided to go round to Evie's to sort things out in person; but when he got there it didn't look like anyone was at home. He waited a few minutes then got back in his car and drove home. Brilliant plan, genius! he told himself, you just thought you'd rock up and expected her to be in and fall into your arms – how bloody naïve. You're not 17 again. He was angry with himself this time. Another wasted day they could have spent together.

Boy was he in a foul mood on Monday, even his secretary Margaret who had worked for him for over ten years knew when to leave him well alone. He was worse than a bear with a sore head. Obviously he didn't have a good weekend, so no-one asked. Evie went through the motions in her two morning classes; but her heart just wasn't in it, she didn't want to be there but she didn't want to be at home either. She'd lost her appetite and just felt rubbish. Everyone noticed she wasn't her usual happy self, this wasn't like her, no not like her at all. She showered at the gym, just letting the water run over her.

She stood there for so long her fingers went all wrinkly until she shook herself and turned the water off.

She dressed on auto pilot and walked through into reception where she bumped into Miles and Stacey. Stacey produced a box which had been delivered to the gym for her that morning. She just stared at it – 'Oh My God', surely he hadn't sent flowers to apologise yet again? Evie didn't want whatever it was; but opened the box anyway. Sure enough, there were flowers, flowers from Jonathan with a note saying sorry. Her shoulders slumped. She was weary of this endless circle of mistakes and apology, flowers to solve all their problems. She felt tired and emotional and asked Stacey to get the number of the courier. Miles asked her if she wanted to stay and have lunch with him and she agreed. Just have a quiet lunch with a friend, maybe that would do the trick. Evie rang the couriers first and headed out to lunch with Miles.

"So what's new with you, then?" she asked Miles. She hadn't seen too much of him lately and felt a bit guilty. They chatted about work and then his family and what he wanted to do with his degree. They got onto the subject of girlfriends and it turned out he had a sweetheart back home in Chicago and they were trying their hardest to make it work by using Skype to keep in touch every day if possible. Evie was envious of them, they were thousands of miles apart and yet they had committed to each other. They obviously trusted each other and talked every day – see it could be done; but just not for her.

Evie mooched around the house. She'd forgotten what this felt like when you'd been dumped or just finished a relationship, it was always the worst. She couldn't concentrate to read or watch TV, she didn't want to eat, she didn't want to do anything. She put some clothes on to wash and steamed the kitchen floor; wow, was that really the highlight of her day: doing domestic drudgery whilst trying not to cry, boy she knew how to live the high life, she thought wryly to herself.

Unbeknown to her Jonathan was struggling just as much as she was. He'd waited to get her text thanking him for the flowers but none had come. He'd even checked with the delivery company that she'd received them. Maybe she was busy and would text him tonight? He wasn't in the mood for his workout at the gym with Mike, but at least it gave him something to do whilst trying and failing not to think of her. Late Monday evening and still no text from her. He was exhausted as Mike had really put him through the wringer. Jonathan had lost his appetite and stared at the steak in front of him, he closed his eyes and rested his head in his hands. Relationships were so difficult sometimes; it was very easy to walk away when it was obvious it was going nowhere; but he didn't want to let this one go, maybe you only felt like this if was worth fighting for – he didn't know – he'd never watched Oprah, for fuck's sake, maybe things would look better in the morning?

Tuesday and Evie felt like it was groundhog day. Get up/shower/go to work/ shower/come home and try not to cry for the rest of the day. Look in the fridge and not want to eat anything that was in there. Why was it that some people lost their appetites and others ate for England when relationships failed? Jonathan's secretary brought a package into his office before noon and left it on his desk. He was in a meeting elsewhere and would be back after lunch. She hoped it would be a good surprise because if it wasn't then she desperately didn't want to be there when he opened it. Just after 2.30 and Jonathan returned to his office, he saw the parcel immediately and his heart sang. Maybe it was from Evie? He checked the sender and, yes, it was from her. Not waiting for scissors he tore off the parcel tape and looked inside. Jonathan couldn't believe his eyes. She'd sent his flowers back to him.

He sank into his office chair, then stood up again. Maybe there was a note? He found the note with the word sorry that he had written and turned it over. Nothing, not a word, it was blank. This couldn't be right; maybe there had been a cock up with the couriers after all? He sat down again and just stared at the box. Now what? Calling the couriers who told him yet again that, yes, the parcel had been delivered and then collected yesterday afternoon with instructions to be delivered to his office, he realised there had been no mistake.

His secretary buzzed through to say his 3.00pm appointment was here and should she show them in. Right at that moment he didn't care two jots about his bloody appointment; but had little choice but to move the box to behind his desk and carry on with his afternoon. He had to talk to her, make her talk to him. Yes, looking back, flowers had been a predictable and lazy option, but it had worked for him every time up until now; no girl had ever sent them back to him, ever.

That night he sat in his apartment drinking tea and eating the biscuits she had baked for him. He couldn't face a proper meal. Everything was just a mess. One minute they had been eating dinner, everything was great, more than great it was fantastic. He'd spent the night with her albeit on the sofa, but he'd slept well with her in his arms. Then she'd kissed him all afternoon and given him a wonderful back massage and he'd drifted off to sleep – it was like the best dream ever which then slowly turned into a bloody nightmare and he was absolutely clueless as to what to do next.

Chapter 18

Early Wednesday morning and Evie was on the train to London. It was the first Wednesday of the month and the routine was always the same. Meeting at 10.00 with Peter, lunch with Alice if she was free and then meeting with Ian at 3.00pm. Well maybe it would beat being stuck at home all day as she didn't think she could cope with that. She met with Peter who, although didn't say it, thought she looked terrible and wondered what was going on.

Lunch with Alice who took one look at her and demanded to know who or what was responsible for her friend looking so 'bloody awful' and should she send the boys round to sort out whoever it was? Evie had perked up and without mentioning names said yes, it was boy trouble again and she wanted Alice's advice on what to do next. Some of which wasn't very helpful like stringing him up from his balls; but she did listen when Alice asked her gently what did she want to do, did she want to walk away or try again? Evie felt the tears well up and she wiped away a lone tear that had escaped and was running down her cheek. The truth was she didn't want it to end; but had no idea how to fix things, it had gone from great to grim in a blink of an eye. Alice hugged her and said she was welcome to come and stay with her anytime she had her free weekend and to think seriously if Evie wanted this loser roughed up a bit as she was sure she would find someone to take it on.

Next it was Ian at 3.00. This hour was always the hardest, as he was a nice chap and they'd known each other for nearly four years now. Ian just let her talk. It was obvious to him that she was struggling yet again on the relationship issue; but the ball was in her court and although he couldn't tell her what she should be doing he tried to steer her in the right direction, whatever that was.

Relief flooded through her finally she was on the train home and was glad it was all over for another month, except for meeting Alice whom she would love to see more of. She chided herself to make more of an effort to see her, especially as Alice was now engaged and it would be harder to get single girl time with her alone once her and Harvey were married. Emotionally exhausted, she drove home wanting a hot bath and hoped Henry would be home wanting some attention from her. That was the thing with cats: they only wanted you on their terms and you just had to get used to that.

Some time later she was soaking in a hot bath full of lovely bubbles not caring how wrinkly her skin was becoming. She'd put more hot water in twice now and realized that she had to get out soon, as much as she wanted to stay in there preferably for the next month! She always felt so grubby after her day in London and she had double cleansed her face just to make sure. Evie chose her favourite pyjamas and wrapped herself up in her blue robe and padded downstairs. Typically Henry was no-where to be found and she made herself a piece of toast, not really even wanting it if she was honest.

The courier would have returned Jonathan's flowers to him by now and she wondered what his reaction had been. Maybe he'd been angry or maybe he'd just shrugged his shoulders and thought there were plenty more fish in the sea, she didn't know anymore; but she did care. She took her phone and her book back upstairs and brushed her teeth. She would be in bed early yet again.

Jonathan was pacing the floor of his apartment. Never in a million years had he expected her to return the flowers; she loved flowers. Maybe that was the message – oh he didn't know. Idly he switched on his laptop and started to search. This had been bothering him since Saturday night and he couldn't bear it any longer. He typed in MFEO and waited for the answer. What popped up next on the screen took his breath away, for staring right back at him was the answer. He ran his hands through his hair. This is what she was hoping they'd be, she hoped that they'd be together and he'd ballsed it up right in front of her. Now he had a plan and, he smiled to himself, you're not getting away from me that easily, Evie Wallace. He continued to work on the computer and when finished smiled to himself; there would be no way she would be sending this present back. No way at all.

Thursday afternoon and Evie arrived at work before 5.00. She had some paperwork to complete before her class at 6.00 and didn't want to give Steve any excuse for bollocking her again. Stacey handed her a large brown soft jiffy envelope and Evie took it, puzzled at what it could be. It definitely wasn't flowers that was for sure – she felt relieved, she loved flowers; but you could have too much of a good thing after all. It would have to wait until she got home and had some privacy.

Jonathan knew Evie was working and wouldn't be home until after 9.00pm. His session with Mike had gone well and he felt energized and alive for the first time in nearly a week. He would wait another half an hour and then start texting.

Once home Evie showered, put on her pyjamas and then sat in bed staring at the package. She was dying of curiosity, but felt almost torn in two: what if it was something awful? On the other hand it could be something wonderful. She couldn't stand the suspense any longer and ripped it open. What was inside took her breath away. He'd remembered and he did care, hell he'd even figured out what she was trying to tell him – oh yes, he'd been very clever indeed and she did a little happy dance with her feet under the duvet. Lying on the bed was a short sleeved t shirt, in navy blue with white writing on the front, writing that spelled out, "I have a boyfriend and we are Made For Each Other." She hugged herself, grinning like a maniac. She hoped he would text her as she was definitely going to reply this time.

Shortly after 9.30 her phone pinged and there it was, those two little words that meant so much.

Missed you x – SEND

She typed back: Missed you more x – SEND

Yes, yes she was back, for once he had got something right.

Did you get my present? – SEND

Yes it's wonderful, thank you – SEND

Why am I such an idiot!? – Send

How long have you got? – SEND He laughed, yes okay, she was right.

How have you been this week? – SEND

Not good, mostly sad, you? – SEND

Bloody miserable without you – SEND. She sighed. So it wasn't just her, then.

Did you eat your biscuits? – SEND

Yes, every one of them – thought about you each time I took one out of the tin – SEND. She grinned for that had been her intention all along.

Glad you liked them. Where are you? – SEND

In my apartment texting my girlfriend. Where are you? – SEND

In bed, in pyjamas texting my boyfriend – SEND. She felt brave tonight, very brave indeed.

Is Henry with you? – SEND

No, he is out living up to his name tormenting some poor creature, so it is just me on my lonesome – SEND

Which pyjamas are you wearing tonight? – SEND

My my!, you are making up for lost time. Am wearing a new set; thought I would treat myself after latest dating disaster-yes I do mean you! It is a deep v top with lace and matching bottoms, both in very soft dusky lilac fabric – SEND

A cami top? – SEND. Boy, he wanted to see her both in and out of those too!

Well, you have been paying attention, and yes, you are spot on! What are you wearing? – SEND

Am in jeans and t shirt after session with Mike in the gym – SEND

By the way how is that going, are you enjoying it? – SEND

It's fine; but enjoy is too strong a word – SEND

Maybe you need a different trainer? – SEND

Who did you have in mind? – SEND

How about Miles? – SEND. No he didn't want bloody Miles not for the training he had in mind anyway.

Was thinking about a female trainer with a more personal touch! – SEND

What kind of personal touch? – SEND

Perhaps I can demonstrate tomorrow? – SEND

Why what is happening tomorrow? –SEND

My girlfriend is coming over to mine after work – SEND

What's she like? – SEND

She is the most amazing girl I have ever met, you'd like her a lot as you are very similar. – SEND

She does sound great. – SEND

Evie I am so happy we are back on track, I mean we are okay aren't we? – SEND

Yes we are very okay – SEND

I don't suppose you can get anyone to cover your shifts tomorrow night? – SEND

I could try; but it's very short notice. Why? – SEND

Am going crazy just thinking about seeing you, was hoping for more time together to make up for last weekend –
SEND

Let me make some calls right now and I'll come back to you, okay SEND

Okay – SEND

Evie started to call the other trainers, but either they couldn't cover her classes or they didn't reply or pick up her message. It was no good, she would have to work and go to Jonathan's afterwards. Ten minutes later she texted him.

Hi. Sorry, but I can't get anyone to cover so I'll see you just before 9.00pm – SEND

Really no-one? – SEND

My my! I had forgotten just how impatient you can be Mr D? – SEND

You have no idea! – SEND She laughed. Oh she had a pretty good idea alright.

I'd better go soon – SEND He groaned, already.

Go where? – SEND

To sleep, as am already in bed – SEND He would have given anything to be right there with her.

Can I join you? – SEND

As I recall we did spend last Friday night together or is your terrible memory playing tricks on you again? – SEND

No haven't forgotten, loved every minute of it. Can we do the same tomorrow night? – SEND

Maybe, depends. – SEND

On what? – SEND

Depends on how comfy your sofa is! – SEND

Do we have to use the sofa? – SEND How was she going to reply to that one?.

For now, yes. – SEND She was nearly ready to share things with him and then they could move on to the next level.

Okay, no problem – SEND. Oh good, he wasn't going to pressurise her. She would plan to open up to him soon.

Until tomorrow then; goodnight Jonathan x – SEND

Night Evie xx – SEND She noticed he'd signed off with two kisses and not just one he was definitely trying harder and about time too.

Jonathan was ecstatic. She sounded happy and his present had been genius, bloody genius; and, what's more, she'd agreed to stay over – albeit on the sofa; but it was a start, yes a very good place to start again .

He typed, Miss you xx – SEND His phone pinged almost immediately.

Missed you more.xx – SEND

Chapter 19

Friday and Evie woke early. She felt a bit odd; it couldn't have been anything she'd eaten as she hadn't been eating much of anything lately. Going to the bathroom she realised she had started her period. Could the timing be any worse? she groaned to no-one in particular. She took her morning classes as usual and then went home again before her evening shift began. Evie pottered about and planned what to wear to Jonathan's tonight.

Arriving at the gym just after 5.30 she went into the ladies' changing room and sat down. She did feel weird and had already taken two painkillers before she'd left home. She might have to do a slightly different type of class with the clients tonight. She couldn't wait for 8 o'clock to come round as she really was struggling now and needed to go home.

Arriving home, she looked in the bathroom mirror and a very pale looking face peered back at her. She definitely wasn't looking her best; maybe after a shower she would feel better. It was nearly 9.00pm now and she was not well, not well at all; there was no way she could go to Jonathan's tonight. She took two more painkillers and called his phone.

"Hi, it's me."

"Hello. Are you on your way over?"

"Umm no, not exactly. Sorry, here's the thing: I'm not feeling very well, I've been like this all day and just about managed to get through my classes. Am so sorry. I don't want to let you down; but can we take a rain check on tonight?"

"Do you need a doctor?"

"No. I've just taken more painkillers and am going to bed, I feel awful about tonight." She sounded sad and forlorn and he just wanted to wrap his arms around her and hold her.

"I'm more concerned about you. Do you want me to come over?"

"Not sure there is anything you can do, I just need to lie down."

"Okay well text me if you need me – promise?"

"Yes I promise, am so sorry Jonathan."

"Stop saying sorry, it's fine you're not well. I'll call you tomorrow okay?"

"Okay thanks for understanding – night then."

"Night Evie."

He ended the call. He hadn't known her be unwell before, it must be bad for her to cancel as he was sure she was just as keen to meet up tonight as he was. Evie settled down to sleep. She had a hot water bottle but it really wasn't helping much. Why did this have to happen now, tonight of all nights?. She slept fitfully and made frequent trips to the bathroom, but at 7.30am she heaved herself out of bed to get ready for work. She was going to need to put on some makeup this morning otherwise her clients would turn around and leave before she'd even begun. She showered and put on her gym gear. Just two more classes and then she'd be free to go to Jonathan's. She texted him. See you before 12.00 at yours if this is okay? –SEND

The morning was indeed a struggle, but she got through it and showered at the gym. She felt a bit woozy but convinced herself that was probably a combination of exercise and her period. Dressing carefully in a patterned maxi dress as she couldn't bear anything tight today, she swallowed two more tablets and walked out to her car. Sat in her car she took some deep breaths, she'd be fine, just fine, she repeated to herself.

She arrived at Jonathan's and he was out the door practically before her car had come to a halt. He opened her car door and helped her out." Are you okay, I was worried about you?"

"Yes I'll be fine," she smiled at him. He did look very handsome today. He thought she looked very pale, she'd lost weight in a week too and he wasn't convinced that she was any better than she had been the night before. Once inside he offered her a cup of tea, but she asked for a glass of water instead. He took her hands and rested his forehead on hers, "I'm so glad to see you, you have no idea how much I missed you," and he kissed her soundly on the lips. Her arms curled over his shoulders and she responded, her kiss telling him she had missed him too. Eventually they broke apart and smiled at each other; it was going to be okay.

"So Mr D," she teased him, "what delights are we having for lunch today?"

He hadn't given it a lot of thought but he did have some chicken and salad and he'd raided the fridge in the main house for some extra things. Evie sat at the kitchen table. Her offer of help had been refused and she watched whilst Jonathan prepared their lunch. Excusing herself she went to the cloakroom; she was gone quite a while but reappeared seemingly okay. She looked out of the window and then was suddenly gripped by a shooting, stabbing pain. "Aarrgh oh my God!" She clutched her tummy and bent over holding onto a kitchen chair for support. Jonathan was beside her in a flash. "Evie are you okay? You don't look very well. Here, sit down. She was breathing heavily now and felt a bit sick too. How embarrassing, she wanted the ground to swallow her up. "Evie, Evie look at me. What do you need, what can I do?" He was very worried now; she looked terrible. She didn't reply for what seemed like ages but truth was she was concentrating on not throwing up. "I'm sorry but I think I need to lie down, I don't suppose you've got a hot water bottle, have you?" her voice was quiet and strained.

"Okay, let's get you upstairs. I'll help you."

Jonathan draped one of her arms over his shoulder and gingerly helped her to climb the stairs. He was going to take her into his bedroom, but she asked him to take her to a guest room instead. She didn't want to spend her first time in his bed looking and feeling like this.

He opened the door of his largest guest room it had its own en-suite and a large king sized bed. Evie put her hand out on the chest of drawers to steady herself, "I'm going to need a bath towel please," she asked staring at the floor; honestly, could her embarrassment be any greater? He made sure she was steady and then dashed out to the linen cupboard on the landing and grabbed the first towel he saw. Back in the bedroom Evie hadn't moved an inch, almost like she was using all her concentration on just standing still. She asked him to leave her for a few minutes. He didn't want to go but she pleaded with him, "Just for 5 minutes whilst I sort myself out. I'll yell if I need you, I promise." He left but waited outside the door. Surely this wasn't normal? Evie slowly slipped off her sandals and placed her maxi dress over the bedroom chair, next she pulled back the duvet and folded the towel in half and placed it on the bed before climbing in and pulling the duvet over herself. Keeping her underwear on she curled up on her side pulling her knees up towards her chest. Evie called to Jonathan that he could come back now and he knelt by the bed. Concern written all over his face. She smiled weakly at him, "Not quite the romantic date we were planning?"

"I don't care about that, I just care about you, what's going on?"

She took a deep breath. "Well, here's the thing. I'm just losing a lot of blood, too much I think; I didn't want to not turn up again?"

Jonathan stroked her brow, "You should have stayed at home. You're not well. I'd have survived, you know."

"I didn't want to disappoint you for a second time. Can I have a glass of water and that hot water bottle now please?"

"Sure, sure, I'll be back in a sec." He bolted down the stairs. This wasn't right. He was calling David and then he'd look for a bloody hot water bottle. David picked up on the third ring. Jonathan explained as best he could whilst David listened, "I'll be there in 20 minutes," then he hung up.

Next he got her a glass of water and took it up to her, placing it on her bedside table. She had her eyes closed now; but if anything she looked worse than ever.

Leaving his house, he ran over to the main house. Luckily Jamie was home for the weekend and he went straight in to the TV room which was where he found Jamie and his friends. They were watching football as Jonathan practically burst through the door.

"Hi Jon, where's the fire?"

"It's Evie. She's at mine and she's not well; do we have a hot water bottle anywhere?" He had all their attention now and they all jumped up, the football game forgotten.

"Um not sure, but the kitchen is probably the best place to look." They all piled into the kitchen and began to rummage through cupboards and drawers. "So what's happening exactly?"

"She looks terrible, she's in pain and losing a lot of blood. I've rung David and he's on his way."

Jamie looked shocked. "Look, we'll find it and I'll bring it over to you okay, you go back to her now."

"Right, right, good plan," and with that he was gone running back over to his house.

Jamie and his friends just stared at each other. This sounded bad, very bad. They continued to search until Francis pulled out a square cushion type thing. "I think this is a heat pad. You put it in the microwave. My sister has one of them." Jamie grabbed it from him and put it in the microwave. None of them knew how long it should be in there for so agreed on 2 minutes and then they'd take it from there. That two minutes was the longest two minutes they had ever endured. The microwave pinged and Jamie removed it and ran over to Jon's. Whilst he was gone George, Will and Francis stood in the kitchen in silence. Eventually George said, "It doesn't sound good does it?" They agreed it didn't sound good at all. Francis took a deep breath and said to no-one in particular, "Do you think she's having a miscarriage?"

Jamie just happened to be coming through the door at that moment and stopped still. He hadn't thought of that – bloody hell, bloody hell!

Evie clutched the heat pad to her tummy. There, that should help. She'd drunk some water and was enjoying the relief of her head lying motionless on a cold pillow. Jonathan had left the front door unlocked ready for David. Where was he, for God's sake? she needed him now. Less than twenty minutes passed and David's car appeared outside. He ran up the stairs and in through the first door. He opened his case and knelt on the floor beside the bed. "Okay Evie, I'm here now. Let's have a look at you, shall we?" Evie opened her eyes. Thank goodness David was here. He'd make this pain all go away. He turned to face Jonathan, "You have to leave us now." Jonathan wasn't going anywhere anytime soon, but David insisted he had to leave, quoting doctor patient confidentiality. Reluctantly he left; but sat at the top of the stairs straining to listen. He shouldn't really be eavesdropping, but he wanted to hear what was being said.

David began asking Evie questions in a quiet and thorough manner: when did this start, has it been like this before, are your periods regular? She replied that, no, they weren't particularly, in fact they hadn't been since well since you know David knew what she was referring to and then continued, "Okay I'll need to take a look etc. then he said, "I need to ask you something. I don't want you to be embarrassed, but I need to know okay?" Bloody hell, her embarrassment was sky high already she thought but if you must. She nodded her head at him to continue.

"Are you and Jonathan having sexual intercourse?" – she mouthed 'no'.

"Sorry Evie, but I have to ask, are you having sex with anyone else?" – She looked agitated now, 'no'! A lone tear trickled down her cheek and she swiped it away with her hand.

"Okay, I just needed to ask these things, let's get you into the bathroom." He helped her get out of bed and made her lean on him whilst they moved slowly towards the en-suite. Once inside he placed a cardboard pan in to the base of the loo and lowered her carefully down and told her to wee, as he needed to take a sample. "Don't pull the flush, okay?" She nodded back at him. Suddenly she felt very hot and said, "Oh I'm feeling sick." David just managed to grab the plastic bin and hold it in front of her as she threw up in it. Jonathan could hear retching now; it sounded awful, so he was so glad he had called David and thanked God she had not been on her own.

Retching finished, she pulled on clean pants which she'd had the foresight to bring with her and David helped her to lean against the basin, staring back at her in the mirror was a deathly white face with huge eyes; oh great, didn't she just look peachy today? She washed her hands and put some toothpaste on her finger and cleaned her teeth the best that she could. David steadied her and then left for a moment to get his bag and as she leaned against the cold basin all she could think about was having a little lie down on the cool tiled floor.

Chapter 20

Jonathan heard a loud thud and then David's voice calling her name over and over. Sod this, Jonathan thought, and ran back into the room. Evie was lying on the floor, her legs in the bathroom and her body through the doorway on the bedroom carpet. Shit! she was out cold. David motioned for Jonathan to help him lift her up and they carried her over to the bed. Jonathan then noticed two things: firstly, she was wearing some very sexy underwear, navy blue bra with flowers and matching shorts; but as they laid her down his eyes were drawn to the second thing: her body, for staring back at him he saw scars, lots of scars covering her torso with a particularly nasty looking one running down the side of her tummy towards her belly button.

He stood back just staring down at her. So this was what she wanted to show him? Bloody hell, did she really think that in seeing these he would dump her and leave – maybe so – for she had intimated that it had happened repeatedly in the past. Now he just wanted her to wake up so he could hold her in his arms and tell her just that or that they were going to be okay. David asked him to fetch some clean bathroom towels and a soft t –shirt. He did so in a daze and then was asked to leave to make David a cup of tea, for he had things to do that didn't involve Jonathan standing and staring at Evie. Reluctantly Jonathan left the room and made his way downstairs. He put water in the kettle as if on autopilot and just stood there. He had so many questions: what had happened to her?, when? where? how?, all these things were racing round his head until he thought it might explode.

Back in the bedroom Evie was awake and David was talking to her, soothing her, explaining he had to take a blood sample from her and then he helped her change out of her underwired bra and into the soft T-shirt to sleep in; it was more comfortable for her. This done, he gave her one Tranexamic tablet followed by two more tablets to make her sleep. She needed to rest and stay still, very still and making her sleep was the safest way to do this.

David cleared up, closed the bedroom curtains and made his way downstairs to see Jonathan. He knew he'd seen the scars and would have a lot of questions for him; but as a doctor he technically wasn't allowed to answer them, at least not to him. He sighed. This was turning into a tough afternoon.

Jonathan passed David his mug of tea and they sat facing each other. David started to talk and soon realised that Jonathan wasn't really listening, so he pulled out a sheet of paper and began to write things down. What was it with these city boys? he wondered. They could run huge businesses but give them some simple list of instructions and you may as well be talking to them in a foreign language. List finished, he made a call and then started to talk.

"So the courier will be here soon to take the samples to the lab, you just need to give this package to him okay? Evie needs complete rest, she isn't to get up at all except for using the bathroom. You need to help her with that. She can't be left alone at all; whatever you do don't let her lock the bathroom door. Fiona will get her things from Evie's home and bring them over to you in the morning and will arrange for her neighbour to feed Henry. She needs to drink plenty of fluid, preferably water. I've left these tablets for her, three times a day after meals and two of these before she goes to sleep, okay? He continued, I'll come back and see her Monday evening after surgery and I'll also call her work and tell them she won't be in until a week on Monday at the earliest. You're going to have to feed her though. Remember she can't eat wheat." He passed the list over to Jonathan, "Okay, read this out loud to me whilst I drink my tea."

Suddenly Jonathan was jolted back to reality and began to read the list aloud. Okay he could do this, yes he could do all these things; the only tricky one was her food; maybe he could persuade Jamie to go to the supermarket for him and get some basics just until he came up with a better plan. Finally he looked over at David, who took a deep breath he knew what was coming next and decided to pre-empt it somewhat.

"I know you've seen her scars and that was unfortunate. You'll have a lot of questions for me; but you know as her doctor I'm not allowed to answer any of them don't you?"

"Seriously, I can't ask you one thing? I'm going crazy here imagining all kinds of shit?" He was angry now, he wanted answers and fast. "What if I ask a question and you just nod or don't answer? Can we at least try that? I'm going out of my mind here with worry?"

"Okay I'll try."

"So I've seen her scars. Are they what she wanted to show me?"

David nodded, "Yes, you'll need to tell her what you've seen and how you saw them so she doesn't freak out, okay?"

"Yes okay I'll do that; but not until she's better. Was she in an accident?"

David paused. "Evie calls it an accident, yes," – he just looked at Jonathan in silence. Come on! he thought, you're a bright boy, you can surely figure this out?

"But it wasn't an accident was it? He asked slowly.

David repeated himself, "That's what she calls it, okay?"

Jonathan thought for a bit. So if it wasn't accident then it must have been something else. Something much worse. This explained why she was still having counselling every month. Suddenly things became a lot clearer; this thing whatever it was, this was what she needed to talk to him about before they took things further. She'd already tried to give him a chance to walk away and now he was so glad he hadn't taken it; it would take more than this to break them up. "So who exactly knows about all of this then?"

"Her family, Fiona and myself, Ian her counsellor and two family friends – that's it. She calls it Team Evie and, believe you me, that team would do anything for her and I mean anything. I assume you'll be staying with her for the next week?"

"Yes of course. I am I'm not going anywhere," he said defensively.

"Okay just checking. In that case you need to know that when she gets stressed her anxiety nightmare might return, it's the same one that pops up from time to time and if that happens you need to wake her up straight away – okay?"

"Okay got it." David had given him a lot to think about; but his thoughts were interrupted by a motorcycle courier arriving outside. David picked up the package and dealt with that, he hoped Jonathan was up to this.

"Call me if you need me any time okay?"

"Okay thanks David. I really appreciate this."

"No problem, she'll be asleep now until the morning so you can go through that list I gave you, right?"

"Yes, yes right. I'll do that and thanks again." With that David got into his car and drove away.

Jonathan closed the door and leant against a kitchen chair. Blimey, what had just happened? It was a lot to take in. There was a knock at the door and Jamie burst into the kitchen.

"I saw the doc leave, is she going to be okay?"

"Yes I think so; yes, of course she will."

"God that's a relief. We're so worried, especially me," he paused for a second. "One thing though, Jon, did she lose the baby?"

Suddenly Jonathan was jolted back to reality, "Umm no, she..." Jamie didn't wait for him to finish his sentence, but grabbed his brother and held him tightly in a big bear hug.

"Oh bro, that's great, no it's bloody fantastic news. I'm going to be an uncle and you're going to be a dad! isn't that just bloody brilliant news?" There was no reply from his brother, "Jon, aren't you pleased?"

"You don't understand J, she didn't lose the baby as there was no baby, Evie wasn't pregnant," – as soon as he said it he realized he was devastated, devastated that she wasn't in fact pregnant with his baby. He quickly sat down and put his heads in his hands; what a bloody nightmare.

"Oh Jon, I'm sorry I just thought, well we all thought... I was so excited about it too, can you imagine what Evie's baby would be like, all happy and smiley just like her, running all over the place here? it would have been great," – he sounded so disappointed; Jonathan was really surprised by his brother's reaction and most of all by his own reaction too.

He asked Jamie if he would go to the supermarket and get Evie some food. Jamie didn't even hesitate, of course he would, they all would go right now. Sod the footie, this was far more important. After Jamie had left clutching £100, Jonathan ran back upstairs to check on her. She hadn't moved an inch, but was just sleeping quietly as if she didn't have a care in the world – if only that were true, he mused to himself. She must be one tough cookie and since she'd met him he'd done nothing but piss her off and make her cry. Well not any more; he would show her he could be a great boyfriend and would look after her until she was better. Then, and only then, would he tell her about what he'd seen. Yes that was a good plan and he pulled up a chair to sit and watch her sleep.

Chapter 21

Jonathan looked at his watch. It was after 7.00pm now and he realised he hadn't eaten since breakfast. He went downstairs to make himself a sandwich and then sat and stared at it. He wished he knew what had happened to her, it was driving him mad, all the different scenarios that kept running through his head and some of them were scaring the shit out of him. Jamie and his friends had come back from the supermarket with an assortment of food; it wasn't too bad, they'd tried hard and it meant she would have something to eat tomorrow before the real stuff arrived. He'd used the time watching Evie sleep, to email both Edward and Robert at work and tell them he wouldn't be in for at least a week due to a family emergency. Jonathan sent a similar message to his secretary, she would cancel everything and rearrange meetings if necessary.

Then he'd had a brainwave about her wheat free food and had rung the concierge service on his black card. He told them what he wanted and when, and then left them to organize it; he'd also ordered flowers to be delivered on Monday. He was aware he'd done nothing but send flowers to her, mostly as an apology and that she'd actually returned the last ones to him. This made him smile, only Evie would have done that; still, he thought, she would like something pretty to look at whilst she lay in bed and flowers were a good bet. Her phone was pinging like crazy but she had a security code on it so he couldn't do anything about that. He texted Jamie

Do you know the code to Evie's phone? –SEND

No, why? – SEND

She's getting a lot of messages and stuff. –SEND

That's cos she's popular – unlike you! – SEND Jonathan smiled; yes, that was true.

Why does she have a code anyway? – SEND

Told me cos if it ever got stolen then it would be useless to the little fuckers who took it! – SEND

Seriously, those were her exact words? – SEND

Yeah, me and Evie we're pretty tight – thought you would have realised this by now! – SEND. Jonathan laughed out loud, oh yes he knew that now and began to eat his sandwich. He would have an early night after all the drama of today, plus he would be sleeping in the same bed as her for the next week and although she was ill he couldn't help but be happy to be lying next to her.

Meanwhile David had rung the gym and spoken to the assistant manager. He explained that Evelyn wouldn't be at work for at least the next 7 days, maybe longer, and that he would update them when he knew more. Kevin put the phone down and looked at Stacey. "Blimey that was Evelyn's doctor, he's been out to see her and she's off sick for at least 7 days, maybe more… Steve's going to go mental when he finds out." Stacey looked worried. "Do doctors still do house calls? I thought you had to be nearly dead before they visited you and on a Saturday too." They looked at each other; this didn't sound good.

"Okay so let's get cover organized so that his majesty doesn't blow his fuse when he gets in on Monday," They started to make arrangements, neither of them willing to guess at what was wrong.

MUSIC: – LAY ME DOWN – SAM SMITH.

9.00pm and Jonathan had finished in his bathroom and walked along the landing to Evie's room, as he was now calling it. He switched on his bedside lamp and got into bed beside her. She smelt of her perfume and he wanted desperately to hold her; but annoyingly he couldn't even do that at the moment. So he covered one of her hands with his. This would have to do for now, he groaned to himself. She was so soft and warm; how was he going to get through the next week? He switched the light off and closed his eyes.

Evie had a little stretch she felt as if she had been asleep for a week and she was lovely and cosy under the duvet; she opened her eyes. It was morning; but she didn't recognise where she was. She turned her face and found Jonathan looking straight back at her, "Hello sleepy, feeling better?" Yesterday's events suddenly popped into her head. Oh my God, she thought, it had been a dream.

"Um hello you," she mumbled, praying he wasn't naked under the duvet. "Feeling a bit woozy to be honest."

"What would you like for breakfast this morning? I have fruit and yoghurt and juice, how does that sound?"

"Very nice," she squeaked, "I'll be down in a minute."

"No you're not allowed to leave this room for a whole week; don't you remember anything David told you yesterday?" He sounded cross already.

"Can you just give me a hint – it must be the medication?" Phew, what a great come back.

Jonathan quickly filled her in, so the upshot was she had to rest here for at least a week, be on medication (which she hated) and that Jonathan would be looking after her. Best news was that Fiona would call in today and bring her some toiletries, underwear and pyjamas – Thank the Lord!

"Okay I see, I need to use the bathroom now, so if you don't mind." She gestured for him to leave.

"No, no, no you're not allowed to walk there by yourself you have to let me help you!" He leapt out of bed and walked round to her side. Thank God he was wearing pyjamas, she couldn't face him being half naked, not with her like this.

"Seriously not even 10 steps to the bathroom?" –she was exasperated already.

"Yes, David will have my guts for garters and Fiona will probably do something even worse." She laughed, yes she could just imagine what Fiona would want and it involved trees, rope and his balls.

Moving the duvet aside she sat on the edge of the bed. She was wearing an unfamiliar T-shirt which came to mid – thigh and just her pants; God, how embarrassing. She stood up and swayed a little, Jonathan made her put her arm around his shoulders and they started to move in slow motion just like in the movies. If they didn't hurry up, she thought, she would wet her knickers and that wouldn't be the best start to their patient/nurse relationship. He helped her to steady herself by holding onto the basin and then she asked him to pass her bag to her and then leave her just for 5 minutes; when he hadn't moved she looked at him, "Seriously you have to go, I'm closing the door and you're going somewhere else for 5 whole minutes. If I'm here for a week, then this is how it's going to be, okay?"

Reluctantly he agreed and left her whilst he went downstairs to prepare her breakfast. He was going to need to be patient with her and patience wasn't exactly his strongest virtue.

Jonathan helped her back into bed where she sat up and pulled the duvet up under her arms. She was very aware that she wasn't wearing a bra and didn't want him staring at her breasts whilst she ate. He placed a tray on her lap and left her to eat in peace whilst he showered and dressed. She ate and drank a little of everything and swallowed one tablet with water after she'd finished. Sighing to herself she wondered what she was going to do for the rest of the day.

Jonathan removed her tray and sat down on a chair, "What would you like to do now, the newspaper is here if you want to read that?" Ah bless him he was trying really hard, his little face was all serious and earnest wanting to please her.

"Yes okay but you'll need to place an old towel on top of the duvet first though."

He didn't understand. "What for exactly?"

"To protect this lovely clean white duvet cover from the newsprint of course."

"You don't have to worry about that, it'll be fine."

She laughed. "My mother would tear me off a strip if I didn't cover the duvet."

"But Evie, your mother isn't even here!"

"I know but I will feel so guilty if I don't do that then I'd rather not bother – hasn't Jamie told you about my mother's interesting little foibles?"

"No he hasn't – are you serious?"

"Yes, you have no idea and I'd like my phone please to call her and check on my messages and stuff." She smiled sweetly at him. He brought her phone, the newspaper and a blue towel.

"I could help you with that."

"You want to reply to my messages from say my girlfriends?" She could have some fun here, Truth was, she was a bit bored already.

"Well I could try?"

"Okay then let's see. Oh, Rowan is asking for advice about the guy she saw last week, wonders if she should give him a second chance; hmm, what would your advice be about giving second chances?"

Now he saw she was playing with him again; well, at least that meant she was feeling better.

"I would say yes, she ought to give him a second chance as you never know, just because he was a – now what's the term again – oh yes, a fuckwit, on their first date he may be able to redeem himself on the second!" There, that was a good answer.

She laughed; he was playing along. "Oh good answer, Mr D, I'll text her right now – do you want to go and eat whilst I do that and call my mother?" She wasn't really asking him, but dismissing him and he left her to it.

Evie rang her mother who wasn't picking up so she left a message and then went through her e-mails and texts. There was one from Jamie asking if he could come over and see her sometime today. Maybe after Fiona had been, she would text him later. Jonathan was back and seemed determined not to leave her for one second. "Honestly I'm not going anywhere. I promise I'll text you if I need anything or if I need to go to the bathroom." He insisted on staying so she sat back and flicked through the paper; after a bit she felt a twinge and put her phone down on the bedside table. She needed to lie down again. Jonathan was all concerned, but she told him she was fine and closed her eyes. He thought she looked very far from fine.

She woke again and realised she needed the bathroom, Jonathan wasn't there so she sat up and moved her legs out from under the duvet, and as if by magic he reappeared with a face like thunder.

"Evie what are you doing?"

"I was just going to text you to help me to the bathroom," she lied through her teeth. He didn't believe her for one second, but decided not to push it.

"Okay so lean on me," as she did so she felt a terrible pain again in her tummy.

"Oh my God I've got to sit down," she gasped, slumping back onto the bed and holding her stomach. This was intolerable, she was in such pain and all in front of him too. Honestly, could it get any worse? Just then there was a knock at the door. Evie gestured for him to go and answer it as she wasn't going to be standing up any time soon. Fiona breezed into the bedroom, dropped the overnight bag she was carrying, took one look at Evie and glared at Jonathan.

"Oh sweetheart are you okay?" She sat on the bed holding Evie's hand. Evie nodded, afraid she might actually start to cry again.

"Tell me what you need." Fiona was all 'there, there' and soothed her, tucking her loose hair behind her ears. Jonathan, realising he was superfluous, left them to it; God, that woman hated his guts and given the tiniest excuse she would take Evie away from him. Fiona helped Evie to the bathroom, left her to go to the loo and then put the chair in front of the basin. She placed a folded towel on it then she helped her to cleanse her face /brush her teeth / have a general wash and then brushed her hair for her. That felt so much better. Evie changed into clean pants and put on a pair of her pyjamas. She was still in pain and Fiona persuaded her to eat something so she could take her next round of tablets. Fiona called out to Jonathan who was only too happy to make Evie some lunch and even brought Fiona a cup of tea, much to her surprise and displeasure. Fiona had told herself he wasn't right for Evie and here he was waiting on Evie hand and foot and even being nice to her in to the bargain; she would sort out Mr bloody Dempsey. Fiona kissed Evie goodbye and told her if she wanted to go and stay with her she only had to text and she'd come straight over and collect her. She'd said this deliberately loud enough for Jonathan to hear as a kind of warning to him, and then she was gone. Jonathan breathed a sigh of relief, Evie was dozing and he went downstairs to fix himself some lunch. He wasn't actually very hungry but ate some scrambled eggs on toast; that would do for today his priority was Evie. He couldn't believe his ears when Fiona had given Evie the option to leave with her at any time, cheeky cow.

Late afternoon and Evie stirred. Jonathan was sat in the chair just watching her, "Hello. What time is it?"

"It's after 5.00. You've had a good rest, do you need anything?"

"Um, bathroom again sorry."

"Don't be sorry; let's get you up." He was gentle with her and she felt less exposed now she was wearing her pyjamas. Five minutes later she called out to him that she was finished and they started the slow walk back to bed. Once settled she pleaded with him to let Jamie come over and see her. He wasn't too happy about it but agreed Jamie could come but only for 10 minutes. In a flash Jamie was in the front door and up the stairs. He sat in the chair at her bedside and grinned at her.

"Hi sis, how are you?"

"Oh you know, being lazy really; just to get a week off work – you know how it is?" She was joking with him and he relaxed.

"Yeah I thought as much, oh the guys say hi, by the way." He filled her in on his weekend and the football results.

Jonathan was sat at the top of the stairs listening yet again; this was turning into a bad habit of his. They were just idly chatting when Jamie suddenly got all serious.

"I suppose Jon told you we'd all jumped to the wrong conclusion yesterday, you know $2 + 2 = 100$?"

"No but go on; as I told you before, you can't tell me half a story and leave me hanging."

"Well okay; but don't get mad. Jon came over shouting about hot water bottles; he was in a bit of a state actually, he told us you were very ill and losing a lot of blood. Next thing you know, Francis says out loud maybe you were having a miscarriage. Blimey Evie, I was so worried, then after the doc had gone I came over and convinced myself I was going to be an uncle and bear hugged Jon until he told me that I'd got the wrong end of the stick entirely. Never been so gutted – actually had been looking forward to it and everything."

Evie started to cry. So this was what they had thought, foolish boys. She was touched that Jamie was disappointed and thought about what Jonathan's reaction had been, of course he already knew it to be impossible; but it didn't stop her from wondering.

"Evie please don't cry or Jon will throw me out, please stop."

"Sorry," she sniffed. "Am very emotional, it's all the medication; it's fucking me right up," and she gave a small laugh and wiped her eyes.

Jonathan was all ready to chuck his brother out but decided to leave them alone for a while. Yes her emotions were all over the place, David had warned him to expect this. Best to let her compose herself. After 20 minutes Jamie left and as if by magic supper appeared. Evie ate the smallest piece of chicken she thought she could get away with. Jonathan noted her small appetite, but decided to let it go, after all as long as she ate something then she could take her tablets.

It had been the longest day and Evie couldn't wait to wash and get ready for bed. She let him help her into the bathroom, but asked for 20 minutes this time. She had her phone so would text him when she was done, she promised. She sat on the chair and as she went through her night-time routine she wondered how the hell she was going to get through another 7 days of this; it would drive her slowly mad. The only thing she couldn't do was clean her feet. She had a packet of baby wipes, but couldn't see quite how she was going to manage this. She sighed and sent Jonathan a text.

Am done but need your help with something, please. – SEND

He was there right away and they figured out that the best solution was if he sat on the closed toilet seat then he could gently lift her feet one at a time and wipe them with a baby wipe. To lighten the mood she joked that it was just like Jesus in the bible and was looking mockingly askance when she had to explain what she meant.

"Didn't you go to Sunday school? – I'm very surprised at you."

"Oh Evie, that was a long time ago."

"Yes keep forgetting how old you are and what a terrible memory you have."

He smiled at her; they were making progress of sorts, she'd asked him for help and was letting him give it. So far so good. Once finished they did their usual slow walk back to bed and he settled her down for the night. He kissed her forehead and left the room.

Chapter 22

He was asleep when a loud noise woke him. What was that? Switching on the bedside lamp he saw that Evie wasn't in the bed. He leapt up and discovered her lying on the floor in a heap by the chest of drawers. He ran over to her and gently picked her up.

"Evie what are you doing?" He was exasperated with her, honestly he thought they were past all this nonsense.

Oh shit, he sounded really mad, but she'd woken up and saw that he was fast asleep and not wanting to wake him up. She had thought she could make it to the bathroom by herself, after all how hard could it be?

"Didn't want to wake you, thought I could manage."

"Well that is the whole point of me being here with you? Honestly, anything could have happened; if I hadn't woken up you could have stayed on the floor all night. I am losing patience with you, you must start doing as you are told."

Yep he was mad with her alright. She didn't reply and waited until she was in the bathroom and closed the door,

"Call me when you're finished, okay?" – he went downstairs to get a glass of water. For heaven's sake, how many more times were they going to go over and over the same things? She was worse than a small child.

Evie waited until she heard Jonathan go down the stairs then she locked the bathroom door. After weeing she washed her hands and then sat on a folded towel on the closed toilet lid. Taking a smaller towel from the rack she folded it into four and buried her head in it and began to cry. This was so awful; she hated being ill, just hated it and she just sat there sobbing her heart out. Jonathan came back up the stairs. It was 1.30am and he was tired and wanted to get back to sleep, but she was taking her time. He knocked on the door, "Evie are you okay?" There was no response, but he could hear muffled sounds, so he tried again. "Evie! answer me or I'm coming in." Again, nothing. He tried the door handle, shit she had locked the door – he'd explicitly told her not to and she'd disobeyed him again. He banged on the door with the palm of his hand. "Evie, I told you not to lock the door what the hell are you playing at?"

Fed up with him shouting at her, she raised her head from the towel and yelled at him to go away.

Jonathan realised she was crying; but she had to open the door.

"Evie open this bloody door right now or so help me I'll.." he trailed off – what exactly was he going to do?

"No," – she shouted right back at him. How dare he started shouting at her, he was supposed to be looking after her not shouting at her. She continued to cry, whilst he banged on the door and continued to shout –any other time this would have been amusing, but not now.

"Evie if you don't unlock this door I'm going to call the fire brigade and then I'm calling Fiona to come and fetch you, do you understand?"

"So it's true you can't wait to get rid of me is that it? Messing up your busy schedule am I? Well sorry to be such an inconvenience to you. I'll call Fiona myself actually, she wants me with her, she'll look after me, she wouldn't shout at me and bang on the door and do you know why?" – Now her voice was barely above a whisper. "Because she loves me, that's why," and then she sobbed even harder. He was being a pain in the arse.

He rested his head on the door and three words ran across his mind 'so do I' – yes he was in love with her, he needed to tell her; but had to get her to unlock the door first. This was getting them nowhere, so he took a different tack, he stopped banging on the door and talked to her quietly hoping she would listen to him. "Evie tell me what's wrong please, I don't want to shout at you, but David said you can't lock the door; it's dangerous, in case you pass out again – do you understand? Please Evie tell me what's wrong."

She stopped crying and took a few deep breaths, her voice was louder now. She was as mad as hell; how dare he, how bloody dare he! "What's wrong, what's wrong? Okay I'll tell you what's wrong. I tried to manage on my own because I didn't want to wake you, so sorry for being so selfish. I'm humiliated beyond belief, my embarrassment levels on a scale of 1 to 10 are at about 1000, I have no bloody dignity left, I can't even go to the loo by myself, you're shouting at me and banging on the door and I can't even bloody cry in private that's what's wrong with me. Now go away and leave me alone."

He listened to her; he hadn't thought about it like that, he hadn't realized how embarrassed she was by the whole thing and yes if the tables were turned he would have hated to have to ask for help to use the bathroom; but she was unwell and needed help.

"Evie I understand now, but you have to unlock the door, please!" .He waited, nothing not a word, he tried again in a slightly louder voice, "Evie please unlock the door and we'll talk about it okay, just unlock the door." Nothing not a peep; if he didn't know any better he half expected her to have climbed out of the bathroom window and be making a run for it by now. "Evie I'm running out of patience here now so for the last time will you please open the door?" Nothing, zero, nada. "Okay young lady you've left me no choice – I've tried to be nice;" quick as a flash, Evie shouted out, "I must have missed that," he chose to ignore her outburst and continued, "So I'm going to count slowly to 10 and if you haven't unlocked the door then you leave me no choice. Firstly I will call the fire brigade and then we'll see just how embarrassed you can be. And secondly I'll call Fiona who by the way has been just dying for me to fuck up again with you and will be over the bloody moon that I have failed and will be absolutely delighted to come and take you away – do you understand?" Still nothing, fuck he was actually going to have to start counting; he didn't think it would come to this, but boy was she pushing his buttons and all at the same bloody time too.

"Okay 1... Nothing 2...nothing 3...nothing 4...nothing 5...nothing 6...still nothing...7 nothing he was panicking now 8...nothing 9 ...nothing just as he said t for ten he heard the door unlock, thank goodness for that, now how was he going to get her out of there?.

Silence. Neither of them said a word, then Evie slowly opened the door just wide enough to get her hand through and she switched off the light; she didn't want him to see her eyes all red and puffy, she just wanted to get in to bed and pray for this all to go away. She opened the door wider and stared down at the floor, then in complete silence he helped her walk back over to the bed and climb in. Evie pulled the duvet over her and shuffled so that she was right on the edge of the mattress as far away from him as she could possibly be without falling on the floor. Jonathan got back into bed switched off the lamp and stared at the ceiling. What the fuck had just happened? Yes he'd been mad, but only because he was worried about her, why didn't she get that? He sighed. She hadn't wanted to wake him, but that was precisely what she should have done, by trying to let him sleep she had stumbled and fallen and could have hurt herself even more – foolish girl. He strained to listen to her; she was completely under the duvet, but he was sure she was crying again. Slowly he turned onto his side and moved over towards her, he touched her arm with his hand, she flinched and told him to leave her alone, hadn't he done enough for one night? He kept his hand on her arm slowly stroking it up and down.

"Evie," he said softly, "please don't be mad, I don't want you to let me sleep, if you need me then you must wake me up; that's why I'm here with you, lying next to you, wanting to hold you so badly and make this all go away." He listened again, her crying had subsided. "Just so you know I would never have called Fiona the last thing I want is for you to leave, I want to look after you; but you have to let me."

Just when he thought she was going to continue to ignore him, she moved, ever so slightly, but she moved towards him. It took her about 12 little careful movements to turn over until she was facing him in the dark, a bit like when you first learnt to drive and a 3 point turn took you about 15 steps. He pushed his arm underneath her neck and pulled her into his arms; her head rested on his chest, but he was careful not to touch her lower body with his. He could feel her damp cheeks through his T-shirt as he held her and stroked her hair kissing her head, soothing her tears away. They stayed like that for such a long time, she was content to be there and he was happy to hold her and try to make it all go away. Slowly he started to kiss her face and then inched his body down so that he could kiss her mouth. He kissed her softly at first and she responded kissing him back enjoying every touch of him on her. His chest was gently pushing against her breasts and he could feel her reacting to him. Her arm crept around his waist and her hand moved to caress the small of his back. He groaned and kissed her more forcefully now, she responded and finally they were where they had wanted to be last weekend. They continue to kiss and Evie slowly moved her hand from the small of his back and slipped it underneath his pyjama bottoms she let it rest casually on his bum and then slowly started to gently massage his bum cheeks with her hand. It took Jonathan a little while to realise what she was doing, he pulled away slightly.. He whispered to her, "Evie what are you doing?"

"Oh nothing," she replied softly and continued to massage his bum; he had a great bum she thought to herself. He returned to kissing her more thoroughly now and Evie slowly moved her hand down the side of his thigh, stroking it until she reached between his legs and started to move her hand firmly up and down. She felt his response; oh yes he was beginning to enjoy it now, He pulled away again. "Evie what are you doing?"

"Oh nothing much."

"It doesn't feel like nothing much to me."

"You just seemed a bit tense and I thought this would help with that, so stop talking and kiss me.".

She was right he was enjoying it, very much, he was kissing her ear then her neck and her shoulder when suddenly he gasped and told her if she didn't stop then he was going to come in his pyjamas. She giggled and asked him if he had another pair of pj's.

"Of course I do."

"Well then what's the problem?" She whispered to him and she continued to stroke him until he came and cried out. She squeezed him firmly and then let him go.

"Better now?" she asked him

"Oh Evelyn Wallace you are such a bad girl. What shall I do with you?"

"I have a few suggestions actually."

"I bet you do," – he laughed with her now, their fight all forgotten.

"So shut up and kiss me then."

"I am kissing you."

"No not here," and she moved her mouth away from his, "but here." She took his left hand in her right hand and slowly moved it until it covered her breast. He pulled the flimsy fabric of her pyjama top away and started to move his hand over her breast feeling the nipple harden under his fingers then he took it in his mouth, caressing it letting his teeth nibble it, she arched her back and pushed her breast towards him; my oh my, this was good.

Suddenly without warning she cried out in pain and lay very still. He stopped what he was doing. "Evie. Evie are you okay?"

"No not really," she had flooded everywhere, through her pants, through her pyjamas and onto the folded towel she was resting her bottom on, she was flooding and it felt like it was never going to stop. "Oh my God, oh my God," she kept repeating over and over again. Jonathan got out of bed switched on the lamp and went over to her, "Do you need the bathroom?"

"I don't think I can move," Evie replied in a small voice, "I think I need David."

Shit, shit, shit, not again. Jonathan went back to his bedside table and scrolled down his mobile until David's number was on the screen. He was willing him, pick up, pick up, pick up; after what seemed like hours but was only seconds David's sleepy voice was heard.

"It's Evie," David was wide awake now and swung his legs out of bed and turned on his lamp. Fiona groaned and turned away from the light. Jonathan passed the phone to Evie who gestured for him to go away whilst she spoke to her doctor, David listened and said twenty minutes and then was gone.

"So?"

"He'll be here soon, you need to open the door for him though." She was breathing faster now through the pain, willing both the pain and the flooding to stop.

Jonathan raced downstairs turning on the lights as he went, he unlocked the front door then took the stairs two at a time. He ran into his bedroom and pulled out some clean pyjama bottoms and then went into his bathroom to sort himself out. Less than five minutes later he was back knelt on the floor beside Evie.

"I'm feeling a bit hot and clammy. Can I have a cold flannel on my forehead, please, and could you bring the bin out too I feel a bit sick?"

He did as she asked and then they waited for David to arrive. Sure enough David's car pulled up outside and he was up the stairs and in the bedroom. Jonathan knew the drill by now and left them alone. He took up his familiar place on the stairs and waited.

David examined Evie and before he could help her to the bathroom she was sick in the bin. She was in a bit of a mess, but this happened sometimes, usually brought on by stress. Her pants, pyjamas and the bath towel were all ruined and in the bathroom he carefully helped her into fresh underwear and pyjamas. She brushed her teeth and then all cleaned up he walked her slowly back to bed where he placed a fresh folded towel before she lay down. He gave her two different tablets and then started to ask her some questions. David ascertained that they had had yet another fight – boy did these two do anything else? Then they'd kissed and made up and Evie swore that was it. He made her drink some water and then went down to ask Jonathan for his version of events. Jonathan made David a cup of tea; he was getting used to this routine now and then David started to ask some questions.

"So Evie tells me you had another fight and now let me get this right. You shouted at her, made her cry, banged on the door threatening to call the fire brigade and my wife before making up and kissing her, is that about the size of it?" Secretly David was amused; no harm had been done, Evie would be fine if she would just do as she was told and he wanted to make Jonathan squirm as much as possible

Jonathan looked sheepish. "Yes that's about right, she locked the bathroom door and I kind of lost it with her I'm afraid."

"Well this kind of thing can be brought on by stress so no more banging on doors/ shouting or threats I don't care how much she winds you up you have to be the grown up here understood?"

"Yep got it, won't happen again." He felt like he was back at school in the headmaster's office.

"As far as the kissing goes, no heavy stuff; in fact no excitement at all, understood? Not until she's better. Honestly, you two it's like herding cats! Oh and these things need to go in the bin, couldn't save the towel or her pyjamas-sorry."

"But they're one of her favourite pairs."

"Can't be helped I'm afraid."

David got up to leave, "One more thing – absolutely no more making her cry or I will send Fiona round to take her away got it?"

"Yes loud and clear," and with that David was gone. Jonathan went back upstairs. What a night. Evie was asleep and he climbed into bed next to her; so no excitement for 7 days, that was some penance; but he snuggled up close to her, well that wouldn't hurt surely? As David drove home his mind wandered back to a spectacular fight between him and Fiona; she rarely got cross but on this occasion she was incandescent. They had angry make up sex which resulted in their second child and he wondered if they could do it again when he got back, for he was sure she wanted more children – so maybe this morning they'd start trying?

Chapter 23

Jonathan checked his watch. It was a little after 8.00am and normally he would be in the office by now, but this Monday morning he was at home in bed with Evie. He wanted her to wake up and didn't want to get out of bed until he'd spoken to her. Maybe he would try and wake her up himself, first he tried whispering to her; nope, nothing. Then blowing softly on her face; nope, still nothing. He started to stroke her arm with his hand, still nothing. Feeling frustrated he turned and looked at his bedside table and gently pushed a book on the floor. Turning back to her expectantly, no there was still nothing; just how strong were these tablets David was giving her? He tried again stroking her arm and nearly jumped out of his skin when she said, "Jonathan what in God's name are you doing?" and opened her eyes. Her face was about 10 inches from his and he just grinned at her looking into her big brown eyes. "Morning gorgeous."

"Good morning handsome," was her reply and they just continued to stare at each other. Finally he asked her if she wanted breakfast or the bathroom first.

"Neither actually. I need something else."

"Oh what's that?"

"This," and she moved slightly forward and kissed him. "My good morning kiss of course."

"Evie," he warned. "David said no stress and no excitement remember?"

"Well David's not here is he?" Realising he was having none of it: "Oh you're no fun," she pouted back at him.

"Now which is it to be, food or wash? Come on, I've got a lot of surprises for you today."

She groaned. "Didn't we have this conversation about surprises before? Now I will have to make 'that face' even if I hate them."

"You won't hate them, you'll like them – really you will."

She'd washed and was sat up in bed eating her breakfast from a tray whilst he sat in a chair tapping away on his laptop. After a while he left her so he could shower and dress. Then there was someone at the door; she could hear voices and then silence again. She could hear him making a noise in the kitchen and finally when she couldn't wait any longer she sent him a text.

Hi whatcha doing? – SEND

Unpacking groceries for your meals for the week, now leave me alone or it'll take twice as long. – SEND

Okay but what sort of groceries? – SEND She wanted to know if she would be eating well or if she would need to disguise the fact that it was all perfectly dreadful.

Evie please, just give me ten minutes and then I'll come back up and tell you okay? – SEND

Okay – SEND.

Eventually he was back and told her he had got some special food to be delivered for her. She wasn't convinced, but decided to give him the benefit of the doubt until she had tried some of it herself. The morning passed in mostly companionable quietness; she read or sent texts and emails whilst he worked tapping away. He brought her some lunch and it was good, no better than good it was great. Maybe her week's stay with him would have some benefits after all.

Flowers were delivered in the afternoon whilst she was asleep and when she woke they were the first thing she saw. She smiled. They were lovely, just lovely and she wouldn't be asking him to take them back any time soon. She'd just finished some delicious chicken soup for her supper when David appeared.

"So how's the patient today then?"

"Much better thank you doctor," she was behaving herself which made a change!

David examined her and asked her some more questions. Once satisfied he let Jonathan re-join them.

"So what happens next?" –she was hoping for some good news, maybe about when she could go home; sooner rather than later fingers crossed.

"Well the test results will be back tomorrow and I'll call you with the results and we'll take it from there. You'll need to come into the surgery on

Thursday afternoon, I'll make you an appointment. So just carry on same as today really until I tell you otherwise."

"That's it?" She had hoped for better news than just stay put and carry on. "When can I have a shower?"

"Saturday at the earliest and you'll need help with that."

"Saturday! But that's 5 days away," she cried out petulantly, "and what do you mean, I'll need help?"

"Evie," he warned gently, "Saturday means Saturday and you'll definitely need someone there so who do you want?"

"Don't know, really; do I have to have someone there?"

"Yes you do, so no arguments," he turned to look at Jonathan and raised his eyebrows. Suddenly he had some sympathy for what he'd been dealing with. Jonathan then made the mistake of chipping in trying to be helpful: "How about your mother or a nurse?"

"I don't want my mother. Are you mad! and I don't think nurses will come out on a Saturday." This was getting them nowhere and she was annoyed at having to wait five more days and then be treated like a child who couldn't be left on her own.

Jonathan tried again, "Evie don't be difficult; just choose someone."

And there it was, so she was being difficult was she, well she'd show them just how difficult she could be.

She picked up her mobile and began to type. "It's fine, I know just the person and believe me they would be only too happy to help me.". No-one said another word as she typed away and they heard the text whoosh sending it away. They heard her phone ping within seconds and she put her phone down and grinned at them. "There all sorted."

"So who did you choose?"

"Miles!"

Jonathan's face was a picture of amazement and thunderous anger. "Miles, Miles the guy from the gym? Absolutely no way Evie, no bloody way." He was apoplectic, seriously she was going to let Miles, who was a man, see her naked in the shower. "David, tell her that's not going to happen."

David looked at Evie; was she telling the truth here? because he knew her probably better than anyone and he was pretty sure she wouldn't let a guy from the gym be with her in the shower, it seemed extremely unlikely, so he decided to step in. "Evie are you just kidding around because it doesn't sound like the best idea?" She knew he knew it was a joke, problem was Jonathan didn't. She passed her mobile to Jonathan. "Here, read it if you like – I don't mind." Jonathan hesitated. The last time he had read her text messages it had nearly been the end of them.

"David can you read it please?" he was barely able to speak. David took her phone and began to read. A smile passed his lips; it was exactly as he'd thought, of course she wasn't going to let Miles help her. She'd texted Fiona.

Hi Fiona, your husband has just informed me I can't have a shower for 5, yes, 5 more days and that I need someone there to help me when I do. Don't suppose you would volunteer, would you? I promise to bake you a dozen of your favourite chocolate cheesecake brownies as a bribe and deliver them to you personally next week when I am back in my own kitchen. What do you say? Pleeeease Fiona? – SEND

For 12 bites of heaven –count me in! – SEND

There, she was just messing with the two of them. "Oh Evie you're not playing fair," David ticked her off gently and passed the phone to Jonathan. "Here, read this and try to remain calm."

As Jonathan read, Evie spoke to David, "Look I'm sorry but you know how much I hate being ill and I normally shower 2 or 3 times a day so this is tough for me."

David sighed, "Evie can you just give Jonathan a break, please, just for me. He's trying very hard and you're not helping at the minute."

"Okay yes, I suppose that was a bit naughty of me – sorry doctor it won't happen again I promise."

Jonathan having read the text realized she had been winding them both up, but especially him and wasn't sure whether to laugh or, if the circumstances had been different, put her over his knee and give her a jolly good hiding. Of course she wouldn't let Miles help her to shower; she hadn't even let him see her naked yet let alone Miles. She'd pushed his buttons yet again! He passed the phone back to her as David stood up to leave. "Well David let me show you out. I'm sure you've got better ways to spend your evenings than to keep coming over here. And you, young lady would try the patience of a saint," – he looked pointedly at Evie.

As the two men went downstairs, Evie could hear them talking and laughing in the hall then the front door closing and then silence. What was happening now, why hadn't he come straight back upstairs to see her? Perhaps she had gone too far this time. She picked up her mobile, thank goodness she had a phone plan with masses of text allowance, otherwise her bill would be sky high this month.

Am apologising, was just having a bit of fun, sorry – will try very hard to behave for the rest of the week.x –SEND

She waited and waited, but silence; nothing pinged into her in-box. She couldn't decide whether to try again or just wait and see. He would have to come back soon for her evening routine of washing etc., He was making her wait for him for a change. In the kitchen Jonathan reheated some soup and ate some bread. All this caring for her was exhausting, not the physical side of helping her to the bathroom, but all the other stuff. Maybe what they both needed was just a good night's sleep. Reading her text, he realised she was sorry. He should have known from the minute she said Miles' name that it was a joke; but he'd taken it at face value and overreacted again. He needed to try and stay calm around her; all this activity wasn't good for her health, it certainly wasn't good for him, but he thought he'd make her wait for a bit just so that her behaviour could sink in.

Time ticked by. It was nearly 8.00pm now, the tablets were making her feel sleepy and she would need to visit the bathroom soon. Yes, she felt contrite; it was just a little joke, surely he could see that? She sent another text and waited.

Am very sorry to bother you but I do need to go to the bathroom before I'm too sleepy, could you come and help me please? x – SEND

Jonathan read it and rose from his chair. Okay he had made her wait long enough. On entering her bedroom he stayed quiet and helped her to her feet and they did the same routine as the night before only this time in complete silence. He walked her back to bed and pulled the duvet over her, said goodnight and left her alone.

Evie was confused. This was much worse, yes he was still helping her but nothing more, nothing less. She was too sleepy now to try to talk to him again so she would go to sleep and hope things were better in the morning. Sleep was the one thing that just wouldn't come. She turned over carefully time and time again, but just couldn't settle; what was the time now? Where was he? Surely he wasn't going to sleep in his own bed tonight? Suddenly she felt very alone and a bit scared. She switched on her bedside lamp blinking in the light and sent him a final text.

Hi it's me – can't sleep – wondered where you are? –SEND

Am here – now go to sleep. – SEND. Oh that was a bit grumpy, so he was punishing her for the little stunt she'd pulled earlier; although she couldn't really blame him, however she wanted him here, next to her.

Can't sleep. Are you coming to bed soon? – SEND She was missing him and felt sad.

Count some sheep, – SEND

They keep running away! – SEND. Jonathan smiled to himself; gosh, she was infuriating sometimes, funny but infuriating.

Try harder, goodnight Evie. – SEND. Then nothing, no reply. Finally she closed her eyes.

Jonathan was sat in his bedroom thinking and waiting for her to fall asleep before he joined her. They just needed one night, just one quiet night. It was only Monday, there were 6 more days of this. He was starting to feel a bit mean though, just leaving her alone and after 20 minutes or so he made his way along the landing and into her room.

Evie was dozing when she felt him get into bed next to her. So he was going to be lying next to her all night; and she exhaled softly, now she could go to sleep, it was all okay.

Jonathan lay on his back staring at the ceiling in the dark. He needed to have a serious talk with her but it never seemed to be the right time. He eased himself onto his side so that he was facing her and put his hand over hers, they needed to talk and soon. At some point during the night they had both moved closer to each other. His arm was now around her waist and their legs were tangled together, they were sleeping peacefully at last.

Chapter 24

At some point in the night Evie stirred. She was still asleep, but she felt hot and trapped, there was something heavy pinning her down. All she could see was HIM touching her face, gripping her arms, talking to her, starting to hurt her. She tried wriggling and twisting gently, but nothing happened. She hadn't moved an inch, and slowly she began to panic – oh my God – oh my God, her breathing was faster now and she needed to be free. She was thrashing about and then suddenly she woke with a jolt and cried out. Jonathan was awake in a flash, "Evie it's okay, it's okay, I've got you." He heard her whimpering. "It's okay you're safe, you're with me it's okay, it's okay." Slowly she woke properly and realized where she was; it was alright, it was okay, she was safe, she was safe with Jonathan and she buried her head into his shoulder. She couldn't stop trembling and Jonathan continued to hold her and soothe her, stroking her hair until finally she quietened down.

He felt guilty now, he knew she was sorry, but he hadn't replied to her texts and all this stress had resulted in her having a nightmare. She was soft and warm in his arms, breathing slowly now, not fully relaxed but calmer. At some point both of them realised they were tangled together but neither pulled away; it was the only place they wanted to be. Evie placed small kisses on his chest and felt him tense slightly and inhale. She moved herself upwards and kissed him gently on the mouth. He responded instantly, it was just the perfect kiss, all soft and tender. There was no drama, no talking just kissing and touching.

Eventually they broke apart. Even though it was still dark they both knew they were smiling at each other. Jonathan decided it was now or never, he couldn't wait any longer. He stroked her hair. "Hey do you need anything?"

Evie shook her head. "No – am just glad you're here with me."

"Me too, me too." He paused and took a deep breath. "Evie I need to talk to you and I can never find the right time; hell maybe this isn't the right time either, but I need to tell you, do you think you're up to this now?" He held her even tighter to him. He didn't want her to turn away from him, but to stay and listen.

Evie was confused, talk to her, tell her what things; honestly he was as bad as Jamie for these half stories. "Tell me what, bad things or…?"

"No silly not bad things, things about us." He felt her relax slightly.

"Okay what things?"

He continued talking slowly and softly to her, "Do you remember on Saturday …when you fainted in the bathroom?"

"Not really no, why?"

"Well… David and I had to pick you up … and carry you back to bed."

"Yes so, I still don't get it."

"Well… you were in your underwear and I, I saw you."

"You saw me in my underwear… So…oh, …oh my God …you saw, …you saw…," Suddenly she knew exactly what he was trying to tell her and she tried frantically to pull away, but he wouldn't let her go.

"Yes I saw and it's okay, well not okay that you've been hurt, but I saw and I'm not leaving you I'm staying right here and do you know why?"

"But you only saw the front, there's more on the back too, they're ugly… really ugly."

"Evie listen to me you're beautiful, smart, funny, impossible at times, but never ugly Evie, never."

"But don't they bother you-they must do?"

"All I'm bothered about is you and what's in here," he placed his hand on her chest and took a deep breath, "and the reason for that is because I love you. I love you Evie and have done for a while now. I just didn't realise until, well until the other night when you locked yourself in the bathroom, I was so worried about you, so worried…"

Evie couldn't take in what he was saying. Until there was no more fighting, no more arguing, no more apologizing, no flowers and no talking…if Evie hadn't been unwell there would have been a whole lot more too.

Chapter 25

The next day set a pattern for the remaining six days she spent at his house. They'd called a lovable truce, Evie was on her best behaviour and did exactly as she was told, well more or less. Jonathan spent every night with Evie asleep wrapped in his arms, not wanting to let her go for a second. Officially they were a couple in love and didn't care who knew it. Evie had a talk with Jonathan and told him part but not all of the things she felt it was time he needed to know.

He drove her to her appointment on Thursday afternoon with David, annoyed he couldn't go with her into the consulting room. David examined her and asked her some more questions. He seemed pleased with her progress and agreed that on Friday she could get up for the day as long as she sat downstairs and only went back upstairs once at night. She probably didn't need help going to the bathroom and the tablets had worked for now. Fiona was coming over to help her shower on Saturday morning and she could go home on Sunday. He would sign her off of work for another week and even then she was to be on light duties only.

"So any questions for me?" asked David. Evie squirmed on her seat; yes she did have questions and although she'd known David for a few years she was still embarrassed to be having this conversation with him.

"Umm yes I do as a matter of fact, well the thing is, um here's the thing I was umm wondering if...if I could umm go on the pill and if so... how soon I could... Well how soon we could...?" She tailed off. Surely he knew what she was asking?

"I see, well yes you can go on the pill I'll write you a prescription now. But I know I don't have to tell you with your medical history it's extremely unlikely you'll get pregnant and you'll need to use a condom to prevent STD's okay? You won't be able to start taking it until Monday at the earliest, then you need to wait 7 days. The pill may help regulate your periods a bit we'll have to wait and see."

"Yes okay, umm one more thing I don't want to collect the prescription today, can you get Fiona to bring it with her on Saturday but don't tell her what it is?"

"Of course I can; but Evie you're absolutely sure about this next step, he hasn't pressurized you or anything?"

"Yes I'm sure, and no he hasn't, it's okay. Can you tell him I don't need bathroom help and stuff cos he probably won't listen to me," she was mumbling now, just wanting this conversation to be over.

David called Jonathan back in and relayed the new information to him.

On the drive back Jonathan was pleased she could get up tomorrow, but was also a bit down in the dumps in that she would be going home in 3 days' time. Yes her stay with him had been unexpected and boy did it get off to a rocky start; but they had been cocooned in their own little bubble and the truth was that he was going to miss her like crazy once she was home and he was back at work. That night as Evie got ready for bed, she wasn't sure where Jonathan would be sleeping as she didn't need his help. She needn't have worried for he padded into her room and got into bed beside her just as before. She turned to him. "I thought you might be sleeping in your own bed now I don't need so much help from you."

Smiling, Jonathan wrapped his arms around her. "Now why would I want to go and do a silly thing like that when all I want is right here?" Then he kissed her and that was all she needed to know.

Friday and Evie was allowed downstairs. After washing, she put on her maxi dress and sandals, pleased to be fully dressed for the first time in nearly a week. She sat at the kitchen table and ate her breakfast – just like a normal person she mused whilst Jonathan put the radio on for her. He continued to type on his laptop whilst she read a book curled up in a chair in the living room. They only had two more nights together before they had to go back to reality and they both ignored that topic of conversation not wanting to spoil things. Evie was so pleased to be finally be feeling better; Fiona would be here tomorrow and she was allowed to shower and wash her hair; umm, she thought to herself, absolute bliss. Then her final night and off the medication on Sunday night. She thought about checking in with Steve at the gym; but couldn't face it, no plenty of time for that particular delight on Monday morning.

Fiona breezed in on Saturday morning all ready to help, the truth was though that she just sat on the downturned toilet seat and chatted whilst Evie showered herself, Fiona was only there as a precaution. Evie did ask her to help dry her hair as even though it was just a shower and hair wash it left her more tired than she'd expected. When her hair was half dry she twisted it up into a low ponytail and that way it would dry naturally with a wave in it by suppertime. It being Saturday Jonathan's laptop stayed firmly shut and he kept out of Fiona's way by reading the newspaper. Jonathan was on his best behaviour with Fiona; but when she left before midday although they were polite to one another there was no chumminess on either side; they were carefully watching each other for the smallest slip up with Evie but none came.

Evie ate a small salad for lunch, but afterwards she found she was too tired to read much. She hadn't expected her shower to use up so much of her energy and finally she realised and accepted that although she hadn't wanted to be off work for another week that it was probably a good idea.

"So what would you like to do this afternoon, it's a lovely day outside?"

"Well I'd really like some fresh air so maybe a walk round the garden if that's allowed?" She was hoping he would say yes as being cooped up inside was now starting to drive her a bit crazy.

"I think that'll be okay, "Jonathan flashed her one of his smiles. When he was all charming like this he was hard to resist, "Just give me ten minutes okay?"

They walked round the garden hand in hand in the sunshine and instantly Evie felt her spirits lift. This was so much better, besides although David had said no to her running he'd said that walking every day would be fine. Jonathan had laid out a picnic rug under a shady tree and they settled down her head on his lap just talking and being together. Neither of them alluded to the elephant in the room, namely her departure tomorrow for they both knew it would come round all too soon. She started to doze and drifted off to sleep in the warm air. He was happy just to be with her, to sit and watch, stroking her soft hair with his hands. After an hour or so she stirred and found him lying next to her, his arms around her looking into her eyes.

"Hello, enjoy your snooze?" he laughed at her.

"Umm yes sorry about that, I was more tired than I thought; but it was a lovely snooze though all I seem to have done is sleep and antagonize you for a whole week." She paused, "It's nothing short of a miracle that you're still here at all. I owe you an apology for my behaviour. Here's the thing: I once spent so long in hospital that now I can't bear to be ill and this was just the most frustrating thing for me, so I'm sorry I took it all out on you. You've seen my scars and I told you I still have counselling and that I can't have a baby and you're still here, which is nothing short of a miracle really." She had a little stretch and reached over to kiss him. There was no more talking; but eventually the sun had gone in and she shivered. It was time to go back to the house. She wondered if she should tell him about her going on the pill; but decided that too could wait a bit.

Their last evening together, Jonathan had saved the best meal from the food delivery service, hot smoked salmon with spinach, baby new potatoes and vegetables; afterwards there was a wheat free chocolate cake. "Oh thank you, that was such a lovely meal." She groaned out of pleasure, "too bad it's back to reality next week for me."

Jonathan suddenly looked pained. "Don't, don't say that, I don't want to even think about next week." He took hold of her hands in his, "What am I going to do, you'll be at home I'll be at work – Jesus, life's so unfair sometimes!"

Evie released his hands and went round to him, curled up on his lap and nestled her head into his shoulder. "I know, I know we've come such a long way in a week, even though I behaved terribly," she giggled, "but just think I'm nearly better so things can move on again can't they…if you want to that is?"

He tilted her face up and looked into her eyes, "Oh Evie of course I want to – was there ever any doubt?"

"Well here's the thing: you know I'm a complicated sort of girl, so yes I would say that there was doubt, a lot of doubt." He interrupted her, "Well not any more, as soon as you're well again we'll.." and then she interrupted him by kissing him; they didn't need to spell it out. They spent their last night together in the guest bedroom wrapped in each other's arms, both thinking about the week gone by and the week ahead.

Sunday afternoon and she'd packed and was ready to go home. Jonathan followed her in his car just to make sure she was okay and helped her out by her front door. Henry came running round the corner and she picked him up holding him tightly to her, "Henry, oh Henry it's okay I'm back now, hey did you miss me? Well I missed you too, you know."

Once inside she put Henry down and now it was time for goodbye, at least until next weekend.

"So I'll text you later shall I?" Evie's voice was quieter now. She couldn't look at Jonathan so stared at the floor, thinking to herself: please just go now before I start to cry again.

"Yes I'll let you know I'm home…promise me you'll call me in the week if you need anything, anything at all?"

"Okay, … look, about next weekend. I can't and don't want to leave Henry again, I've really missed him so how about you come to stay here with me? Come over on Friday once you're home from work, just bring an overnight bag… what do you say?"

Jonathan took two strides towards her and held her, "What do I say? I say just try and stop me." And taking her face in his hands kissed her softly, stepped back and said, "I'm going now. I don't want to, but if I don't leave now then I'll never go."

"Okay then." Evie smiled and with that he'd gone, and it was her and Henry, just like old times.

Chapter 26

Evie spent the week spoiling Henry rotten, well he'd had to put up with a lot recently and he did get pretty anxious when she was away. Still her neighbour feeding him was way better than putting him in a cattery. She'd been over to Mrs Harris to thank her yet again for feeding her cat and had ordered some flowers and chocolates to be delivered with her groceries as a thank you for her trouble. Evie walked every day and gradually felt much stronger; although she wasn't allowed to run she did some toning exercises with light weights as she would have to be fit enough to get back into the swing of things at work next week come what may. Steve had been pretty grumpy when he found out she would be off another week; but had no choice but to manage without her. Every night she'd sent Jonathan a text message and he'd called her back after his PT session was over and he'd eaten. They talked every night for over an hour, just wanting to hear each other's voice, ending each chat with their words of "Miss you – Miss you more." Both of them were counting down the days until Friday night; but only Evie knew just how much there was riding on Friday – she thought she would surprise him for a change.

Jonathan spent his week making up for lost time at work by deliberately filling his diary to the brim so he didn't have any free time to just sit and think about this maddening girl who was now his girlfriend. The last few days they'd had together had been amazing, lots of talking and kissing plus other things for him but no sex as per doctor's orders. Every night he waited for her text and then they talked and talked; it was so good to hear her voice and count down the days until he would see her again. He'd never even spent one night at Evie's apart from when they fell asleep on the sofa together so he was – now what was the word exactly? – excited made him sound like a teenager; but he was excited. They would have the whole weekend together – just the two of them with hopefully no dramas, shouting or banging on locked doors with idle threats, no just two days of being utterly loved up or whatever the phrase was these days? Jamie would know; but he certainly wasn't calling Jamie to ask him.

Friday morning and Evie was so happy she thought she might burst before he arrived that evening. Jonathan had told her he was finishing work early so would be leaving London at 3.00 so would be with her before 6.00. He was on cloud nine himself. Everyone in the office had noticed this change in him; whatever the crisis was last week it had improved his mood. His secretary was relieved as it meant a much easier time for her and everyone else.

Everything was going to plan; he'd left the office on time, Evie had chosen their supper and had decided which pair of pyjamas to wear tonight, not that she'd be wearing them for long, or if at all she giggled to herself.

Jonathan's car ground to a halt a little after 4.00, maybe they had just hit the motorway at the wrong time; but as they sat there still going nowhere it began to look like something more than just the usual Friday night exodus. Another half an hour and they still hadn't moved an inch, a police car had roared up the hard shoulder a while ago, but since then nothing; they were stuck. He sent a text to Evie.

Hi you it's me – not sure what's happening but we are stuck on the motorway going nowhere, so will be later to see you than planned. Will text again when I know more. – SEND

Okay no problem am not going anywhere, will just be sat waiting for my boyfriend to arrive! – SEND

He smiled at that, it sounded like she was in a good mood, but oh why did this have to happen today? He just couldn't catch a break with this girl. It was beginning to look like they wouldn't be moving for a long time; they'd seen an air ambulance hover overhead and a lot of people had got out of their cars and were stretching their legs on the hard shoulder. This was turning into a nightmare. Finally, a little before 7.00, they were aware of some activity happening behind them. A police car was making everyone turn round and go back the way they had come –problem was, they would all be following the same diversion signs so it was going to be a very slow journey home. Sighing, he called Evie, "Hi it's me. We are eventually moving but in the wrong direction I don't know what time I will make it to yours, do you still want me to come over tonight?"

"Yes of course I do, I'll get ready for bed and cook you some eggs or something light when you get here. These things can't be helped. I'll sit and read or watch some TV, main thing is that you're okay."

"Okay that'll be great, sorry to mess you about, I'll text you again when I'm home then I'll be with you 30 minutes after that."

"Don't worry. I'll still wait up for you, see you soon," and she was gone.

Jonathan was not in the best of moods as he drove down the lane to Evie's house; his watch now said 11.30pm and he was tired and frustrated by the whole process of just getting home on a Friday night. He'd texted her 30 minutes ago and she was still waiting up for him, so that was a good sign at least. Shame about their supper being ruined, but she assured him that she would cook him some eggs and that there was plenty of hot water for him to shower off the grime of London so all was not lost. It dawned on him that she really was a glass half full kind of girl as other girls would have told him not to bother tonight. She opened her front door as he got out of his car and then he was standing in her hallway looking weary.

"Hi," she smiled at him suddenly feeling nervous which was quite ridiculous considering they had spent every night last week lying in bed together.

"Hi."

"So, eggs or a shower first?"

"Neither," in a flash he placed his hands either side of her face and her body slammed into the back of the door as he kissed her as if his life depended upon it. His tongue explored her mouth and she groaned and ran her hands over his shoulders and into his hair. This is what she'd been waiting for all week. On and on they went, the pressure of his body on hers leaving her in no doubt as to how he was feeling. Eventually he pulled away, breathing heavily.

He grinned at her, his hands still on her cheeks, "Sorry, got a bit carried away."

"So I see. I gather from that little display you're pleased to see me after all?"

"Oh yes indeedy?" He kissed her again quickly and then said, "I'm starving. What's for supper?"

She cooked some scrambled eggs on toast and made him a cup of tea. It was too late for wine and he was hungry. Watching him eat she had a chance to study him again. After a week apart he looked exactly the same, a bit tired though, but after a long week at work and then tonight's journey that was to be expected.

He finished his meal and groaned. "I was so hungry, that was just what I needed."

"So go and shower and I'll clear up here and be with you in 5 minutes."

"Okay, see you in five, I take it I'm allowed to use your shower?"

"Yes, you know where it is." This told him she had known all along, he'd used her shower before.

Less than 10 minutes had passed and Evie went into her bedroom. She pulled the duvet to the end of the bed, switched the lights to dim and taking a deep breath made her way into the en-suite. He was brushing his teeth and she stood next to him washing her hands in her basin. Their eyes met in the mirror and both of them knew exactly where this was headed. She left him to finish. Taking off her robe she hung it in the dressing area just as he came through the door. He had a towel wrapped round his waist and his hair was still damp. Pulling her towards him he grinned at her and said, "Well, then."

There wasn't any need for them to speak as his arms wrapped around her and they took up exactly where they had left off in her hallway less than 30minutes ago. His towel was now on the floor swiftly followed by her pyjama bottoms. She could feel his erection pushing against her and she moaned softly. They stumbled around to the edge of the bed and he sat down holding her between his legs. Jonathan pulled her cami top off over her head and then they were together on the sheets, touching and kissing, moaning and exploring. He moved over and asked her, "What about protection?"

"Top drawer," she motioned to the bedside cabinet and turned the lights off.

Chapter 27

Jonathan lay awake watching Evie sleep. Finally they'd gone to bed. For their first time together it had been good, very good. He smiled to himself; at one crucial point she'd asked him to stop and he thought it was all over before it had even begun, but Evie just needed to wriggle a little bit to get into a more comfortable position and then they picked it right up again. He wrapped his arms and legs around her. It had taken them so long to get to this point, but it had been worth the wait and hopefully it was only going to get better and better. Breathing deeply he inhaled her scent. He'd been dreaming about the two of them being naked together in her bed for far too long and he was in no hurry to let her go.

Evie woke and turned to look at the clock. It was early barely past 7.30am and she snuggled back into Jonathan's arms. Last night had been good, yes very good. He'd been taken by surprise as she came closer to her orgasm she got noisier and noisier, but he'd come shortly after and she'd squeezed him whilst he was still inside her making him cry out her name. Jonathan was tired and they slept soundly, legs all tangled together. Not wanting to wake him she stayed where she was, just watching him sleep. This is what he must have done every night she was at his house recently, only now they'd had sex and it had brought them as close as you could be. He hadn't shied away from touching her scars and for that she'd been thankful. She reached up to smooth away his hair from his face and to her surprise he caught her hand and kissed it.

"Morning sweetheart."

"Hello handsome." They were both in a playful mood it seemed. "It's early go back to sleep."

He moved swiftly so she was now underneath him; "sleep wasn't quite what I had in mind," and began to kiss her over and over, touching every part of her body.

She was dozing now in a post sex haze of contentment, her head was on his chest and she didn't care what time it was; they had the whole day and nothing planned at all – how heavenly. Stretching out against his body she realized he was awake and watching her.

"Oh hello just having a little stretch," she said lazily. "Do you want to shower first?"

"How about we shower together?" He pulled her on top of him now so that she could feel he was ready for her again and raised his eyebrows, making his intentions crystal clear.

Laughing they made their way into the en-suite and Evie turned the water on. They took it in turns to massage creamy shower mousse onto each other; it took them quite a while as there was a lot more kissing to be had in between. Finally Jonathan couldn't stand it a moment longer and grasped her bum lifting her against his erection. She wrapped her legs around him and leaned her shoulders against the tiled wall as he started to thrust inside her. When she climaxed she cried out, feeling wave after wave of pleasure and then he came, filling her deeply, shouting out her name and then nuzzled into her neck not wanting to release her from him.

The morning was nearly over by the time they made it downstairs. Henry was glowering at them all huffy at having been made to wait for his breakfast. They were like teenagers and couldn't keep their hands off one another. This was such fun, they only made it from the kitchen to the sofa and back all day, the longest gap being for when Evie had to prepare supper. Jonathan had brought some wine and poured two glasses for them whilst he watched her cook. God he thought to himself I could watch her all day just moving gracefully between the hob and sink stretching up to reach into the cupboards, that tight little bum just itching to be fondled. At one point he moved up behind her pulling him against his chest, then wrapped one arm around her waist, kissed her neck and placed the other hand over her breast. Evie moaned; this was torture of the best kind. Feeling her legs start to buckle he moved to sit at the table with her on his lap and kissed her passionately.

"This won't get the supper cooked," she whispered quietly when he had released her mouth for a second.

"Not sure I'm very hungry, at least not for food," came his reply, followed by his hands now reaching inside her t – shirt and making contact with her soft skin.

"How about a compromise?" She could barely string a sentence together. "We eat now and then take a bath before an early night?"

He broke off from kissing her neck and murmured his agreement. "You have all the best ideas."

"You're going to have to put me down now though I'm afraid or there won't be anything to eat at all."

Reluctantly he released her and put his hands behind his head lazily stretching out. Boy, this weekend had been worth the wait; a few weeks prior he thought they would never get to this stage and now it was even better than he could have hoped for.

Evie cleared the dishes away and fed Henry before closing the utility door. He could have a night out on the tiles and leave her and Jonathan in peace. She had a feeling that neither of them would want any interruptions tonight. They made their way upstairs and Evie ran a bath, she poured in some moisturizing bath foam and left it to fill. Jonathan meanwhile had drawn the curtains and stared to undress.

"Here let me do that." Evie proceeded to loosen his belt and undo his shirt buttons. Eventually he was left in just his boxers and then it was her turn to be undressed by him. She stood before him in just her bra and knickers. She'd deliberately chosen one of her sexiest sets of underwear in the hope it would get him all excited and so far it seemed to be doing the trick. He reached inside the back of her panties and pulled them down whilst kissing her hard on the mouth. She moaned and he pushed his tongue inside probing her soft flesh, then he unhooked her bra and pulled it over her arms.

She was naked in front of him and he had never wanted her more. Her breasts were free from scars and just fantastic. Evie yanked down his boxers and his erection sprang free, God he was so ready for her and they hadn't even got in the bath yet. Pulling away she took his hand and he followed her to the bath. It was full enough now and she stepped into the warm water and sat down letting the bubbles caress her skin. Jonathan got in behind her and she rested her back on his chest, their legs touching together skin on skin. She sighed. Oh his was so good, she could still feel his erection on her bum and then he started to massage one breast with his hand whilst his other hand reached down between her legs and began a whole other type of massage. He nuzzled her neck and whispered in her ear, "This is to thank you for all the pleasure you gave me last week when I could do nothing in return for you." She couldn't even speak as her desire began to build; she started to moan louder and louder. Jonathan knew what this meant and he didn't stop until she cried out her orgasm quivering inside her. Standing up to get out of the bath he held her tightly to him, pushed his thighs onto her and then kissed her. "I love you so much, you do know that don't you?"

"I know," she whispered. "I love you too."

They dried each other with soft fluffy towels and then had sex again. It was his turn now. They snuggled under the duvet, naked skin touching naked skin, legs tangled together. Evie was dozing, finally she'd found someone who didn't recoil at the mere sight of her naked body and who seemed to accept her for who she was, trouble and all. She drifted off to sleep and Jonathan just held her to him not wanting to let her go even for a second.

Sunday followed a similar pattern: wake up/ make love/ eat/ have hot shower sex/ eat, and so on. Evie insisted on them using condoms. Yesterday they'd been careless and although she was on the pill she didn't want them to take any more chances. The day flashed by all too soon and neither of them wanted it to end. They were a couple in love and were enjoying this honeymoon period. Just before Jonathan left he asked her if she still had Wednesday free.

"Yes of course. I do I have classes on Thursday night but nothing Wednesday. Why?"

"I was thinking you could come up to London and we could spend the day together, I don't think I can manage a whole week without you."

Evie grinned, "I'd love that; but we are going to have to find a way to manage for 5 days after that don't you?"

Jonathan groaned. "I know but can we just get through the first week, please?"

Monday afternoon and Fiona answered her mobile. It was Evie calling. She hoped everything was okay?

"Hello you, everything okay?"

"Hi Fi, yes don't panic. Everything's fine, in fact," she giggled. "Here's the thing: everything's better than fine."

Fiona was intrigued. "Evie what's going on?"

Evie was back at home, sat at her kitchen table fit to burst if she didn't tell someone soon. "Well I just thought you ought to know that Jonathan and I have um taken things to the um… next level…"

"Oh my goodness," Fiona sat down, "So am I allowed to ask… How was it, you know?"

Laughing, Evie said, "Well the first time it was good, you know it's always a bit tricky, but after that it was very good, yes very good indeed."

"Oh sweetie I'm so happy for you. I don't need to tell you I wasn't at all sure about you and him together but you sound happy, really happy and that's great."

"Yes I am happy, the happiest I've been in such a long time." They continued to chat and Evie explained she was going up to London on Wednesday to spend some more time with him.

Chapter 28

So it was all agreed. Wednesday morning found Evie on the train to London. She didn't know what he had planned and she was excited. Pulling her wheelie case behind her she went through the barrier and looked for a sign with her name on.

Unbeknown to her, THE MAN was there already taking discreet photos ready to send them over to HIM.

Jonathan's driver Alan picked her up from the station and explained they were going to meet Jonathan in his office. She was to leave her overnight bag with him.

THE MAN smiled to himself. So Dempsey and HER were together again, well this made his life a whole lot easier than trying to tail them separately.

She found herself in the lobby of SCD, (Smith Cable Dempsey) and made her way to the lift. Margaret, Jonathan's secretary, knocked on his office door and showed her in.

"Miss Wallace is here for you sir."

"Thank you Margaret. Hi come on in, Edward and Robert were just leaving."

Edward put his hand out, "Not without an introduction we're not, and smiled at her." Introductions made Jonathan indicated the door, "Now you two get lost; we've got plans."

Alone with Jonathan Evie looked around his office. It was very nice, not much of a view, but very corporate all the same.

Jonathan went to hug her but she stepped back. "Not in front of everyone, they're all looking through the window," she pleaded.

"Well I could close the blinds if it bothers you." He smirked.

"No, that's even worse. I don't want you getting the sack."

He threw his head back and laughed. "Oh Evie you say the funniest things sometimes; but seriously just a quick kiss and we'll be on our way." He kissed her and wouldn't let her go; eventually she managed to pull away.

"That was very naughty" she admonished him.

"Oh you haven't seen anything yet, now let's go. I see you brought your sexy shoe boots up to town for the day."

Evie looked down at her shoes, "Yes, they get terribly lonely and when I told then I was off to the bright lights and big city, well they just begged to come along too."

They walked through the office hand in hand, "Goodbye Margaret. I'll be in for 2.00pm tomorrow."

"Yes sir; enjoy your day." she watched them leave and thought now that explained everything; she caught Selena's eye and they nodded in agreement – that was it then – it was a girl after all.

They were driven to a small intimate restaurant for lunch. It seemed that Jonathan was known there and they were done within an hour. Back in the car the next stop was The Royal Albert Hall, for a matinee performance of Madame Butterfly. As soon as Evie saw the posters she turned and hugged Jonathan; oh this was just the best surprise ever. They had a private box and it was just so beautiful, it was such a sad tale of forbidden romance and although she'd seen it before Evie cried at the end every time. Leaving the venue they emerged out into the sunlight.

THE MAN was there again taking more photos, this time of the two of them.

Alan drove them to Jonathan's apartment and once inside Evie realised he wasn't exactly struggling to make ends meet in the city, as this must be costing him a pretty penny, unless it belonged to the business of course. He showed her the master bedroom and she unpacked her things, kicked her shoes off and padded out into the kitchen. Jonathan had opened some wine and she took a sip; oh lovely and cool. They were going out to dinner at 7.00 and she wondered where he was taking her, somewhere nice she hoped.

"Would you like to shower before we go out to dinner?"

"Um yes please, I'll only be ten minutes."

He reached for her. "Of course we could always shower together."

Evie laughed. "Well we could, but then we'd probably never make it to dinner and I want to go out so... Ten minutes okay." Reluctantly he let her go, "Okay you can go first but if you take too long I'm coming in," he warned her.

Evie stood under the warm water. She'd been looking forward to this night away ever since Jonathan had suggested it. She'd bought a new outfit and hoped he'd like it; although she planned to wear a silk kimono jacket over the top and then reveal the surprise once they were sat in the restaurant – boy if that didn't get him all hot and bothered then nothing would. Dressing with care she brushed her hair and settled on a half up half down style and applied some light makeup. Why did the no make – up look take twice as long as the fully made up look? she wondered. Back in the bedroom she zipped up her shoe-boots, dabbed on some perfume and put in her earrings; there, all done. Jacket in place, she went out into the living room to finish her wine.

Ten minutes later Jonathan appeared looking very fine, oh yes very fine indeed in a navy jacket and trousers; smart casual, but very expensive smart casual, Evie mused. He smiled when he saw her. "You look so beautiful," he put his arms around her and nuzzled her neck, "God you smell divine too… are you sure you still want dinner?"

She laughed. "Yes please I'm getting hungry now." Just you wait until we're at the restaurant, she thought, you won't be thinking about food at all.

Alan drove them to a very discreet looking restaurant and it was obvious to Evie that Jonathan was a regular diner here too. They were shown to a corner table and Evie took the chair facing into the room; she liked to see all the comings and goings whereas boys just weren't that bothered by all that. She kept her jacket on until after they'd ordered their food and their wine had been poured. Reaching over the table for her hand Jonathan asked if she was glad she had come up to London now?

"Oh yes I've had a lovely day, just lovely thank you." She smiled and stared at him with her big brown eyes. Jonathan suddenly felt a bit hot under the collar; those eyes of hers, she really didn't have a clue what they did to him.

Without dropping eye contact and explaining she was a bit warm she slipped her jacket off and waited for his reaction. She didn't have to wait for more than a nanosecond, his eyes nearly popped out of his head. She was wearing a very discreet navy jumpsuit but – and here's the thing – it had a large rectangular cut-out panel that skimmed over both sides of her breasts, showing her cleavage and hinting at what lay either side of it. It made it look as if she wasn't wearing any underwear. She was of course wearing just a very clever bra.

"Bloody hell, Evie! that's quite some outfit," he exclaimed; he couldn't tear his eyes away, no wonder she'd worn a jacket over the top, as if he'd seen this before they'd left the apartment they sure as hell wouldn't be sat in the restaurant now.

"I'm glad you like it," she murmured, pleased it was having exactly the reaction she was hoping for.

The waiter reappeared with their starters and they began to eat. Jonathan was mesmerized; he knew she was a sexy little thing; but she mostly wore jeans or tight Lycra, but this well this was something else entirely. He was stunned into silence and in two seconds he would have had sex with her right there and then on the dining table. Jonathan swallowed hard he just had to get through dinner and then he would definitely be having his cake and eating it too.

Plates cleared away Evie murmured her excuses and sashayed out to the ladies' room. Jonathan sighed. It was getting so damn hot in there and he was pleased to have a few minutes' respite. His penis was already primed ready for action and he would have to make sure they got back to the apartment in double quick time or else they would be having car sex in front of his driver, which wasn't a very good idea. He drank some cool water and steadied his breathing; he thought this little trip to London would be good for them both, but he had no idea just how good until five minutes ago. Evie sat back down again; yes he looked a bit tense and was breathing faster too, so the jumpsuit was having the desired effect on him. Bring it on she thought; I've spent too long waiting for someone like him to come along, she sure as hell wasn't going to mess this up.

Their main courses were served and they ate in companionable silence; they didn't need to talk they both knew how their evening was going to end. The waiter reappeared, "Can I offer you the dessert menus?"

Evie didn't want dessert at all but was intrigued to see what Jonathan's reaction would be, so she took a menu and said, "I don't know, what do you think darling, are we having dessert here or back at the apartment?" As she asked Jonathan this question she began to move her foot up and down against his ankle and lower calf making him jump to attention.

Sounding strained he replied, "Oh I think we'll just get the check please." She smiled back at him. "Good choice Mr D as always." Jonathan thought he might self-combust and concentrated on calling Alan to say they were ready to leave and paying the bill.

As they stood up to leave, he placed his hand in the small of her back as she had decided to leave her jacket off and they made their way outside. Evie's legs felt like jelly, she had never been so brazen before and it wasn't a role she was entirely comfortable with; but she smiled to herself – she had pulled it off-just.

Sat in the car together, they held hands, careful that their legs weren't touching. At the hotel they made it across the lobby and into the lift. Luckily for him, two other people joined them in the lift and they just concentrated on reaching their floor. As soon as the apartment door was closed Jonathan pulled Evie into his arms and kissed her hard, pausing and kissing her neck intermittently he whispered: "Well that was quite some display there Miss Wallace. Part of me wanted to cover you up and the other part of me wanted to rip it off you; now which option do you think I might take now?"

Evie pulled back slightly, "Well seeing as we're back here why don't you peel it off me ... slowly and then we'll see." Jonathan needed no encouragement and they stumbled into the bedroom. He unzipped her boots and she undid his shirt whilst he slipped off his shoes and socks. Next she loosened his belt and undid his trousers, "My, my, someone is all hot and bothered, aren't they? she whispered to him, seeing his erection underneath his boxer shorts. He turned her round and unzipped her, whilst she removed her earrings. Then she wiggled out of it until she was standing there in her bra and knickers. Now he saw she'd worn underwear all along, but that soon ended up on the bedroom floor until there was just naked skin on naked skin and they sank onto the bed together.

THE MAN checked his watch. Hmm, they would be here for the night, he may as well send what photos he had and call it a night.

Chapter 29

The following morning they made love again. All too soon Evie would be on her train home and he wouldn't see her until the following evening. They were tangled together under the duvet and he groaned to himself, why couldn't every morning be like this one, with long lazy lie-ins and sex with Evie? They showered together and ate a late breakfast, but she needed to be at the station before 12.00 as she had to teach that evening. Jonathan wrapped his arms around her and nuzzled her neck, "Are you sure you can't stay another night and then we could drive back together tomorrow?"

"It's a lovely thought but no I really have to get to work and you Mr D (she was laughing at him now), have a job to do too as I recall."

"Spoilsport," he sighed and released her.

All too soon the car pulled up outside the station and Jonathan took her bag and they walked in to check the digital noticeboard. Her train was on time and the barrier would be lifted at any moment to start boarding. Jonathan put her bag down and hugged her. They looked like any other couple saying goodbye at the station. "How am I going to get through tonight without you?"

She laughed, "Oh I'm sure you'll think of something, I'll text you when I'm home and then again after work; honestly it's only another 24 hours and we'll be together again."

"Well it's 24 hours too long," he grumbled.

Sensing his mood was changing Evie quickly kissed him and he kissed her back hard, squeezing her bum, then she pulled away picked up her bag and scampered through the barriers leaving him there with a thunderous look on his face. "See you tomorrow, I'll text you," she grinned. Always leave them wanting more, wasn't that the phrase, well something like that? She located her seat and settled down for a couple of hours' peace; it had been a great trip, but truth was she was tired, must be all the sex she giggled to herself.

THE MAN watched this play out and then followed Jonathan back to his car and then back to his office.

Her phone pinged and it was Jonathan.

That was very naughty, I hadn't finished with you? – SEND

Well I didn't want to be arrested for indecent behaviour at a railway station now did I? – SEND

Just you wait until tomorrow night. I'll show you what indecent behaviour is . – SEND

(Oh blimey this was very hot and steamy for a lunchtime train journey and she squirmed in her seat. Best to cool things down).
Am not sure what you mean; can you tell me tonight when we text? As am going to have a little nap now, can't imagine why I should be so tired?! – SEND

Jonathan laughed. Oh he had a pretty good idea alright; but she was right he needed to get to work; although he'd never felt less like work in his life.

Okay will leave that discussion for tonight. Miss you xx. – SEND

Miss you more xx. – SEND and she was gone.

Much later that evening Evie snuggled under her duvet and began to type.

Hi it's me, whatcha doing? – SEND

Hi am waiting for my girlfriend to text me so that I can explain what will be happening tomorrow night! – SEND

Can it be a surprise? – SEND

Do I have to remind you that you hate surprises, – SEND

Yes I know but I have a feeling that I might like or rather enjoy this one! – SEND

Oh that's guaranteed. – SEND

You sound very sure of yourself, sir. – SEND

(She was teasing him now, why had he let her go home it was so frustrating.)
Yes I am, now are you coming over to me or am I coming over to yours? – SEND

Well I have to work on Saturday so can you come over to me then you can stay here whilst I pop out and I'll be back before you know it – SEND

Okay what time? – SEND

Should be home just before 9 if I shower at home that is? – SEND

Yes, you or rather we are definitely showering at home! – SEND

I have a surprise for you too! – SEND

Good job one of us likes surprises isn't it? Any clues? – SEND

Well here's the thing I don't want to give too much away but it does involve some new items of clothing. – SEND

Evie please stop as I'm now imagining all sorts of things . – SEND

I aim to please, just thought you might like to think about it whilst you are going to sleep tonight. – SEND

Am not sure I'll be getting a lot of sleep! – SEND

Oh dear that's a shame, I don't want you running out of energy before I have given you your surprise. – SEND

(Jonathan groaned – this was bloody torture; in one second he'd get in the car and be at hers n two hours from now and call in sick tomorrow).

Don't you worry about my energy levels, do I have to remind you that I have been working out a lot recently. Did you notice? – SEND

Yes indeedy, I noticed and I have been paying a lot of attention to exactly which parts of your body you have been focusing on! – SEND

I would like to be focused on your body right now. – SEND

Oh! Well with that in mind, I'm going to sleep and suggest you do the same. You can dream of what my surprise to you might be. Night Jonathan.xx –SEND

Night Evie xx – SEND

Miss you xx – SEND

Miss you more xx– SEND

Chapter 30

Evie arrived home at 8.30, just time to sort a few things out before her boyfriend arrived. She smiled to herself; yes her boyfriend who so far hadn't run screaming for the hills and would be here soon to hopefully pick up where they left off in London. Less than ten minutes later there was a knock at the door. Blimey he's early and he's very keen, she laughed to herself. She opened her front door and he swept her into his arms kissing her like he hadn't see her for a week or even a month. She eventually pulled away, "Hey I'm all sweaty remember.?"

"Oh I know, I was counting on it – now how about that shower you promised me?" He closed the door and took her hand pulling her up the stairs and along into her bedroom with indecent haste. Evie turned the shower on and began to strip off her exercise gear, whilst Jonathan undressed not taking his eyes off of her. They were under the warm water in seconds and he started to wash her back with shower mousse, kissing her shoulders as he was doing so. Then he soaped her legs and moved his hand round to her tummy where he held her against him soaping and caressing her until he couldn't stand it for a second longer; oh yes he was ready for her alright.

Cuddled together under her duvet she stretched and raising her head from his chest asked, "Would you like something to eat now… just to recharge your batteries for later?"

He turned over catching her out as she was now firmly underneath him, "I'm not sure – I haven't had my surprise yet."

"Oh yes, that. Well I'm hungry so I'm going to eat and then I'll let you have your surprise are you coming?"

"All the time with you," he answered smuttily.

"Jonathan really? You're impossible, now let me go I need to use the bathroom and I'll see you in the kitchen okay?"

Reluctantly he let her go and watched her saunter away from him and into the bathroom. 'God how bloody good was this, she was a great cook and they had really good sex together; what else did a man need?'

In the bathroom Evie had a wee, washed her hands, dabbed on some perfume and then took out her surprise from the drawer, wriggled into it and then wrapped herself up in her blue robe and padded downstairs. He was already there, dressed in boxers and a shirt, looking at the contents of her fridge.

"See anything you fancy?" she asked. He turned and smirked at her. "I take it you don't mean food?"

"Honestly, what's gotten into you?" she enquired pretending to be cross.

"Well you mostly..."

"Jonathan behave, I need to eat or else I won't have any energy for later, I have been to work you know."

He felt guilty now, "Yes of course I'll have whatever you're having."

She took a variety of things out of the fridge and the cupboards and laid out a mini picnic on the kitchen table, "There. I thought we could just help ourselves."

Jonathan raised his eyebrows; but wisely said nothing and began to serve himself. There was quite a choice, baby mozzarella, sun dried tomatoes, Parma ham, parmesan cheese, focaccia rolls, cheddar, goats cheese, herb crackers, apples, mixed nuts, all simple food but delicious none the less. She opened some chilled white wine and they sat opposite each other eating and sipping wine. A while later she jumped up, "Would you like dessert?"

"Only if it's you?"

She laughed, "Okay, okay I get the message, just let me clear these things away and we'll take our wine upstairs, how about that?"

"Perfect." He sat back and watched her move gracefully around the kitchen. To think if she hadn't given him as second chance after their disastrous coffee shop date he wouldn't be here now like the cat who got the cream waiting for her surprise to him.

Wine glasses in hand they climbed the stairs for the second time; Jonathan brought up his overnight bag and he dropped it on the floor besides the bed. Evie went into the bathroom and brushed her teeth she hoped he was going to like his present. When she came back he'd removed his shirt and was unpacking his things, he looked up when he saw her.

"So I thought you might like to unwrap your surprise present yourself," she whispered to him. He was by her side in a flash and proceeded to untie her robe and let it drop it onto the floor. Jonathan gasped as he took in what she was wearing. Evie had really gone to town. Firstly there was a silky chemise in a pale coffee colour with delicate straps and lace on the bodice. Jonathan slipped the straps off her shoulders and it slipped silently onto the floor. Underneath Evie was wearing matching knickers and a bra with lace and boning over her breasts. It was amazing what you could order online in the privacy of your own home without any knowing looks from snooty sales assistants. Gasping he put one arm around her waist and pulled her onto him, then he kissed her on the mouth whilst cupping one of her breasts through the delicate fabric. He moved his mouth from hers and began to place featherlight kisses on her neck and shoulder. She whispered to him, "So what do you think, do you like?" He didn't reply, just took her hand and led her over to the bed where he proceeded to unwrap the remaining layers.

Midnight and Evie was still awake. She would be so tired at work tomorrow, but for once she didn't really care. Jonathan had been pleased, yes very pleased and excited about unwrapping his present and she was happy too. She snuggled into his body and closed her eyes. Jonathan had one arm around her and was absentmindedly stroking her arm; wow he did not see that coming not for a second, he thought it might have been some sexy pyjamas if such a thing existed but not, well not that. He thought she was so lovely, so lovely, he couldn't quite believe she was his girlfriend. She was full of surprises that was for sure, he'd have to up his game if he was to hang onto her.

The alarm made Evie practically jump out of her skin and she almost fell out of bed and walked through into the shower in a daze. She stood under the hot water, trying to wake up; but her mind and body were still in a delicious sexual haze. They'd had so much fun and pleasure last night it was almost too much, she smiled to herself; was there a thing as too much sex she wondered? Evie began to soap herself and then something touched her arm, her eyes snapped open startled, but she relaxed when she saw that Jonathan had decided to join her under the water. She mustn't be late for work today, but she had a bit of spare time to make this shower more interesting. Jonathan washed her in double quick time for he wanted her right there, right now and didn't want to wait. Placing his arms underneath her bum he lifted her up until her shoulders were resting against the cool tiles and she wrapped her legs and arms around him. She was so ready for him too and carefully he entered her, he wanted her to feel all of him inside of her and then began to thrust. Evie arched her back and moaned, Jonathan kissed her and continued to thrust; she cried out loudly as they climaxed together in an earth shattering explosion of pleasure as wave after wave flooded through Evie and she rested her head onto his shoulder. They were both breathing heavily and he carefully eased out of her and held her to him under the water.

"Well good morning to you too," she smiled at him as he peered into her big brown eyes.

He groaned, " Evie don't look at me like that or you will never get out of the house this morning."

Laughing she moved away from him and wrapped herself in a bath towel and proceeded to brush her teeth.

Evie left Jonathan eating breakfast as she drove into work. She planned to shower at the gym after her classes as she didn't think she could take any more hot shower sex, well not until tonight anyway. Maybe they would have a bath together – yes a bath would be just as much fun if not more. Jonathan picked up the newspaper, but he couldn't concentrate, he wanted to buy Evie a gift, not flowers as he had bought too many of those and mostly for all the wrong reasons too, no he would have to start thinking. She was quite a difficult person to buy presents for and nothing run of the mill was going to work. He had an idea and picked up his mobile. Well what was the point of having some fancy concierge service on his black card if he hardly ever used it? He would get them to think of something amazing; but he ended the call before it had been picked up. No he was going about this all wrong, she didn't like big gestures she wanted something more personal and unique like the t – shirt he'd had printed for her. Think he needed to think, so he made himself a coffee and walked into the garden to ponder on it.

Evie was back home before midday and he was so pleased to see her; but disappointed that she'd already showered – he'd been looking forward to picking up exactly where they had left off this morning. Lunch was a repeat of their supper last night and she'd planned to cook a hot steak salad with wild rice for their supper. Later that afternoon they went for a walk, well it was a very slow walk as they kept stopping to kiss every few yards eventually they had to give up and walked back. They spent some time making out on the sofa before Evie announced she was having a bath and did he want to join her. He didn't need to be asked twice and they undressed each other kissing and laughing whilst waiting for the bath to fill. Evie sank into the warm water and laid her head on Jonathan's chest. This weekend had been simply one of the best she'd had in such a long time. To think that at the start all they did was fight and yet now look at them, all happy and in love she couldn't stop smiling.

Jonathan lay back in the bath with Evie against him. He was so lucky she'd given him a second chance as they certainly wouldn't have been here otherwise. He still hadn't decided what present to buy for her, maybe when he was back in London he would find some inspiration. Sighing he began to soap Evie's back and after rinsing it started on her front. He didn't get very far and in no time he had moved in front of her and they were facing each other. He pulled her legs over his and then lifted her on top of him. Oh wow they were both so needy for each other and the sex was definitely getting better and better each time.

A new week and Evie was back at the gym trying to focus on her classes, but kept getting confused when her mind switched back to her weekend. It had been the best and she didn't know how Jonathan was feeling but she felt great. In London Jonathan was trying to keep his diary full to stop his thoughts drifting back to Evie, he loved her so much, even though they had only been together such a short time. Her other boyfriends must have been crazy not to stay with her, she was the best thing that had ever happened to him and he intended to keep it that way. He still wanted to buy her a gift and was very undecided.

Jonathan walked down to his hotel gym; it was Wednesday night and his trainer Mike would be waiting to put him through his paces. The receptionist smiled and told him that Mike had been detained and there would be a replacement trainer with him shortly; if he'd like to start to warm up on the cross trainer they'd come and find him. He was a bit annoyed as they could have sent him a message about Mike, he could have had a night off for a change. Still if Evie continued to give him tins of baked treats every Sunday for him to eat during the week then maybe he would need every session just to work them off.

Suddenly he was aware of a girl on the cross-trainer next to him. Not really looking at her, he thought she reminded him of his girlfriend. She stared right at him and said, "Hello I thought you might like a more personal workout tonight Mr D." He couldn't believe his eyes: it was Evie. He stopped immediately and pulled her off her machine, hugged her to him and proceeded to kiss her like they hadn't seen each other for a month, not two nights. Finally he let her go.

"So do you like your new trainer Mr D?"

"Do I, come on were not wasting any more time in here." And they practically ran to the lift to take them up to his apartment. Luckily they were alone in the lift and there was a lot more kissing and running of hands over each other until the doors opened and they had to stop.

In bed later that evening, Evie stretched out lazily against him. This had been a good idea of hers, she didn't have to be at work until the following evening and he'd had the best surprise ever. Jonathan lay there; she'd surprised him alright whilst he had been thinking of expensive gifts she'd given him the one thing she knew he'd like – her –making a surprise trip to spend one night with him –this had been the best gift ever. Smiling he turned towards her and started to kiss her again; he was going to be so tired tomorrow; but right now he really didn't care.

THE MAN sent over more photos of Jonathan and Evie in the hotel gym, then called it a night.

Chapter 31

Friday night and Jonathan was back at hers. No delays on the motorway so he was nice and early. They ate together, salmon with new potatoes and salad, plus Evie had baked a delicious cherry cake for dessert. Well she loved cherries and he loved cake so it was a win, win. Their honeymoon period showed no signs of stopping and they had sex everywhere, in bed, on the sofa, at the kitchen table, in the shower and in the bath. Evie's favourite place was the bath, it was so sexy and intimate and her boyfriend was always more than ready for her. She asked if they could go out for a meal tomorrow evening just for a change – nothing fancy the pub would do. Jonathan said okay and thought to himself, yes nothing fancy that was just so her. He would have been happy to eat anywhere if she was going to be with him.

The following afternoon passed quietly with her reading a book and Jonathan supposedly reading the newspaper; but he was constantly distracted by staring at her every few seconds. About five-ish, she announced she would be taking a bath before they went to the pub and did he want to join her. Yes, he bloody well did, and they practically ran up the stairs together. Her bath was very large and very modern but it did take a while to fill, so she busied herself with pouring in some scented bath foam, tying her hair up and brushing her teeth. She undressed and put on her blue robe, swishing the water with her hand she tested the temperature; it was a bit hot, why was it that girls loved hot baths and boys liked cool ones? very odd really.

Eventually it was ready and she called Jonathan in who'd been lying down on the bed waiting to be summoned. When he entered the bathroom Evie was already lying in the bath under a layer of bubbles with her eyes closed. Jonathan stepped in in front of her and lay back against her warm, wet, soft skin, her breasts were against his back. He closed his eyes – this was just the best. Evie began to wash his back and then reached around his waist and started to soap his tummy, avoiding any region below his belly button as she didn't want to be hurried tonight. Once she'd rinsed him off he stepped out and got in behind her and she moved forward and they repeated the process. He left soaping her breasts until last, which was a good idea as by this time they were both so needy for one another again it was almost obscene. Quickly he stood up again and moved so he was facing her, and pulled her legs over his; their noses and foreheads were touching and he began to kiss her softly at first but building with more intensity. Evie couldn't bear it any longer, she wanted him now and she pulled away so he could lift her up and towards him and placed her gently down on top of him. She felt him inside her, filling her deeply, she moaned loudly then they began to move together up and down rocking back and forth until they were both so close – he grabbed hold of her hips and pulled her down onto him hard and they climaxed seconds after one another in the most delicious way possible. Her arms were around his neck and they remained together feeling every wave of pleasure.

They dried each other and Evie chose her underwear carefully. Jonathan took one look at her in her white lace bra and panties and started to kiss her determinedly. They both realized it would be a bit later than planned before they left to go out. He slid one hand underneath the top of her panties and began to caress her bum whilst his other hand moved slowly across her back and unfastened her bra. He moved them both slowly across to her bed and they sank down on it, he whispered to her, "Oh my God do you know how I feel about you?" Evie could only murmur, "I think so."

Finally getting dressed to go out, Jonathan watched her as she opened her wardrobe and picked out some tight jeans and a boyfriend white shirt, understated but classy; well that was so Evie after all. She wriggled into her jeans, until Jonathan stood in front of her, "Jesus do you have to do that?"

"Um yes it's the easiest way to get them on –sorry," she grinned at him, God he was insatiable this weekend, well anymore would have to wait until they were back from the pub. They left in his car, for some reason Evie didn't think this would be a particularly late night. Smiling, she said to herself: umm now I wonder why that would be.

The Lamb Inn was getting busy, well it was a Saturday night after all. They had last been here together when he had turned up at her gym unannounced. They found a table and Jonathan went to get them some drinks and menus. Less than ten minutes later Jamie turned up and joined them. This time Jonathan didn't mind one bit, he'd had Evie all to himself for what felt like ages so a shared meal in a pub really was no big deal. They chatted and Jonathan went to order food for the three of them. Jamie was pleased as it was another free meal.

"So Evie how've you been, sis.?"

"Well busy with work and I went to London last week and of course your brother takes up a lot of my free time," she raised her eyebrows and laughed. "How about you, studying hard I hope?"

"Yes uni is okay; got a few girlfriend problems at the moment, maybe we could have a chat about it when it's just you and me?"

"Okay sure, why don't you text me during the week and I'll see what pearls of wisdom I can dish out."

Jonathan watched Evie and his brother whilst he was waiting to be served. He had no idea that she would have affected his life so much, everyone adored her, even Jamie who'd never shown the slightest interest in any of his previous girlfriends before. He wondered about planning a romantic weekend away just the two of them, yes that would be perfect; go away just the two of them somewhere romantic. Once he was back in London he'd spend a few hours in the evenings seeing what was available. Hotels were all on-line these days; but he wanted it to be somewhere really special, yes he thought that would be the perfect next step. Lots of room service, champagne, showering together, taking baths together, sex –oh yes a lot of sex and just being with her. Evie, his Evie, he still couldn't quite believe his luck.

Jonathan returned to the table and the conversation turned to his parents who were due back from their world trip next week.

"So you'll finally be able to meet them. Shall I arrange a meal or something?"

"No that's a bit formal. Why don't I just call in for a drink when I'm at yours, you know keep it relaxed, after all they might not like me and I can bale after a drink without being rude."

"Oh Evie you're insane, why wouldn't they like you?"

Jamie chipped in, "That's impossible and no I don't want to bet on it thank you!"

Evie laughed, "So you've finally realised that some bets are not to be taken at any price-hallelujah."

"Yep pretty much. Oh here comes the food, I'm starving."

"Jamie you're always hungry. I don't know where you put it all."

"I'll have you know I'm a growing boy." They all laughed together and began to eat.

Evie excused herself and made her way to the cloakroom. There was always a queue at the ladies, men were so lucky they never had to queue at all. Once done she brushed her hair and tied it back neatly and made her way back to their table. It was very busy now and a bit of a tight squeeze past the bar. Suddenly she felt a hand pinch her bum hard, she whirled round to be met by some young lad grinning from ear to ear.

"Sorry darling didn't mean to make you jump – just couldn't resist could I – that gorgeous bum just ripe wanting to be squeezed." He demonstrated by using both his hands in an obscene manner; he was obviously well on his way to being drunk; but instead of giving him a tongue lashing Evie beckoned him to come closer so that she could whisper in his ear."

He thought all his Christmases had come at once; but on listening to what she said he turned a nasty shade of purple and pulled sharply away.

"Alright, keep your hair on. I didn't mean anything by it." And then he turned back to the fruit machine.

Luckily Jonathan and Jamie hadn't witnessed this exchange and she sat back down at their table.

A few hours later and they decided to leave; the three of them walked out to the car park. Unbeknown to them the lad who had pinched Evie's bum and his mates followed them out. They hadn't gone more than ten yards when a voice slurred, "Yeah that's the little uptight bitch with the tight arse who can't take a joke, looks like she's having both the brothers tonight though," and his group all sniggered. Jamie whirled round, "Oh Gary Pearson I might have known it'd be you! What rock did you slither out from you little fucker?"

Well that was all it took and the two of them began to brawl. Gary was no match for Jamie; but Gary's mates decided to level the playing field. Two of them held Jamie whilst Gary took a swing at him, luckily Jamie moved just a fraction so that Gary ended up hitting his mate instead. Jonathan stepped in to get Jamie away as Evie looked on not sure quite what to do.

"That's enough okay, come on J, just come away." The three of them went to walk towards their cars when all of a sudden Gary came bowling right back at Jamie and went to grab him from behind. Once again Jamie was too quick for him, but they tussled just as Evie turned round to meet someone's fist in her face. She was thrown backwards banging her arm against the bonnet of a car closely followed by her torso, then her face finally she crumpled onto the ground banging her head on the tarmac in the process. Jonathan watched this play out as if in slow motion one minute she was next to him and then she was lying lifeless on the ground. Suddenly for a second there was silence before all hell broke loose again. The landlord appeared and with the help of two of his regulars restrained Gary (who was well known to everyone in the village), someone called the police and an ambulance and Jonathan just stood over Evie talking to her, holding her hand. But she was out cold.

There was a small crowd now gathered in the car park. THE MAN took a few sly pictures. These should make HIM happy, yes very happy indeed.

Chapter 32

First to arrive on the scene were the police. They knew Gary Pearson of old and hauled him into the back of the police car. Next they questioned Jamie and decided to take him into custody as well, calling for backup. Meanwhile an ambulance had arrived with blue lights flashing into the car park and Evie was examined and placed onto a stretcher. Jonathan sat with her in the back of the ambulance not wanting to leave her for a second. One minute she'd been next to him and then, well, then she was lying on the ground eerily still. He was shaken and wouldn't let go of her hand until the paramedic threatened to throw him out of the vehicle unless he let them do their job. The police took his details and said they would want a statement from him in due course, but allowed him to remain with Evie.

Stirring himself he rang David; yes, he knew he wasn't at A&E anymore but thought he might be able to help.

David picked up after the fourth ring, listened and then said 'Okay I'll meet you at the hospital'. Fiona had wanted to go with him, but they didn't have a babysitter and he promised to call her as soon as he knew anything. The trip to the hospital felt like the longest 30 minutes of Jonathan's life. There was still no response from Evie and they refused to let him go with her as he wasn't family. He had to remain in the waiting room as they took her into A&E and there was absolutely no choice but to sit and wait.

David arrived after half an hour, spoke briefly to Jonathan and then went through to find out what was going on. He still knew a fair number of the staff in that department and it wasn't long before he'd spoken to the registrar on duty and they let him into the screened off cubicle where Evie was being treated. His first thoughts were: bloody hell! she looked a mess, a real mess, what had she been doing? He would need to call her mother once her injuries had been assessed and wasn't looking forward to that one little bit.

Evie was still unconscious but she was in a queue to be taken for x rays on her arm, her ribs and also to have a CT scan on her head. She was oblivious to all of this and once she was placed on a morphine drip for pain relief she wouldn't know anything until at least 24 hours later. One side of her face was a mass of black and blue mixed with purple and red, quite a colour combination. She was admitted and was to remain in A&E until she could be moved. There was nothing more that David could do for the time being so he left her in the capable hands of his colleagues and went to find Jonathan.

"Okay so here is how it's looking at the moment, we'll know more once she'd had her x rays and CT scan and once she's awake. Possibilities are broken or cracked ribs, obviously she has bruising to the face, broken or fractured arm and she's had a nasty bang to the back of her head-that's the most serious out of everything. They'll need to keep her in for observation for internal bleeding so there's nothing more to be done tonight, probably not for 24 hours. I'll call her mother and I suggest you go to the police station, make your statement and get Jamie out of there. Then go home get some sleep and I'll call you tomorrow to let you know when you can come back and see her okay?"

"So there's nothing I can do for 24 hours – are you serious?"

"Very, sorry Jonathan, but you have to let my colleagues take care of her now, I won't tell you not to worry as I know that's exactly what you'll be doing but honestly the best you can do for her now is listen to what I've said and go to Jamie, okay? Jonathan okay? Did you hear me?"

"Um yes, yes go to the police station and get Jamie out and you'll call me. I just feel so helpless, she was standing there next to me and the next minute she was on the floor. It all happened so fast it's a blur. Jesus what a mess, her mother is going to be apoplectic and will blame me no doubt and I haven't even met the woman yet." Sighing he ran his hands through his hair; how did an innocent meal at a pub result in this bloody mess?

David rang Fiona on the way back to his car and relayed the information. Hopefully she'd be just fine but she'd be out of action for at least 4 weeks, possibly 6. He'd let Fiona see her as soon as he could, but it may not be for a couple of days at least. Driving home his thoughts turned to Jonathan, when he'd first started to date Evie, David hadn't been sure that they would get very far; but he'd been proved wrong. In some ways she'd been the making of him over the past few months and to see him so worried about someone other than himself for a change could only be a good thing. He would call Evie's mother once he was at home, he might need a stiff drink before he picked up the phone just in case. Also he'd call the gym tomorrow. Goodness only knows how her boss was going to react as she'd been off work for two weeks only the other month, now this. Well there was nothing more to be done tonight.

Chapter 33

Twenty-four hours later and David and Jonathan were both back at the hospital. Jamie had given the police his statement and been released; but until they'd spoken to Evie he wasn't sure what action if any would be taken. Jonathan had given his statement too; but had been careful not to implicate his brother but had stuck firmly to the line that it all happened so fast blah, blah, couldn't tell who punched who kind of thing, so basically a waste of time on everyone's behalf. He wasn't going to land Jamie in trouble, not that he was entirely sure if it had been Jamie's fault anyway.

The police were really wanting to take Evie's statement but would have to wait like everyone else until she regained consciousness. The CCTV cameras in the pub car park were temporarily out of action so it was all relying on witness statements. David had rung Evie's mother only to discover she was abroad again and had left her a voicemail message to call him back. The worst call ironically had been to Steve, Evie's boss. He was such a nasty little shit, he never even asked how she was, just moaned on and on about how he was trying to run a business, she'd only just recently had two weeks off and now this did he realise just how inconvenient it all was? etc. David had kept his tone polite but had told Steve in no uncertain terms that Evie was lucky to be alive – well okay, that was a huge exaggeration but he'd had it up to here with him and his whining.

Her test results were back and they made for an uncomfortable read: bruised and fractured arm, bruised and cracked ribs, her head injury thank goodness wasn't serious just severe concussion, which could lead to possible dizzy spells, nausea and amnesia, not forgetting the mess that was the left hand side of her face which looked as if she'd done ten rounds in the boxing ring and come off worse by a mile. She bruised easily as it was so her face would be painful and take a while to heal. Her arm was strapped up and she was on pain relief for pretty much everything. There were no signs of internal bleeding and she was going to be released in 48 hours. Not that Evie knew any of this, she was being sedated, but was going to be brought round gradually the next day.

David had made it known that her mother was abroad and had cleared it for Jonathan and Fiona to visit. So on Sunday evening, David took Jonathan to see Evie. At first he thought they'd made some mistake. This couldn't be her surely; but it definitely was. She looked very small and pale, apart from the rest of her face that was black and blue. He took her hand in his and kissed the back of it. He'd always made fun of her small hands, asking for smaller cutlery etc., but now he'd give anything for her to squeeze his hand and let him know she was okay. David checked with the nurse and she assured him that yes, Evie's arm was already strapped up; but they didn't strap ribs anymore and as long as she was awake enough tomorrow then she would be allowed home but with lots of rest for at least a week. He rolled his eyes at that; the last time she had needed enforced rest it had been an absolute nightmare! She would have a weekly visit from a nurse to help her and David was sure that once Evie's mother had been in touch then arrangements would be made for Evie to be very well cared for.

They left together as there was nothing more they could do apart from wait until she had been assessed in the morning and then they had to accept the results whatever they might be. The police were still keen to talk to her but had also been told to come back tomorrow too. David had persuaded Fiona to wait until Evie was at home before seeing her; he didn't want to scare her into thinking it was going as bad as four years ago when she'd ended up in hospital, mind you that had been 1000 times worse than this. Jonathan e-mailed his office and quoted yet another family emergency and he'd be in touch when he knew he'd be back, but it didn't look likely he'd be in this week at all.

So Monday morning and Evie was being brought round gradually. She'd only been aware of bright lights, people talking about things that she couldn't understand and then nothing apart from a sense of drifting which felt very weird. By lunchtime she was awake and so thirsty, the nurse let her take sips of water when what she really wanted was about two litres of the stuff, so frustrating. She was very sore and her ribs ached every time she moved, so no laughing for her for a while. They hadn't given her a mirror as they felt that could wait until she was a little stronger. The doctor had been to see her and said that yes she could go home but not until Tuesday afternoon at the earliest. There were visitors waiting to see her; but the police wanted to speak to her first so he'd show them in; but made it clear it was only for 10 minutes at the most.

Jason Bellamy only had 15 minutes left on his shift when he got the call to interview a witness at the hospital. He was already there having just brought in a suspect who needed to be treated before being taken to the station. He groaned; he could do without this today, now he'd be late finishing and he wanted to get home and do some prep for his Sergeant's exams. He left his colleague Robert and went to locate a Miss E Wallace. He spoke to Evie's doctor who repeated he had 10 minutes and not a minute more and then the curtain was swept back and he came face to face with Evie. She couldn't really see out of one eye as it was bruised and battered but her other eye saw a policeman in uniform and she struggled to sit up.

"No, no don't move, it's fine, I'm Constable Bellamy and I've come to ask you some questions about the incident at The Lamb Inn on Saturday night." She looked a mess make no mistake. Surely she hadn't been fighting? she didn't look the type, but then in his line of work you never could tell these days.

Evie put out her right hand and introduced herself, "How do you do Constable, I'm Evelyn Wallace. How may I help you?"

"I need to find out exactly what you saw and heard that night, are you feeling up to this right now?"

"Well here's the thing: to be honest it's a bit of a blur, but I'll do my best officer," and she gave him a wobbly smile.

He smiled back at her. No she definitely wasn't he fighting type he'd lay money on it. Taking out his notebook he asked her to begin whenever she was ready.

Chapter 34

Evie gave the police officer the barest of information. She had no intention of giving her formal statement until she had spoken to both Jonathan and more importantly Jamie. Citing memory loss and general wooziness she made it clear she was more than happy to help with his investigation when she was feeling up to it. Jason left her well before the ten minutes were up and went back to find his colleague, he was sure there was more she wasn't telling him; but time would tell, after all she was on some quite strong medication.

Finally late on Monday morning Jonathan was able to talk to her for the first time. He took a deep breath and opened the curtain; Jesus she looked worse than he remembered, but he tried to smile and not scare her too much by his reaction.

"Hello sweetheart, how are you feeling?" he took her hand in his and kissed it.

Evie gave the best smile she could give in the circumstances, "Well to be honest I've had better days." She gave a little laugh then immediately grimaced as it hurt so much.

Jonathan was concerned. "Are you okay, should I get the nurse?"

"No, no it's just my ribs hurt when I laugh so no more jollity for me for a while, which will be a struggle. Do you have a mirror – they won't give me one and I want to see how bad it is?

"No, no mirror and don't worry about that, you'll soon be as right as rain." Bloody hell if the nurse wouldn't get her a mirror then there was no way he was going to either.

"How's Jamie, is he okay?"

Trust her to be more worried about someone else, "Jamie's fine, worried about you naturally, well we all were, are if you see what I mean?"

"I think they're letting me home tomorrow, can't wait to be in my own bed with Henry, it's so noisy in hospital I'd forgotten about that."

"Has the doctor spoken to you yet?"

"Yes he's told me about my injuries and he'll give me a list of medication and instructions tomorrow before I'm discharged. Oh and the police were here earlier wanting to talk to me, but I was deliberately very vague so they'll be back later in the week I expect. Why aren't you at work, it's Monday isn't it?"

"Evie are you kidding me, do you honestly think I'd be at work whilst you're lying here in hospital?"

"Well you have a very busy job and it seems to me you are forever taking time off just to look after me and there's only so much slack your boss will give you. Talking of which has anyone called Steve, I bet he's hopping mad?"

"My job is just fine and yes David called Steve. He's a piece of work isn't he, I don't know how you put up with him? Just so you know I'll be looking after you this week at your house and then David is making arrangements." Evie went to interrupt him, but he stopped her, "One thing, you have some very nasty injuries so you can't misbehave as you did before, understood? You've got to behave and let me look after you, okay?" He hoped he sounded firm enough without trying to upset her. To his amazement she agreed without any argument at all; blimey, he thought, she must really be feeling ill if she gives in as easily as that.

Evie was very tired and Jonathan left her with a promise he'd be back tomorrow to collect her and take her home. He bent down to kiss her cheek and realised she was close to tears; he so desperately wanted to take her in his arms, but with her injuries it just wasn't possible, so he squeezed her hand and left. Outside he paused and took some deep breaths; she was hurting a lot more the he'd realized, both physically and mentally. She seemed very fragile and he would do his best to look after her. The fact she'd acquiesced so quickly meant she understood there was to be no messing him about this time.

THE MAN was there again, a few photos later and he was done for the night.

Tuesday afternoon and Jonathan helped Evie out of the car. They were at her house and she was so happy to be home. She walked gingerly to the front door and once inside made straight for her bedroom. She felt peculiar and wanted to lie down, maybe it was all the medication. Jonathan left her to undress; but she called him in to help her with her arm. Dressed in pyjamas she got into bed and was relived just to lie back and rest her whole body. Five minutes later she was asleep. Jonathan made himself at home, he'd checked in on her and she was sleeping, maybe this time there wouldn't be any dramas? He found himself smiling thinking back to the locked bathroom door incident, now it seemed quite funny but at the time it was anything but. Evie slept right through to the following morning. Jonathan slept next to her, careful not to touch her, which was agony of the worst kind. The last time they'd been here together they had, well they'd simply had the best time; he couldn't keep his hands off of her, and now it would be at least 4 or even maybe 6 weeks before they could entertain those thoughts again. Still it would give him plenty of time to decided where to take her on their romantic weekend away; although he wasn't quite sure when she'd be up to that trip now.

The next few days passed off quietly and without any dramas. The worst point came on Wednesday morning when she finally saw her face in the bathroom mirror, she'd been so shocked she couldn't speak and had to sit down.

It was like the elephant in the room with no-one mentioning just how terrible half her face looked. The doctor had given her medication and instructions plus the nurse was calling in on Friday.

Friday turned out to be her favourite day. Fiona came round and they chatted for ages, then the nurse arrived and groceries had been delivered followed by a visit from Constable Bellamy. Citing amnesia, she wasn't any more forthcoming and he'd promised he'd return next week to try again. She desperately wanted to talk to Jamie but that wouldn't be until Saturday at the earliest.

Chapter 35

Jamie knocked on Evie's front door. He'd been desperate to come and see her, but his brother had told him the earliest would be Saturday and not to come a day before.

Jonathan opened the door, "Hi J come on in."

"Hi can I see Evie now?"

"I ought to say no, but I think you need to see her so yes go on up, but she needs to rest okay."

"Okay."

Jamie knocked on her bedroom door and went in; blimey what he saw was so much worse than he'd been imaging. He took in her black eye and could only imagine the rest of her injuries. "I am so bloody sorry. Are you in pain?"

"A bit."

"I ought to go."

"No don't go, I want to talk to you, I'm going crazy just lying here and it's your penance," she smiled, "for doing this to me."

Jamie smiled back, "Okay if I must."

"Just don't make me laugh, it hurts too much."

"Oh fuck I'm so sorry, sorry about everything."

"Jamie stop, it was an accident okay?" An accident plus I am on these amazing meds and am feeling quite peculiar too. "So this Gary, have you known him long?"

"Just some local guy, always seems to wind me up and get under my skin."

"Yes I noticed."

"Sorry."

"Jamie please stop saying sorry; but what have I told you about choosing your battles?"

"I know, but I could have flattened him."

"I know that's probably true, but look what happened instead – you have got to be more careful."

"Yeah I know."

Jonathan entered the room. "Not annoying you is he, cos I can chuck him out if you like?"

"No I want him to stay. We are having a lovely chat aren't we Jamie?"

"He's not supposed to be having a lovely chat – he's supposed to be apologizing for what he's done and feeling remorseful."

"He is, he is, just let us talk please, please?"

He smiled, "Okay, okay; but I will chuck him out if I think he deserves it okay?"

"Okay thank you."

"Oh Jamie. What am I going to do with you? Can you pass me my bag please?"

"Sure where is it?"

"Um over on the windowsill, I think." Jamie passed her the bag.

"Thanks, now I just need to give you a pound."

"A pound. Are you delirious or something?"

"Not quite, but something similar – these meds are a bit strong to be honest, but I think it's time we had a proper chat. Have you told your parents yet?"

"No, they're away until tomorrow and I'm putting it off as quite frankly they will go ballistic."

Evie gave Jamie £1.

"What's this for?"

"Well in order for me to hire a lawyer I think the minimum fee is £1 so once I have given this to you, you are bound by law to listen to what I have to say and cannot under any circumstance repeat it to anyone client/lawyer confidentiality thingy, am I right?"

He smiled, "Kind of, but I'm not even qualified yet."

"I know, but that, young Jamie, is the whole point."

He looked at her. "I don't understand."

"Jamie, just take the pound and I will explain everything to you okay."

"Okay."

"Okay, so now you are my lawyer."

"Right," he smiled

"And I am going to tell you something which you cannot repeat to anyone okay?"

"Okay."

"Okay here's the thing. The reason the police keep calling me is that I haven't made a formal statement yet. Every time they ask me I give them the same reply, I can't remember /it's all a blur/very fuzzy etc., etc."

"Well that's true isn't it?"

"Umm no not entirely."

"Go on."

"Well the thing is I do remember, I remember everything that happened well at least until I blacked out."

"You do?"

"Yes."

"So you know it was me that hit you and not Gary?"

"Yes that's right."

"I don't understand."

"Oh Jamie for a bright chap you can be a bit dim sometimes." she took his hand.

"Let me explain. If I give the police the true version on my formal statement and tell them I don't want to press charges there's no guarantee that the CPS won't ignore my wishes and decide to make an example out of you so you'll be charged and have a criminal record."

"Yes but I don't see."

"Quiet, let me finish – if you're charged and found guilty you can't practice law anymore it's all over and I won't and I can't let that happen to you."

He slumped back in his chair. She was right; he hadn't even thought about that until now. "I can't let you do this, Evie, you can't lie to the police."

"I admit I thought long and hard about it," she smiled, "now if you had been studying a different degree well that would have been a whole different ball game and I may have chosen to come clean, but no, Jamie, I have never been more certain of anything."

"You'd do that for me, you'd lie to the police, which I don't have to tell you is also an offence?"

"Yes, but I am thinking of it as a white lie and you are far too smart not to get a brilliant degree and become an amazing lawyer and I for one want to see that happen do you understand?"

"Yes I think so."

"So you cannot tell anyone about this – ever. If you tell the police I will deny everything and say I was high on medication and didn't know what I was saying so we have a deal?"

"I don't like it."

"You don't have to like it – just live with it, you must start to choose your battles Jamie."

"Does Jonathan know?"

"No and he must never know, the best thing you can do is learn from this get your degree and pas the bar and have a wonderful career as a top lawyer. Jamie you can't throw away opportunities like this; although my mother would be livid of she found out."

Jonathan entered the room, "Now can I throw him out?"

"No we are just getting started."

"You're overdoing things."

"No I am only using my tongue and my tonsils and believe you me us girls are well practiced in the art of waggling both of them all of the time."

"Okay okay."

"I would like an orange juice though – Jamie glass of juice?"

"Yes please."

"You're kidding you actually want me to bring him juice?"

"Yes do it for me please Jonathan for me?"

"Okay okay," he left, poured out two glasses of juice but on climbing the stairs he decided to stop and sit on the top stair listening, he was intrigued what did she want to talk to Jamie about?

"Now for the second secret."

"There's more?"

"Oh yes indeedy. You remember a few weeks ago your brother took me for a track day at Silverstone?"

"Yes he said you had the best time, even though he lost."

"Yes well he was always going to lose."

"How so?"

"Well I used to have an Aston myself; she was so beautiful, I loved that car so I had a lot of experience driving her on track days and such like and I couldn't believe it when that was our date I was so excited."

"They're very expensive."

"So what's your point?"

"Sorry, just not sure ow you could afford one that's all."

"Oh there you go assuming again. It's a very dangerous thing to do; that's secret three, but you are getting way ahead of yourself here."

Jonathan was all intrigued now. What was the first secret, he wondered?

"How come you don't have it any more?"

"Oh lots of reasons," she was deliberately vague – "not very practical for where I live, fed up of being chased around and tailgated by young boys just too much hassle. So you see Jonathan was always going to lose that battle, do you see what I am trying to tell you, you can't know everything, but when you're a lawyer you'll need to find out everything you can about your client; not just what they decide to tell you but more importantly about what they are not telling you and never ever make any assumptions do you see.?"

"Yes I am beginning to. But Jonathan has," he didn't finish his sentence

Jonathan came crashing through the door. He didn't want Jamie to tell her he had lied to her about his car not now anyway.

They were both startled. "Oh my, it's like a herd of elephants," she laughed, "oh oww oww mustn't laugh too much, forgot it hurts."

"Juice, you two?"

"Thank you."

"Now please tell me I can throw him out?"

"No not yet. I haven't finished my talk and I need him to realise the error of his ways. I promise I will be super quiet tomorrow to make up for it."

Evie she looked at him and pleaded with her eyes.

"Well if you're sure?"

"Yes very sure."

"Okay then," and he left the room and took up his position on the stairs; he didn't like being left out

"Now secret three. When I first met Jonathan I couldn't work out why he was still single."

"Oh I can tell you."

"Jamie behave."

"Okay sorry, go on."

"Well it occurred to me that maybe he was very picky or maybe your parents didn't approve of his choice of girlfriend."

"My parents, God you haven't met them yet have you? Don't approve! You're not wrong there. They see every girl as a potential gold digger, they don't stand a chance – oh sorry Evie, wasn't thinking."

"So they think every girl is after his money?"

"Yeah something like that."

"Jamie you are priceless. –You haven't met my mother. She is super protective of Thomas and me and she would eat Jonathan for breakfast without batting an eyelid. She's quite amazing and I love her to bits, she was very strong when my dad died."

"How did he die?"

"In a plane crash. There was nothing anyone could do; but the hardest thing was not saying goodbye to him; that still hurts even now. And now as you're my lawyer I can tell you that I don't need Jonathan's money – if he had any that is because I have my own money; it's not outrageous or anything, I mean I'm not a bloody arms dealer or anything; but if anything my mother should be grilling him, not the other way round. You look confused. Look, when my father died it turned out he had some investments which we didn't know about and I have to say they have done rather well so I am well and truly provided for."

"But you live in a small cottage, drive an old car and work at the gym; is this a wind up?"

"No it's not scouts honour."

"Girls can't be scouts."

"Good point." Jamie opened his mouth to speak she held her hand up, "Just let me finish okay?"

"I don't need a big house; there's only me and Henry, maybe someday when I have a husband then yes I'll think about it, but I'm very happy in my home. I've ordered my new car, but I get very attached to the silliest of things and it just seems so wasteful as there's nothing wrong with my car and the reason I work is that I love my job, I love the people and it's very uplifting exercising every day, I did have a professional career once, but decided to take a different path."

"How come?"

"Oh something happened. I won't explain now, but one day I might tell you although I probably need to tell Jonathan first."

"Fair enough."

"I want people to like me for being me not because I live in a fancy house and drive a flashy car and sit on charity committees with my picture in the paper; don't get me wrong I give to charity. I meet with my financial advisor every month and we decide what to do etc."

"You have a financial advisor?"

"Yep I sure do."

"Do you trust him?"

"With my life."

"Right."

"So you see Jamie you must never assume anything about anyone until you know all the facts and the best thing you can do for me right now is get a first class degree, pass the bar and start your career, I won't let you throw that all away before your life has truly begun, but if you make another stupid mistake remember you may not be so lucky next time. Now I need to tell you more about my mother and what you're up against."

They laughed together

"She sounds interesting."

"She is she's amazing."

Jonathan was still and thoughtful on the stairs. This girl, this wonderful girl just got even more amazing. But he still didn't know what she'd done for his brother.

"God Evie you're the best can I hug you?"

Jonathan entered the room, "No you definitely cannot now bugger off and leave Evie in peace."

Chapter 36

The rest of Saturday flashed by. Evie would be allowed to get up as from Monday and her mother would be flying back and be with her from Tuesday. She knew that Jonathan's parents were due back tomorrow but she had never felt less like meeting them. Oh she was sure they were very nice and all that, but looking like she did was hardly going to make the best first impression. Jonathan only had one more day with her before he too had to return to work. She had assured him she would be just fine and they would call and text all week until he was home again on Friday. He didn't like it, but had no choice but to put up with it.

His parents were back too and he'd been over to see them on Sunday evening explaining how they wouldn't be meeting his girlfriend after all as she'd been involved in an accident. He left Jamie out of the picture for the time being, they needed to wait to see what action if any would be taken by the police and the family lawyer seemed to have everything under control. He'd stressed that their lawyer wasn't to mention any of this to his parents, not until they knew for sure what the outcome would be.

Jonathan said his goodbyes to Evie; he'd never felt less like leaving her; but David assured him that everything was taken care of and she would be perfectly okay until her mother arrived. On Monday evening Evie and Jonathan spoke on the phone. She told him she was just fine, she'd been up and about and had spent some time in the garden with Henry and that yes she was taking her medication.

Evie's mother duly appeared on Tuesday, took one look at her daughter and promptly burst into tears. This was so unexpected that it took Evie by surprise.

"Hello Mum, sorry you had to cut short your holiday."

"Oh Evie, I leave you for 5 minutes and look what happens, what am I going to do with you? I want to hug you so tightly, but I'm guessing I can't do that without hurting you at the minute?"

Evie smiled, "That's right, but enough with the tears okay, I'm going to be just fine, it's just going to take a few weeks for everything to heal that's all. And before you ask, yes I am eating properly and taking my medication, Henry is just fine too. He was a bit freaked out when he first saw me as he recognized my voice, but I guess I don't exactly look the same as before."

"Sweetheart, what do you need me to do? Would you like some juice or something to eat?"

Evie laughed quietly, "Oh mum I'm fine, why don't you unpack, have a shower and I'll meet you in the kitchen then we'll have some tea and a good catch up okay?"

Later that day, Evie and her Mother were sat outside in the sunshine. It was just so good sometimes to feel the warmth of the sun on your skin, made you feel relaxed and at ease with yourself.

"So when am I going to meet this new boyfriend of yours? You haven't exactly told me a whole lot about him you know. So come on all the details. Plus, is he the one to blame for you looking like this?"

Evie smiled, she had left this conversation for too long and so duly told her mother the usual things, where he lived, what he did for a living, how they met etc. And that no he wasn't responsible for her injuries, again she was careful to leave Jamie out of it. Her mother didn't need to know all the finite details, just the gist would be more than enough for now. Her mother seemed satisfied.

They spent the rest of the week just pottering about. The only thing Evie needed help with really was washing her hair and she assured her mother that the nurse would be in every Friday to help her with this until she was able to do it for herself. It was agreed that her mother would stay until midday on Friday as to be honest there wasn't a whole lot she could do. Evie had it all under control. Her groceries were being delivered and everything else was only either a phone call or the click of a mouse away. So Friday came and she said goodbye to her mother, she promised she would call her if she needed her and kissed her before she drove away. Having waved her mother off, less that ten minutes later a police car was outside and Constable Bellamy was back yet again to try to take her formal statement. Realising she'd fobbed him off for too long she welcomed him inside and made him some tea before beginning to talk.

Evie started off by explaining about her bottom being pinched and then leaving the pub, "So you see I can remember so much up to the point of the three of us walking across the pub car park and then nothing. The doctors did say this was perfectly normal in the circumstances and that my memory of the remaining night may or may not return. I hope this has been helpful?"

Jason looked down at his notes. Well it looked as if they wouldn't be able to charge anyone with her assault, and the landlord didn't want to press charges as there wasn't any damage to his property, so unless they charged the two lads with breach of the peace or something then it was just not worth the paperwork. He'd follow this up when he typed her statement later at the station. Then he'd have to come out to her just once more to get her to read and sign it as she wouldn't be able to drive for at least another 3 weeks at the earliest. He noticed she was healing well; there wouldn't be any lasting damage she'd just been in the wrong place at the wrong time kind of thing. Making his excuses he left her to the rest of her day and drove back into town.

Chapter 37

Shortly after 6.00pm and Jonathan's car was outside. He couldn't wait to see her, hopefully she would be feeling a whole lot better and look less battered and bruised than a week ago. Evie opened her front door and he was there in the hallway as if he'd never left 6 days before.

"Hello, you did you miss me?" she asked him shyly.

He held her very gently as she was much too sore for his usual welcome tonight, "You have no idea." And then he kissed her softly.

She grimaced slightly as her face was still a mess, but that would heal soon enough and then they would pick up exactly where they left off hopefully. He was a little relieved that her mother had left earlier that day, there would be plenty of time for the meet the parent's ordeal.

They spent the weekend just being together, listening to music. Evie despaired when he had no clue about popular music, but she relented and let him choose his favourite radio station. They ate and read and even Henry seemed to be more at ease with Jonathan this time too. At night they held hands in bed until one of them fell asleep and then woke together with a gentle morning kiss to start the day. She texted Jamie giving him some advice about his current girlfriend troubles. She smiled to herself, thank goodness she wasn't that young again when everything seemed like the world depended on just the tiniest thing. All too soon, their weekend was over and it was back to work for Jonathan and back to her new routine at home for Evie. She had initially thought that being at home for an enforced period of time would drive her crazy but she had amazed herself when she found she was actually quite enjoying it.

Jason Bellamy was sat at his computer. Bloody thing was playing up again and it kept freezing and then losing the last thing he'd typed. This was driving him nuts; it was bad enough to be stuck there on a Sunday evening as it was without this to annoy him too. Swearing out loud at the screen his colleague called over, "Look I'm off now. Do you want to borrow my computer, just remember to sign me out before you leave okay?"

Jason shouted over his thanks. At least he would be able to finish his report and then move on with something else. He moved desks and began to type. Something strange appeared on the screen. His colleague had a higher security clearance than he did, and it was asking him if he wanted to see the EW case file that would have normally been off limits to him. Looking round the office to check that he was alone, he thought: well why not? He was curious to see that she even had a previous case file on record and he clicked on the word yes and began to read.

Fifteen minutes later and Jason clicked on the final page which brought up countless photos of her injuries when she had arrived at hospital over four years ago. He couldn't take it all in. This case had been on the news, but her identity had been protected and yet here she was. This was definitely the same Evelyn Wallace that had given him her formal statement such as it was only two days previously. Resting his hands behind his head he sat back in his chair and exhaled. Bloody hell, bloody hell! He did not see that coming in a million years.

Late on Tuesday afternoon Jason arrived back outside Evie's house. He'd brought her formal statement which he needed her to read and sign and then he'd be on his way. Question was could he treat her in exactly the same way as last week before he'd seen what he shouldn't have seen on her file? Taking a deep breath, he got out of the squad car. Evie opened the door and offered him some tea or coffee. He accepted coffee as he still had another 4 hours remaining on his shift plus her coffee was actually really good. Making himself at home sitting at the kitchen table, he thought this was a very nice home and it always seemed to have a very welcoming atmosphere. Still compared to a lot of the shitholes he found himself in on a fairly regular basis it was a little slice of heaven. Accepting the cup he noticed that her face was looking a lot better now, soon she'd be able to go out and with a bit of make up on she would look almost back to normal.

He passed the statement over for her to read and let his mind wander. So this girl had been in the wrong place at the wrong time twice now; this recent pub fracas was relatively minor and she'd be absolutely fine after a few weeks of rest; but he began to wonder about the first time. How did you get over something like that, was it even possible to move on? It didn't bear thinking about. He shook his head, refocused on Evie and drank his coffee.

During the next few weeks Evie stuck to pretty much the same routine and the bruises were fading nicely. She'd purchased some expensive cream for her face and was pleased to see that it was working well. The nurse was no longer needed so it was just her and Henry for most of the time, plus Fiona when she could spare the time to pop over. Her friends dropped in unannounced any evening they were free and she caught up on all their girly gossip. Who needed to go out, she thought, when everything and everyone came to you? Jonathan arrived every Friday night and although he wasn't happy to be away from her it was just the way it was going to have to be. Obviously he missed being intimate with her especially after their recent weekends together, but he had no choice but to be patient.

After 3 weeks she arranged for a taxi to take her to see David at the surgery. He wanted to check on her progress and general health. She'd been feeling a bit odd lately, but put it down to her coming off her medication and her body starting to cope by itself. David was pleased she was healing well and in another three weeks she'd be almost back to normal. He told her that there was to be no sex for another couple of weeks and although she'd blushed until kingdom come she was glad he'd spelt it out, It would give her something to text Jonathan about tonight, she thought. She wandered into the High Street, glad to be out of the house and making the most of the fresh air. In the supermarket Evie smiled to herself. This had been where she had first met Jonathan; it seemed like ages ago now. They'd come such a long way together in such a short space of time; she was happy, so happy for the first time in years. Her taxi dropped her home; she felt suddenly tired, it had been quite a day all in all and she thought an early night wouldn't hurt.

Chapter 38

Evie was so excited, she could hardly contain herself as she settled into the first class seat. The 7.12 was due to depart in few minutes and then she would be in London to see Jonathan after 9.00am. Boy was he in for a surprise. Hopefully he'd be pleased to see her, after all it was her who didn't like surprises; he didn't share her loathing of them. Mind you when she thought back to her last surprise she'd bought for him he was almost speechless; the new lingerie had been money very well spent she giggled to herself. Her train was on time and she hailed a taxi to take her to his office although once in reception his secretary informed her that he wasn't due in until 11.00 and had she forgotten? Thinking nothing of this, Evie hailed yet another black cab and was in the lift up to his apartment within ten minutes.

THE MAN was loitering outside the hotel when he saw her pull up in a taxi. Well well then, this was unexpected, he'd hang about for a bit and see what was happening.

She had a piece of luck when on rounding the corner to his door she spied a cleaner going into the opposite apartment and begged her to use her pass key to let her in. Yes she knew it was against all the rules, but she wanted to surprise her boyfriend, surely she understood? It was a done deal and in seconds Evie was stood in Jonathan's apartment.

Strange but she could hear voices as she made her way into the living room, maybe he had the TV on? Suddenly she heard a woman's voice say, 'Have you seen my earring?' Evie froze and her overnight bag plopped on to the floor beside her feet. She couldn't move. What was happening? Then the bedroom door opened and a woman wearing just her bra and pants came through the door, but stopped abruptly when she saw Evie.

"Oh hello," she purred, then shouted through to the bedroom, "Darling you have company."

Jonathan's voice rang out, "Look Alexa I've had enough of your games. What's going on?" and he appeared next to her wearing his boxers and trying to do up his shirt buttons. He saw Evie and stopped dead in his tracks. He swallowed hard and felt faint. Evie had turned a shade of white and couldn't get her mouth to work, her head was meanwhile working overtime.

"Evie what are you doing here? It's Thursday. You know I'll be home tomorrow. Is everything okay?"

Still nothing from Evie, no movement no sound; just her face struggling to take in the scene in front of her. Then Jonathan made the biggest mistake, "Look Evie I can explain," and he took two steps towards her.

MUSIC: – LEAVE RIGHT NOW – WILL YOUNG.

Evie turned and ran, not stopping to pick up her bag. She ran out of the door and along the corridor round the corner to the lift, luckily someone was leaving the lift and she shouted to them, "Please hold the lift I'm coming." Once in the lobby she went out of the side door and walked quickly away; she needed to leave and hailed a taxi. The cabbie asked her where she wanted to go but she had no idea and said the first thing that came into her head, "Big Ben please." She sat back, her ribs ached as she shouldn't have been running anywhere. Over and over in her mind she was asking herself what to do now, where to go. She needed help and fast.

THE MAN saw her leave and waited for Dempsey to follow. He had a bit of a wait but he did emerge eventually.

Suddenly she knew and gave the cabbie a different address and sat back feeling sick, numb and in a daze. She arrived at Peter's office and explained that no she didn't have an appointment, but that it was very urgent. She only had to wait a minute before she was ushered through to Peter's office. Immediately she sat down to wait before her legs gave way.

Peter rushed in. This was unexpected and he had a very bad feeling about it. He couldn't get any sense out of her, so he gave Evie a glass of water, held her hand and said, "Okay just tell me." In less than quarter of an hour Evie was in Peter's chauffeur car being driven to her mother's house. Next he called Fiona and gave her a list of instructions, he spoke to Evie's mother and then finally he called Ian.

Meanwhile Jonathan was dressed, called his office to say he won't be in today after all and then called Alan his driver to take him straight to Evie's. En route he called Jamie who surprisingly picked up, "Hey J do you know the address of Evie's mother?" Jonathan didn't know if Evie was there, but it was worth a try.

"Um no sorry I don't, hang on I'll ask the guys." Jamie turned to his friends, "any of you know Evie's mum's address?"

Will asked why, Jamie just shrugged and said Jon needed to know. They all shook their heads. Francis looked down at the floor, he didn't know what was going on, but it didn't look good, he did know the address, but figured if Evie hadn't given it to her boyfriend then it must have been for a good reason and he certainly wasn't going to let on he knew it.

"Sorry Jon but no we don't, is everything alright?"

Jonathan sighed, "No not really J, in fact it's all gone wrong." Then he hung up.

After what seemed like the longest two hours of his life Jonathan's car pulled up outside Evie's house. He found Fiona's car there plus another car he didn't recognize. Fiona was in the kitchen.

"Is she here, I need to see her talk to her?"

Fiona glared at him. "No she's not here," she spat at him.

"I don't believe you."

"Okay then knock yourself out and go and look, but I'm telling you she's not here."

He saw Henry in his travel basket and bag of groceries, Fiona was putting things into a small wheelie case, books, hairbrush etc.

"Okay if she's not here then where is she – you must know that?"

"Even if I did I wouldn't tell you."

"Won't or can't?"

"Both."

"Where is Henry going?"

"Oh he's going on his holidays aren't you?" and she pushed her finger through the front and tickled his head.

"I need to see her we need to talk."

"Well you should have thought about that before."

"I don't need a lecture from you."

"No probably not, but if I was a man I'd have punched you by now."

Fiona went outside carrying Henry. "Hello if you could take Henry then I'll bring out the rest?"

Fiona took out two more bags and said, "That's everything now thank you."

Jonathan went outside and asked the driver, "Where are you going, I have to know?" But the driver didn't answer, got back in the car, started the engine and drove away.

Jonathan walked back inside to the kitchen.

"Happy now?" He shouted at her

"Oh yes I'm ecstatic," she shouted back at him, "my best friend has been fucked over." She laughed despairingly. "God, how ironic that is, yes she has literally been fucked over by you and you think I'm happy – you don't know the half of it-it's not all about you, you know?"

He slumped into a kitchen chair, "You don't understand."

"Too damn right I don't understand."

"I need to show you something."

"Well funnily enough I'm not in the mood for show and tell, I'd have thought you'd have figured that one out by now."

"Please Fiona. I have to show you something, just one thing and then I'll leave I promise."

Fiona sat down, "I don't know why you're even still here, but go on I'm listening."

"Wait here," – he went to his car and brought out Evie's bag

He placed it on the kitchen table – "She left this at my apartment."

"No surprise I bet she couldn't get out of there fast enough."

"Fair point but I couldn't understand why she was there, it didn't make sense."

"Believe you me nothing makes sense lately."

"I didn't look in the bag until I was on the way here," Jonathan took out a small oblong box, "I found this," he placed it on the table.

"God she'd even brought you a present, priceless bloody priceless."

He continued, "The thing is the message on the tag didn't make any sense, it says for us... normally...," Fiona interrupted him

"Believe you me none of this is normal."

He waited for her to shut up.

"Well it would say to you from me or to Jonathan from Evie, but it doesn't. It says for us, and then I opened it."

He pushed the box over to Fiona, "Look inside."

God she didn't want to look; but had to, she opened the box and her eyes nearly fell out of her head for wrapped in a box in pink/blue striped paper was a pregnancy testing stick with the words 3-4 weeks.

Evie was pregnant.

Chapter 39

As soon as Jonathan had left, Fiona called her husband, "Hi it's me. Things have just got a whole lot worse."

David listened and after ending the call was thinking 'Shit, shit, shit.' He needed to make some calls and fast.

Evie had arrived at her mother's and using her key went inside to wait for Henry and her luggage. She'd had a couple of hours or more to start to think things through and it had been surprisingly simple. She would raise the baby herself, she didn't need Jonathan bloody Dempsey for anything, not his money, not his fancy cars, his stuck up parents – nothing.

Her mother would be home tomorrow, Friday and they would talk things through together just like the old times. They had been through tough times before with the death of her father and Evie's accident so this would be just another thing to get through. The Wallaces were made of tough stuff and wouldn't be fucked over by anyone. It had been a stroke of genius for her to go to Peter, he knew exactly what to do and he was always so calm about it too.

Henry had duly arrived and she let him out into the utility, giving him his favourite food and some milk. She would spend maybe a week or so here, as she wasn't expected back at the gym for another two weeks.

Jonathan was driven back to London. He had to be in the office for tomorrow as they had an important meeting which he just couldn't miss. In the car he let things play over and over in his head until he thought he might actually throw up. When she'd been ill and had to have enforced bedrest at his house Jamie had assumed Evie was pregnant and Jonathan had been devastated that she wasn't pregnant with his child. Only now due to some miracle she was expecting their baby and he'd fucked everything up in the most dramatic way possible. He spent a sleepless night tossing and turning. He had no idea how to fix this, none what so ever. The following morning, Margaret knocked on his office door, "Sir, there's a courier here with a letter; but he won't accept my signature it needs to be yours." Sighing Jonathan made his way over to the reception desk, and signed for the letter. Taking it back into his office he saw it was from London Lawyers Digby and Brown. They had a fierce reputation. Ripping it open he started to read the contents then sank into his office chair and had to read it all over again. It was an official letter known as 'Cease and Desist'; it explained there was to be absolutely no contact in any form what so ever between himself and Evelyn until after the birth of the baby. Now what was he going to do?

THE MAN had watched the courier arrive at SCD with a letter, he wondered what it was; but that was going to be impossible to find out.

Evie spent time just relaxing at her mothers, who was naturally over the moon about the baby and a lot less so about the boyfriend who was by now ancient history. Visits from both David and Ian helped enormously; but most days she just felt numb and went for long walks until she was able to run again. David made her turn her phone on and they went through it together. So after 6 weeks of recovery from the pub accident she wanted to go back to work on Monday, she needed her old routine and was allowed to drive.

Once back at home Evie volunteered for any classes she could, trying to make up for taking a lot of time off recently. She made her class work harder whilst she took it slightly easier, not that her pregnancy was common knowledge, it was far too soon for that to be shouted from the rafters. Her boss Steve was away for two weeks' holiday and the whole staff had two weeks of peace; there was a brilliant atmosphere and the clients were cheerful and happy. Two weeks later and the gym was closing up, it had been a busy Saturday and Sean the assistant manager had left Miles in charge.

"Goodnight Miles, oh I nearly forgot. I just need to get something from my locker, I won't be a sec."

"No Problem." Miles was happy to wait, he hadn't got any plans for that evening anyway.

Time ticked by and Miles was thinking how strange that Evelyn didn't say goodnight, it wasn't like her and he went to set the alarm. Just before he pressed in the code he couldn't escape a niggling feeling, something wasn't right. He walked towards the ladies changing room and pushed the door open, on seeing that the lights were still on, "Evelyn are you still here?" No reply, but he wasn't convinced so he opened the door to the ladies' cloakroom and tried again, "Evelyn are you still here?" At first there was nothing then a muffled sound, he walked in and called her name trying the doors, the second one was locked, "Evelyn are you in there are you okay?" He could hear her crying now and talking to herself.

"Evelyn I'm getting worried now," he tried the door but it was locked. "Evelyn can you open the door? Evelyn can you open the door please?" he spoke quietly, but he thought she needed his help.

Ever so faintly he heard her voice, "No I don't think so."

"Okay I'm going have to open it myself is that okay?" No response. "Evelyn did you hear what I just said, I'm going to open the door now?"

He lifted himself up over the top of the door and saw her, holy mother of God what had happened? She looked white as a sheet, she was crying and distressed, he leant over the top of the door and reached to the catch; good job he had long arms. Dropping himself down he opened the door, it wouldn't open fully but it was enough to be able to see her and talk to her

"Evelyn I want to help you, tell me what I can do, Evelyn tell me what you need."

After what seemed like an hour but could only have been 20 seconds or so she said so quietly he could barely hear.

"I need a doctor."

Oh she was sick. He felt relieved, almost. "Okay I can take you to the doctors."

"No you don't understand. I need to go to the hospital."

"What's wrong, is it serious?"

She gave a small laugh. "Yes you could say that." – Then silence

"Evelyn, you're not making any sense."

"I think I'm having a miscarriage. I'm losing the baby."

MUSIC: – EVERYBODY HURTS – REM.

Chapter 40

Miles didn't have a car and wasn't insured to drive Evie's so he called 999 and waited for the ambulance. It was early on a Saturday night so there might be a delay; but it pulled up within 30 minutes and he let the paramedics into the gym. After what seemed like ages, they took Evie out in a wheelchair and he locked the gym and went with her. On arrival at hospital they wouldn't let him through so he sat in the waiting area; he wasn't going anywhere until he knew she was going to be okay. Sometime later a nurse came out to find him. "What did she tell you?" Miles briefly explained. "Okay we need to contact her family. There's nothing more you can do here tonight so I suggest you go home okay?" Reluctantly Miles left. Why do some people get all the bad luck? he thought to himself. She'd been in and out of hospital for weeks now. When was she going to get a break?

David got the call at home and made his way to the hospital. On arrival he spoke briefly to his colleagues and then called his wife and then Evie's mother. The question now was should he call Jonathan; on that issue the jury was well and truly out. Evie's miracle baby was lost and she had never felt so lost herself either. In the days that followed she was really struggling and Ian had to be called out more than once to see her at home. Her friends were supportive but none of them really understood what she'd been through. There was no word from Jonathan which surprised her immensely; but she decided that ship had long sailed.

THE MAN watched as Dempsey went through airport security. So he was off to New York, by himself too, maybe his romance had bitten the dust. If it had then HE would be elated and might even give him a bonus.

Weeks later and Evie was at home. She'd resigned from the gym as she just couldn't take any more. She didn't really need the money, so removed herself from all social situations and became focused on running and keeping her mind active on a day to day basis. Henry was her single most steadfast companion, almost sensing her loss he wouldn't be parted from her for a second and would wait anxiously for her to return from her daily run. She spent hours in her small gym trying to get herself back to her physical peak, but it was a struggle. Jason Bellamy was still popping round from time to time, saying he was just passing and how was she doing after the pub fracas. No charges had been brought and the whole thing was forgotten. She always made him some coffee and offered to help him study for his sergeant's exams. She encouraged him to join her on her runs as you couldn't really run and talk at the same time so it didn't make any difference to her really. Evie had gone to her friend Alice's wedding. She hadn't really wanted to go at all; but this was Alice who had stuck with her through thick and thin and once she was there she almost began to enjoy herself. She danced with Mr Hunter and with Alice's brother Angus too. She would have felt so guilty if she'd baled plus that just wasn't her style, or at least it never used to be.

She went to see Fiona. On opening her front door Fiona was shocked to see just how terrible her best friend was looking. Over a cup of tea they began to chat.

"So it's all over yet again, why do I keep putting myself through this Fi why? I should have listened to you and David; but oh no I knew better and I gave him a second chance after the coffee shop nightmare – why will I never learn?"

Fiona held Evie's hand, she was hurting so much, both with Jonathan cheating on her and then her losing the baby, this would be a lot for anyone to cope with; but after what her friend had already been through well it was too much, way too much.

"Well far better to find out now that he's a cheat I suppose. Yes, I know it doesn't make it any easier and right now you're feeling low and lost; but it will get better you just need some time." Fiona took a deep breath, "As for losing the baby, I know it's devastating for you; but generally there's a reason. I know it was your miracle baby; but I think you need to see Ian and talk this all through. Promise me you'll call him and if there's anything you need you call me or David day or night?"

"I was an idiot, I really thought he was the one, I really loved him-I gave him so many chances-chances to leave; but he didn't take any of them and what with the baby well it would have been perfect – too perfect I suppose."

Evie left after an hour there were more tears; just when she thought she was all cried out, they reappeared like some nightmare pantomime constantly calling out, "They're behind you!"

One Saturday afternoon her mobile pinged. It was Jamie. Now she felt really guilty as she hadn't been in touch with him since, well since that day in London. Reading the message, he wanted her to go over and watch the footie with them he hadn't see her for ages etc.; it would be fun! Texting him back she wrote:-

Hi J. Sorry, not great company at the moment. Can I take a rain check? – SEND

No, am not taking no for an answer, it's been far too long Wallace so am coming over to pick you up in 30 mins, no arguments! – SEND

J I don't know – who's with you? – SEND

Just me and the boys. They've missed you too. – SEND

She had to ask but this would be the first time she mentioned his name in months.
Is Jonathan going to be there? – SEND

No he's still in New York –SEND

What was he doing in New York? she wondered, but it didn't matter he wouldn't be there, so okay she would go.
Okay you've worn me down, come and get me – SEND.

Jamie waited outside her house and she was out the door in seconds. On getting into his car she remembered the last time she had been in the black Golf and what had happened with a pair of knickers; that was such a long time ago now. Jamie thought she looked terrible, but wisely kept that thought to himself. As he had promised it was just him and his mates, who were very glad to see her, but also thought she looked a bit grim, not the lively Evie they remembered. Sitting in an armchair with her feet dangling over the side she watched her team play quite well. They were leading two nil at half time and Jamie had been right, she had enjoyed it. They wandered out into the kitchen and helped themselves to beer and Evie had a glass of water. She caught up on all their news; they were in their final year now and they had to actually do some serious studying.

Will, George and Francis went back to watch the second half whilst Jamie and Evie remained at the kitchen table. She hated to ask, but needed to know, "So what's Jonathan doing in New York then?"

"Um I thought you knew, he's been there for weeks/ months ever since you and he, well you know broke up – kind of thing."

"Oh, we broke up kind of thing. I see…"

"What do you mean?"

"How much did he tell you?"

"Not a lot, well nothing really, only it was over between the two of you – he didn't elaborate."

"No I bet he bloody didn't."

"What do you mean? I just thought it was the weirdest thing though to be honest."

"I'm not sure I should be telling you any of this."

"Well I'd like to know, I'm a pretty good listener."

"Okay but just for the record you asked me to tell you, I'm not out to deliberately make anyone look bad."

"Fair enough – I know you wouldn't; but I would like to know the truth."

"Well as you know I was recovering from that incident in the pub car park, things had been great between your brother and I up until then. I don't know maybe he got bored of waiting, but we couldn't… well we weren't allowed to have sex for 6 weeks."

Jamie put his hand up, "Too much information," and laughed.

"Sorry but I have to spell it out otherwise the rest of it won't make any sense."

"Okay go on."

"So after 3 of 4 weeks I decide to go up to London for the day to surprise him as I had some exciting news, I get a very early train and he's not at his office so I go to the apartment and basically find him with another woman."

Jamie looks stunned, "Really …another woman …oh my God Evie I'm so sorry… he never mentioned that."

"You've nothing to be sorry for Jamie. So naturally I leave, I'm a bit shy not like the fast city girls he's obviously used too. Maybe he missed all that, I don't know but I haven't heard a word from him since. Didn't know he was in New York or anything. There's more if you feel up to hearing it?"

"Um yes of course go on." Jamie's thoughts were reeling, Jon never mentioned he'd been having an affair.

"Well here's the thing, the exciting news I went to tell him was that I or rather we were going to have a baby."

Jamie excitedly interrupted her, "Oh my God, for real?"

She interrupted him again, "Not so fast Jamie, okay? So yes I went to tell him the news, but obviously he literally had his hands full with other things so I decided to bring up the baby by myself. Only… only… (Evie began to cry) about four or five weeks later I was at work and I had a miscarriage, I lost the baby and now I'm a bloody mess to be honest." She wiped her eyes. They chatted for a bit more until Evie said, "I think I'd like to go home now if you don't mind?"

Jamie drove her home in silence. His head was spinning. What had his brother been thinking? He only had to wait another two weeks and then they'd have been back together. As for Evie being pregnant, well she'd told him it wasn't possible so she must have been elated to find out she was having a miracle baby only for that to be taken away from her too. No wonder she hadn't been in touch, his brother had behaved appallingly, Jamie didn't know if he would speak to him ever again. If Jon knew that Evie had lied to the Police just so that Jamie wouldn't have a criminal record – would it have made any difference? Who knew?

Evie got out of the car, thanked Jamie and went inside. She thought it would've made her feel better to get it out into the open, but if anything it had made her feel worse. Why did she feel so guilty when she'd done nothing wrong?

Chapter 41

Jamie had hardly slept all night. He just didn't know what to do. Realising it was now the morning he padded downstairs to the kitchen and turned his mobile over and over in his hands. Eventually he scrolled down his contact list and pressed call.

In Seattle Jonathan was in bed but not asleep. This conference had been dull, if this was how life in the USA was going to pan out he'd rather have been at home. His mobile began to vibrate and thankful of the distraction he swung his legs out of bed and walked into the living area pressing accept.

Hey Jon it's me.

Hey J are you okay?

Yeah well no, well not really

You're worrying me now, are you hurt?

No I just need to talk to you, is now a good time?

Well it's 1.00am here in Seattle but don't let that bother you.

Seattle I thought you were in New York?

Long story, go on. Are you in trouble?

No no, nothing like that.

Okay so what's this all about then?

We umm I had a visitor this afternoon.

What kind of visitor?

A friend came over to watch the footie.

And you're calling me at 1.00am for this – seriously? J are you still there?

Yes, the thing is, well the thing is… it was Evie.

(Jonathan felt like he'd been punched hard in the stomach and sat down, only to immediately stand up again)

Evie, oh my God. How is she, I mean does she look well? I mean bloody hell.

How honest do you want me to be?

Totally.

Okay then no she doesn't look at all well, in fact she looks bloody terrible. (In Seattle Jonathan groaned and placed his head in his hand). You know how when she was with you or she'd walk into a room and all of a sudden people would be smiling and laughing with her? You know … well that's all gone…her … her I don't know… her sparkle has all gone.

Is she ill, it doesn't sound good?

No, no not sick-sick but there are a few things that don't make any sense. For example, she had no idea you were in New York, I mean surely she must have known? but it was a complete surprise to her. But the weirdest thing.. she didn't know about the letter.

Letter? what letter? J you're not making any sense.

The cease and desist letter (Jonathan sat down again). I had to explain to her what it was, she'd never seen it, she'd never sent it.

Really?

Yes, honest to God, you should have seen her face she had no idea, she just thought you didn't care.

I expect one of her Team Evie group sent it.

Who?

There's about eight of them and after her accident or whatever it was 4 years no 5 years ago now, they form a kind of wall or barrier around her to protect her.

Well I'm telling you she didn't know a thing about it.. not a thing.

Jesus Christ. Is there more… J are you still there?

Yes, but I'm not sure if I should tell you the rest or not.

Whatever it is you have to tell me, don't forget you called me remember?

Okay if you're sure?

Just tell me J.

Firstly you remember the incident in the pub car park?

How could I forget?

Well the thing is she lied on her formal statement to the police… she lied to protect me.

What do you mean?

Well she knew that it had been me that hit her and she wouldn't drop me in it otherwise I wouldn't have been able to practice law, so she lied to protect me.

Bloody hell J, were you ever going to tell me this?

Um no I swore to her that I wouldn't tell anyone. Are you sure you're ready for the rest?

There's more-Jesus! Not really but yes go on.

Well four weeks after she surprised you in London – which by the way she told me she'd found you with another woman ... well four weeks after that she lost the baby, her baby... Your baby.

Jonathan couldn't breathe. No Evie. No baby.

Jon are you still there?

Yes I'm still here. It's just a lot to take in.

Why did you cheat on her Jon, why? I just don't understand?

Honestly I don't know – don't you think I've asked myself that question a million times already? Thing is I'm not even sure I did cheat on her, I was so drunk I can't remember a thing, only waking up in bed next to her, Christ what a bloody mess.

You're not mad at me for telling you all this are you?

No J I'm not mad.. in fact I'm glad you did.

So what are you going to do now?

I need to think.

Were you having an affair with that woman in London?

No no; it was a one off, kind of odd thing, inexcusable really, but no.

So you're still going ahead with this marriage to Paige?

Honestly after what you just told me I'm not sure J... I need to work some things out.

Jamie ended the call. He'd done the right thing, he knew he had, but he had no idea what his brother was going to do with the information he'd just have to wait and see.

MUSIC: – SUGAR – MAROON 5.

Chapter 42

Shortly after arriving in New York, Jonathan had been set up on a blind date with Paige. He wasn't in the mood really, especially after everything that had happened with Evie, but it was through a good business contact and he couldn't really refuse. Well Paige Adler, a Park Avenue princess, had taken one look at Jonathan and decided this was the man for her and wouldn't let him go no matter how hard he struggled to break free. So much so that now after only three months they had got engaged to a rapturous response from her family. She was heiress to a wealthy grocery chain and marrying an English gent was all her dreams come true. Jonathan thought it was alright, they could probably make a go of it; but truthfully his heart wasn't really in it. She'd practically marched him into Tiffany on Fifth Avenue and demanded he buy her an engagement ring and then an announcement was made in the New York Times and the wedding would be in 6 months' time. Fait accompli.

Staring out at the Seattle skyline Jonathan began to wonder what he was doing in America in the first place. It had seemed like the perfect place to escape to; he couldn't bear to be anywhere near to Evie and when his office had asked for one of the three partners to go it made sense as he was the only single guy. He couldn't get his head around it. Evie had lost the baby, his baby, their baby and no-one had thought to tell him. Jesus he'd been so excited planning when he would see Evie and their baby after the birth; but now that day would never come. Was he to blame for the miscarriage, who knew? He certainly felt responsible. God what a mess, he was booked out on an early flight back to New York in the morning and he needed to think carefully about what his next move would be.

On entering his rented New York apartment Jonathan was relieved that Paige was out, he needed a shower, something to eat, go through his mail and then decide. He should have had plenty of time to think on the plane journey, but it had been too distracting with people moving around the cabin the whole time. He spent the whole flight thinking about Evie, his Evie. How was she, where was she, what was she doing? He'd been only too glad to get off and hop into a yellow taxi. Showered and fed he picked up his pile of mail.

Nothing looked very interesting until he saw a small brown jiffy bag with an England postmark. He tore it open and found it was a CD for a wedding he'd been invited to, but had declined as he wasn't in the mood to be around happy people. Taking a sip of red wine and then not really thinking he put the CD into his laptop and pressed play, it was the usual footage of the bride and her father, at the church etc. He pressed fast forward and it stopped at a still of the dance floor with the bride and her father dancing together and he pressed play.

The video camera followed the bride until the music stopped and then there was laughter as the camera panned over to the bride persuading someone to dance with her dad. Jonathan turned the sound up and listened, "Oh go on, you're his favourite you know, you can't come to my wedding and refuse to dance with my dad, it's just not allowed," more laughter then the reluctant participant was hauled up and was dancing with the father of the bride. The music was a beautiful waltz and Jonathan was transfixed, whoever she was she was a great dancer. He couldn't see her face though as she was a lot smaller in height than Alice's father. Suddenly the sound picked up two voices whom he recognized as the bride and her brother Angus. He turned up the volume to the highest setting.

"So sis, how come she's single and do I have a chance?"

"Oh Angus, she's had such a rough time I think you ought to let the poor girl be."

"What do you mean, maybe she just hasn't met the right guy yet?"

"And you think that's you do you?"

"It could be… what do you mean rough time?"

"Her boyfriend said he loved her, got her pregnant, cheated on her, dumped her, fled the country and then she lost the baby, rough enough for you?"

"Bloody hell he sounds like a right shit."

"So promise me you'll leave her alone at least until I come back from my honeymoon – Angus promise me."

"Okay, okay ; but now I'm dancing with her, it's my turn. And I'm definitely going to ask her out once you're back."

The music finished and Angus went over to the girl and there was obviously some more persuasion needed. Finally he had his arms around her and they were moving slowly to the music, Angus's hand was in the small of her back and he was holding her so tight, too tightly in Jonathan's mind. Finally Jonathan saw the girl … it's Evie, his Evie. He couldn't breathe, she was right there in front of him-like a dream. They'd been talking about him, he was the shitty boyfriend. Suddenly he'd never felt so ashamed in his whole damn life. Running his hands through his hair Jonathan made his decision. He'd got a lot of calls to make but he'd never been so sure of anything before. Stirring himself into action, well this was supposedly the city that never slept so he wanted to see who was awake.

Chapter 43

Jason Bellamy had just ½ an hour to go and then his shift for the day was finished. He was tired and was looking forward to watching some football and having a pizza. Driving his squad car back towards the station he spotted Evelyn walking along the road, immediately he pulled over and got out of the car.

"Evelyn hi, I thought it was you, how are things?" It had been a while since he'd last seen her and she was looking better he thought, yes a lot better.

"Oh hello Jason, I'm fine just out for a walk, clear my head sort of thing, How are you, how's work?"

"You know busy busy, always some low life up to no good."

Evie laughed, "If you say so."

"Look I tell you what, me and some of the guys are off to the pub to watch the footie and then we all go for a pizza afterwards; why don't you come along, it'll be fun?"

"That's nice but I'm not really in the mood for company right now, things on my mind kind of thing you know how it is?"

"My shift is over in about 25 minutes what say I meet you for a coffee and then we'll go from there, come on it's just a coffee… please?"

Evie smiled. "Oh okay coffee it is then, where shall I meet you?"

And it had been as simple as that. Jason arranged to meet her in 30 minutes at a well know High Street coffee shop, somewhere where they would have fruit tea and soy milk, as he now knew those were the things she liked.

Entering the coffee shop, Jason was relieved to see that Evie was already there. He thought she looked very pretty today in an orange top with grey trousers. "Hey, can I get you something to drink?"

"No I'm fine, let me get you a coffee or something; you must be dead on your feet after your shift." Evie jumped up and went over to the counter. Less than five minutes later she was back with a large cappuccino for Jason, with some brown sugar sachets on the side.

"So what's new with you then, still studying hard?"

"Yes I've got just over a month until my exams so it's pretty full on, plus I'm trying to get into peak physical shape just in case it comes down to two of us. I need to be the fittest so there's an extra reason for picking me kind of thing."

"Oh I see that's very smart officer?" Evie winked at him; this was a good idea just a coffee with a friend.

"So how are you – still at the gym?"

"No not exactly I resigned from there a while ago; but I'm ready to get seriously fit again and I've heard they're thinking about re-advertising my old job so if they do then I might reapply – you know get back on the horse kind of thing. Not that Steve my old boss is likely to give me the job but I thought I might try anyway."

"Is there anything I could do to help?"

"Well I do have a question for you actually. Here's the thing, what do you know about Donnelly's gym on the industrial estate?"

"Why?"

"Just tell me what you know first and then I'll explain okay?"

"Okay he's a good bloke, straight as they come, takes in kids who are in danger of going off the rails; you know the sort, why?"

"Well I was thinking of asking him to help me get my fitness back, I mean really get it back, sort of high intensity for a month or 6 weeks ."

"Okay, but I don't think he trains girls and I wouldn't park your car on the estate; you need to go in daylight, park ten minutes away and walk over. I have to say I wouldn't be happy about you going there really."

"Oh Jason, it's just a sweaty gym and I haven't even spoken to the guy yet. I'll be fine."

They finished their drinks and then Jason tried to persuade her to join him and his colleagues at the pub for the footie. "Come on I know you like football, there's a whole group of us that go and then we all pile into the Italian down the road, it's just harmless fun please say yes?" He waited and just when he thought she would say no she replied, "Oh okay then you've worn me down, now do I need to move my car?"

Half an hour later they squeezed their way into the Queens Arms to join Jason's colleagues. The match had already started but the score was still nil-nil so nothing was lost. Jason introduced her to everyone and bought her an orange juice. He found Evie a spare stool at the bar and she sat down to watch. The match was quite good, the usual mix of missed chances coupled with some unbelievable refereeing decisions, but at half time it was one all. Jason was very attentive and never left her side, he made sure she was okay and had a drink, his colleagues were very nice and there was the usual banter between them all. Evie was actually glad she had joined them, there was no pressure just watching footie at the pub, it had been a long time since she had enjoyed such a simple pleasure.

She went to the ladies' cloakroom and whilst she was gone, Andy, one of Jason's workmates, asked him how long they had known each other and how the two of them had met. Jason just said she'd been a witness to a fracas in a pub car park a while ago, but he decided to leave out the stuff about Evie being hurt as he didn't want to rake all that up again. But he did imply that that he'd known her for quite a while and deliberately didn't correct his friends' assumption that they were actually boyfriend and girlfriend.

The match was over and everyone bar a couple of them made their way out onto the street and down to the Italian restaurant. It was obvious when they walked in that they were regulars and soon tables were moved to accommodate all 15 of them. Menus were produced, wine, beer, plus water were ordered and Evie scanned the menu to see what she could eat.

"Are you okay? Just so you know, we've tried nearly everything and it's all good here."

"I'm sure you have, but I just need to look at wheat free options, I'm sure it'll be fine."

"Wheat free, I didn't know, so no pizza, pasta or bread?" Jason sounded incredulous; how could he not have known this about her? Was she going to be able to eat anything at all? It had been going so well now it looked as if he'd stuffed everything right up.

Evie saw his face and laughed, "It's fine; there's always something, don't worry okay?"

Eventually everyone had ordered, Evie chose a caprese salad to start and then chicken with tomatoes, a green salad and Mediterranean vegetables. The noise levels were rising and Evie discovered she could just sit back and listen, there was no pressure for her to join in. At one point Jason casually covered her hand with his on the table and Evie waited a few moments before moving her hand slowly onto her lap. She was sure he was just being friendly but she didn't want any complications tonight or any night, she'd had her fill of relationships for quite a while. Jason had been right the food was very good and although she declined dessert it didn't stop a lot of them from tucking into three courses with gusto.

The meal ended and they piled out into the car park. Evie had moved her car there before the football match so she could hop in and go home. She said her goodbyes and the group began to disperse. Jason was in a very good mood, he'd had a good day and then bumping into Evelyn had been the icing on the cake. She seemed to enjoy the football and dinner so now he was trying to move things on.

Unbeknown to Evie, Jamie's friend George had been into the restaurant to collect a pizza to take out. He'd spotted Evie but not wanting to interrupt her evening had sat and watched her with this large group of people. George wasn't sure who they were but she looked a lot better than the last time he had seen her, more like her old self again and for that he was grateful. He didn't know all the ins and outs of why her and Jon had split but the general consensus between the four friends was that Jon had been a bloody idiot. George was sat in his car and was just about to drive away when the group including Evie spilled out and he decided to sit for a minute and watch. Evie was talking to some bloke who looked vaguely familiar but he wasn't sure where he knew him from. He saw him go to kiss Evie but she deliberately turned her head so he kissed her cheek and then she walked over to her car, got in and drove away. The guy looked disappointed and shook his head, obviously that wasn't what he had wanted. George knew that as soon as he got back to his parent's house he would call Jamie and fill him in.

Chapter 44

Evie drove home. It had been an enjoyable night, but she'd felt a bit awkward when Jason had leaned in to kiss her; she didn't feel that way about him at all and hoped he'd got the message without her offending him.

Jason meanwhile was already at home, kicking himself for forcing the issue when obviously she wasn't ready for that. Hopefully he would get another chance soon he just had to convince her they made a good team.

Jamie's mobile vibrated, it was George. "Hi mate what's up?"

"Hi J, just got a pizza but saw something weird in town."

"Go on."

"Well I saw Evie."

"That's not weird. How was she?"

"Well actually she was in the Italian restaurant with a big group of people and she looked really well, J, really well, just like her old self."

"Wow that's great news... is that it?"

"Um no not exactly; when they all left some guy tried to kiss her, but it looked to me like she deliberately turned her face away so he kissed her cheek, you know what I mean? we've all been there before. Then she left and he looked cross kind of thing. Funny thing is I've seen him from somewhere I just don't know where from."

"Okay can you describe him to me?"

"Sure, about 5 feet 8 or 9 inches tall, late twenties, short dark hair-kind of regulation cut, good physique but not really the gym type and they all seemed to be part of a work group or something. Does it ring any bells?"

"No let me think on it for a bit, did you talk to her?"

"No I didn't want to intrude or embarrass her. When I was sat inside waiting for my pizza I thought he was her boyfriend; but thinking about it she moved her hand away from his at the table. And just now in the car park that was obviously not the case – just thought you'd like to know. What's the news with Jon is he coming home?"

"Yes I never thought I'd say this but I can't wait for him to be back."

Jamie started to think. This bloke with Evie, it definitely didn't sound like he was her boyfriend. He was thrilled she was looking good and soon Jon would be back and who knew maybe they'd get back together? So this bloke: how would Evie and George know the same bloke? He couldn't get his head round it, he'd have to try again tomorrow once he'd had some sleep.

The following day Evie drove round to the industrial estate. It looked okay in the daylight and she circled round before spotting Donnelly's Gym in the corner. She'd been a bit cross when Jason said he wouldn't be happy about her going there, but she wasn't silly she would park five minutes away and walk over just to be safe. She'd deliberately worn her scruffiest gym gear, no make – up or jewellery and had her speech all rehearsed. On entering the gym it was pretty much what she'd been expecting. It wasn't a gym in the usual sense, but it had a boxing ring, free weights, punch bags, areas with skipping ropes and a row of lockers, basic but effective none the less.

It seemed pretty deserted and she made her way over to what looked like an office and knocked on the door. A booming voice rang out, "Piss off, we're not open yet."

Undeterred Evie opened the door and stepped inside. A chap in his mid-50s was sat behind a desk with his feet up and his eyes closed, looking as if he was taking a nap. Suddenly he said again, "Are you deaf? we're not open."

Evie took a deep breath and piped up, "Yes Mr Donnelly I heard you but I was hoping you would help me?"

Patrick Donnelly opened his eyes and took in the view. A girl, possibly twenty something stood in front of him. She had a slight smile on her face, wore very old gym kit and carried a battered holdall. It didn't look as if she was selling anything so what did she want? He took his feet off the desk and looked Evie straight in the eye. "And what the fuck makes you think I would want to help you?"

Evie threw her head back and laughed, "Well that's a very good point Mr Donnelly; but here's the thing, my mother always told me if you don't ask then you don't get. So I'm here to ask."

Patrick Donnelly instantly liked this girl. She had spirit and he was intrigued. "Okay so sit down and ask me."

"Okay well firstly my name is Evelyn Wallace and I need your help." Evie explained briefly about her miscarriage and the fact she had lost her sense of direction since resigning from the gym. She wanted, no needed, to get fit again for her job as well as her sanity and yes she knew he probably didn't train girls but she would do as she was told, work hard, try not get in the way and it would only be for 6 weeks' maximum.

Patrick thought about this, in his experience girls in his gym were nothing but trouble; but she didn't look like a trouble maker. "So if all this is about some guy, what do you need from me exactly?"

Evie explained and then played her trump card. "If you help me then maybe I can help you. I can do some office stuff, paperwork or some fundraising or whatever you need kind of thing? And the guy to keep it short, said he loved me, got me pregnant, cheated on me, dumped me, fled the country and then I lost the baby, so yes a real charmer."

They chatted for a bit and Patrick sighed, "I'm guessing that if I say no that you'll be back here every day asking me the same thing until you've worn me down and I've agreed anyway?"

"Um yes, pretty much," she laughed.

"Well okay then I'll give you a week's trial from tomorrow and we'll go from there. You've got to do as you're told mind? I'll call you Wallace, can't be too over friendly with these boys. Now make yourself useful and make some tea, milk two sugars in mine."

Evie smiled and walked over to the kettle, "Yes coach."

Donnelly smiled to himself, the next six weeks could go one of two ways. Either it'd be a fucking disaster and she'd only last a day or it would work out just fine and he'd get his tax return done for free. Either way he'd give her a go.

Chapter 45

Evie was excited about her first day at Donnelly's. They'd agreed she would go in at 2.00 do some tiding and office work for a couple of hours then at 4.00 he'd start her off on weights, punch bags and things she could do by herself before working with him or one of his other guys from 4.30 until 5.30. This was Monday to Friday with the first Wednesday of the month off too. He didn't want her hanging about in the evening it would be too distracting for the boys plus she'd have had enough of it by then anyway.

She started off by making Patrick Donnelly his afternoon cup of tea. She'd brought some homemade biscuits with her as a sort of sweetener for him. When she placed his mug and biscuits down he didn't say anything; but thought well if he was getting free biscuits he hoped she'd at least last the week. Evie cleaned up and tidied round, she would need to bring in some proper cleaning stuff for the men's toilets, it needed to be hygienic as a bare minimum. Looking at Patrick's desk, well it was a mess so she just rolled up her sleeves and got stuck in. It was already gone 4.00 before she started some exercise, Donnelly had left her to her own devices, but came over from time to time offering advice regarding weights and technique. She was a quick learner and then he kitted her up with junior gloves and let her throw some punches; she wasn't too bad and would probably be okay if she did as she was told. All too soon it was 5.30 and Evie got ready to leave, a couple of lads came in glanced at her and then carried on much as before. It was obvious that Patrick ruled them with iron discipline and they respected him all the more for it.

Once back at home, she fed Henry and had a long soak in the bath; first day done, once she'd eaten she'd write a list of things she needed to do and then e-mail Peter, she needed to call in a few favours. Texting Jason, she was brief in saying that Mr Donnelly had agreed to take her on for just 6 weeks and that so far she was enjoying it, not to worry, she'd taken his advice and parked elsewhere etc.

Jason read her text immediately. He groaned loudly; he didn't think for a minute that Donnelly would let her in the door let alone offer to train her for six weeks. As soon as he passed his exams he would lay his cards on the table and pray that she would say yes. She was definitely headstrong and spirited, well he'd seen some of that before her boyfriend had dumped her, but obviously she was now picking herself up and what was that annoying phrase everyone used these days – oh yes getting her mojo back-whatever the fuck that was when it was at home.

The same night Jamie was at uni trying to study but he just couldn't concentrate. He'd been racking his brains for who Evie had been at the restaurant with; how would George and Evie both know the same guy? it just didn't make sense. Knowing full well he wasn't actually achieving anything he took out his mobile and texted Evie, he'd just come straight out and ask her she wouldn't mind – would she?

Her mobile pinged just after 9.30; who was this now, oh it was Jamie. He wanted to ask her something.

Hi sis, just doing some studying – yes really-wanted to ask you something though? – SEND

Okay ask away. – SEND She smiled, well at least he said he was studying.

George said he saw you at the Italian place the other night with some bloke – which is fine by me by the way; but he thought he knew him from somewhere. Odd? – SEND

Evie laughed; oh so she'd been seen and they couldn't work out who the guy was, she knew Jamie hadn't judged her by what happened with his brother so she thought she'd come clean.

Oh that guy! Sorry but he's just a friend, no gossip for you tonight, the reason you recognize him is cos he's the policeman who kept coming by to take my formal statement after the pub fight. I expect he came to see you at the house when the boys were with you. – SEND.

Oh the policeman, are you and him together? – SEND

No as I said we're just friends, nothing going on at all and don't worry your secret is still safe with me, cross my heart etc.! – SEND

Okay any other news then? – SEND

Um yes I'm training at Donnelly's gym five days a week and thinking of reapplying for my old job back in town. I've spent too long moping about, time to get back on the horse – fitness wise at any rate. – SEND

Where's Donnelly's, I don't think I know it? – SEND

No you probably don't; it's a sweaty boxing gym run by an Irish guy for lads who need a bit of direction – SEND

So it's a boy's gym – how come you're there? – SEND

Needed to work out some aggression and get super-fit, also I'm helping him with his office stuff and general cleaning etc., so win-win for me. – SEND

Is it safe? – SEND

Oh J – what are you like? Yes, I park 5 minutes away and am usually gone before the lads show up for the evening. Don't worry I can take care of myself. – SEND

They continued to text, mostly about his friends and love life. Jamie didn't mention that Jonathan was due home soon, he didn't want to get involved plus it wasn't strictly his news to tell.

Two days later and Evie submitted her online application to her old gym. If she didn't try she would never know. All she could do now was wait and see if Steve even gave her an interview. She had included details of her latest training courses and hoped this would give her an advantage depending on who else applied. Stacey had been in touch and Evie had asked why there was a vacancy so soon; it turned out that her replacement had been disliked by practically everyone and numbers had slipped back dramatically. Evie thought this would play in her favour as her classes had always been full with even a waiting list for some of them.

She pulled on her running gear and set off just for an hour; she wanted to think about the other night. Jason had been attentive but she hadn't given him any encouragement so had been thrown when he'd put his hand over hers and then tried to kiss her in the car park. Evie hoped he wasn't going to be difficult, she was so off men, that was the last thing she was looking for. She needed and wanted to try to get back to work and start to feel better inside. She'd spent too long feeling like crap and she didn't like it one bit, she was at her best when she was fit, healthy and in a good place mentally. Ian had been helping her with some online counselling and it seemed to be paying off. That coupled with Donnelly's would sort her out hopefully.

Chapter 46

Two weeks later and Evie had been granted an interview back at her old gym and although she'd been surprised she was apprehensive at having a meeting with Steve. Most of the time he was such as arse and she would have to be on her best behaviour. She dressed carefully, there was bound to be a practical assessment and she wanted to be fully prepared and not give Steve any reason to discount her before she'd been given a fair chance. Driving into the car park it was like she'd never been away and she was surprised at just how much she'd missed everyone.

Waiting in reception she was greeted with enthusiasm by her old team mates and clients who assumed she was already back. She was called into Steve's office and was very surprised to see not only Steve but another man sat next to him. This was a Mr Granger from Head Office and all hiring and firing had to go through him now as well as the gym manager. It turned out that he was a very nice man, Steve looked less than thrilled to see her and she guessed that her being granted an interview hadn't been Steve's decision. After 30 minutes she was given a ten-minute break and then told she would be taking a class of her own choice at 10.00am; this was music to Evie's ears so she would be able to show them just how good she was after all. Walking into the studio she saw a lot of familiar faces who all said hi and how nice it was to see her. Some of the male gym instructors had been roped in as well so she decided to do a HIT class, followed by abs and then stretch to finish. She set her music to play and began.

An hour later and she was done. It had gone very well in her eyes and she couldn't do any more except wait and see if she was to be offered her old job back. The hours were to be the same and she had stressed that apart from the first Wednesday of every month she was more than happy to cover for sickness and holidays. Steve had been itching to ask about all her recent time off sick, but regulations meant that he wasn't allowed to so he just sat back and looked miserable throughout – no change there, then. thought Evie uncharitably. Miles had gone back to Chicago a couple of months previously and she was sorry not to have said goodbye, but she hadn't been in any fit state to do anything of the sort – maybe she would write to him if Stacey would give her his address as she was sure he would appreciate it. They had two new personal trainers at the gym focusing on one to one and group sessions. One was to replace Miles and the other was to replace Jack who had decided he was destined for bigger and better things. Evie was more than happy to see the back of him.

At home that night she texted Rowan, but she was out and about so didn't reply. Alice too was busy and so she tried Fiona. "Hi Fi it's me do you have time for a quick chat?"

"Sure how are you, when are you coming over for supper?"

"Anytime you like." Evie laughed. She loved Fiona, she was always exactly the same.

"What about tomorrow night?"

"That would be lovely, I have some news."

"Ahh well so do I actually, so we'll do a swap."

"Okay what shall I bring?"

"Nothing just bring yourself; why don't you come over earlier about 6.00 and then we can have a chat before David arrives?"

"That sounds great, see you tomorrow. Bye Fi."

"Bye Evie."

Supper at Fiona's was such good fun, although neither of them were drinking it didn't stop them from having just as much fun gossiping and generally putting the world to rights. Sat at the kitchen table Fiona couldn't wait any longer she was bursting to tell Evie her news.

"Come on then Fi, out with it what's going on?"

"Well I'm pregnant with baby number 3," she squealed with excitement.

Evie got up and hugged her friend, "Wow that's just fantastic news! Are you pleased, when's it due?"

"Yes we're both thrilled to bits, as you know I always wanted more children so this is just the best news, I'm only 10 weeks gone, but I had to tell someone." Fiona was grinning from ear to ear and Evie was really happy for her and for David. A thought entered her head if she hadn't miscarried then the two babies would have been very close in age together, how much fun would that have been. She shook her head wryly, these things always happened for a reason didn't they? and her miracle baby was not meant to be. David arrived home and more congratulations were in order.

"Sorry Evie I haven't asked what your news is I'm so excited about mine, so go on."

"Well it's not as exciting of course, but here's the thing; I reapplied for my old job back and I'm waiting to hear. I feel good at the moment, stronger, fitter, healthier, I've been working out at Donnelly's plus Ian has been helping me a lot too so I figured it was time to get back on the horse so to speak."

Fiona was pleased for her friend. There'd been times when she thought that Evie would never be like her old self again, but looking at her now she was sure, Evie was back.

Chapter 47

Another couple of weeks passed and Evie hadn't heard anything about getting her old job back; maybe they'd decided to give it to someone else after all. She was still at Donnelly's, the toilets were spotless, everything in the gym now had a place and Patrick's office was ship shape too. Evie had persuaded Patrick to apply for some charity funding, well she talked and he agreed she could fill in the paperwork kind of thing. Four weeks in and she was staying a bit later every day, the boys had just accepted her as she kept her head down and was generally smiley and polite.

Patrick had a rule that if you used obscene language you had to drop and give him 20 press-ups, even her. When she'd been frustrated by her lack of ability to punch hard enough she'd found out the hard way, so she'd dropped and given him twenty just to show she was one of them. Since then the boys had been friendlier, wanting to know how come she was there and why wasn't she at some fancy spa etc.?

Generally she liked the boys a lot; yes, some of their language was a bit ripe from time to time, mostly under their breath to avoid punishment, but they generally seemed to thrive on the discipline. She put up a rota for the toilets which was met mostly by 'in your dreams' kind of thing; but she pointed out that she was only going to be there another couple of weeks and it was important not to let standards slip. Tony was one of Patrick's most reliable helpers, he'd been going to Donnelly's for years and was good with the lads and fine with her. They were chatting one night about girls. Tony had a steady girlfriend, but things weren't moving as fast as he would like. Evie gave him some advice and he listened and thanked her, said he'd try it and let her know. She was really going to miss the gym once her time was up, so much so that she persuaded Patrick to let her drop in whenever she had some free time to help out. He'd been quietly surprised she'd lasted the course; now he had better mugs and chocolate biscuits too, plus his paperwork was all up together and she'd done some great stuff with simple wall planners to keep track of everything and everyone. His tax return had been filed and they were waiting to hear if they'd been successful with their charity funding application as it would make a huge difference to them.

MUSIC: – SO STRONG – MECK FEAT DINO.

On her last day she had baked a big chocolate cake. It was Tony's birthday and she hoped Patrick wouldn't mind too much. It was her last time in the ring and Tony decided as a farewell gesture to take some punches with her. She was a lot stronger and fitter now; but still she would never punch as hard as a guy. It was going well and then Tony lost concentration for a split second and Evie threw a right punch and he fell over onto his backside– he looked as surprised as she was – then mayhem broke out followed by hollering and whooping. Evie smiled, well it had been about time, she deserved a break for a change.

Out of the ring she gave Tony his cake and left him and the boys with paper plates whilst she said goodbye to Patrick. Yes she'd pop back in from time to time, but decided to come clean and told him that not for a second did she think he would ever have agreed to let her train with him and for that she was very grateful. She kissed him on the cheek and left his office. He was touched by her sincerity, the boys all liked her and as for baking Tony a cake; Patrick doubted that Tony had ever had a birthday cake before so that was another first at Donnelly's gym.

Arriving home there was a letter on the doormat. It was an offer of her old job at the gym in town, they wanted her to start next week and could she call them to either accept or decline asap. She called them the next morning to accept and sent a text to Jason. She wanted to tell him the good news in person. Jason was thrilled to get her text, he had some news of his own and arranged to come round to her house the following evening. Evie had been busy spreading her news; Fiona had been very happy for her and her friends, Rowan, Viv and Claire were promising a big night out to celebrate. Life was good, finally she was moving on and felt better about herself, both inside and out.

Jason knocked on Evie's door. He felt oddly nervous, but it was good news right – yeah of course it was? Evie opened the door and welcomed him in, he kissed her on her cheek and she led him into the kitchen. She'd already put the kettle on to boil and they sat at the kitchen table.

"I have some news, good news I wanted to share it with you first, I've been dying to tell someone all day."

Jason sounded excited, Evie guessed this was his promotion he'd been hoping for. "So I...well I passed my exams and I'm getting promoted... how fantastic is that?"

Evie got up from the table, walked round and gave Jason a hug. He was a good man and he deserved it.

"Well done you, I knew you'd do it, they'd have been mad to pick anyone else. So what happens now?"

"I'm waiting to hear what division I'm going to join and which force that'll be with, I find out in a few days. I'm just so excited, at last something is going my way." He couldn't stop grinning at her, he was simply having the best day ever.

"Well I've got some news myself actually; you know I told you I was reapplying for my old job, well here's the thing: I had a letter a couple of days ago and I'm back, they want me to start next week. Isn't that just brilliant?"

Jason was struggling to take it in, hadn't she just heard him say he may get posted away? She couldn't take her old job back, not if she was going to go with him. "Um yes that's great.... Well done...but you do realise that you're not going to be able to accept it if I get transferred away from the area don't you?"

Evie looked stunned and her brain wouldn't connect with her mouth. Hadn't he just heard her news? she was starting back next week. Yes he'd done really well, but where he was posted to had nothing to do with her – she wasn't going anywhere. Neither of them spoke and then Evie said quietly, "Look Jason. I'm thrilled, no I'm beyond happy for your promotion, you deserve it, you're a good man and a great policeman. You've become a good friend to me; but I think there's some confusion because I'm not leaving. Next week I'm going back to my old job and it's what I want."

Now it was Jason's turn to look confused. He grabbed her hands across the table. "But Evie you must know how I feel about you, you must. I love you, in fact I've been in love with you for ages. I was just waiting for the right time to tell you and I thought or hoped you felt the same about me too. This promotion means a new start for both of us, away from here and all those memories, I thought you'd be genuinely happy to leave?"

Gently Evie removed her hands from his. Oh no this was awful; he'd been so happy to tell her about his promotion; but how could he have just assumed she was in love with him and that she would drop everything and move away – it was bonkers. "I don't know what to say, I never expected you to say you're in love with me, this is going to sound harsh, but here's the thing – I don't love you and yes, I was a mess when we first met; but I'm so much stronger now, ready to move forward, but that doesn't mean move away with you. I'm sorry but the answer is no, I'm not going anywhere."

"Look I wasn't going to mention this, but it's okay you know. I've seen your file. I um know everything about you, so there's nothing to be scared of, you don't have to tell me anything because I already know and it doesn't bother me. Please say you'll at least think about this, think about us moving away together it could be just what you need."

Evie was stunned, how long had he known everything? She didn't know what to say so got up from the table as if to silently intimate that the conversation was well and truly over. Awkwardly she hugged him goodbye and closed her front door. She leant against it and closed her eyes, God what an evening.

Driving back into town, Jason still couldn't get his head around it. He loved her, he thought she had feelings for him too, okay maybe not as deep as his but surely that would change with time? If he moved away it was the perfect opportunity for both of them to start over, new place, new jobs, new relationship in fact new everything. He'd left pretty much as soon as she'd said no, he needed to give her some time to think it through, maybe tomorrow she'd wake up and realise it was all for the best – yes he'd give her some time and then once he found out where his posting was he'd call her again.

Evie got ready for bed. What a mess; it was too late to call Fiona, she needed her rest before baby number three came along. No, she'd call her tomorrow. But honestly what was Jason thinking? They'd never even kissed, well, only on the cheek let alone gone to bed together. Yes he'd confessed he knew all about her about her issues and stuff, that whole other chapter of her life wasn't closed to him. She knew he was giving her some space to think it through; but to be honest there was nothing to think about-she didn't love him it was that simple. They wouldn't or couldn't be happy with that – well she certainly wouldn't be, it wasn't fair to him. No he needed to start afresh, new job, new town even new girlfriend; but not with her. She wasn't going anywhere, the sooner she told him the better. She'd call him tomorrow and tell him again that she wasn't leaving with him.

Chapter 48

It had been a very long day. Evie was tired, she'd taught her two usual Friday evening classes, Steve her boss was being an arse again so same as usual and as she drove home all she could think about was a long soak in a hot bath. She'd been back at work for two months now and was so happy, a lot of her old clients were still there and she was enjoying life again. It was getting dark and had been raining steadily since lunchtime. Tomorrow was her weekend off and although she hadn't made any definite plans she hoped the weather would buck up as there was nothing worse than a crap weekend.

She drove steadily, she had to be a lot more aware of her speed as this model was a lot quicker than her old car. Suddenly in her rear view mirror she saw a car approaching her from behind it seemed to be moving very fast and within seconds it was right up behind her, almost hitching a ride on her bumper. Evie could hear the loud beat of the car's music coming out of the darkness pounding incessantly. It continued to dodge out and in, out and in trying to manoeuvre to overtake; but this road was windy and tricky at the best of times even if you were familiar with it let alone on a night like tonight.

Holding her breath she started to panic. The car was making her very nervous and she knew there wasn't anywhere for her to pull over for at least a couple of miles. Her heart was beating so loudly in her head it was making her ears hurt. Suddenly its lights vanished from her mirror as it jerked out and past her, whomever was driving surely had a death wish she thought to herself as it sped past. Gently she squeezed the car brakes to give the vehicle more space as it narrowly missed crashing into another car coming in the opposite direction. That was a close call, if it had been daylight she was convinced the driver coming towards them would have had a face as white as a sheet. Stupid dickhead, she thought, next time they might end up killing someone as well as themselves.

Less than a mile later as she rounded a bend, out of the corner of her eye she thought she saw the brake lights of a vehicle to the left of her; but that was impossible she thought as this part of the road veered to the right so there couldn't be a car to the left of her. She slowed down checking there was nothing behind her and pressed the button for her passenger window to lower and squinted out into the darkness. Oh shit, it was that car, it had gone through the hedge and was now lying on its roof in the field. Slamming on her brakes the ABS kicked in immediately and she moved her car over to the left hand side of the road. Grabbing her mobile and a torch from the glove box she switched on her hazard lights and got out of her car. She scrambled through the gap in the hedge that the car had made and slipping and sliding across the muddy field made her way towards it. When she reached the car, it was an absolute mess, buckled metal and smashed glass everywhere. Evie shone her torch into the windows there was a young lad upside down in the driver's seat but she couldn't see anyone else. Evie tugged at the door handle but it was stuck fast. Using her phone which miraculously had a faint signal she called for all three emergency services describing her location as best she could and then tried the handle again. She had to get the door open; it could be at least 20 minutes if not longer before any help arrived out here and just one look at the boy confirmed that he would need help much sooner than that.

Ben was so fucking angry, he'd been back in the UK for less than ten days and hadn't wanted to go to this stupid bloody wedding in the first place. Charlotte had been very persuasive, saying it would be fun and didn't he need some fun after 6 months in Afghanistan? She'd pouted and fluttered her eyelashes at him promising him all sorts of things as they were staying the night at the wedding venue; eventually and against his better judgement he'd given in and they'd driven over three and half hours to make it to the church for 1.30pm.

Well he should have stuck to his guns. Charlotte had taken forever to get ready changing her outfit at least twice and then redoing her makeup. The Friday traffic on the motorway had been horrendous and they only just squeaked in to the church seconds before the bride was due to arrive, as it turned out the bride was 45 minutes late so there was a lot of hanging about for nothing.

After the ceremony everyone went back to the reception venue and whilst endless photos were being snapped. They checked in and discovered they'd been given a twin room in the oldest part of the hotel, which was on its last legs 30 years ago, he reckoned. He'd taken one look at the bathroom and wished he was back in barracks as it would have been a lot cleaner. Why oh why did he agree to this?

Things didn't get better any time soon. He knew no-one there, the other guests were an unfriendly and quite frankly unlikeable lot. The cheap wine was disgusting and from his point of view they had been seated on a table with a collection of oddballs and nutjobs each trying to outdo each other in getting drunk the fastest. Charlotte had wandered off somewhere and when people asked him what he did for a living and he replied he was a soldier all they wanted to know was if he'd killed anyone –for God's sake, this was even worse than being deployed.

The food was inedible, not that the other guests at his table seemed to notice. He wondered idly why it was called a wedding feast – maybe it was someone's idea of a joke. The only highlight was a particularly terrible speech from the best man who although pretty much worse for wear managed to stand and proceeded to tell everyone about the time the groom had hooked up with what turned out to be a lady boy on one of their boys holidays away. Ben had laughed at that; although the bride was a sour looking girl he didn't think she deserved to be humiliated in such a blatant fashion.

The tables were cleared and then quite possibly the worst DJ from about 1976 started to go through his tired and not even fashionably retro playlist. Eventually he'd found Charlotte in a dark corner wrapped around one of the ushers who was in the process of sticking his tongue down her throat. Taking one look at them he decided they were welcome to each other and left them to it. He couldn't even be bothered to stay and have a row about it. Exhausted and pissed off he grabbed his things from their bedroom and got back in his car. He had no idea how Charlotte was getting home and right now he didn't give a damn either way. Let the usher sort that out – she was not his problem anymore.

On the drive home he wondered to himself why things turned out the way they do? The deployment had been tough, much tougher than the previous one and 6 months was a long time to be away from family, friends and his girlfriend. He'd missed her a lot, just wanting to be with her, hear her voice and have lots of sex obviously; but now he was wondering why he'd thought she was even his type in the first place. Shaking his head he concentrated on the road, the weather was grim and he put the radio on eager for anything to make the miles pass quicker.

As he rounded the corner he saw a car's hazard lights flashing. Some idiot had run out of petrol no doubt, well let the AA or whoever go to their rescue he wasn't stopping tonight not for anyone or anything. His car drew nearer and he slowed down. The parked car didn't have its bonnet open and he could see no sign of the driver, then he looked to his left, shit what was that? Parking in front of the 4x4 he turned on his hazard lights and scrambled out. He ran towards the upturned vehicle where he saw a girl frantically trying to open the driver's door, she had her foot up against the car and was tugging and tugging but nothing was happening. He heard her shout out, "Oh come on – I need to open the bloody door."

Evie wasn't aware of anyone else until she heard a voice saying "Out of the way, let me try". She stood aside and wiped her hands over her face and through her hair, thank God someone else had stopped maybe now they could get this lad out of danger. Ben tried the door, but it was stuck fast he needed a crowbar or something to try to open it.

"Don't suppose you have a crowbar or something similar in your car do you?"

"Um no but let me see if there's anything we can use that's fallen out of this one." Evie shone her torch to illuminate the cars' interior she could see rubbish strewn about and then caught sight of something. It looked like an old fashioned crook lock but it had a long slim piece of metal at one end that might just do the trick. She shouted, "I see something we could use, but I'll need you to lift me up so I can lean into the car to reach it."

Ben stopped tugging the door handle and went round to where Evie was, she shone the torch for him, "See? I think that thing there might work." He nodded, "Right but let me try to reach it first, okay?"

"Be careful, there's a lot of broken glass everywhere."

Ben tried to reach it but it was no use he was just too big, "No good; it's going to have to be you I'm afraid."

Evie didn't hesitate and moved into position, Ben lifted her up and she squeezed through the broken window stretching out her hand towards the Holy Grail; it was no use, she needed to be further inside the car. "I need to be about another foot inside the car and then I think I can reach it." Ben shifted his weight, he had to give it to her, she was a trier. Evie inched forward but caught her jacket on the glass in the window she heard the fabric tear – "Aargh just a bit more" – and wriggled free. Then reaching out her hand she tried again. By this time Ben had moved his arms from her waist to her bottom for support. "Another 3 inches and I can get it," – now was not the time for laughing, but Ben had been in worse positions than this and had never had a girl ask him for another 3 inches of anything. Re – focusing he lifted her further into the car until he heard her say, "That's it. I've got it," carefully bringing her out she handed it to him and he went back to the driver's door sure enough two tries later and the door was open.

In the car was a young lad maybe 17 or 18. He was upside down, unconscious and looked to be in a very bad way. "Have you called the emergency services?"

"Yes at least 10 minutes ago, but it's quite rural out here so it'll be a while longer before they arrive assuming they can find us first time that is." She felt for the boys pulse it was very weak. She started to talk to him. "Hello, can you hear me? my name is Evelyn and I'm here to help you okay? I need you to try to open your eyes for me do you think you can do that? Try really hard just for me? Tell you what let's have a bit of a chat whilst we're here, so my name is Evelyn, but special friends are allowed to call me Evie and I guess that could include you too if you like? Do you have a job? I teach fitness classes at the local gym, luckily for you I was on my way home – had an awful day mind you – my boss is a right pain in the arse. What football club do you support, come on, you can tell me, I support Chelsea so you see I do have a sense of humour."

Whilst Evie was talking to the lad Ben had taken her torch and was looking round the vehicle; there was smoke coming from the bonnet and he noticed a strong smell of petrol. Shit, they needed to get the boy out and fast.

"We need to get him out of the car."

"Is it safe to move him, what about his injuries?"

Quietly Ben said, "We don't have a choice, this car's going to go up in flames pretty soon." Evie was stunned for just a moment and then focused her mind into action.

"Okay so what do you need me to do?"

"I'm going to move his upper body and I want you to reach in and grab his legs okay?"

"Okay."

Quickly and carefully they started to move the boy who had started to come round and was groaning. "It's okay, we're just moving you out so you'll be more comfortable," she told him. "What's your name?" she heard him say 'Matthew'. "Matthew that's a lovely name. Okay, so Matthew just stay still and let us move you okay don't try to help just remain still." Ben lifted the boy's upper body whilst Evie reached up and took hold of his legs. Matthew shouted out in pain, "It's okay, it's okay you're going to be okay just a few more seconds and we're done here okay?"

After what seemed like hours but could only have been two minutes at the most Matthew was free and out of the car. Ben and Evie carried him towards the hedge and laid him down away from his car. She took his hand again and felt for a pulse, she couldn't find one. He was fading away. Evie pulled back his shirt and began CPR, counting out loud, 1 2 3 4 5 6 7 8, 1 2 3 4 5 6 7 8, 1 2 3 4 5 6 7 8, suddenly there was an almighty explosion as the car burst into flames. Ben threw himself down on top of Evie and Matthew. All the air was pushed out of her and she couldn't move, couldn't breathe, slowly Ben eased off of her, "Are you okay?"

"Yes I think so." She began compressions again counting 1 2 3 4 5 6 7 8. Ben then saw the flashing blue lights and ran up towards the road to flag them down. A few minutes later the fire brigade were scrambling down into the field towards her followed by a paramedic. Ben pulled her away. "Let them take over now." Then it was all a blur with an ambulance and the police arriving together. A blanket was wrapped around her shoulders and they helped her up to the road.

The tailgate of the police car was open and she sat on the edge of the boot her mind a blank. Ben noticed her feet didn't even touch the ground but were dangling over the edge. She was aware of someone sitting next to her and she could hear voices but they sounded like they were under water and she couldn't make out the words. Suddenly she jumped up and ran towards the hedge, bent over, her hands on her knees and began to retch, a strong arm was around her waist supporting her and holding her ponytail back. Evie was trembling and retching until there was nothing left, she leant back against someone's body grateful for the support as her legs buckled under her. She heard a voice say 'it's just the shock it's a perfectly normal reaction'.

Someone helped her to sit back down and she was given some water. Ben was wearing a white shirt that was wet through and covered in mud, but he noticed there was a large streak of blood across it now. He turned to look at the girl next to him she must be bleeding from when he lifted her into the car through the broken window, he jumped up and shouted, "Paramedic we need you here now."

The paramedic appeared and persuaded Evie to lie down into the boot of the police car. He noticed the blood trail from around her waist. Her jacket zipper was stuck and he was going to cut it until Ben reached over and ripped it from top to bottom to save time. Slowly the paramedic pulled up her top and began to wipe away the blood. Evie was lying there with her eyes closed, she tensed as something cold was wiped across her tummy, tears pricked her eyes and she put her arm across her face. It was all just a blur of noise and talking, she couldn't concentrate and just blanked everything out. She was exhausted. The ambulance left with its blue lights flashing in the darkness.

The paramedic noticed a lot of old scars, but the fresh ones were only superficial and she'd be fine. Ben was staring at her stomach; it looked as if she had already been in quite a fierce accident already so for her to have rushed in to help the boy at all was impressive. She was cleaned up and sterile pads taped to her tummy just to stop any further bleeding, then it was just the two of them sat together in silence.

Suddenly a fire officer appeared in front of her; he was tall and blonde and began to talk to her.

"I just need to talk to you, okay; then the police will need to ask you some questions?" He leaned in closely, a bit too close for her liking

"Is he going to be okay, is Matthew going to be okay?"

"He's pretty badly injured, but you did a great job, you both did and he's in good hands now. In fact, little lady, it's Evelyn isn't it? or should I call you Eve or Evie, you did a great job. It was a pretty reckless thing though all the same, the car could have gone up at any minute. Matter of fact we could do with more girls like you in the brigade. I'd be happy to talk you through it next week if you like or we could even go out for a drink you know have a chat about your options?"

Evie's brain was suddenly wide awake; did he just say what she thought he'd said? She bristled with indignation. "Well firefighter ... umm sorry I don't think we've been introduced."

"Oh it's firefighter Laing, Kevin but everyone calls me Kev." And he grinned at her

"Well Firefighter Laing, firstly I'm not a little lady which quite frankly is extremely patronising. Secondly my name is Evelyn, thirdly as far as being reckless goes, if we hadn't done anything then Matthew would now be dead which surely would have been the worst possible outcome. Fourthly I have no intention of joining the brigade not now not ever. I have a job which I love thank you very much and don't need any careers advice from you. And last and by no means least I certainly will not be going for a drink with you to (she made invisible quotation marks in the air) chat about my options whatever they may be– am I making myself clear?"

Sat next to her Ben was struggling to keep his laughter under control. She may be in shock but goodness was she putting God's gift to firefighting in his place, it was hilarious.

"Um yes, very clear."

She made a shooing gesture with both her hands and dismissed him. "Okay so now we've got that clear, Firefighter Laing, off you go." He turned and walked back to his crew who were getting ready to leave the scene.

She put her head between her knees and took some deep breaths. "Cheeky bastard – brave little lady indeed, reckless am I? Go for a drink, bloody nerve. Options, yeah my knee and his crotch that's an option."

Ben couldn't bottle up his laughter anymore and threw his head back. He would love her in his regiment.

Evie suddenly turned to look at the man who'd stopped to help; he smiled at her.

"Hello, he's right you did a great job you know."

"It was you, all you. You saved him, I couldn't open the door, it just wouldn't open," she repeated. "I'm sorry I don't even know your name."

"It's Ben, Ben Shaw."

Evie put her hand out. "Nice to meet you Benjamin Shaw, I'm Evelyn Wallace."

Chapter 49

A police officer was then standing in front of them. "I just need to ask you some questions, routine mostly but we'll need a formal statement too. So if I could start with your name, are you Miss, Mrs or Ms?"

"Evelyn Wallace – Miss." The policeman jerked his head up. "Evelyn is that you? Oh my goodness I didn't recognize you-sorry."

Laughing she said: "Not surprising really Robert, I'm trying out a new look; it's called 'Covered in mud, blood and smelling of eau de shitty field' – it's all the rage in *Vogue*, don't you know?" She realized she must look a fright, but was past caring after the events of the previous hour.

"Oh my God, Evelyn, I had no idea. What you did was amazing, Jason would be so proud you know."

She murmured, "Well it wasn't just me, it was mostly Ben really."

"We were sorry to hear that the two of you had split up. We all thought you'd go with him once he was promoted. Do you still hear from him?"

"Not for a while; we texted for a bit, but he's super busy and loving the job, he has a new girlfriend –Shona –she sounds nice and he seems very happy which is great isn't it?" She didn't really want to discuss that topic not now.

"Right, right okay so back to business; address, telephone number, mobile, occupation, one final thing when did you last have a drink?"

She racked her brains but nothing would come, "umm about 6 weeks ago I think."

Robert laughed," I meant in the last 24 hours."

"Oh sorry, can't think straight must be the shock or something."

"We'll need you to come down to the station to make a formal statement."

"Can I come in tomorrow, I just need to go home now – please Robert – I'm not going to do a runner now am I?"

"No no, of course not. How about 10.00ish?"

"Can we say midday as I think I might need a lie in after tonight?"

"Yes, sure, no problem." Ben had been listening to all of this, so she'd been going out with a copper, but not anymore; he wondered why?

"So now over to you, sir, starting with your name;" and he proceeded to ask him the same set of questions. Evie was listening now, so he was an Army Officer, what was he doing on this road tonight she wondered.

"Again we'll need you to come into the station tomorrow to make a formal statement so I'm afraid you'll need to stay locally; also when did you last have a drink sir?"

"Well I'm on my way home from a wedding, so yes I've had a drink today."

"Okay well we'll need to breathalyse you, sir – just routine procedure."

Evie placed her hand on Constable Blake's arm, "Robert can I have a quick word? Ben could you just give us a minute please?"

Ben moved away, what was going on now; although the last thing he needed was a drink driving charge that really would have been the end to a great day. Evie spoke quietly to Constable Blake for a couple of minutes. Robert indicated for Ben to rejoin them, "Well sir in light of tonight's dramatic events we'll skip the breathalyser. Evelyn assures me you were the main reason that boy got out of the car alive so we'll leave it there. Now sir, where will you be staying?"

Ben had no idea, all of this was unplanned, "Umm not sure actually, are there any hotels near here or something?"

Evie stood up. "It's no problem Robert, Captain Shaw can stay at mine tonight and then we'll come in together tomorrow to do the formal statements, if that's okay with you that is?" she motioned to Ben.

"Yes thanks that would be great."

Robert didn't think this was a good idea and intimated as such.

"Oh Robert, it's fine I have spare bedrooms and separate bathroom. Besides, don't army personnel have to swear an oath to serve and protect or something?" She looked at Ben who was trying hard not to laugh.

"Err yes that's right, at least it's something like that."

"Okay so we're all sorted. Just one thing, Robert; can you drive my car to mine, I don't think I can right now?"

They set off in a small convoy. Robert drove Evie's car with her sat in the passenger seat, followed by Ben in his car and with Constable Wyatt bringing up the rear. In less than ten minutes they pulled up outside Evie's house, the light above the front door flashed on and then it was just her and Ben.

"Welcome to chez Wallace," Evie laughed as they stepped into the hallway. She shut the front door and started to take off her shoes, socks and jacket dropping them into a pile. "I don't think anything here is salvageable – feel free," she intimated for him to do the same. "Okay so I'll show you to your room and bathroom. I don't know about you, but I need one hell of a shower and then some food. I'm starving." Ben followed her up the stairs.

Evie looked at Ben. He must be 6 feet tall so a single bed was not an option. She opened the door of the biggest room, "Here we are this should be okay, I don't think you'll fit in a single bed, I'll leave you fresh towels in the bathroom which is next door, do you need any toiletries or anything?"

"No I'm all sorted thanks."

"Okay so meet me in the kitchen when you're done, no rush. Oh any dirty clothes you want washing just leave them in a little pile outside your door and I'll pick them up on my way down?" She left him to it and padded away down the landing into what he assumed was her bedroom. He looked at his bedroom and bathroom; both were quite luxurious and 1000 times better than that shitty hotel he would have stayed in if he'd remained at the wedding.

Evie washed her hands and then grabbed some clean towels and took them to the guest bathroom then returned to her en-suite. She began to peel off her remaining clothes when she caught sight of herself in the mirror. Bloody hell, who was that girl staring back at her? She was unrecognisable from the Evie who had left home a few hours previously. She let the hot water wash over her; wasn't it amazing about the restorative power of water to make you feel 100% better?

Ben stepped into the shower picking up the gel and shampoo that he found inside the cubicle. Well what an evening it had turned out to be; he was glad he'd stopped to help now. She'd been amazingly calm, no sign of panic, followed his instructions even when faced with seemingly impossible tasks. They made a good team he mused, and as for tearing a strip off that firefighter, well he had deserved it, fancy trying to hit on her after what she'd just done; the man was a prick. He remembered her words about her knee and his crotch being an option and he laughed forgetting he was in the shower and got a sudden mouthful of shampoo. Smiling to himself he thought she obviously had no idea about the army, yes they did swear an oath; but that wouldn't have kept her safe from anything.

Evie dried herself and put on some soft pale blue sweat pants with a matching top. She needed some comfort tonight, and picked up her hairdryer; she felt better already. Twisting her hair up into a lose ponytail at the nape of her neck she went out on to the landing and collected a pile of muddy clothes Ben had left for her. In the kitchen she put on some music and went into the utility room to sort out the washing. Ben wandered down to find her peering into the fridge. Over her shoulder she asked him if hot steak salad with jacket potatoes and rolls would be okay. He said that sounded great. "Okay ten minutes then," and she proceeded to remove things from the fridge setting them down onto the worktop. He'd already seen the back view of her, in fact less than an hour ago he had one hand around her bum and his other hand under her waistband supporting her through the broken car window; however, her bum definitely looked better in soft sweatpants he reasoned. She turned to ask him about the wine and caught him staring at her. "Wine is in the utility, just choose something you'd like, it'll be fine, how do you like your steak?"

Ben shook himself. This couldn't be the girl from the field, it wasn't possible, "Um medium is fine thanks," he mumbled and went to fetch the wine. Bloody hell he hadn't been expecting that, where was the girl from the field and who was this in front of him? It couldn't be the same girl, she was, well she was, what was she exactly? He was flummoxed.

Evie put the potatoes in the microwave and prepared the salad. He had scrubbed up very well she thought, yes very well indeed. He must be at least six foot with brown hair and hazel eyes, very nice build too, probably fit; well he was in the army after all. Not drop dead gorgeous, more boy next door, well rugged boy next door maybe, still she was hardly a supermodel herself and she smiled. Fifteen minutes later they were sat eating as if they hadn't had a meal for a week. Finishing her plate, she sighed, "Whoever had invented frozen jacket potatoes must be a fine man, as aren't they just the eighth wonder of the modern world?"

Ben laughed. The meal had indeed been good and they'd eaten in a companionable silence. She decided to just rinse and stack the plates in the dishwasher and leave the rest for tomorrow. They took their wine into the living room where she'd already lit the wood burner so it was toasty and warm. Indicating he take the sofa she curled herself into an armchair.

"So Captain Shaw, tell me how you came to be on that road just at the exact same time I needed you?" Ben explained about the wedding, it sounded truly awful she thought and although she'd never met Charlotte it sounded unfair of her to practically force him go with her; he was only home ten days after all. They talked loosely about their respective jobs and families, all safe topics as they had had quite enough drama for one night.

"Can I ask you a question now, it's a bit personal?" Ben was intrigued to know about the policeman.

"Um okay as long as you know I might not answer it then go ahead," she grinned at him. The wine was having a relaxing effect on her.

"Why didn't you go with that policeman to start over?"

"Ahh I see – well for a start we weren't actually a couple, not that his work colleagues ever really knew that. Jason helped me through a very difficult patch after a very nasty break up. I was a bit of a mess actually and he helped me pull myself together and get my fitness levels back and I helped him study for his Sargent's exams."

"There must be more to it than that?"

"Oh you're very perceptive aren't you?" she smiled at him. "Well here's the thing: yes, if you must know he said he loved me and wanted me to start over in a new place etc., but I just didn't feel the same way about him. It wouldn't have been fair on me and definitely not on him – it's a bit like when you do a jigsaw puzzle, you know – there are a few pieces that if you try really hard they will fit together, but they don't really fit there. They belong somewhere else. Does that make any sense?"

"Yes actually it does, when you say nasty break up what happened?"

"Gosh you do ask a lot of personal questions don't you?" she mocked him. "Okay if you really want to know but fair warning. Guys don't actually come out of it very well."

"Fair enough, I asked."

She began to talk, quietly and slowly. "I met this guy, um a city boy and he seemed great, but for the first few weeks all he did was fuck up-excuse my language and send flowers to apologize. My house started to look like a florist shop. I actually sent one bunch back to him as I was so fed up of this endless fuck up /fight/apologize/flowers merry go round – so not a brilliant start. Gradually we fought less and things were going well, really well, then I was poorly for a while and had to have enforced bed rest for a week. He took a week off to look after me at his house, told me he loved me and things stepped up if you know what I mean everything was fantastic. Sometime later I got hurt in a fight in a pub car park, I wasn't fighting I hasten to add (Ben smiled to himself wondering what that would have looked like); but I stepped in to break it up and got walloped, so cracked ribs, black eye, fractured arm, bang on the head, so again was out of action for 4 weeks.

I discovered I was pregnant, which with my medical history by the way was nothing short of a miracle. It's been made very clear that me having a baby is not going to happen and so I went up to London to surprise him with the news." Evie took a large gulp of wine and continued. "Well it was me who got the surprise as I caught him with another woman and it was over just like that," she clicked her fingers. "Maybe this is what city boys do all the time, I don't know I'm not a fast sort of girl more a slow wait and see type. Then the icing on the cake was that a few weeks after that I lost the baby – so all in all a bit grim. Jason was the officer who took my statement about the pub fight so that's how we met."

Blimey he hadn't been expecting that, "One more thing, those scars on your tummy are they from the pub fight?"

Evie didn't answer straight away. "No …they're from…an…accident a few years ago. So tell me about Charlotte." It was obvious the subject was closed, Christ he thought she'd been through some shit make no mistake.

Ben described their relationship. They hadn't known each other long before he got deployed and that's tough on anyone; but he'd made it back home and couldn't wait to see her. She on the other hand had obviously not been missing him half as much whilst he was away and this wedding was just the final straw.

"Why are relationships so hard?" he asked out loud.

"You're asking me after what I just told you, what makes you think I have any idea, after all I'm still single?"

"Because it doesn't sound like any of it was your fault."

"Believe you me I'm a lot for anyone to take on, my love life's been a disaster, it's complicated what with my medical issues, my physiological issues and after that break up now my trust issues too. I mean, bloody hell, where's it going to end?" she laughed wryly. "Mind you it's like I am always telling people you have to choose your battles, so there's the small stuff and the big stuff."

"Go on," Ben was happy to sit and listen, maybe it was the wine or maybe it was because of what they'd been through together that night but no topic was off limits.

"So small stuff, who puts the rubbish out or she wants to see a rom – com but you want to see an action movie, you just alternate. Same as who's driving to the pub and who's drinking; you take it in turns, she wants to paint your bedroom a horrid – in your eyes – shade of let's say purple, so you paint three walls a neutral colour and one wall behind the bed purple and that way you don't have to look at it very often." Evie paused. "Well only when you're you know," and she laughed, "you can always shut your eyes or make her look at it if you see what I mean." Ben smiled. She was funny and yes shy too, but there was something about her, he just couldn't put his finger on it. "So that's all the small stuff, the big stuff involves what house you buy or what area you live in, marriage, babies, money;, that's a whole other level of things; but if you can't get the small stuff right then I don't think there's a lot of hope for the big stuff do you?"

Ben pondered what she had said. it sounded like common sense but life was never as easy as that, surely. Evie was suddenly very tired, "Sorry but I need to get some sleep now, stay up if you like, just watch out for Henry if he comes in to see you."

"Who's Henry?"

"My cat. I've had him about 4 years or so, he's a rescue cat and he doesn't like loud noises or sudden movements."

Ben smiled, "Sounds just like me in Afghanistan! No I'm happy to turn in it's been quite a day one way or the other."

They said their goodnights on the landing and went their separate ways.

Evie crawled into bed. Tiredness had washed over her suddenly and she could hardly keep her eyes open. The one recurring thought was that Matthew had been very lucky that her and Ben had been in the right place at the right time or goodness knows what the outcome would have been. She needed to go to the hospital tomorrow to check on him too.

Two doors away, Ben lay in bed. It was very comfortable and big enough for him to stretch out. What a day!. He pondered on Evie's description of her nasty break up as she had described it. The guy sounded like a total bastard, fucking city boys. She was way too good for him; fancy cheating on her whilst she was pregnant and then for her to lose the baby too. Some people just wouldn't have come out the other side from that. But she seemed okay, sounded like the baby would have been a miracle baby too. She was a trier that was certain. If she hadn't wriggled through the broken window hurting herself in the process then who knows where that kid would be now? He smiled to himself thinking of his hand holding her bum then sighed and turned off the light, still thinking about her.

Chapter 50

Evie woke and stretched. Oh what a lovely, lovely sleep; if it wasn't for the fact that she had to feed Henry she would have stayed in bed a bit longer. Yawning she pulled on a robe and padded downstairs. Sure enough Henry was just coming in through the cat flap and didn't want to be fussed with he just wanted milk/food and sleep, preferably in that order. That done she opened the fridge door; 'now for breakfast.' She nearly jumped out of her skin when a voice said, "Good Morning."

"Oh my God, you made me jump." She turned round to see Ben grinning at her.

"Well I wouldn't be much use in the Army if I couldn't creep up on people unannounced, would I?"

Laughing now she replied, "Um no I suppose not – what would you like for breakfast?" They settled on eggs and toast for him and fruit and yoghurt for her.

"Did you sleep well?"

"Like a baby. That's a very comfy bed right enough."

"Good." She changed the subject – "I've done the best I can with the washing; but it's not looking good for your white shirt I'm afraid, the rest will just need ironing when we're back from the station and then you're good to go."

"Okay thanks that's great." He wasn't sure he actually wanted to go anywhere right now. He snuck a furtive glance at Evie. She looked very pretty this morning; she'd obviously just got out of bed so she was all soft and lovely. He shook himself he had to get a grip.

They ate and then after she'd showered and dressed they were ready to leave for the police station. "Would you mind if I drove this morning just to make sure I'm okay driving again after last night, then if I start to panic you can take over?"

"Sure, no problem," it sounded like a good idea, they only needed the one car after all. Sat in the passenger seat he noted she was a very good driver, even better than some of his mates and was happy for her to just drive whilst he peered out of the window.

Just before Midday they presented themselves at the police station and were shown into separate interview rooms where their statements would be taken. It didn't take very long as it was quite straightforward and Evie waited outside for Ben to finish. She'd already asked if she could visit Matthew in hospital but was told he was currently in the ICU and the earliest he could have visitors would be the middle of the week.

On the way back to her house Evie and Ben were happy just to listen to the radio and she caught herself singing along at one point much to his amusement. Once through her front door she offered him a cup of tea and then got out the iron and ironing board for his things. She was sure he wouldn't want to hang about with her for much longer and would be keen to get going.

"Here let me do this, you've washed them after all."

"Well I didn't exactly wash them by hand did I, are you sure?"

"Yes you can sit and watch if you like."

"Okay then if you insist." Of course he could iron he was used to taking care of himself wasn't he, she scolded herself. He was probably better at ironing than her!

She offered him some lunch and asked him about his plans, "I need to go and visit my parents as I haven't been home to see them yet."

"You're kidding – you've been home, what was it? ten days and you haven't seen them. My mother would be so angry with me if I pulled that stunt."

"I've called them of course, but to be honest they're just glad I'm back home alive and well."

"Sorry I didn't think of that; of course they are." She felt bad now. Why did she always have to put her foot in it, usually right up to her neck.

Evie placed a selection of bread, meat, cheese and fruit on the table and indicated he should just help himself when he was ready.

An hour later he was all packed and ready to leave, his bags were thrown in the boot all that was left was to say goodbye. He couldn't figure out why he was finding this so difficult, but they exchanged mobile numbers in case there were more questions from the police and he got in his car. Evie closed the door. That was that little adventure over with, now what was she to do with the rest of her weekend?

Less than five minutes later there was a knock on her door. She opened it to find Ben standing there, running his hands through his hair, "Sorry but my car won't start. It must have been all that rain and everything last night."

"Okay, well come back inside then and we'll think of a plan." She closed the door again and they went into the kitchen.

He leant against the worktop, "So do you have any ideas?" he asked her.

Evie thought for a bit and then smiled and said, "As a matter of fact I do. Just give me a minute to make a few phone calls. How many days were you planning on staying with your family anyway, and where do they live exactly?"

"Just two nights or so, I have to be back to base on Wednesday night and they are about 4 hours from here."

She picked up her mobile and began her calls. Less than 15 minutes later she had a plan, all she had to do now was to convince Ben that it was a good idea.

She took a deep breath, "Okay so what I was thinking was, I can drive you to your parent's house this afternoon, if you give me your car keys I will drop them into Graham in the village when we go by and he'll look at your car first thing on Monday – he owes me a favour. Then I can come back and collect you Tuesday afternoon. I've persuaded a colleague to take my Monday and Tuesday night classes so I don't have classes until Thursday evening and you can make it back to camp easily for Wednesday night –what do you think?"

Ben pondered on what she had said. "That's a lot of driving back and forwards for you which I'm not too happy about; but apart from that it could work I suppose. I really do want to go and see them. Can I just make a quick call and I'll let you know?"

"Sure no problem," and she left him to it. There was quite a bit of toing and froing but she figured she owed him after his help last night. She heard him finish his call and she went back into the kitchen. "Everything settled then?"

"I have a counter proposal which I think makes more sense if you agree?" He held his breath. He wanted her to agree to it more than anything.

"Oh okay, I'm intrigued so go on then, what's this master plan of yours?"

"Well we'll drop the keys off with Graham and then drive on up to my folks. We can stay with them until Tuesday and then the rest is the same as you suggested–what do you think?"

Oh blimey, she hardly knew him and now he wanted her to stay with his folks; this was a bit weird wasn't it? "Um I'm not sure, here's the thing you're a nice chap and everything; but I'm not sure I'd feel comfortable meeting and imposing on your parents, especially as they just really want to see you etc." There she'd said it, he had to decide what he wanted to do.

"I've just called them and they're more than happy for me to bring a friend to stay. You can have the guest room as it has its own en-suite and everything. They're pretty easing-going and I think you'll like them. You may have to bring some of your special food, but apart from that I think it's a good plan." He waited for her response; he'd said as a friend and separate room with en-suite; but there was still no reply from Evie. Finally he spelt it out, "Look just so you know -- in case you're worried there won't be any funny business okay? It's just a trip away with a friend no more no less." He waited again.

Evie was thinking. He certainly sounded like he was on the level and after all she'd got her classes covered so what was she going to do with all that time off if she didn't go with him? Finally she said, "Okay but give me five minutes to check that my neighbour will feed Henry, otherwise it'll have to be my plan or no plan?"

Ben was crossing his fingers that her neighbour was okay to feed the cat as he thought the trip would be fun for both of them. "Okay I'll wait here whilst you go and ask." He was surprised just how much this mattered to him but all he could do now was wait and see.

Chapter 51

They'd been driving for a couple of hours now and were at ease in each other's company. The time passed easily enough, they talked, laughed, listened to the radio and sang along to the music. Her car was eating up the miles and it was a very easy way to travel, suddenly her sat nav announced there was standing traffic 10 miles ahead and did they want to detour.

Evie laughed, "I don't know why they always ask you that question as who wants to sit in traffic, it's bizarre?"

"Yes I suppose it is. This is a nice car, have you had it long?"

"A bit over a year I suppose. It's just the updated version of my old car really, but just with a few added bells and whistles." She had a flash back to that scene in Jonathan's apartment. A lot had happened in a year.

Ten minutes later the traffic ground to a halt, the car automatically switched itself off and there was nothing to do but wait along with everyone else on an early Saturday evening. After an hour of going absolutely nowhere they swapped over seats, Evie was tired, she'd been to work that morning and soon realised they weren't going to get to his parent's house by 7.30 as originally planned. Ben called his mother to let her know they were delayed and not to wait up if they were very late. Eventually a police car appeared and made all the cars merge into one lane before pulling off and then sent them on a massive detour. They had no choice but to follow everyone else-very slowly. After an hour or so Evie wondered, why was travelling so tiring when all you did was sit there? Five minutes later she was fast asleep. Ben drove on, every so often turning to look at her sleeping next to him. He was undecided – should he make his move or wait? She'd already told him she wasn't a fast sort of girl more slow and wait and see; but he didn't want to wait too long.

Just before midnight Ben pulled on the driveway to his parent's house. The lights were still on so it looked as if they had ignored his advice about not waiting up for them. Evie was still asleep and he unloaded the car before opening her door. He watched her for a few moments, just looking at her and wondering. Gently he shook her arm and called her name until she stirred.

"Oh sorry, where are we, and what's the time?" she said sleepily. What he really wanted to do was to pick her up in his arms and carry her up to bed, his bed preferably; but he was getting way ahead of himself.

"We're finally here, come on I'll introduce you, it looks as if they've waited up for us." With that, the front door opened and what looked like a small crowd piled out onto the porch. Ben was hugged and gripped in bear hugs by various members of his family, there did seem to be a lot of them she thought. Finally everyone was inside and made straight for the kitchen. Introductions were made, his mother and father seemed very nice, then there was his older brother William and his girlfriend Daisy, and finally his little sister, April and her boyfriend Craig, so a total of eight. Bottles of wine were opened. Everyone was around the kitchen table all talking at once. The family cat, Monty, made an appearance and headed straight for her legs, obviously sensing a cat lover amongst the group. She watched Ben with his family, lots of joking about and laughing. As the noise level increased she motioned to Ben that she would like to leave him to catch up with his family without her.

"Okay everyone, just quieten down. I'm just going to show Evelyn to her room and then I'll be back." Before he had a chance his sister April had jumped up and grabbed Evie's hand, "No need I'll take her, you stay here and chat," and with that Evie said a general goodnight and followed April. She collected her bag at the bottom of the stairs and then they made their way to the guest room. Ben was quietly cross he wanted to be the one to show Evie to her room; but April had got there first, he'd have to be quick on his feet tomorrow.

It was a lovely big room with its own bathroom too. From her initial glance it seemed like quite a large house; she reasoned it must have at least five bedrooms just to accommodate everyone who was here that night. Thanking April, she asked what time breakfast was in the morning, "Oh we don't stand on ceremony here. The earliest anyone will be down is 9.00ish in their jim jams so just whenever you want really. I'm glad you're here, we really miss Ben when he's away and it's great for him to bring a girl home. If you need anything in the night then Ben's just next door." She waved her hand towards the bathroom wall and with that she was gone, not giving Evie a chance to say that they were just friends; but surely that was obvious, wasn't it? She was in the guest room, after all. Before she could close the bedroom door Monty squeezed through the gap and making straight for her bed, jumped up and gave her a look which she took to mean: hurry up, then! and get into bed, I'm ready to curl up and sleep. Laughing she hung up some clothes, sorted out her toiletries, cleansed her face and brushed her teeth. Leaving her door slightly ajar in case Monty wanted to leave in the night she climbed into bed and switched the light off. Oh sleep! she thought, sometimes it was her best friend in the world. Monty chose his spot carefully, snuggling into the space by her tummy and settled down with a loud purr.

Some time later the Shaw family decided enough was enough and gradually made their way to bed. Ben paused outside the guest room and noticing the door was ajar peered in. Two green eyes met his and if he wasn't mistaken the message was 'sorry, you're too late. I got here first and I'm not leaving anytime soon'. He noticed Evie was curled up obviously in a deep sleep. Frowning he was still cross he hadn't had the chance to show her to her room; if he had, he would he have given her a goodnight hug, well he was never going to know now was he? Ben made his way next door to his bedroom. Tomorrow was another day.

Sunday morning at the Shaw house and no-one was in any hurry to get up and start the day. Evie showered and dressed in faded jeans and a lilac sweatshirt, tying her hair into a low lose ponytail. She thought that although they were comfortable sitting around the kitchen table in their pj's, she definitely wasn't, not in front of people she had only met briefly the night before. She made her way down to the kitchen to find Mrs Shaw making coffee.

"Hello Evelyn. Did you sleep well?"

"Yes thank you, I was so tired. I hope you didn't think it rude of me to leave you all to it last night?"

"No not at all, there's a lot of us and we're just so happy to have Ben home. I expect you'd figured that out already. So, breakfast?"

She was eating fruit and yoghurt when Ben appeared, dressed in sweatpants and a t–shirt, his hair damp from a shower. My oh my, he was looking good this morning, more relaxed somehow now he had his family around him.

"Morning Evie, sleep well?" Were his eyes twinkling at her or was it just her imagination working overtime?

"Yes thanks, very well. I had Monty for company so just like being at home with Henry, really."

"Who's Henry?" Mrs Shaw asked and before Evie could reply Ben piped up: "Oh that's Evelyn's cat, named after Henry 8th. So what would you like to do today?"

She hadn't really thought about it, "Um well I'd like to go for a run before lunch if possible, if you just point me in the right direction I'll only be an hour." Yes, she thought, good plan: get some distance from Mr Twinkly Eyes himself.

"Sounds good. I'll join you." Oh no, she hadn't imagined he'd want to come along too.

"Well only if you're sure. I think your family want to spend as much time with you as possible." She was desperately wanting his mother to insist he stay with her, but nothing was forthcoming.

"True, but an hour won't hurt now will it?" Before she could reply William and April staggered into the kitchen in their dressing gowns.

"Oh my goodness how do you two manage to look so disgustingly healthy at this time in the morning?" grumbled William.

Ben stretched out lazily in a chair with his hands behind his head and replied, "What can I say, it's a gift, some of us have it and some of us don't." and then he winked at Evie. She decided to stare very decidedly at her fruit and let the conversation mill around her. Immediately he realised she really was a bit shy and it was very appealing, yes very appealing indeed.

"We're going for a run at midday, care to join us?"

"Are you insane? That sounds like far too much hard work. Are you sure you want to go Evelyn, cos don't feel you have to do everything Ben wants to, you know?"

"Actually it was Evelyn's idea wasn't it, so the more the merrier." He knew damn well no-one else would be joining them and was secretly very pleased it would be just the two of them.

The kitchen then filled up with the remaining family and partners and there was general banter and laughter all round. Evie was happy to sit and listen, she helped to clear the table and when she turned round Monty was sat in her seat waiting for her. She picked him up and plonked him on her lap where he made himself at home. This hadn't gone unnoticed by Ben who thought she was looking very pretty this morning and seemed right at home with his family, pets and all.

At 11.45, Evie excused herself and went upstairs to put her running gear on. Thinking about it, how it was going to be fine as you couldn't really run and talk at the same time, so although Ben would be accompanying her there wouldn't be too much chat thank goodness. Back in the kitchen April was grilling Ben about Evie: all the usual stuff girls like to know, how had they met /how long had they been seeing each other? She wasn't getting very far as Ben was being very evasive and eventually said, "I'd forgotten just how nosey you can be, okay I'll tell you over lunch. Right now I've got to change for my run. Are you sure I can't persuade anyone to join us?" and with that he was gone.

Ben found Evie laughing in the kitchen with his mother. She was dressed ready to go. He looked appreciatively at her Lycra clad figure. She looked good this morning. After saying their goodbyes he shut the front door behind them and they set off slowly jogging down the drive. His stride was naturally a lot wider then Evie's so he made allowances, just like in the Army with recruits they all had to stay together; but she was pretty fit so it should be just fine. Evie was glad to be out in the fresh air; it was a bit of a dull day, but wasn't freezing cold so good for running. Ben obviously ran this route regularly and she was happy to just follow his lead, each of them listening to their own thoughts running through their heads as the countryside went by.

Suddenly she was jolted back to reality as Ben asked her, "So do you want the easy route or the harder route with a great view?" They were running on the spot and Evie took a few moments to do some stretches.

"That depends on what your version of hard is, I'm not actually in the Army don't forget?" She smiled at him.

"True enough, but do you trust me, I wouldn't suggest it if I didn't think you could do it?"

After the events of Friday evening Evie realised that yes, she did trust him. Putting her head on one side she replied, "Yes I do, so okay let's do it."

"Good choice." He knew she would step up and they set off again.

He wasn't kidding about this being the hard route, it was uphill for most of the way. Her legs began to ache slightly but she pushed on and pushed herself hard. After another twenty-five minutes or so she was rewarded with the most amazing view and they slowed to a halt to catch their breath.

"Wow you weren't kidding, were you? This is fantastic." She spent a while just drinking it in. The countryside was beautiful even on a day like today, in the summer it must be even better.

MUSIC: – WHAT CAN I DO TO MAKE YOU LOVE ME? – THE CORRS

Ben wasn't looking at the view, after all he had seen it hundreds of times before. He was watching her, he wasn't quite sure whether to push his luck and see what happened or just to bide his time. If he got it wrong now she'd be gone and he'd be stuck with no girl and no car either, so he decided to play it safe for now. "Told you it would be worth it didn't I?"

They made their way back. It was much easier on the return journey as most of it was downhill and then on the flat. Arriving back at the drive they slowed their pace to cool down and stretched on the porch. She'd enjoyed that, her mind was clear and she felt refreshed and energized. Taking off their shoes they went inside and made for the kitchen to get some water. Everyone seemed to be exactly where they had left them only they were all dressed now and reading the Sunday papers.

They'd been out for more like an hour and a half and Evie realized she was hungry. Lunch was going to be at 3.00, giving the boys time to go to the pub for a drink if they wanted.

"Did you enjoy that Evelyn?" enquired Mrs Shaw.

"Yes thank you it was great, you have an amazing view from the top."

"Oh Ben you didn't make the poor girl run all the way to the top of Roman Hill did you? Just because you do it all the time doesn't mean everyone else wants to" she scolded.

"Evie did just fine mother, don't forget she's a fitness professional herself, plus we wouldn't have gone that far if I didn't think she could do it."

"Honestly Evelyn – boys what can you do with them they're impossible aren't they?"

Evelyn and Mrs Shaw laughed conspiratorially together.

"Don't worry Mrs Shaw I was fine. I was more worried about Ben being able to keep up with me to be honest." She winked at Ben, two could play this game. Ben grinned back at her, if they'd been on their own he would have thrown caution to the wind and pulled her to him and kissed her hard. As it was he had no choice but to take a shower set to cool and go to the pub with his father, William and Craig.

Chapter 52

Evie stood under the hot water in the shower. She felt great; exercise, fresh air and now hot water followed by lunch. She was glad she'd decided to accompany Ben on this visit. Sometimes, the best times came when you least expected them. Dressing in her best jeans and one of her favourite tops she rejoined the women in the kitchen. April and her were tasked with laying the table, whilst Daisy was in charge of tableware. Evie wondered if she should ask for smaller cutlery, eventually plucking up the courage to ask April. Luckily April thought this was funny and found her a smaller set. They were interrupted by the men returning from the pub and the conversation changed to football and when could they eat.

The eight of them were sat at the dining table passing bowls of vegetables between them. Again there was plenty of chatter and it was easy to just sit back and listen. Evie complimented Bens' mother on the delicious meal, the only thing she couldn't eat was the gravy; but it was no hardship given the scale of the feast presented to them. After the main course had been cleared away they took a break before dessert and April, seizing the opportunity, took up questioning Ben where she had left off this morning.

"So come on Ben, you promised to tell me how did the two of you meet? Don't keep me in suspense."

Ben grinned at Evie who was sat on the opposite side of the table a few places down from him. "Well do you want to tell them or shall I?"

Evie though about it for a second and then said, "I'll start and then you can fill in all the details okay?" He nodded.

"Well I first met your brother last Friday night in the dark, in a field and I was all covered in mud." There – she left it hanging, letting the words sink in. He started this so he could take it from here she thought.

April looked confused and before she could speak William had butted in, "You mean Friday, two days ago Friday?"

"Yes that's right."

April said, "I still don't understand, what were both of you doing in a muddy field in the dark?"

Evie left it to Ben to tell the whole story, complete with details of how he happened upon the scene and everything that had followed from there.

The table was stunned into silence for a few seconds before the questions started again coming thick and fast. Eventually Ben's father said, "So the reason that boy is alive is down to the two of you?"

"Pretty much dad, yes I suppose so."

Evie felt obliged to chip in at this point, "It's really down to your son, as without him I couldn't get the car door open so things could have been very different."

"She's being modest, don't listen to her. If she hadn't climbed through a broken window, hurting herself in the process then I never would have got the door open. So sister dear does that answer your questions?"

"Yes and no; but I'll save the rest for later."

Ben said, "Thank the Lord for that." And everyone laughed. Dessert was brought in and the subject was changed.

Ben's mother cleared the table. So her son had done yet another heroic deed, this time in partnership with this girl called Evelyn, whom he'd only met two days ago. She didn't see that coming although that explained his request for her to have the guest room. Helen Shaw thought they seemed good together, even though it was just after knowing each other for two days, how strange but fascinating all the same. Evelyn was a surprise and a delight, (very different to Charlotte whom she had met only once and didn't take to at all), it was clear her son liked her; but the question was, did Evelyn feel the same way about him?

The boys settled down to watch the football and Evelyn joined them after being shooed out of the kitchen by Mrs Shaw. She settled into an armchair sitting crossways with her legs dangling over the side. Ben stole a glance at her. She was here until Tuesday and then he had to travel back with her, collect his car and go back to the Army. This time spent with her would be over all too soon. She'd made it clear she had issues, a lot of issues, and trust seemed to be the biggest obstacle for her at the moment. He would have to give her some time; but not too much.

At some time after 7.00pm April and William started to make noises about having to leave, not that any of them wanted to break up the party so to speak; but they all had work tomorrow and needed to get back on the road.

Goodbyes and hugs all round. Soon it was just Ben, his parents and Evie. Mrs Shaw fixed them a snack, luckily Evie had brought some of her oatcakes so she was happy with an apple and some cheese to go with them. They discussed plans for Monday. She thought that Ben ought to spend some time with his parents without her and decided to take herself off for the morning on the pretext of doing some urgent clothes shopping in the nearest town, insisting she go on her own. Besides she needed some space; the group had halved from 8 to 4 and as per usual she was feeling a bit uneasy, so no change there she smiled wryly to herself.

Brushing her teeth, Evie pondered on the day. She'd enjoyed herself. True, she still didn't really know a great deal about Ben, but she was happy to be here. His family were lovely and had made her feel very welcome. She thought back to the surprise on their faces when it was explained they had only met two days ago and the circumstances that had followed. Going back into the bedroom she noticed that Monty had already taken up his position on the bed the same as the night before. She smiled. Cats were so much simpler than people, weren't they?

Ben lay down on his bed. Today had been a good day, everyone happy, relaxed and laughing, it had been just what he needed after his last deployment. They didn't get any easier in fact they seemed to get tougher. Maybe he could persuade Evie to keep in touch by text and email once he was back on base. He couldn't imagine her not being part of his life. He'd read an article somewhere about people saying that the first time they met someone they just knew they'd be great together which he'd thought was utter bollocks; but now he wasn't so sure.

Monday was just as she'd planned. She took herself out of their way for the morning and then went for a run with Ben in the afternoon. By 11.00am the following morning, Evie had packed her things and was putting her bags in the car. They would need to stop for fuel, but other than that she hoped it would be a good journey home. Much as she'd enjoyed her trip away she wanted to get back to see Henry and besides her class rota was jam packed for the next two weeks especially after all the favours she'd had to pull in for this trip. She said her goodbyes and then it was just the two of them setting off back the way they'd come only four days before. His parents were emotional at his leaving, but told her she would be welcome to stay with them again any time, how did families cope with this time after time she wondered.

They hadn't been on the road for more than 15 minutes when her phone rang. She pressed the hands free button on the steering wheel. It was Graham. There was good news and bad news about Ben's car. The good news was it was fixable the bad news was he needed to order a part and it wouldn't be in until Thursday so he wouldn't get his car back until the weekend. Evie listened and thanked Graham, ended the call and manoeuvred the car into a side road.

"So what do you want to do now? There doesn't seem to be much point me driving you home to mine as you need to be on base tomorrow and without a car I'll just have to drive you back again; but you'll be back a day too soon?"

Ben thought about this for a moment. "Yes, good point, how about we stop somewhere nice for lunch today and you drop me back at base early this evening then we'll figure out the rest once my car is fixed?"

"Good idea, so where are we going for lunch?"

Ben suggested a pub he'd been to before. He knew it was open all day so there wouldn't be a rush to leave. He was disappointed not to be going home with her; but he knew it didn't make any sense to do that plus he'd have to go and collect his car when he was next on leave so he would see her again then. He was used to plans changing at the last minute; but it didn't make it any easier sometimes.

Evie entered the location of the pub into the sat nav and let it guide her there. She put her favourite CD on to play and let Taylor Swift's voice fill the car. The pub was very nice. As the day was chilly they had lit the open fire and it was just the place to hunker down for the afternoon. Ben bought the drinks, large orange juices for them both and they read the menus in silence. Evie would need to choose carefully, but usually she could get them to tweak a meal for her if she asked them nicely enough. It was a very pleasant way to spend an afternoon. Once the lunchtime service was over the pub was deserted and it was just them and a couple of diehard locals filling the chairs until the evening rush began.

Neither of them were in any hurry but as time went by it was obvious they would need to make a move soon. Even after Evie had dropped Ben back she would still have to drive an hour and a half until she was home. Reluctantly they set off once again. Ben gave her directions to the camp and silently prayed for roadworks or any diversion that would make their journey longer; but sod's law dictated that wasn't going to happen today and they pulled into the gate of his camp a little before 6.30. He showed his ID and the barrier was lifted for the car to drive through. Ben directed Evie to pull up outside a nondescript building where she parked and turned off the engine. They both got out and he grabbed his bags from the boot.

"So thanks for the lift and everything, I've enjoyed the weekend, hope my family don't give you nightmares?" he joked, although he wasn't really in the mood for jokes now. Another member of Army personnel walked past and saluted Ben. Evie smiled; she really had no idea about the Army and found it slightly amusing to see Ben being saluted when she thought back to his appearance in that muddy field.

"Well it's been fun Captain, hasn't it?" she joshed.

"Safe journey home, text me when you're back will you?"

"Okay, but I've got Taylor for company so I'll be just fine," she smiled back at him.

"Taylor who?"

"The CD silly, I usually have it playing a lot louder than today so you've had a lucky escape."

It was funny, but he really didn't feel very lucky at all right then.

This done, Evie suddenly felt awkward. Ben stepped forward and hugged her, released her far too quickly but it was too late to hug her again. She got back in her car and drove back towards the barrier and the road home.

Ben lugged his kit though the door and made his way up the stairs. On entering the office he found a colleague, Lofty grinning at him, "so Benny boy – three things I've been wondering, firstly why you're back 24 hours early, secondly who's that lovely lady down there, and thirdly what the fuck is she doing with you?"

Chapter 53

Wednesday and Evelyn went into town to the hospital. She wanted to see if they would allow her to visit Matthew. She wasn't a relative but hoped for even five minutes just to see how he was doing. Well he was still in ICU and visitors were strictly limited; however once the nurse knew who she was she asked Evie to wait and went off up the corridor. A few minutes later a man and a woman returned with the nurse; it was Matthew's mother and brother who wanted to thank her for all she'd done.

Introductions made, it turned out that Clive his brother was a solicitor and would be handling the case. He would need to get in touch with her and Ben in due course and Evelyn said anything they could do to help etc. She made her excuses after a few minutes and left them to it. Evie spent the day doing domestic drudgery: food shopping, cleaning, stripping the sheets from the guest bed and although it was productive enough she couldn't shake the feeling that had circumstances been different then who knew what could have happened? Shaking her head, she sighed – Matthew was one lucky boy.

Ben discovered that he was due on a training exercise first thing Thursday morning for the next 6 days. So much for collecting his car at the weekend, his car would have to wait. Evie had texted him once she was back home last night and so now he sent her a message saying plans had changed and was there any news about his car. His car was still with Graham and not to worry for when it was fixed it would be just fine parked outside her house until they had a new plan of how he would collect it.

The following 5 days passed quickly enough for the two of them. Evie was flat out doing both morning and evening classes so had no time to think about anything else really. She was going to see her mother soon and they'd chatted on the phone about the accident, her mother scolding her for getting too involved yet again. Evie had deliberately kept some of the details from her mother as if she knew the whole story she would have been even crosser with her. Evie and Rowan had a late night drink together on Friday and Evie didn't want to discuss Ben; but rather moved the conversation round to her friend's new boyfriend. Rowan was only too happy to fill Evie in on all the juicy news.

Meanwhile Ben was on Army Exercise and had no time to think about Evie at all except just before he fell asleep every night. The accident seemed almost like dream now and he was very aware that he would need to call her to sort out plans to collect his car. Turning his phone on briefly Tuesday morning, he saw Evie had sent him a text; she'd given him a choice of either her collecting him on Tuesday night after she finished work so about 10.00pmish or Wednesday evening, all he had to do was text back which option suited him best. Instantly he replied that Tuesday night would be fine if it was still okay with her. She would have to report to the barrier and he'd leave instructions for her car to be allowed through onto base. Smiling, after he pressed send he thought it hadn't mattered either way, but this way meant he would spend more time with her so it was a win, win in his eyes. Phone now switched off, he dragged his mind back to the final days' exercise.

Evie parked her car at the gym just after 5.30, allowing herself plenty of time to organize both her and her music before her first class began at 6.00. On entering reception she was met with a chaotic scene with members of staff running up and down the stairs in a panic. It turned out that a water pipe had leaked into the studio and that part of the ceiling had fallen down. She went up the stairs to assess the situation. Steve the manager was doing his usual headless chicken routine and after asking Stacey what was going on. It was clear that the studio would be out of action until Monday at the earliest. Stacey had been tasked with texting the regular clients so they wouldn't have a wasted journey and put a notice on the glass front door of the building explaining the situation. Steve wasn't happy; there would be no classes for at least 5 days according to the insurance company and their builders; but then as Evie told herself, that was nothing new as he was never happy. The cloakrooms and showers were also out of action until tomorrow as they had to turn the water off. Steve reluctantly agreed she wouldn't be needed until Monday morning; but to make sure she was in early that day just in case things still needed to be sorted. As she walked across the car park she smiled to herself and thought, 'Thank you, God, for this little intervention'. Maybe her good deed with Matthew had been rewarded after all?

Back in her car now she swung into the supermarket car park. She would need to use the loo and get some fuel before she set off and texted Ben to let him know she would now be with him a lot sooner, possibly 7.30/7.45 ish instead and was this okay with him?

Ben read her text. Was it okay with him, yes it was bloody brilliant news! If he planned things correctly they could spend a few days together, yes, life was suddenly very good to him. He simply texted back, 'Yes fine see you soon'. Earlier that morning Lofty just so conveniently happened to glance at Ben's phone when it was left on the dashboard of their Land Rover. Oh so he was having a visitor, was he, and if he wasn't much mistaken it was the girl from the other day. Well, well he thought; we could have some fun with this.

Evie's car easily ate up the miles towards the camp. She was very happy just singing along with Taylor tonight. She'd decided to remain in her gym kit as it was clean and she didn't see the point of wasting more time just to stop and change. Earlier that day Graham had parked Ben's car on her driveway. It was as good as new and she'd given the outside a wash to make it all shiny, not that he would see that in the dark; but never the less she owed him one for stopping and helping her the other night.

Pulling up to the barrier she opened the passenger window and gave her name to camp security, who after checking her ID and her vehicle directed her up the same way she had been last week. Getting out she was met by another soldier who told her she was to wait in Captain Shaw's office as he had been temporarily delayed. Lofty spied her pulling up outside and had sent Private Turner to escort her into the building. Unbeknown to her Ben was on the other side of the camp having been told that he was needed urgently.

"Um are you sure that's allowed, I can just wait here in my car?"

"Sorry Miss I'm just following orders. If you'd like to come this way."

She followed Private Turner up the stairs and he knocked on what she assumed was Ben's office door, waited until he was told to enter then announced Miss Wallace for Captain Shaw. Evie stepped into the room and was surprised that three, no four, men immediately stood up.

"Good evening Miss Wallace. Captain Shaw has been unavoidably detained and asked us to look after you until he returns."

"I see. Thank you." Evie wondered what was going on, this seemed to be a bit odd; but they seemed friendly enough and once introductions had been made they offered her a chair and all sat down. They offered her a cup of tea which she declined, but she asked for some water instead.

On the other side of the camp Ben had arrived only to be told there must have been some mistake as he wasn't required after all. Cussing for what was a complete waste of his time he turned round and started to walk back the same way he'd just come. Soon he could see his office building in the distance and the closer he got he realized that Evie's car was parked outside, but that she wasn't in it.

In his office it soon become clear to Evie that these guys had sent Ben away somewhere just so they could find out more about her, or rather her and Ben. She guessed that Ben had been vary cagey when Lofty had asked about her and he'd hatched a plan to get him out of the way once they knew she was coming back to camp to collect him.

Lofty thought he would try out some subtle interrogation questions on her whilst they had the time. "So Evelyn, Ben has told us a lot about you; but why exactly are you acting as his chauffeur tonight then?"

"Well his car wouldn't start after the accident so he left it with me to get it fixed." She wasn't going to tell them anything that wasn't common knowledge.

"I see, so were you on your way to the gym tonight?"

"Yes I only wear this kit for work and exercise. Are you sure it's okay for me to be here in his office as I'm happy to wait in the car?" She pretended to stand up.

Lofty jumped in way too quickly. "Yes it's fine, not a problem at all, sit down, sit down." She caught a glance between two of the guys; it was just as she expected, they really didn't know anything at all. Ben had told them precisely nothing so this was an exercise in pure nosiness,

"So do you think you could... for example help me to get into shape, you being a professional and all?

She decided to have some fun at their expense. "Well maybe. I do HIT, running, general stuff, weights, a bit of boxing too; but I'm a bit concerned to be honest?"

"Oh concerned, what about?"

"Well I would only be too happy to whip you into shape, but to be totally frank I'm worried that you just wouldn't be able to keep up with me!"

The other men sniggered but Evie continued, "Ben has told me all about the four of you, naturally I'm only too happy to help of course; although I'm still a bit confused maybe you could help me out? So tell me which one of you is as slow as a snail and who is just being a lazy bastard?"

After a tiny pause then there was laughter all round. She had sussed them out, alright.

Before they could answer another man dressed in army uniform walked unannounced into the office, the four men immediately stood up and so Evie did too.

"At ease gentlemen, oh I see we have a visitor." Oh gosh this didn't look good, not one bit.

"Sir this is Miss Wallace for Captain Shaw."

Evie turned to face him and put out her hand, "Evelyn Wallace Sir, how do you do."

He shook her hand. "Are you being entertained Miss Wallace?"

"Yes thank you Sir, it's been… very entertaining." She bit her lip – hard, now was not the time to be getting the giggles.

"Miss Wallace, Miss Wallace… now would that be the same Miss Wallace who helped Captain Shaw at an RTA a few days ago?"

Evie swallowed. How did he know? "Yes Sir that's correct."

"Ah very good, well gentlemen this lady could probably teach you all at thing or two about keeping calm whilst under pressure." At that precise moment Ben entered the now somewhat crowded room.

"Ah Captain Shaw there you are, your visitor has arrived. I won't keep you, Miss Wallace. Gentlemen." Everyone stood up again as he exited the room.

Ben was angry. So this was what they'd planned and he knew just who the ringleader was too. Before he could say anything Evie walked over to him, put her arms around his neck and said, "Oh there you are baby. Did you miss me?" winked at him and then put her lips on his.

He looked startled, pulled back from her slightly then guessed what she was doing and played along with it, "Oh you have no idea," he replied, kissing her back. Evie was the one who was startled and went to pull away, but Ben wasn't having any of that. She'd started it so they'd better finish it, although she still wasn't responding to him as he would have liked. His arms were around he and he squeezed her bum; God, life was good. Eventually someone cleared their throat.

"Gentlemen if you'll excuse us, we have to be on our way, things to do as the saying goes, say goodbye now Evelyn."

She grinned at them. "Gentlemen, it's been a pleasure." And with that Ben and her exited the room and ran down the stairs trying not to laugh before they were out of earshot.

Once in the car they dissolved in laughter, "Oh my God, did you see their faces?" whatever they were planning it had backfired.

"I got sent on some bloody wild goose chase just so they could invite you in and ask you questions, Christ they're nosey. Just you wait I'll get them back soon enough."

"Don't worry I didn't tell them anything," She told him the gist of the conversation he'd missed. She was more than capable of looking after of herself he realised, funny too. She followed that up with, "Not that there's anything to tell is there?" Evie was just spelling it out; but just in case he hadn't or didn't want to understand she continued with: "Just to be clear, I was just playing them at their own game, okay? You know we're just friends don't you?"

"Yeah of course I knew that." Ben agreed with her but silently was wishing she hadn't spelt it out quite so definitively, so she still wasn't interested in him, he'd kissed her and had really enjoyed it too; what did he have to do for goodness sake? She'd told him she was complicated; but he couldn't see it. Yes, she had major trust issues so maybe he would have to get her defences down.

The drive back to her house was quick and uneventful, Taylor kept them company and they chatted about what Ben had been doing on his latest exercise. Once home she gave Ben his car keys and they sat and had a glass of wine in the living room.

"I do appreciate you doing all this."

"Well it wasn't much really, just a few lifts here and there and getting your car fixed. Oh by the way, I washed your car today so it's all shiny and ready to go."

He didn't want to go anywhere. "Did you? You didn't need to do that."

"Yes, well, call it a thank you for stopping to help me last week. So tell me, what are your plans now? ".

It turned out that Ben had two days off before going back to camp; however, Evie had already planned to spend the following day with Rowan and then she had to cover classes on Thursday morning so that she could have Sunday off to visit her mother.

In that case he would go and visit his brother William. He couldn't just hang around at Evie's not if she wasn't even going to be there. They said goodnight and went their separate ways along the landing. Ben pulled back the duvet and lay on the bed. He'd been so excited about spending more time with her, he thought the more he did that then the better chance he had of changing her mind about him or rather about the two of them. That obviously wasn't going to happen now, it was so frustrating, William would naturally be glad to see him; but it wasn't at all what he'd planned.

The following morning they said their goodbyes after breakfast and promised to keep in touch by text, as Ben drove away all he could think of was when and how he was going to get the chance to see her again.

Chapter 54

THE MAN yawned. He was fed up at getting to the airport before 5.00am still he didn't have much longer to wait as he spied Dempsey meeting his driver at the arrivals barrier. Taking a sly photo he sent a quick text to let HIM know that Dempsey was back in the country. Great, now he could go home and take a nap.

Evie enjoyed her day with Rowan. They always picked up exactly where they left off, talking and eating all day long. Although she mentioned the accident she didn't give Rowan too many details about Ben, she just wanted to keep them to herself for a bit. She'd thought about their recent time together and wasn't sure if: A he wanted to go out with her in the first place, B: if she was ready to put herself through all of that again after Jonathan or C: if he was just being kind after stopping to help?

Friday morning and Ben was back at base. He'd been summoned to a meeting and told he was going to be sent on a special deployment, this time for three months. He couldn't believe his bloody ears, not again and so soon too, he felt like he'd only just got home, but apparently he'd been chosen following his outstanding performance on the last deployment and had no choice but to make plans to leave in exactly a week's time.

Over the weekend he had time to think about him and Evie; but just saying those three words together didn't mean it would happen. He knew she had Wednesdays off so maybe he would turn up and surprise her, he hadn't told her yet that he was going away again. His parents had been supportive when he'd rung them with the news; but he knew they'd worry from the time he left until he called them to say he was home again – still that was life in the forces for you. Just because this was a regular thing didn't make it any easier to bear.

Ben set off very early on Wednesday morning. He hoped to arrive at Evie's just after eight, to get the best possible chance that she would be home and they would have the whole day together. Plus, he needed to tell her he was going away again. He knocked on her door but there was no reply; the curtains were open so she couldn't still be in bed, eventually he sent her a text.

Hi it's me, where are you? –SEND

Hi, on the train, why where are you? – SEND

I'm stood outside your front door, what train? – SEND He was outside her front door, she hadn't been expecting him, it didn't make any sense.

The train to London. I have to go up for meetings on the first Wednesday of every month. What do you mean you're on my doorstep? – SEND Oh shit she wasn't even here, she was on a train going to London, now what was he going to do?

I wanted to surprise you, plus I have some news. –SEND

Well that's the trouble with surprises isn't it – they don't always go to plan. What news? –SEND

Should he just tell her by text? Somehow it just didn't seem right.
I'd rather tell you in person than by text. – SEND

It sounds serious, should I be worried? I'm usually on the 5.15pm train home so won't be back until 7.15pm. What will you do for the rest of the day? – SEND

He had no idea. He'd thought it was such a brilliant idea, but now he was here and she was there and he didn't have time to wait until tonight as he had to report back on base by 6.00pm.
Don't worry, can I call you once you're off the train so we can talk properly? – SEND

How about I call you after my first meeting? I'll see if I can use one of their offices so it'll be nice and quiet and private too – SEND

He sighed. He didn't have a choice but it was probably the best solution. He was kicking himself now why hadn't he called her last night instead of trying to be clever and surprise her?

Okay call me when you can. – SEND

They both hung up. Evie was worried, what was he going to tell her? Any other Wednesday she would have been at home; how bloody annoying! Ben sighed. He had no choice but to turn around and make his way back to camp. He'd stop at a pub for lunch and hope that Evie would call him so they could talk properly.

His mobile rang just before midday and he hurried out into the pub car park to answer it.

"Hi it's me. Are you okay to talk now? You sounded kind of tense before, I was worried"

"Um yes. I'm in a pub car park just a sec and I'll get in the car – so how did your meeting go this morning?"

"Oh you know. Same old, same old," she wasn't giving anything away, same as usual he sighed; there was no easy way to tell her, he'd just have to blurt it out.

"Evie I found out yesterday that I'm being deployed again, for three months this time that's why I was on your doorstep this morning. I wanted to tell you in person." He waited for her response – nothing came, "Evie are you still there, did you hear what I just said?"

In a small voice Evie replied, "Yes I'm still here, I'm just surprised that's all, obviously I'm not sure how these things work, but I take it this wasn't exactly planned – have you told your parents?" She didn't know what to say, he'd been back less than a month and now he was going away again. Her feelings took her by surprise, she didn't think this would matter quite so much to her.

"Yes it was a surprise to me too. I called them last night, they're worried of course, but it's my job so we've all just got to accept it."

"When do you leave, or is that top secret?"

He smiled. She really didn't have a clue but rather than get cross he found it strangely endearing. "Sunday, I leave on Sunday, but I'm back to base tonight to get prepared, so I won't see you before I leave." There he'd said it.

"Oh … I see…," She didn't know what to say; what did people say in the circumstances? It was so different to anything she'd ever known and she didn't want to make a bad situation even worse.

"I wanted to ask you a favour actually."

"Okay go on."

"If I text you the details will you write to me whilst I'm away? Letters from home are one of the best things to make it bearable?" He waited with baited breath; at worst she would refuse, at best she would agree and it would make his day, if not his year.

There was relief in her voice when she said, "Oh letters …of course I can do that, in fact I'd love to write to you. I thought you were going to ask me something else entirely." Letters – he wanted her to write letters – now that she could do no problem at all.

Ben was ecstatic: she was going to write, but what in God's name did she think he was going to ask? He decided not to risk anything by asking her so decided to let that bit go. She was going to write and he couldn't wait to get her first one.

MUSIC: – HOW YOU GET THE GIRL – TAYLOR SWIFT.

Sunday morning found Ben ready at the airfield for the flight out of the UK. He wouldn't be back for three months this time, just when he wanted or needed to be at camp. He had plenty of time during the flight to think about Evie, this funny girl from the muddy field had appeared out of nowhere and he'd been intrigued and entranced from the word go. She was easy to be around, hell even his family really liked her. Best of all Evie had promised to write to him every two weeks and she didn't strike him as someone who wouldn't keep a promise. It didn't sound like she was in a hurry to get involved in another relationship anytime soon; but still he hoped she wouldn't meet anyone whilst he was away.

Chapter 55

Ben was in a foul mood and was taking it out on his men. It wasn't actually their fault, but their post from home had been delayed yet again due to bad weather. He still hadn't heard from Evie and now he was beginning to wonder if he ever would. Wouldn't that be just his luck to be away from her for three months and not to hear a single word from her; how in hell's name was he going to cope with that? There was a knock on his door and Private Turner stood there, Ben told him to come in, he'd brought the mail, at long bloody last. Ben could see immediately there were letters from his parents and brother and sister too, at the end of the pile there was another letter; but he didn't recognize the handwriting and holding his breath he tore it open. He smiled and relaxed; it was a letter from Evie, she hadn't let him down at all and he lay on his bed and started to read.

LETTER 1.

Dear Ben (Hello Captain),

I promised I would write and well here I am – well just in words if you see what I mean; but my friends tell me that I write like I speak so you should be able to feel like I am right there with you. Not that I know exactly where that is but that's okay, as long as you are safe and well then I don't need to know the details. I must warn you that this letter will not be very exciting on account of the fact that you are living in a real danger zone and I live here in the sleepy old countryside. So by my reckoning I will write five letters assuming you get them all before you return, of course if they are terrible then tell me to stop and I will.

This is this first time I have written to anyone in the forces so I am not sure what they will let me write and what will be crossed out – it could be a very disjointed letter as you will have to play "Fill in the missing word," which I suspect might start out as fun; but will become very tiresome very quickly. Although you could do this with your platoon as a form of punishment which could be quite funny depending what words they come up with – keep it clean boys keep it clean! (He smiled at that). Also I do not want to wake up to find two burly officers on my doorstep here to arrest me for breaching official secrets act or such like so I will have to take a chance and keep my tiny fingers and toes crossed. Although having tiny toes makes it nearly impossible to paint tiny toenails-still this is not something you and your lads have to exactly worry about, now is it? At least I hope you are not sat there painting each other's toenails! (He laughed, she did have tiny fingers but he wouldn't be seeing them any time soon as he wasn't due home for another 3 months. He'd never seen her toes so that would be a surprise).

So back to me; yes I know it's all about me really isn't it? ha ha! I am waiting for the postman to bring me my new book from Amazon; oh! I hear you cry, is there no limit to the giddy heights of excitement in her life? Well I do feel very guilty not to have ordered it from Jean in my local book store, but it is the latest one from one of my favourite authors and I'm afraid that impatience got the better of me – I know, I know, I will not get to heaven at this rate which will be a shame as I am not keen on the heat and I have heard it said that hell can be a little too hot to handle most of the year – so I must try harder – yes a lot harder. It's raining here so a bit dark and damp – see not all sunshine and flowers – I expect you are enjoying the weather in somewhat sunnier climes; although with my pale skin Mr Sunshine and I have never been the best of friends. So whilst you are – and I make no apologies for guessing here, shouting at the lads and working on your tan, all I am wanting to do is to curl up on the sofa with a blanket, my new book and Henry (God I am already jealous of her bloody cat) – you see what excitement you are missing; you must already now be feeling very envious?

I'm also very excited about my supper tonight, yes I know it's only 10.30am and it sounds a quite pathetic; but I do like to have a lovely meal to look forward to on Wednesday's and tonight it is one of my favourites. I am cooking chicken in ras-el-hanout spices with salad and sweet potato falafel. Ooh so yummy, I can almost taste it already. Two things have just popped into my head now, firstly that you may not have the faintest idea what ras-el-hanout is, it's a blend of Moroccan spices with rose which by the way it is way nicer than it sounds too (he made a face it really sounded a bit yuk if he was honest) and secondly I don't know what food you get to eat where you are and that for all I know it may be a bit on the crappy side so I mustn't boast about the lovely things I am having here so sorry about that. Maybe you could tell me if I'm allowed to send food out to you and if so what would you like, I could definitely do that. See, I'm not ashamed to try bribery and corruption if required! (Yep definitely send me some food and when I get back I'll try the corruption!)

I am going out with the girls on Saturday night for a couple of drinks, some dancing lots of talking – my tonsils and tongue are resting now in preparation for the big day and definitely no throwing up afterwards I promise. God when I think back to my 21st birthday I was so ill that night the memory has stayed with me ever since. I will tell you all the gory details in another letter in case I run out of exciting things to tell you, (he didn't care, just to read her letter as if she was sat next to him was a great place to start but it did sound intriguing) but even just thinking about it makes me queasy. It will be great to just go out and have some fun, you would like them all and again I will introduce you to them etc.

Haven't been up to much else, just work, going running which I love and general domestic drudgery; although I was glued to new thriller which started at the weekend. I love a good drama-well murder, preferably, and I hate it if I can't guess who the killer is. I won't watch horror movies though, oh no, never ever not even if you paid me – will tell you funny story about this next time (must ask her about this). This is quite a different show, lots of sub plots and a bit dark too and I am intrigued already. Oh there will always be critics who can't wait to write negative things; in fact, I am convinced that it is their sole reason for being, they won't watch a few episodes first they just steam in after one – tell you it's shite and then off to the next thing. Well I lose patience with overhyped nonsense too, why people just don't use their off button on their TV is still a mystery to me? It's all fiction none of it is actually real, I feel like shouting at them; and I don't care if they use the wrong type of car or the wrong bus appears in shot – again it's not real life. I do think some people can't distinguish between the two things at all.

Sports news now. By the way, how are you liking this bulletin form of writing? Yes its very good isn't it? (Ben smiled, yes he liked it a lot). It is helping me to focus on all the menial things that have made up the last ten days but seriously I hope it is not too trying for you to read and stick with? So onto football, omg my team were useless at the weekend and I do mean bloody USELESS. They ended up losing 1 – 0 to Burnley, yes you read that right, ruddy Burnley. I was beginning to think that they must all have a real passion for Am Dram, what with all the falling over and histrionics on the pitch; in fact maybe some of them should go into acting they'd be bloody good although the pay is lousy in comparison.

At half time I was completely exasperated. Their manager, you know the one, good looking, great accent, twinkly eyes, he who blames everyone and anyone for any mistake and never his team or himself well he looked positively apoplectic with rage and I suspect they got a right old half time bollocking or as we polite people say a half time motivational pep talk with segments of orange all round! (She was so funny sometimes, she said the oddest things but when she said them they just made perfect sense.) Well they were better in the second half but they missed chance after chance it was a relief when the ref blew his whistle.

Have also been watching England play rugby; nice guys in tight shorts, what's not to like about that from a girl's point of view naturally – they didn't play too well, so spent a lot of time with my hands in front of my face – yes I know I'm such a wuss sometimes!

Right I am signing off now as the postman has just brought my book and I want to start reading it straight away. I know, I know, it's the little things right? To be honest I am not quite sure how writing to someone in the forces actually works or how often you even get mail so I won't wait for a reply from you. I'll write the same time every two weeks and then you can catch me up with all the larks from your destination. Don't forget to let me know if you would like food or other things sent as I would be only too happy to do this for you. I have just downloaded a new running CD which has got some great tracks. I could always send you a copy if you like, assuming you have a CD player out there – you see I really know very little so may be safe from breaking official secrets act after all! Will post this tomorrow

Stay safe,

Evelyn. (Private Wallace).

Ben read the letter 3 times over. It was so good to hear her voice and she was right she did write as she spoke so it was the next best thing to having her there with him in person. He would drop her a line back and ask her to send some things. The worst thing was he would have to wait another 14 days before he got to hear from her again assuming their mail was delivered on time. He sighed; this deployment could be the toughest yet and not for the obvious reasons.

LETTER 2.

Dear Ben (Hello Captain),

Only me. Time for another letter I hope you are safe and well. I don't know how families cope when their son/brother/husband/wife etc. is on active duty – I am only a pen pal and am already feeling the stress. (Only a pen pal!)

Now to bore you with the minutiae of my life since I last wrote

Breaking news: I actually prayed last week; I know: 'shut the front door' as they say on those annoying American reality shows. Now I know you think I am a thoroughly good person who was an angel in a previous life and who is only ever one step away from a church and prayer book and kneeling for forgiveness. (A rude thought popped into Ben's head concerning Evie on her knees in front of him, preferably in her bedroom; God, he had to stop thinking like this it would drive him crazy and this deployment was far from over.) But I don't actually go to church, used to when I was little, Sunday school and all that jazz. (He laughed. He couldn't imagine her at Sunday school.) But today I actually had to pray; I was on my way home from particularly trying morning at work, Steve like bear with a sore head don't know if he has got girlfriend trouble or what is eating him – thinking about big bear actually eating him now and making all our lives easier – bad thought, Evelyn, bad thought– will need to say at least 6 hail Marys and I'm not even Catholic – or if he even has a girlfriend; my God, I would like to shake her by the hand and wish her all the luck in the world, cos boy is she going to need it.

So anyway! soo glad when shift was over practically, skipped to the car like they do in slow motion movies. Driving home when out of nowhere black hatchback right up my bumper, all over the place trying to overtake, pretty difficult here with windy roads and narrow lanes, so distracting, starting to stress looking for layby, does this overtaking manoeuvre, nearly crashes into car coming the other way; heart in my boots, kind of thing; other driver white as a sheet, eventually pull over as am shaking so much. Turn off engine and pray. Thank you, God, for guy not killing me today; manage to get home and drink glass of water very slowly. Made me think of the accident with Matthew that you and I happened upon, he was one lucky kid.

Talking of Matthew, I called round to see him and his mum the other day. He is on the mend, she offered me lots of tea which I declined; you know how fussy I am about my funny milk, as you call it. Well if I had a pound for every time she said thank you, then I would be a very rich girl – well okay richer by £10 or so. (Ben laughed; this was so good, it really was as if she was right here talking to him). She seems like a nice woman, warning uncharitable thought coming next, those with a saintly nature should look away now: although am not sure about Clive his brother, he is a solicitor and is handling Matthews case etc.; not quite sure what there is to handle when his brother was driving like a maniac and no other car was involved but still I digress. Clive has been calling and texting supposedly to sort out paperwork. Not quite sure why this should bother me so, but it does – I am just being silly I suppose. (Ben frowned; something not quite right there.)

Had great night out with the girls. It seems to be harder and harder for us all to get out together these days. I suppose that is the price we pay for leading modern lives with too many choices on how to fill them. Rowan is as hilarious as ever honestly the things that girl gets up to would probably make even you blush and I kind of think it would take a lot to shock you – am I right? Yes, thought so. (She did this thing – asked him questions and then answered for him; funny really.)

Funny thing happened; we were all sat together and when I returned to our table with some drinks a couple of guys had joined us – Rowan encouraging them no doubt. Anyway more chat/laughs etc. (Ben didn't like where this was heading), when we went to leave I couldn't find my blue scarf, don't know if you know it but it is my favourite one – I think it makes my eyes look more sparkly. To cut a long story short, one of these guys, um Adam, was holding it hostage and he required a ransom – yeah I know; funny ha ha!(Ben didn't think this was funny at all, bloody hell what was she going to say next?). It turns out ransom demand is to go out with him for a date (Ben threw his boot across the room – fucking hell was she trying to tell him she now had a boyfriend?). I declined but wanted my scarf back so was forced to kiss him (Oh for fuck's sake! Ben groaned and threw his other boot across the floor), nothing full on, I just really wanted my scarf back, so kissed him – mouth firmly shut I hasten to add; he wanted my phone number but again I said no, wasn't in the mood really. Maybe when you are back you can teach me some negotiation techniques in case I have to rescue said scarf again from the clutches of a desperate dickhead? (Ben was laughing now, yes she'd kissed this jerk, but it didn't sound like she'd enjoyed it very much. She'd refused to go on a date with him or give him her phone number and yes he'd definitely give her some instruction in techniques when he was back home; but not in negotiation, no in something much more enjoyable if he ever got the chance).

Finished that book I was telling you about, it was great. I am a very quick reader, but I've always loved books, not these e – reader things-don't get me wrong; I love a bit of techie stuff, you know iPhone/iPad/iPod/laptop/Fitbit tracker – but I love books made out of (shock horror!) real paper – there I said it! When I was little I used to love going to the library in town, it used to be in this huge Victorian building and I always took out the maximum amount of books I was allowed. I read voraciously until after my degree in English lit where suddenly you had to tear everything apart and dissect every word: what does this mean? why did he choose to say that? what is he really saying? It quite spoilt the enjoyment of reading just because you love it. What can I say? My relationship with BOOK was not the same and we drifted apart; maybe some things just weren't meant to be – music of sad violins are playing in the background – but I restarted my affair with BOOK and the written word 3 or 4 years ago and haven't looked back since (Bloody lucky BOOK! was what he was thinking).

Although am getting very frustrated with wasting money as I do read the book reviews but they don't bother to tell you the one thing you need to make a decision as to whether you are going to buy it. So you buy it anyway, it arrives then you read something crucial in the first chapter and you think omg what a waste of time. If I had known that it was about – insert things I don't like here: birds/the circus/magic/Valentine's day, I could go on, but too little time etc. – then I would never have bought it. Yes, I know it is a very personal thing choosing a book and you cannot please all the people all of the time. Don't know if you like books or not or even if you have time to read where you are; but I would be happy to send you some volumes of the written word should you so desire. (Oh had desires all right, just not to do with bloody books!)

Had to take Henry to the vets this week, poor little thing. He had something in his eye. Picked up his carry basket, omg he weighs a ton, still a good workout for toning my arms – I suppose every cloud blah blah. Anyway they sorted him out and he is fine now – not very keen on having his eye drops, but am bribing him with prawns for being a good boy and have been letting him sleep on my bed (bloody hell, still very jealous of her cat) – which is normally forbidden; but he is my best friend in the whole world and it is my responsibility to look after him – a bit like you and your lads. Not that I expect you to bribe them with food and let them sleep on your blanket that may be a step too far even for a very modern Army-ha, ha! (He laughed, she wasn't wrong there.)

I am going to visit my mother next week as she is back from her exotic travels. Since she discovered that the world is a much smaller place than she originally thought she has really got the travel bug; although travelling first class cannot be considered too painful an experience by any stretch of the imagination. So I will hear all about her latest adventure – Peru I think it was, honestly I can't keep track. The only thing I know about Peru is that Paddington bear comes from there, you know he of the duffle coat/wellington boots /hat ensemble and his obsession with marmalade sandwiches. God he must be hot in that hat, coat and boots I always thought Peru was a warm country too? Quite where my mother will be off to next I have no idea, me I am much happier at home where it is calm and I can go for a run every day. (He paused for a second – that was a surprise; he thought she would be very well travelled, still it wasn't everyone's cup of tea.)

Got to go (he groaned – so soon – it was like watching your favourite TV show only for there to suddenly be a power cut and leave you hanging – and not a damn thing you can do about it).

Will write soon.

Stay safe,

Evelyn. x (Private Wallace).

He noticed she had sighed off with a tiny x, still a x was still a x in his eyes and he settled down to read her letter all over again. Silently he was so relieved she hadn't enjoyed kissing Adam, because if she had then she sure as hell wouldn't be single once Ben got home and he was desperate to make sure she would be, yes very single and very available – well for him anyway. He closed his eyes and let his imagination run riot in his head, the two of them naked in bed together, her on top of him, them kissing and him squeezing her bum at the same time – bloody hell he needed a cold shower!

LETTER 3.

Dear Ben, (Hello Captain).

Hope you received the chocolates/book and CD – of course I have no way of knowing if you did or if you didn't, but again keeping tiny fingers crossed that you did? I chose chocolates very carefully so they wouldn't have melted into hideous molten pool of yuk before you had a chance to scoff them all – scoff being the best and only appropriate word to use in my book. (He laughed, yes he had scoffed them – all in one go too).

Henry says Hi, yes I know clever old thing isn't he? Have stopped bribing him with prawns as he has finished his eye drops now, he seems a bit miffed at this but it was only a short term solution after all.

All quiet here, work is same old same old, boss still being an arse – sorry being rude already. Been running about quite literally, but I expect it is nothing compared to all your running about – tell Lofty I will personally put together a PT plan for him when you are back, that should sort him out one way or the other – could be fun making him actually do it too! But only if I was the one who was shouting at him and watching him struggle at the same time.

Now for funny ha ha incident, not funny peculiar incident, that happened to me at the end of last week. I will keep it brief otherwise this letter will incur charges for being overweight – a bit like Lofty – ha ha. Seriously don't tell him that or I will be in his bad books and he will only take it out on you I suspect and judging by the last stunt he pulled am not sure how far he would go – again being overweight and not in peak physical condition not very far – ha ha ha!

But I digress. Okay so, was on way to work last Friday evening, pulled into supermarket to get diesel, paid and was walking back to my car when this chap runs over. He starts telling me about how he's on a stag do with 11 other guys in a min van also getting fuel. Glanced over and there they were all watching him like a hawk watching his prey. They were playing truth or dare and they'd dared him to kiss the next girl that he saw – yep I know you are one step ahead of me as per usual – possibly something to do with your big stride compared to mine and also being in the Army have to think ahead etc. Well first off I think he's winding me up then realise he's quite serious, apparently didn't want to go on stag do in the first place blah blah would I help him out blah blah? Turns out his name is Seamus and he's a tree surgeon. He seemed pretty genuine and so actually do start to feel a bit sorry for him. (Ben groaned out loud, oh my God didn't she realise that guys on stag do's pulled this stunt all the time? Honestly she was so naïve sometimes, she would get herself into trouble. She was always saying how her mother scolded her for getting too involved in things she shouldn't, well maybe for once she should have listened to her mother – this wasn't going to have a happy ending for him, he just knew it. Please God this guy Seamus wasn't her new boyfriend or he'd really lose it big time.)

So decide to take pity on him, have to move my car first as it's holding up the queue, so mouthing apologies etc. Cut long story short, I kiss him, (Ben threw his boots across the room; this was becoming a habit-kissed him for fuck's sake!) have to stand on step otherwise I can't reach, that's the problem with only being five foot four inches tall. He begs me not to leave him with other guys, he wants to bail on them as he never wanted to go in first place etc., so we hatch a cunning plan – well maybe not at all cunning in your book, but there again I'm not in the Army. So make it look like he's pulled – me that is, not a muscle – ha ha! He gets in my car, we wave at chaps in mini – van who, by the way, look as if they are going to self – combust –really was very funny. I drive round the block, make sure they've gone and then drop him back at supermarket so he can call taxi home – genius. Cheeky bugger wanted my phone number but I was seriously going to be late for work so declined his offer and left him there. Honestly what a funny thing on a Friday night, made it into work by the skin of my teeth – quite enough drama for one day.

(Phew at least she'd dropped him off after a few minutes and didn't give him her phone number; bloody hell he thought, it was bad enough that she'd kissed him at all. In her last letter it was some dickhead called Adam and now it was another idiot called Seamus, for fuck's sake it was too much, just too bloody much. Was she telling him subtly that she wasn't interested? No it didn't sound like that, it was just her writing what had happened to her over the past two weeks surely? He closed his eyes and began to wonder what it would be like kissing her, properly, really kiss her, run his hands through her hair and then to feel her bum in his hands and squeeze it hard; he wondered how it would feel for her to kiss him back and not want it to stop there-oh Christ he'd have to go and have another cold shower at this rate.)

Clive turned up out of the blue last night to go over Matthew's case yet again. If I was being good cop I'd say fair enough the law's the law, happy to help etc. If I was being bad cop I'd be saying: oh come on! there can't be anything left to talk about – seriously and if I'm just being honest am finding him pathetic, creepy and weird – uurrgghh – yes horrid thought. This is what I get in return for doing good deed or quite possible best good deed of my entire life – what do you think, am I being too harsh? Can't ask anyone else as you are the only person who has met him.

Have just had a brilliant idea for a new business venture: hiring out hunky guys to be pretend boyfriends who could come and throw people like Clive out onto the street – 'Hunks for Hire'-brilliant, now why didn't I think of this before? I would need to do a lot of in-depth very hands on research of course and would need to interview each prospective hunk for hire, but what can I say, it would be a tough job but someone's got to do it! (Ben thought about this, she was a pretty good judge of character he'd say, so if Clive was creeping her out then he was probably up to no good in his books. He sighed. If only he was back home he'd have sorted him out, and as for hunks for hire that just made him mad, and he kicked his kitbag in anger. Why did he have to be away now?)

Was kicking myself last week as I had the chance to do a good deed and it never occurred to me until I was back home, so very cross with myself. Bumped into woman in the supermarket, by chocolate shelves, got chatting, we both laughed yes neither of us should be buying any etc. Then I went and put my big foot, well okay little foot, in it yet again; why will I never learn? – and said something like oh well it's mother's day soon, I expect you'll be getting lots of chocolate, only for her to turn round and say sadly oh I'm lucky if I get a card these days. Made me feel sad and of course don't know whole picture as two sides to every story, but should have bought her some chocs whilst I was there and given them to her just as a gift – see I was so annoyed with myself for not doing this as had a chance to make someone else happy – always someone a lot worse off than me I always think. So frustrating.

Changing the subject ever so slightly: do you need me to send your mother anything for mother's day from you or have you sorted this out with your sister etc. before you left? Tell you what, I'll send something to her anyway with a note from you and if you've already arranged something then she'll get two gifts and you'll be her favourite child for ever – great plan, hey? (Ben re – read this paragraph; yes, Evie's mother was always scolding her not to get involved, but then she was lucky as she had a lovely daughter who wanted to help a stranger as she felt sad for them. This girl had a big heart. He hadn't sorted anything out for his mother so it was indeed a great idea as he was sure she would know just what to send.)

Stay safe,

Evie.x (Private Wallace).

(He noticed she had signed off as Evie plus a small x again; maybe her writing to him was getting him in her good books without him even trying?)

LETTER 4.

Dear Ben (Hello Captain).

Only me again. Weather here is crap – a – doodle – yes new meteorological term, no not really just made it up a bit like the daily weather reports on the news –boom boom – ha, ha, ha! (He smiled. These letters were simply the best thing ever). Still keeping everything crossed you are still okay? I sent your mother a present for mother's day, or rather you did (nudge, nudge, mum's the word) – literally! Hope she likes it; my mother would like it and so would I for that matter – so hopefully you are her favourite child, not that mothers are really allowed favourites I guess; although as it's unlikely I will ever be a mother then can't really comment. (He frowned, yes she'd told him about this).

So on to my exciting day. I'm home all day as it's Wednesday so free from the gym and a Steve free day – big whoop! I know it is perfectly natural to dislike your boss – apart from your boys of course who quite rightly worship the ground you walk on and would literally walk over hot coals for you too I suspect, yes quite right too; but with a few shoves in the right direction Steve could be soo much better at his job and if he was nicer to the staff it would make a huge difference. He's so negative and I find that really difficult to be around. I am a glass half full kind of girl as if you hadn't noticed (he grinned; yep, I had as a matter of fact).Or rather my glass is always full to the top except for a tiny space so as not to spill anything, (yes I had noticed that too) whereas Steve is a glass half empty kind of guy; and well, if I'm being honest I'm not convinced he even has a glass most of the time. For example he would never say 'you're doing a good job' or 'well done your classes are always full and the clients like you' Oh no, instead he will say' got to keep the numbers up you know, get the punters in blah blah blah, can't get complacent', – well that is a downright lie as he wouldn't know what that word meant and then he is always shouting at someone and for most of the time he has no good reason for doing so. Maybe when you are back you could take him for a boot-camp workout just to see what he is really made of? Seriously it's a shame really, as if he was nicer to people then everyone would benefit. There would be a better atmosphere too.

It would be like you for instance – purely hypothetical scenario here by the way – if one of your boys had royally stuffed up – that being a technical term widely used in the Army I believe-? (he laughed).

Option 1 – yes you could shout at him: something like, "Well Jones for fucks sake, what the fuck were you thinking out there? I'll tell you shall I – fucking nothing that's what –what you did was just so fucking dangerous I couldn't believe my fucking eyes – just get out of my fucking sight before I lose my fucking temper – kind of thing, sorry for swear words but am trying to keep it authentic as possible! (was she here in person, because that was uncannily near the mark?)

Or option 2 "Well Jones come on in,"-quiet voice here so he has to strain to hear to you – powerful people use this trick all the time as it gets the person to just focus completely on your words – "Jones I don't have to tell you, that you have let everyone down, you've let the army down, you've let me down, you've let your team down and worst of all you've let yourself down. I'd hoped to see better from you Jones much better, you're bright, capable, a bit too gobby sometimes but on the whole not bad. You have got to stop and think Jones – just think before taking action that puts everyone's lives in danger. I could stand here and give you a right bollocking, which is probably what you were expecting; but to be honest do you know what the worst thing is?" No sir. "No well I'll tell you Jones. It is just that I am so fucking disappointed in you, really fucking disappointed, now go join the others in the canteen whilst I decide what punishment you get. "Sir! yes sir, kind of thing. Using the disappointed word is the worst thing ever, so much worse than shouting and bawling. Maybe you could try this out and let me know how it goes? I hope no-one in your squad is actually called Jones or he will think I am some kind of witch. (He smiled. Maybe he would try this out on Corporal Jones who he was sure would fuck up sooner or later.)

Don't know if you remember but in previous letters I mentioned a few things I would explain in more detail so have decided to fill you in, or as they say on those annoying TV adverts for shampoo 'here comes the science bit'.

A) Getting drunk on my 21st Birthday.

Boy oh boy what an evening that was. I finished uni, went home and changed, ate something or other, as it turned out I should have eaten a whole lot more. Went to pub with group of friends – am using that term of friends very loosely – everyone buying me drinks. My tipple at the time was vodka and orange juice, only thing was I thought I was drinking single ones and unbeknown to me they were actually double and triple ones. Yes, you're way ahead of me aren't you? (Ben smiled; yes he knew what was coming alright). Somehow staggered home, a friend walked me back, spent the whole night/early morning throwing up. Had to be in for 8.45am, and spent whole day throwing up, leaning against desk groaning with a white face tinged with green – nice look. Could hardly wait to finish, got back at 5.45, had bath, drank pints of water and went straight to bed. What a night, have never been so drunk since – hardly surprising really, so now just tend to drink on high days and holidays – safer that way.

B) Scary movies

This is a secret I never tell anyone, but here goes, I have never seen a scary movie in my life! There said it – it's a bit like a confessional in church isn't it? My parents never allowed us to watch them at home, as you may or may not have realised I dream a lot, always in colour and have a very active imagination so don't need any encouragement on this front thank you very much – especially now with anxiety nightmares too following my accident – not ours with Matthew but my other one with scars. (Ben wondered what had happened to her. It must have been pretty bad with the scars he'd already seen and now she was telling him she got anxiety nightmares too, bloody hell).

Well a couple of years ago do you remember that film everyone was raving about, the one shot in a forest on a very low budget with a group of people running everywhere with torches? Well, I Sky + it and one evening settled down to watch it thinking just how bad can it be? Set it to play and before the title music had finished I was so scared about what it was going to be like that I actually deleted it before it even started – there I can hear you laughing your head off from here – (Ben was laughing really loudly. She was hilarious). So really I am just one big scaredy cat – no place for me in her Majesty's Army, methinks. No siree. I'm nervous and jumpy enough without putting myself through any of that, plus I would be having nightmares every night and just haven't got the time as I do need my beauty sleep! You're not allowed to comment on that last bit (he thought she was very pretty and was desperate to wake up in bed next to her, the sooner the better).

C) List of things I hate.

I realise that hate is a strong word but feel it is justified, obviously there are more things I am not very keen on and a whole load of things I love but anyway I promised you so here goes:-

The circus – oh boy how long have you got for this – animals in circus just not right on any level, clowns just really bloody annoying, why can't they find a car that works or shoes that fit their feet, trapeze artistes – don't really care if they fall or not, can't bear the ooh and ahh of the crowd watching – as for those modern cirque du whatsits yuk! yuk! yuk! would be like torture.

Magic – feel sorry for rabbits pulled out of hats, it's all smoke and mirrors anyway, don't care about three metal rings coming apart, card tricks just bore me senseless; all that pick a card, any card, go on any card – bollocky nonsense, I mean please – need I go on – just a waste of time.

Birds – am not a huge animal lover, best ones in my book are cats – obviously – don't mind penguins, polar bears, bunnies, piglets (ohh) and I love cows – that's about it. But birds just really annoying. Only exception is a nice roast chicken-yum yum! (Ben smiled, she was very funny today) Example of this is stayed at very nice self-catering place in Devon, fancy brochure; but they forgot to mention the tens of nesting rooks in the trees at the back who woke you up every morning at 6.00am on your holiday; no thanks, not my idea of a holiday, generally birds just squawk, poo and annoy me. Has put me off of self-catering for life – just too much like being at home when it is in fact just easier to actually be at home. Holidays to me mean long lazy mornings in big beds – yes I know I'm small, but I like to stretch out-, snuggling under big soft duvets, getting up at midday in jimmie jammies, ordering room service, doing whatever takes your fancy, long soaks in big baths – not too big as am a hopeless swimmer, lazy hot showers, movies in bed at night – no scary ones mind you, definitely no rushing about, no noisy birds, just peace, great company, great food – see simple things. (Yes Ben did see he saw that very much.)

Valentine's Day – Now before I start let's get one thing straight – I love flowers all year round, but not red roses, something very fake about having to declare your undying love for someone just because it is the 14th of Feb every year with red roses, whether the person deserves them or not. It is ridiculous, prices go up 1000%, open plan offices full of delivery men all trying to outdo each other with 'ooh look what I've got' bollocky nonsense; hotels cramming in punters with set packages/ set meals so you all get same experience – no thank you very much. It's fine when you are sixteen and you think that the world will literally come to an end if you don't get a card from that boy you've had a crush on for months; but that apart then no. I would love flowers any other time, unless they are to say sorry for fucking up again as I have had so many of those I couldn't bear anymore. Too much pressure to declare undying love on same day every year – who needs that kind of pressure? It's just nonsense would rather have a surprise or flowers on my birthday; they're the best.

Scalp massages – now don't get me wrong I love a body massage- preferably one with hot stones – as much as the next man, but scalp – oh no, no, no it's just too excruciating, can't bear them. (Christ he'd love to massage her body right this second; but what the fuck did hot stones have to do with it?).

Men who wear polo neck jumpers. There I've said it. (Ben threw his head back and laughed until he almost cried; honestly she was bloody hilarious). All I can think about when I see men in polo necks is are they trying to look, A French? B like an architect? C just arty farty in general? Will apologise now if you actually have one, but somehow I doubt it. Also don't they look at themselves in the mirror before they leave the house in the morning? If my boyfriend put one on, I would have to walk five steps behind him and then deliberately shrink it in the wash. (She was so funny, no he didn't have a bloody polo neck jumper, he'd tell her-surely that would count in his favour?)

(Ben read this through, so nothing too surprising there, apart from hating Valentine's Day. He thought all girls loved it. He didn't even know when her birthday was but would find out once he was back for sure. As for massages, he'd have to stop thinking about her and the word massage in the same sentence – he groaned and felt another cold shower was in order).

Stay safe,

Evie x (Private Wallace).

LETTER 5.
Dear Ben (Hello Captain).

Wow this is my final letter before you return home. Doesn't time fly when I am boring you senseless? Still my letters may be a new cure for insomnia – what do you think? I bet you can hardly wait to see your family and friends again. I would struggle with this aspect more than the job itself I think; but as I have no plans to enlist luckily I will never have to find out. Although I would struggle with the discipline too. As I mentioned to you before when I had to have enforced bed rest I was an absolute nightmare for the first three days; I think it's called being a bit feisty? Having spent too much time in hospital in the past I really struggle with being ill and not being able to walk ten steps to the bathroom without help nearly drove me crazy, so no, Army discipline and me will never become bedfellows. (Ben's thoughts immediately went to him and Evie being different kind of bedfellows – oh yes, he would like that a lot.)

Classes are going okay. We had a bit of a sales drive to encourage new clients to sign up and I have got quite a few new people in my classes. We did a leaflet drop and I have the biggest bruise on my hand as I got into a bit of a fight – not with a person as am not the fighting type of girl, hope you know this? (He grinned; yes, he did know this). Anyway got my tiny hand stuck in someone's letterbox. I couldn't get it out and the more I pulled the more it hurt, – stop laughing right now. It wasn't funny Captain, not funny at all – well okay maybe just a little bit. (Ben was laughing, honestly what was she like?) I was wondering just how long I was going to literally be stuck there when all of a sudden it released me – hand looks like I have been boxing without gloves. Now don't get me wrong; I quite like a bit of boxing exercise wise but I do wear gloves – okay they are junior ones – please stop laughing so am in the wars literally! Okay please stop laughing now please! (Ben thought he would be only too happy to kiss her bruise better, and then maybe kiss a whole lot more of her given half a chance too). Don't know if you have ever done an aerobics class but am guessing maybe not, but surely it's kind of obvious that if you go forwards for 4 steps then there is an extremely high probability that you will be taking 4 steps back at some point, quite why this is a huge surprise to some people I will never know. Also why don't people know their right from their left, they must have learnt this when they were children surely? Still they are a lot of fun and we do have a laugh which is just as important some days, as I keep telling them there are no wrong moves as long as they keep moving then they will pick it up – although between you and me I have my doubts about a couple of them. They can't seem to stay on the beat – just had funny thought, it must be so frustrating for your drill sergeant to keep new recruits in time; how he does this day after day, who knows he probably deserves a medal.

I hope your mother liked her mother's day gift, no doubt you will find out once you are back. My mother is such a difficult person to buy for. Don't get me wrong I love her to bits; but sometimes it's impossible to do right for wrong – does that make sense? Anyway I should probably tell you a few of her little foibles and then you can make up your own mind. I have been taught nice manners or at least I hope I have, so I always shake someone's hand, you know, 'how do you do' kind of thing, yes it's a bit old fashioned but you can tell a lot about someone just by how they respond to this. Also I offer someone a cup of tea, you know, if they have come to service the boiler or sweep the chimney, only exception to this is Clive who is still really freaking me out (hmm, still not sure about this guy).

My mother still won't let me eat in the street – yes you read that right – even at my age, only exceptions are an ice cream at the seaside – no cone for me naturally – or a picnic, but a proper one not just a snack on a plate – I know what you are thinking yes but she's not here so does it matter, well yes I feel really guilty like she will find out somehow – I know how nuts is that? Also cannot drink in the street, as am not allowed to drink from a can or a bottle as I would have to have a glass – there you are, laugh out loud stuff. If I read the newspaper in bed then I have to put an old towel on the duvet to stop the newsprint coming off on the duvet cover – see, unbelievable! But I suppose along with all my other issues these are tiny ones. Do you have any foibles I should know about? Answers on a postcard please – do people still send postcards, personally I think they were invented by the postal service so that all the posties could have a jolly good nosey in your business. They must positively hate text messages and emails – probably think they are the work of the devil or something (Ben threw his head back and laughed, she was so funny sometimes).

Have got a sore throat at the moment. Not sure where this has come from, a bit annoying really as need voice to take classes; maybe it's from too much singing in the car? Can there be such a thing as too much singing I wonder – no that must be impossible surely? (Ben smiled to himself – he doubted it) Will be gargling with honey and lemon and keeping fingers crossed it goes away; am upset though as I love a good sing-a–long in the car – you may have noticed this already? (Yes Ben had indeed noticed this, it was one of the things he loved about her – bloody hell, where did that come from? When he was back he'd offer to kiss her throat better, well he'd start with her throat and her neck and then just see where it ended).

How is your tan coming along? Me I am always pale, might have something to do with the factor 50 sunscreen I wear – seriously though with my pale skin me and Mr Sunshine were never going to be best friends; am thinking now about dozing under the shade of palm trees in a hammock, not that I have ever been in a hammock. It's like most things: they look great but then I wouldn't be able to work out how to get in it and then how to get out of it, I would just have to flutter my eyelashes at someone to tip me out into a little heap on the floor; yep, maybe not as romantic as they sound. Do you sleep in hammocks? – if so, I bet you are a dab hand at getting in and out you will have to give me some lessons on your return (Ben thought of the two of them sharing a hammock; well if she couldn't get out without his help she'd have to stay there with him for as long as he wanted. Oh God he wanted to alright.)

Anyway I am signing off now, well this has been fun hasn't it – or at least I hope it has, well it has been fun for me. Please text me when you are back so that at least I know you are safe and sound. I could always send you a short funny e-mail, just like me ha ha ha! Yes a short and funny girl, that's me!

Evie.x (Private Wallace).

(Ben groaned. God, he was desperate to see her, yes it had been fun but all he could think of now was a completely different kind of fun the two of them could be having, not in a hammock; but preferably in her bedroom. These letters had been the next best thing to her being right there with him; good job he'd made a plan – well he was in the Army after all).

Chapter 56

Evie spent Sunday afternoon catching up with Rowan, Claire and Viv. Claire was on a late shift at the hospital so they took advantage of the good weather and sat in the beer garden of their favourite pub.

"Oh my God you didn't... did you? Rowan you are going to get into so much trouble," Evie put on her mock affronted voice, "Just make sure no-one else finds out okay or the doo dah will hit the fan, so to speak."

"Yeah yeah I know I know, but omg it was so much fun." She winked at the others who knew only too well what fun she was talking about. "Anyway enough about me; when's your pirate coming back from the high seas?" she joked doing her best pirate impression complete with parrot on shoulder. They all burst out laughing.

"I've told you I don't actually know, it's not like they can just send you a text or email that would defeat the object of staying incognito; oh and I've told you before, no pirate impressions when you meet him or I will just die. I know we think it's funny him being a Captain and everything, but I expect he has heard that joke a million times before. He's not even in the Navy, he's in the Army," she rolled her eyes and continued, "anyway he's not my (she emphasized) pirate or whatever, he's just a friend who I've been writing too whilst he's away." The other three just looked at each other all thinking exactly the same thing: yeah yeah we believe you but thousands wouldn't.

They went their separate ways just before 6.00 and on the drive home Evie was in a contemplative mood. She honestly didn't know when Ben would be back and she also didn't know what their next step would be if there was to be any, in fact she didn't even know if he would call in to see her. Laughing out loud she told herself that on the face of it she didn't really know much about anything at all and put it out of her mind.

It had been a long evening at the gym and Evie would be glad once Tuesday was finally over and she could get home. She just wanted to shower, eat and fuss with Henry if he was in the mood for a fuss. An hour later she was in the kitchen, music on chopping vegetables for her casserole. She really should have done it before she left for work but maybe she would cheat and cook it in the microwave as she wasn't sure she had the patience to sit and wait for an hour constantly peering into the oven, whilst her tummy rumbled. There was a knock at the door; oh no! she groaned, who was this now? She glanced at the kitchen clock which read 8.45, she wasn't in the mood for visitors.

On opening the door she found Clive stood on her doorstep again but this time with his briefcase.

"Oh hi Evelyn. I'm glad I caught you. Not disturbing you I hope, but I've just got some more things I need to go over with you; do you have a minute?" Inwardly Evie said, no, just bugger off and leave me alone, but outwardly she invited him in into the kitchen. She was very aware she was dressed in her lounge wear, without a bra and it didn't leave a lot to the imagination as she hadn't been expecting company, so she wrapped the drapey cardigan over her chest and folded her arms. There, he could make what he wanted to from this display of her defensive body language.

Clive made himself right at home. Well sod this, she thought. I know my mother would be cross but I'm not offering him a cup of tea. I just want him out of my house, and the sooner the better.

"So Evelyn, or may I call you Evie I feel we have got to know one another quite well these past few weeks," he grinned at her. She didn't say a word; just 'hurry up and leave' was her only mantra repeated over and over in her head.

"Thing is, I'm having a few problems with the insurance company."

"Still." Evie blurted out, they'd already been through this again and again.

"Yes afraid so, we just need to clarify how fast you think the car was travelling as, after all it was dark and the road was slippery after the rain," – not as slippery as you, she thought uncharitably.

Sighing she explained for the umpteenth time that she was doing 45 or 50 at a push and that Matthew's car had come out of nowhere, tearing up the road like a maniac (she watched his reaction to her choice of words – he never even blinked – it made her skin crawl).When he overtook like a madman (again no reaction) he must have been doing at least 60 possibly more as she'd slowed down to let him pass.

"So he could have possibly been doing less than 60 which is the speed limit for that road?"

Oh, now she saw where this was going. Well nice try sunshine but no dice. "Look I've given a written statement to the police, they will have measured the tyre marks on the road or whatever CSI thingy it is they do – I'm not sure what you expect me to say exactly?"

"Well I just need you to be really, really certain as this could have a big impact on Matthew's future record, I'm sure you understand?"

Her elbows were already leaning on the table, Her mother would have had a fit if she could have seen this, she thought wryly. Placing her hands over her eyes she sighed and not looking at him she said quietly, "So you want me to lie is that it?"

"No no, not at all," he said hastily, "just maybe have a think about it. Could you be wrong – after all it was late – you were on your way home from work, you're tired.." He left the sentence hanging.

Oh so now she was in the wrong; she'd stopped to help, quite possibly saved Matthew's life and now she was in the wrong. Tears pricked her eyes, why oh why didn't she have a big hunky boyfriend to throw him out on his arse?

Ben had landed at midday. It was so good to be back, he'd never been so happy just to be home in wet, cloudy England, first thing he did was switch on his mobile and call his parents, They were so relieved, he could hear it in their voices, his mother asking him straight away when he was going to see them. He laughed and told her he'd be there on Saturday evening for 3 nights and she seemed overjoyed with this news. Once he was in his car he made two more calls and then set off.

Just after 8.55pm his car trundled down the driveway to Evie's house. He could see the lights were on so she was definitely at home; but as he turned into the courtyard another car was parked outside, one he didn't recognise. He switched off the car lights and engine and let it coast to a stop. She had company, that was obvious; question was who was it? He got out and walked around to the side wall and peered in. His Army training did come in handy from time to time, he thought. Through the kitchen window he could see Evie with her head in her hands and, bloody hell! it was Clive, that creepy solicitor, back again. Ben knew he'd been right to trust his instincts about that chap; well, son of a bitch, he wasn't going to put up with this for a single second longer. He made his way back to his car grabbed his kit and tried the front door. It opened and he took a deep breath.

Chapter 57

"Hi Honey I'm home." Ben sing-songed as he walked straight into the kitchen. Evie couldn't believe her eyes, 'Oh my God, he's here just when I need him too'. She bolted out of her chair and flung her arms around him.

"I didn't know you were back. I'm so glad to see you." He noticed she was close to tears.

As Ben held her he could feel her trembling, just what had that creepy bastard been doing? "Hi baby, did you miss me?" he asked her, willing her to remember the last time they had played along in his office. Evie looked at him. She was ready to cry, but he just kissed her and then whispered in her ear, "Play along just like last time, okay?" He felt her relax just a bit and then she said, "Oh you have no idea." Just the same as before, only the difference was that this time he was really kissing her and he had no intention of stopping unless he really had to. She wasn't completely responsive, but then he had surprised her. Eventually she relaxed and he seized the opportunity. He'd been dreaming about this for more than the past three months and didn't care who was sat at the table watching disappointedly with a sour look on their face. His hands were in her hair, on her back, squeezing her bum. He'd waited 3 bloody long months for this so he was damn sure he was going to enjoy himself.

Evie's legs were about to buckle beneath her and sensing this Ben reluctantly released her and held her to him. He spoke to Clive next, "Oh it's um Carl isn't it, back again – not sure what you've still got to talk to us about?"

He really couldn't keep the sourness out of his face as he said, "Actually it's Clive, and yes there were one or two loose ends to um…tie up so to speak." Ben was tempted to tie him up alright and dangle him from the nearest tree by his balls if he didn't leave soon.

"Well sorry mate, but we've got a lot of catching up to do haven't we, baby?" Evie was still being held tightly in his arms so just mumbled 'yes that's right'. "So if you've got any more questions I suggest you use the phone or e-mail or I'll tell you what I'll call Constable Blake in the morning see if he can help you tie up those loose ends. Now can you see yourself out or shall I escort you?" Ben kept his voice steady but firm and he left Clive in no doubt he was to leave now and not come back.

Reluctantly Clive shuffled his papers together and made for the door. Over his shoulder he sneered, "Yes, well I can see the two of you will be ...busy...with other things so I'll say goodnight then." They heard the front door slam and Evie almost collapsed. She was so glad he was gone, this time had been the worst ever. Ben moved so that he was leaning against the kitchen table and pulled her against him. She whispered, "Thank you so much, if you hadn't arrived when you did... but do you think he's actually gone?"

"Well I wouldn't put it past him to be down the lane with his binoculars just checking on us. To be frank he's a weird one, make no mistake, so I think we need to do a bit more of this to convince him." With that his mouth was on hers again and both of them just fell into the best kiss – whether it was the fact he'd been away or that she'd needed him so much right at the moment but neither of them pulled away. Ben had been thinking about this kiss, playing it over and over in his head, how he was going to get her to see him as more than just a friend and then tonight he'd shown up just in the nick of time and it had all happened perfectly. Well apart from the fact that Evie was upset, but as he kissed her and she responded she didn't seem so upset now.

Evie was happy on so many levels. Happy he was home safe, three months had been a long time and happy he'd surprised her even though she hated surprises and more than happy he'd got rid of creepy Clive once and for all. And very happy to be enjoying the best kiss she'd had in a very long time. His hand was on her back and slowly it moved down and he slipped it under the waistband of her joggers and into her knickers, gently squeezing her soft bottom. Evie moaned and he kissed her harder. His other hand slowly crept up her back and under her top. Jesus she wasn't wearing a bra. He was getting very over excited very quickly. Slowly he moved his hand around to her front where he placed it over her breast and sighed deeply. At last he was in bloody heaven. He whispered in her ear, "Just so you know I don't own a polo neck jumper."

Evie laughed and pulled away, they just grinned at each other not quite believing what had just happened.

"So I suppose that sex is definitely off the table?" Ben grinned at her now.

"Yes."

"Yes – really?" he sounded thrilled

"Yes it's definitely off, silly." He was impossible.

Ben nodded his head towards the kitchen table they were still leaning on, "How about sex on the table then?"

Evie laughed, "Yes that's off too, now are you hungry? I haven't eaten yet so there's plenty or do you want a shower first –by the way it was just the best surprise ever; and yes I know I hate them normally, but you are forgiven just this once," she joshed with him.

"I'm starving, but I think a shower first, okay?"

"Okay I'll get the supper on. You know the way, don't you? there's more towels in the linen cupboard so help yourself."

With that Ben was gone up the stairs and she could hear him moving about. Evie busied herself with supper. It would have to be microwaved this time but for once she didn't really care. Ben wasn't sure whether to put his stuff in her room or the room he'd had last time. He hadn't really discussed it with her, not yet, so decided to play it safe and used the guest room.

Less than half an hour later they were sat eating supper together just eating and smiling at one another.

"Tell me did you get my letters, cos I wrote to you every two weeks you know?"

"Yes I read them over and over. You're quite the letter writer you know."

"I wasn't sure. I thought you might find them a bit boring actually, ooh did you get the chocolate too cos I sent a lot of that as well?"

Ben laughed. "Yes I got everything you sent to me and yes before you ask I've rung my parents, who by the way are expecting us on Saturday night for a visit."

"Um but I'm working, did you forget?"

"No, but that's another surprise I have for you?"

"What do you mean?"

"Well don't get mad or anything," She groaned out loud. (Evie didn't like where this was going, when someone said 'don't get mad' it was precisely because there was a big chance you'd be getting very mad very quickly so she put her cutlery down and waited); but I kind of booked you a weeks' holiday from the gym from Saturday so we could spend some time together. What do you think?" He waited silently for her to say something, anything. There was quite a pause then she replied, "Kind of – it sounds pretty definite to me. How and why did you do that?"

"I wrote to my brother William and asked him to call your boss and put in a holiday request, but to keep it a secret. Will told Steve I was in the forces and abroad and wanted it to be a surprise for you. No big deal."

"So that's the how and we'll come back to 'no big deal later', so what's the why?"

"Well I figured that we were just getting to know each other, you know, before at my parent's house then I got called away and I had a lot of time to think about us. I gave it a lot of thought plus with your letters I figured when I was back that a week away would be great, you know just the two of us." He waited and waited, "aren't you going to say anything?"

"What if I don't want a holiday, a surprise one at that and it kind of is a big deal to me anyway?" He went to interrupt her, but she stopped him, "Hang on a minute so you've been thinking about this for what 3 months and then breeze in here and tell me it's no big deal?"

"More or less. I thought you'd be pleased." Oh shit this wasn't what he expected not at all; being away he'd only been thinking about what he wanted and now it was all going horribly wrong.

"Do I get a choice, or have you decided what's best for me so no I don't get one?"

"Evie come on. I thought you'd be happy, happy to see me, happy to pick up where we left off, just think about it for a bit, a week off, no work and the best thing is you get to spend it with me." He was grinning at her now.

She wasn't sure why she was mad, she just was – so God's gift to the Army had planned her holiday not even thinking she might say no – unbelievable. "I'm going to need to think about it."

"What seriously, I've got to wait for you to decide." He ran his hands through his hair. "So how much time do you need, bearing in mind it's all booked off from Saturday after you're all finished at the gym."

"Well that's 4 nights from now isn't it? I can't believe you just took me for granted like this and assumed it would all be fine?"

"So you're going to make me wait four nights, bloody hell Evie I just don't get why you're so mad"

Neither did she really. She just felt ambushed and didn't like surprises and being told what to do all in the same sentence too. She sighed and looked straight at him. "Look I've had a hell of a day with work and then bloody Clive turning up and now this. Can we just drop it for tonight please? I just need to think about it, I think that's a pretty reasonable request don't you?"

"So just to be clear: you're not saying no, but you're not saying yes either?"

She smiled. "Yep, pretty much – anyway you haven't told me what we might or might not be doing for a week – I might not like any of it, now would you like some more wine?"

"Well just for the record I think you're going to love every minute of it and yes please I think I might need some more wine now." He was frustrated but happy she hadn't said no so he'd go from there; there was more than one way to convince this infuriating girl to go out with him he'd just have to try plan B – good job he'd had three months to come up with a plan B.

Supper finished they cleared the table and he couldn't resist putting his arms around her waist and kissing her neck whilst she was at the kitchen sink.

"Okay Captain, what do you think you're doing?"

"Just trying out some new persuasion techniques, how am I doing so far?"

God he was just impossible to resist, but she did her best; she'd already decided what her answer would be but wanted to see what he would do in the meantime to win her over.

"Well firstly I don't want to drop this plate so could you stop for a second?"

He didn't move his arms but he did stop kissing her neck, "there is that better?"

"Thank you, now would like coffee or are you just going to bed?"

He nuzzled her ear, "Well now that all depends."

"On what exactly?"

"Whether it's just me going to bed on my own or us going to bed together." Oh she smelt so good he was getting more frustrated by the minute, This was worse than being in Afghanistan.

"It's just you on your lonesome; but I could send Henry in if you want some company." She was toying with him now; but he was just a teeny bit exasperating and she waited to see what he would do next. He didn't say anything so she dropped another hint, "Tell you what. I'll give you my answer tomorrow how does that sound?"

"If that's the best offer I'm going to get then I'll take it," he grumbled.

Breezily she said, "Well you've had 3 months to think about it, so I think I deserve more than 3 hours don't you?"

"Yes okay, you're right of course."

"Good. So that's settled. Don't know about you but I'm ready for bed. Are you staying up or turning in too?" He was leaning against the countertop now and didn't look happy at all, "I suppose I'm going to bed as well."

"Okay well night then, see you tomorrow." and with that she was gone. No goodnight kiss, nothing. He heard her footsteps on the stairs and glumly followed.

Evie got into bed. It was 11.30 and she wondered if he'd figured it out yet, tomorrow was only 30 minutes away, surely he would realise and try again? She dozed off smiling, it was so good to see him too. That kiss in her kitchen, wow that had been fantastic. In the guest bedroom Ben lay with his hands folded beneath his head; gosh, she was exasperating sometimes; but he kind of liked that, being kept on his toes. He hadn't expected her to give him such a hard time over a holiday; but she really wasn't like anyone else he'd ever dated. If he ever got the chance to date her that was.

Chapter 58

The clock said 12.05 and Ben wanted his answer, he didn't want to wait a second longer. Getting out of bed he put two foil packets in his boxer short pocket, opened the bedroom door and padded softly down to Evie's bedroom. Her door was slightly ajar probably in case Henry came up for a visit. He went in and walked round to the empty side of the bed, took the packets out of his boxers pocket and then let his boxers drop to the floor. Lifting the duvet he crept underneath it. She seemed to be asleep so he just inched his way over to her. Oh she was lovely and warm, her skin was so soft and she smelt wonderful too. Then he draped his arm over her waist, placed one leg over hers and hugged her to him.

Evie had heard him come in and get into bed. She stayed relaxed when he snuggled up. Then she waited a few minutes before having a little stretch and easing her body against his, pushing her bum onto his thighs in the process. As she thought, he responded immediately in the only way a guy can. Oh hello, she thought, someone's pleased to see me.

"Evie are you awake? He whispered.

"Well I am now," she whispered back.

"Do you have an answer for me as technically it is tomorrow?" He started to stroke her arm with his hand and felt her reaction to him.

"Getting impatient are we?" she wriggled round to face him in the darkness.

"Evie come on don't toy with me please."

"Are you sure about this, I mean I know I have spelt out my issues and stuff, plus you've seen my scars so…!

"Yes of course I am I wouldn't have booked the holiday if I wasn't sure and anyway you can see my scars in the morning."

"You've got scars?"

He laughed. "Evie, I'm a soldier. Of course I've got scars, so what do you say?"

MUSIC: – BANG BANG – JESSIE J, NICKI MINAJ, ARIANA GRANDE.

She didn't want to make him wait any longer, "I say, where am I going on my holiday?"

He grinned at her, "There are a couple of things I want to do first and then I'll tell you okay?" She nodded.

"So firstly I am going to kiss you, all over, (Evie held her breath: that sounded fantastic) and secondly then I'm going to fuck you into next week," (oh boy!). Ben started to kiss her, taking her a bit by surprise but then his tongue was in her mouth and his hands were all over her body, in her hair on her back, running over her thighs; it all felt so damn good. She moaned and he just increased the pressure of his lips on hers; three months was a bloody long time for anyone to wait. Her hands were on his shoulders then caressing the small of his back before she moved her hands over his bum then between his legs. He pulled down her pyjama bottoms; there was just her cami top now, not that it was presenting any kind of protection from his mouth on her nipples. She arched her back towards his chest and was so needy for him right this minute. Suddenly she pulled away: "Do you have protection?" She was panting already. "Yes," and he rolled away from her whilst she removed her cami and lay back waiting for part two. Part one had been…well…being kissed everywhere was so, was so hot and now for part two, she gulped anticipating that the best was yet to come.

They lay there both breathing heavily. Eventually Evie said, "Well Captain that was, oh boy that was…"

"Yeah I know, Private Wallace the first time… is it usually so… um… so intense for you too?"

"No not like that," and they grinned at each other. It had taken them both by surprise. It usually took a few times with a new partner before it all clicked into place, but this first time had been amazing.

The next few days went by in a blur of sex, kissing, talking, laughing, her going to work and him waiting for her to return so that they could pick right up where they had left off. He was nothing if not skilled in the bedroom department, they were even trying out some new positions, well new to Evie anyway. Thursday morning and Evie wasn't teaching until the evening. Ben stirred and opened his eyes, he was more than ready for his morning wake – up call and turned to face Evie, only she wasn't in bed. He flung his hand over to her side and the bed was stone cold, Oh bollocks! he thought, where was she now when he needed her so badly? Shrugging on some jogging bottoms he looked in the en-suite; it was empty, so he padded downstairs and clocked Henry curled up in his chair in the living room, so she'd obviously let Henry in. The kitchen was empty too, but as he approached the utility room he could hear some music playing and went to investigate. Opening the rear door it led into a small gym and Evie was there on the treadmill working hard, oblivious to anyone and anything. Ben watched her for a while and then casually sauntered over and pressed the stop button. Immediately she wobbled looking surprised and Ben swept her up and off the machine.

"Hi, thought I'd get some proper exercise in for a change you know – just to keep active."

Ben grinned, "Well I thought we might do some proper exercise too this morning – just the two of us." He began to kiss her and pushed his erection into her thighs just to demonstrate just how ready he was for this particular exercise."

Evie kissed him then pulled away. "Um okay but I'm all sweaty."

"Makes no difference to me." Ben knelt down and took off her shoes and socks, then pulled down her leggings and began to kiss her thighs then moved onto the soft skin on her inner thighs. Evie placed her hands on his shoulders and groaned out loud; fuck he was insatiable; but she was loving every minute of it. Ben dropped his jogging bottoms and lifted her top off over her head, Quickly Evie pulled the blinds closed and put her squishy exercise mat on the floor, Ben undid her bra, yanked her knickers down and then proceeded to kiss her. The two of them were getting very hot and heavy when Ben reached over for a condom from his joggers and they started to have sex; but the exercise mat was just too squishy and they had to roll off of it and onto the carpet. Evie was past caring at this point.

Afterwards he wrapped his arms around her and kissed her again, "So Private Wallace, did you enjoy that for breakfast this morning?"

Evie pretended to think about it, "Um yes Captain I suppose it was okay; but why can't you have a bacon sandwich like other guys?"

Ben laughed and started to tickle her, which made her giggle all the more and before they knew it – it was time for round two, followed by a shower – now that was a great way to start the day.

Chapter 59

Evie finished her 6.00 – 7.00 class and showering in double quick time, was out and in her car before 7.15. They would need to be on the road before 8.00 if they were to reach Ben's parents the same day. Last time they were so late she hadn't expected his family to wait up for them to arrive at midnight. His brother and sister plus partners were going to be there too, so the same family group as before. She hoped his mother had made up the guest bedroom for her again as she really didn't want the Spanish inquisition from April – she asked a lot of questions for a young girl.

They threw their bags into the boot of her car and then they were off, so with luck on their side they would be on time for a change. Evie drove and put Taylor on the car's media player, same as before, the only difference this time was that they were officially a couple. Her car ate up the miles, they sang along to the music and with no traffic problems or road closures saw them pulling onto his parent's drive right on time. There was no welcoming committee and they dropped their bags at the foot of the stairs. Ben grabbed her and kissed her hard before taking her hand just as they went through the door to the kitchen where they found everyone sat at the table in the middle of a game of Monopoly.

Mrs Shaw was on her feet in the blink of an eye and Ben had no choice but to drop Evie's hand. She was hugging her son and holding his face in her hands until the rest of the family took over. "Evelyn it's lovely to see you again, how are you?"

"I'm very well thank you Mrs Shaw, it's very kind of you to invite me back again."

"Oh nonsense. We love having you here, and please call me Helen."

Evie let them have their family reunion and sat at the table, picking up Monty as she did so. There was laughter, wine and relief that their son/brother was home safe yet again. The conversation turned to the Monopoly game that had been interrupted. William was cross as he'd been winning, but they promised to have a rematch the next time he was there. There were suggestions of Pictionary for tomorrow and the party eventually broke up just after midnight. Ben carried Evie's bag to her room, "So I'll see you in the morning then, are we running before or after breakfast?"

"Oh after I think, same as last time. You never know you might beat me to the top this time." Ben grinned at her.

He quietly closed the bedroom door and pulled her to him for a goodnight kiss, "Are you sure you're going to be okay sleeping in here on your own?" he was joking with her now. "As I could always come and keep you company if you get lonely."

Evie laughed softly, "Oh don't you worry about me. I'll holler if I need you, plus I expect I'll have Monty to ride shotgun soon." Ben left, checking first that the coast was clear. He left her door ajar and in less than two minutes Monty had jumped up onto the bed and was kneading the duvet. Evie unpacked and got ready for bed, brushing her teeth she looked at herself in the mirror. The last time she'd been here they'd just been friends and now they were together; although Ben was miffed she hadn't let him stay, maybe next time. Snuggling under the duvet her thoughts drifted to the past few days. Ben and her had got to know one another pretty well in a short space of time, she smiled to herself oh yes pretty well indeed and switched off the light.

Sunday morning and feeling more confident Evie padded down to the kitchen in her pyjamas and blue robe. It was perfectly decent attire for breakfast and besides she knew the routine this time. Mrs Shaw was already there and Evie helped herself to juice and fruit.

"So did you sleep well Evelyn?"

"Yes thank you, it's a very comfortable room."

"Forgive me for saying, but I wasn't sure if you and Ben would be sharing this time."

So his mother had noticed them holding hands last night. "The guest room is just fine, it's no problem at all."

With this Ben wandered into the kitchen. He was in pyjama bottoms and a T-shirt. "Morning, mum" and without waiting for a response sat down pulled Evie onto his lap and kissed her. "And good morning to you too, sleep well?" He grinned at her.

She smiled back. "Yes thank you. I was just telling your mother what a nice room that is. Would you like some juice?"

Evie was keen to get off his lap before the rest of the family arrived but he wouldn't let her go and was too strong for her to wriggle free so she stayed where she was. His arms were wrapped around her waist and her arms were around his neck. "In a minute. There's no rush, is there?" and proceeded to kiss her again. William chose this precise moment to walk in. "Oh you two, get a room please. It's too early for PDA'S and before breakfast too."

Ben ignored his brother and carried on until he eventually said, "Morning William. You're so not a morning person are you?" Ben joshed with him.

"Well you two always look disgustingly fit and healthy and it's far too early in the day for all that mushy stuff."

Evie laughed out loud. "So what time is acceptable William, just so I know for future reference, that is?"

William had the good grace to laugh and Evie seized the opportunity to get up and fetch Ben some juice. She knew he was just spelling it out for his family; but there was obviously no need to do so.

"What's a PDA?" asked Ben's mother.

Ben explained, "It's a public display of affection."

As Evie placed Ben's juice down on the table he grabbed her arm and swung her down into his lap again. "Just so you know Will, a kiss is just a kiss but this, well this is a PDA," and proceeded to kiss Evie much more passionately this time. Ben's mother chipped in, "Yes thank you Ben, stop winding your brother up will you? Honestly you two!"

Ben released Evie whose face was now bright red and she wandered over to get some granola and almond milk for herself. Without turning round she asked Ben how many Weetabix he wanted, "Oh three today, no better make it four – I'll need some extra energy for later," and winked at a now grumpy Will sat opposite. Will said under his breath, "Just give it a rest, will you?"

Ben leaned in towards Will and said, "I meant for my run, but you do seem a bit tense; maybe Daisy will give you a massage, I can recommend it as a perfect way to start the day." And he leant back in his chair, resting his head in his crossed arms

"Ben play nicely now." Evie was laughing as she made her way back to the table then realising she didn't have a spoon promptly jumped back up again.

"I still don't see what's wrong with just a morning kiss," sulked William

Ben continued, "Yes, well, you know what that means don't you..?" Evie interrupted and bent down and whispered something in Will's ear, causing him to choke on his juice and go bright red too.

Luckily April and Craig chose that moment to arrive in the kitchen and the talk turned to breakfast and who was having what to eat.

Their leisurely breakfast finished they made their way upstairs to change into their running gear. They decided to wait another ½ an hour or so just to be on the safe side, but then it was a run to the top of Roman Hill again. Ben followed Evie into her room and closed the door. "Do you need any help getting changed because I am an expert in that particular field?" He reached for her again and they kissed, she went to pull away, but Ben held her so tightly she wasn't able to. Suddenly they both felt the tension change and then they were undressing each other with indecent haste before tumbling naked onto her bed not caring about breakfast or running anywhere for the time being.

Lying together in each other's arms, Ben began to stroke Evie's arm.

"I think it's time for our run now don't you? She smiled at him. "Or we'll never get there."

"Spoilsport," he shifted his weight so that she was on top of him now. "I'm curious though what did you whisper to Will to make him go red in the face?"

"Ah I'll tell you at the top of Roman Hill. I have a question for you: now where are we going on our holiday you still haven't told me?"

"Impatience getting the better of you is it?" He started to kiss her cheek and then her nose and her shoulder then he began to nuzzle her ear. "I'll tell you now on one condition?"

"Oh yes, and what pray would that be?" Evie was smiling at him now.

"That I can sleep in here with you tonight, all night and that you give me a massage the same as before."

Evie was enjoying him kissing her body so much she just murmured, "Mmmm okay it's a deal."

"There's just one thing first though."

"What's that?"

"This," and he flipped her over so he was on top of her leaving her in no doubt he was ready for her again. His erection was pushing into her and she groaned. She wanted him so badly and right this second. She broke off from his kiss, whispered 'condom' and in a flash Ben had reached for one in his pyjama bottoms and was back parting her legs and easing himself into her.

Finally they made it down stairs before midday to start their run. They politely asked if anyone else would care to join them, knowing full well what the answer would be, and then set off. Evie loved to be outdoors and she relaxed as they made their way to the start of the climb to the top of the hill. Ben hadn't had a girlfriend who liked fitness before so he was enjoying this so much more then running by himself, even if he did have to slow the pace a bit. Finally the vantage point came into view and Evie slowed down before stopping to rest her arms on her knees. She'd enjoyed that a lot, not as much as what they'd done twice before they'd left, but even so it gave her a rush of endorphins.

"So this holiday; where are we going?"

"Do you remember in one of your letters you wrote to me you described holidays as being, now let me get this right" he took her into his arms and in between every word kissed her, "big beds ....soft duvets... big baths...big .hot showers....room service... movies in jim jams..."

"Yes I think so... so?"

"So we're going somewhere that has all those things, from Tuesday for 4 nights then back here for one night and then home for you."

"So where exactly?"

"Can I keep that part as a surprise... please?"

Evie pretended to think about it and then said, "Okay I suppose so."

"Now tell me what did you say to Will to have such a profound effect on him?" Ben was still curious as it took a lot to silence his brother at the best of times.

"I just finished your sentence, you know, so kiss in the morning and fuck all night."

Ben yelped with laughter and surprise, "Oh my God you are such a bad girl. No wonder he couldn't look you in the eye afterwards."

Evie grinned at him, "Well all this pretend prudish behaviour from him. I expect he's worse than all of us put together if the truth be told, you know the quiet ones are always the worst."

"Yes well you're definitely not quiet in that department are you?" Ben wrapped his arms around her and kissed her hard. "But we may have to keep the noise down tonight, don't want them all piling into your room thinking you're being abducted or anything"

Evie whispered to him, "Why what will we be doing then?" and raised her eyebrows.

Ben groaned with frustration. "God I want you so badly again, right here, right now, just as well I don't have a condom and it's a public place otherwise you wouldn't be safe at all."

She laughed and pulling away from him shouted, "You're insatiable – first one down gets to have their massage first," and raced off. Ben grinned; okay he'd let her go for a minute or two; but he'd still beat her to the bottom and then he'd choose to have his massage first. Oh yes that was a sure thing and he set off jogging slowly down the hill.

Chapter 60

After showering and lunch, a raucous game of Pictionary began with two teams of 4, girls against boys. It was very close, but the girls just squeaked a victory much to the delight of April and Daisy whom Evie suspected didn't get to win much of anything with Will and Craig. It was just after 7.00 and both April and Will were getting ready to leave. There were always arguments and disagreements between brothers and sisters; but they were so happy their brother was home safe and sound and it was an emotional goodbye.

Evie wandered into the kitchen to make some tea, followed by Helen and they began to chat.

"We're so happy to have Ben home and you seem to bring out the best in him. He's very happy and relaxed with you and we love to see that."

"That's a very kind thing to say."

Helen interrupted Evie and said, We worry so much when he's away and the relief when he's back – well I can't tell you; but to see him so happy, you're very good for him you know, you keep him on his toes, he needs someone with a bit of spirit. Ben adored your letters you wrote to him I think they were one of the main reasons for keeping him sane all the time he was away. He told us he read them over and over, so thank you for that, it meant a lot to him and to us too. Also I believe I have you to thank for my mother's day present it was very thoughtful of you."

"I'm glad you liked it and as for the letters, well it was nothing really; just a letter every two weeks. I just tried to keep them light and entertaining, he didn't need any drama from me when he's out there doing such a tough job."

Unbeknown to the two women Ben was eavesdropping outside the door. So his mother liked Evie and liked her a lot, yes she did have spirit and kept him on his toes alright. He smiled, thinking back to when his colleagues had tried to outwit her in his office. She could more than look after herself and as for those letters, well they'd been like Christmas and birthday rolled into one.

Strolling into the kitchen he asked how much longer his tea would be. Evie rolled her eyes at Helen. "So impatient," and they laughed together.

Just before 10.00 Evie yawned and said she was turning in to read in bed for a bit. She said her goodnights, insisted that Ben stay with his parents and made her way upstairs. It must be all the fresh air as well as all the sex she giggled to herself; she was a bit sore too, maybe a bath would help with that. She closed her bedroom door and turned the bath taps on. It seemed to be filling up fast much quicker than her modern bath at home and less than ten minutes later she was relaxing in scented bubbles. There was a knock on the door and before she could answer it Ben was stood in the bathroom dressed in only his boxer shorts. He grinned at her. "Thought you might need someone to scrub your back?"

Evie smiled and sat forward, "Okay then feel free."

"Shove up a bit."

Evie laughed. "Are you kidding? You don't think you're going to fit in here as well do you?"

Ben looked at the bath. No she was right, the bath was way too small for the two of them, "Oh bloody hell I was looking forward to that," he sounded frustrated.

"Tell you what. Once I'm out I'll give you your massage, how does that sound?"

"It'll have to do I suppose." He sounded grumpy, but secretly he was pleased to have been given another option which if he played his cards right might be just as good as sharing a bath.

"Now just be quiet woman and let me wash your back," he pretended to be mad with her but really it was all part of his master plan. He couldn't believe his luck when he'd gone into her room and realised she was in the bath, God, could this day get any better. Ben soaped her back. He didn't really notice her scars anymore and then held out a towel, he enveloped her and kissed her again,

"Okay so now it's my turn."

Once she was dry they snuggled under her duvet together. Monty wasn't getting a look in tonight.

Ben was very keen to have his massage next but Evie pleaded with him for a little bit more time to doze. Honestly, guys they were so ready to go whereas girls just needed a bit longer. Eventually his impatience got the better of him and he pulled down the duvet making her shiver. "Hey I was all warm under that."

"Yes too comfortable by half, so I won the bet and I want my massage now please."

" You can tell you're in the Army, it's all yes sir, no sir, three bags full sir, "she was joking with him and proceeded to straddle him, sitting on his bum and started to knead the tops of his shoulders.

"We have punishments for disobedience you know, "he murmured softly. Her hands might be small but they were so good, but he'd have to be careful not to fall asleep.

She leant forward letting her breasts touch his back and felt his response. "What sort of punishments?" she whispered to him.

Monday morning and Evie yawned and stretched, finding Ben wrapped around her. Last night had been wonderful, they seemed to be on the same page as far as the bedroom was concerned. That bath followed by his and then her massage well it was just all so naughty. She laughed quietly to herself and watched Ben as he slept. She needed the bathroom and started to wiggle her way out from him, "Where do you think you're going, Private?" He opened his eyes and smiled at her.

"Um I need the bathroom and then I'll be right back okay?"

"Don't be long there's something I want to show you when you get back."

Evie laughed; yes, she could imagine just what that would be. She had a wee, washed her hands and for good measure brushed her teeth then climbed back into bed. Ben then jumped out and went to the bathroom and was back in a jiffy, He started to caress her body. "Now where were we again? Tell me about these hotel showers made for two."

"Oh those, well firstly you both have to be naked otherwise it just doesn't work, the water needs to be just right…..then it's all hot and steamy…..and you're all wet …..and slippery and…. then it's all hands and soft lather touching you everywhere……and," Evie didn't get to finish her sentence. Ben groaned out loud and pulled her on top of him, his mouth on hers kissing her deeply, his tongue probing her soft skin, then moved his lips over her body until he turned her over and reached for a condom.

They finally made it down to breakfast after 9.30, but they were both dressed in sweatpants and t shirts. There was far too much temptation to be in their pj's this morning and they didn't want to make his parents feel uncomfortable in their own home. It was a very lazy Monday, spent eating, talking and eventually running in the early afternoon. The four of them ate supper together at the kitchen table and Ben felt totally relaxed at last. No dramas, no Army and the thought of the next four days away with Evie.

Chapter 61

Ben and Evie set off on Tuesday morning. He still hadn't told her where they were staying, but she knew it was in north Yorkshire as he had to give her a tiny snippet of info to program the sat nav. At last fate was on their side and there were no major hold ups and they stopped for lunch just outside York. Ben then took over the driving and within a couple of hours the car made its way up a long driveway towards what looked like a castle.

Evie gasped. It looked incredible; suddenly she felt very guilty as it looked like a very expensive place to stay and she thought she would offer to pay half. She would need to pick her moment though so as not to offend Ben, as she had no idea what the Army paid and didn't want him to struggle to pay for this.

As they pulled up to the front entrance a young guy in hotel uniform appeared. He took the car keys and explained their luggage would be taken straight up to their room. Smiling they held hands and went to check in. That done they were shown to a room on the second floor. It was amazing, their bags were already there and once the reception manager had left them alone Evie just stared. The bed was huge, absolutely huge and she squeezed the duvet; oh yes lovely and snuggly. Next she looked out of the window. They had a spectacular view. Finally she ventured into the bathroom to find twin basins, a massive walk in shower, a huge modern bathtub set in the middle of the floor and masses of fluffy towels. Ben watched her moving round the room taking it all in. He followed her into the bathroom and put his arms around her waist and pulled her against his chest Kissing the top of her head he asked, "So what do you think, is this what you had in mind for your surprise holiday?"

Evie squealed in excitement and turned round to kiss him. "Oh it's just wonderful, how did you find this place?"

"Oh that's a secret, so do you like it?"

"Are you kidding? I love it." She kissed him again, "Just one thing bothering me though – now don't take this the wrong way?"

He frowned. "Sounds ominous – go on."

"Well here's the thing: would you like me to pay half as it looks very expensive and I'll feel guilty if you've spent all your wages on this and on me?"

Ben laughed loudly, "Well I certainly didn't expect you to say that. Of course I can afford it and no I don't want you to pay." He hugged her to him; honestly she was amazing, she obviously had no idea what the Army paid whilst he was on deployment. Secretly he was touched that she'd offered, most girls wouldn't have done this but it was just so typically her and he loved her for that. He stopped suddenly thinking about what he'd just said to himself, he loved her – simple as that, now for four days to show her just how much.

"So what would you like to do first?" Ben was hoping for a certain reply.

"Um unpack, bath and nap – then eat I think. How does that sound?"

"As long as we share the bath then that's fine by me."

Evie turned the tap on, poured in some bath foam and the bath started to fill. It was a big bath so there'd be plenty of room for the two of them in there. She unpacked, noting that Ben had said she wouldn't need any clothes as she'd be lucky to make it out of their room before they had to leave on Saturday morning then he winked at her. Honestly, just where did he get his energy from she wondered?

She sank into the warm water. Ooh this was lovely, just lovely and sighing she thought what a great start to their holiday together this was. To think she'd given him such a hard time about deciding for her. She needed to cut him some slack, maybe tonight she would do just that and she giggled to herself.

"Okay Wallace budge up now, you can scrub my back seeing as how I missed out last night." Ben stepped into the bath and sat down in front of her. She reached for the body mousse and began to soap his back and shoulders followed by the backs of his arms, then rinsed it off with a sponge. She reached around to his tummy and soaped what she could, avoiding his hips and thighs as that would be too much temptation too soon.

"All done, are you going to wash my back now?" She asked him crossing her fingers.

Ben pretended to grumble but moved round and sat behind her and began to repeat the experience. After he'd rinsed her back she lay back against his chest and they both lay there happy together. She could feel his erection pushing against her bum and she wriggled against it letting him know she was nearly as ready as he was. Ben put some more mousse into his hands and began to wash her shoulders and then moved his hands down her chest until his hands were massaging her breasts. Evie groaned; she wanted him so badly, why was she always so needy for sex the week before her period, it was intolerable. Unable to wait any longer Ben stood up and then sat down in front of her in the bath. He pulled her legs over his and then held her up and over his erection and eased her down gently on top of him. Evie groaned, oh my God and then they began to move together, slowly with the warm water caressing their skin until they couldn't bear it any longer and it was faster and more intense. Evie's hands were on Ben's shoulders and his hands were on her hips pushing her down harder so she could feel all of him inside of her. She shouted out as she came followed by Ben two thrusts later. Collapsing onto his chest, she thought, 'oh yes, that had hit the spot, make no mistake'. Holding her tight he kissed her, then resting their foreheads together and noses touching he said, "You do know I'm in love with you don't you?" Evie's eyes flashed open. "Really?" she gasped.

He groaned. "Oh don't look at me like that with those big eyes of yours or else we'll never get out of here. Do you feel the same?"

She smiled shyly at him, "Yes I do. I was going to tell you later anyway I…" He didn't allow her to finish her sentence but started to kiss her again.

Evie woke and stretched. After their bath she'd tumbled into their big bed and been asleep within minutes. Now she felt refreshed and hungry too. Turning her head, she saw Ben asleep beside her and she wriggled over to him. Blimey, but this bed was massive. She started to stroke his arm and then placed her arm around his waist caressing the small of his back before moving her hand down to his bum; oh, he had such a great bum too. Ben stirred. Just what was she up to now? Before she could react he'd pulled her over so that she was on top of him and was kissing her again. Evie wriggled slowly against him and this time it was very leisurely and exquisite. Just think: four whole days of this!.

The next few days they were in their own private bubble, they did what they wanted when they wanted. This involved a lot of baths, showers, massages, sex obviously, room service and all the usual stuff involved with not being able to keep their hands off of one another. They did make it down to the gym once though. Evie left Ben asleep, changed into her Lycra gear and wrote him a note. She made her way down to the hotel gym for an hour. The trainer was overjoyed to see someone who wasn't an overweight business man and gave her all of his special attention. Ben read her note and decided to go and find her. Dressing in camouflage trousers and an army t shirt he found Evie on the rower being encouraged by a very – over keen in his opinion – young trainer. On seeing Ben, he left Evie and walked over to talk to him.

"Hello sir. Are you wanting to work out today?"

"Possibly." Ben nodded towards Evie. "She's pretty good, isn't she?"

"Oh yes, it makes a change from businessman I can assure you, …and …she's very fit."

"Um yes I suppose she is,… very fit indeed." And before the trainer could say anything else Ben walked over to Evie and stood at the front of the rower so she could see him and grinned at her. "That's quite some performance if you don't mind me saying so."

Evie could hardly talk and row so she slowed down and smiled back at him. "Well I have a particularly insatiable boyfriend so I'm trying to keep up with him." She slowed to a halt undid the shoes straps and stood up, whereupon Ben swept her up into his arms and kissed her like they hadn't seen each other for a week. Yes, he thought to himself, you run along now lad and leave this fit girl, who happens to be my girlfriend, to me. Eventually he released her, "So… pleased to see me?"

"Oh yes very…just let me stretch and then I need a shower." She lowered her voice: "don't suppose you know someone who could help me with that do you?" Five minutes later they were back in their bathroom stripping off their clothes and standing under the shower letting the water cascade over them. Hot shower sex to start the day; what could be better?

They had dinner in the hotel restaurant just once. Evie played her jumpsuit and kimono jacket trick, not taking her jacket off until they'd started to eat the first course. Ben was holding a forkful of food half way to his mouth when she slipped the jacket off. His mouth just dropped open and he had to put his fork down; still gaping at her, he whispered, "Fuck me." To which Evie replied quietly, "Oh yes please." And continued with her food. They ate their main course but Ben whisked her away before anyone could mention dessert. She was all the dessert he wanted and he wanted her right this minute.

Their final night together and Evie finally made it into her pyjamas instead of just a fluffy robe. She'd been saving this pair for a special occasion and thought: why not bring them along and see what happened? They were very soft, slinky fabric in a soft wine colour, plain bottoms; but the top had long sleeves with the deepest v edged with wide lace that plunged straight down. She put them on in the bathroom and waited to see if Ben would be in to brush his teeth.

Sure enough, he pushed open the door and picked up his toothbrush. It wasn't until he looked at her in the mirror that he saw the plunging neckline and quickly spat out his toothpaste before pulling her back against his chest and slipping his hands under the lace and onto her breasts. He whispered to her: "So trying to surprise me?"

"Mmm something like that, "she gasped. And before she knew it he'd pulled down her pyjama bottoms and his robe was lying on the floor and it was just his hands moving under the lace teasing her breasts as she arched away from him. In the blink of an eye he had one arm around her back and then he lifted her bum so that her hips were against the washstand and proceeded to ease himself into her, all the time not taking his other hand away from her breast. He began to move slowly inside of her; she was moaning and he kissed the nape of her neck: "Faster?"

"Oh yes ...much faster."

"Happy to oblige," and with that he thrust faster and faster until she was right on the edge and her orgasm exploded into him. He came inside her, shouting her name, and they collapsed clinging to one another. They'd so much sex in the last four days Evie was a bit sore, but sore in a good way; even so this had been the best yet.

Snuggled under the duvet neither of them wanted to leave tomorrow; Evie couldn't keep her eyes open and was asleep in minutes. Ben however stared at the ceiling. Evie was in his arms, her head on his chest and he was thinking this had been the best four days of his life. When he thought how tough his last two deployments had been, if someone had told him just do those two and then this is your reward he wouldn't have believed them.

Chapter 62

Saturday morning arrived all too soon and after sharing yet another bath together they reluctantly packed their bags before checking out. They'd had a fabulous time and neither of them wanted it to end. Just one more night together at Ben's parent's house and then it was back home for Evie and back to Camp for Ben.

Shortly before 6.00pm they pulled onto his parent's driveway and unloaded their bags. They knew that Ben would be sneaking into Evie's room later that night; but there would be no sharing of baths or showers this time. Mr Shaw opened the door and ushered them inside, his wife appeared and they all headed into the kitchen to have a cup of tea. They talked generally about how nice the hotel had been. They didn't want it known that they had in fact seen more of their bedroom than any other part of the hotel, so just said that yes the food had been delicious and the service had been great, all very innocent comments.

They unpacked in their separate rooms and Evie lay down on the bed and closed her eyes, why was travelling so bloody tiring as all you did was sit there? She was asleep in minutes and when Ben wandered in to find her he just wrapped the duvet around her and left her to sleep. Ben and his parents watched some TV before having a late supper. Evie joined them just as they were finishing. "Sorry, it's very rude of me to just fall asleep."

Mr Shaw said, "Not at all, you don't need to stand on ceremony with us, sit down. Would you like anything to eat or drink?"

"Just a glass of water would be fine, thank you."

Both Evie and Ben were a bit subdued. It was back to reality with a big bump from tomorrow night and they needed to figure out just how they were going to see each other over the next few weeks.

Evie offered to help Mrs Shaw clear the supper things whilst Ben and his dad went into the living room. She happily cleared the plates and they stood next to each other at the sink just idly chatting about this and that. Helen was asking her about her brother and Evie filled her in. Yes, he lived abroad and he was married with two children. Helen sighed, "So your mother is already a grandma then? I keep waiting for William to announce that he's getting married so that hopefully I'll be a grandma, but nothing so far." Evie laughed. "Are you in a hurry then to be called granny and what about April? She could beat him to it, you never know?"

"Well I'd like them to be married first but I expect you think that's a bit old fashioned these days?"

"No. My mother would feel exactly the same way if it was me."

"Of course Ben would love lots of children; but then I suppose you've talked about these things already?"

Evie was suddenly stunned; where had that come from? "Um no. It's a bit soon to be talking about children, we haven't been together very long." Bloody hell, talk about a bolt from the blue; but Helen instead of moving on seemed determined to keep exploring the subject.

"Sorry I keep forgetting, it's just that he's so happy and you've fitted in here so easily, I forget that he's been away from you for months. So do you see yourself with a big family – one day I mean?"

Oh shit now what did she say? She didn't want to lie, but she hadn't discussed this with Ben. He knew she'd a miracle pregnancy followed by a miscarriage and she was sure she'd written in one of her letters to him about the fact that she couldn't have any children –she had, hadn't she?

"Um I don't know if Ben has told you this but I have a very complicated medical history and it's extremely unlikely that I will ever have a child of my own." There: she had said it out loud. She exhaled, relieved that now surely the conversation would be over, but it seemed not. Helen just wouldn't let it go.

"Oh no I'm sorry I didn't know that. So is there no chance at all then?"

"No, not really."

"Well there are other options these days aren't there, like adoption? How would you feel about that?"

Evie wanted the ground to swallow her up. "Don't get me wrong; I think it's an amazing and admirable thing to do, but I would find it so difficult not to have a part of me and my husband in our child. I think it would be too much for me."

"How about IVF or what's that other thing called?, they can do wonderful things nowadays, you know"

"Umm well hypothetically if my partner or husband was in the forces I could hardly keep them to my ovulation schedule. Just imagine me calling his

CO and saying 'I know he's on exercise, but I just need him for five minutes and then he's all yours again.' It wouldn't really work if he was abroad either, only if your job was 9-5 Monday to Friday, kind of thing." Surely now this conversation would be at an end.

"So IVF, do you know much about that?"

Oh shit Helen was so determined. "I know a bit yes; but it does put a huge strain on a couple's relationship and there are no guarantees. A lot of people actually split up over the pressure, besides I don't think any of these things are an option for me really." She took a deep breath and continued. "I had a very bad accident about four years ago and it was made very clear at the time about babies....I've seen a lot of specialists."

"Oh well. You never know, they could be wrong."

Evie decided that this conversation was well and truly over so said breezily, "Okay I think we're all done here so I'll go check on Ben." And exited the room as fast as she could. She was breathing heavily now and took the stairs two at a time: bloody hell, bloody hell. Just as her and Ben were finally on the same page. He hadn't told her he wanted lots of kids, how was she supposed to know? Plus, they'd only been together 5 minutes. She had to calm down, but couldn't stop replaying the conversation over in her head. So if he did want a lot of kids it wouldn't be in a relationship with her then – that would be impossible; shit, she'd done it again, fallen too fast and now everything was up in the air. She had no intention of seeking Ben out, she had just needed to escape. She closed her bedroom door and decided to get ready for bed.

Shaking her head, she couldn't face either of his parents again tonight and if there'd been a key she would have locked her bedroom door so she didn't have to face Ben either. Had he spoken to his mother about them or kids or what? Evie was so confused she pulled on her pyjamas and opened the door just in case Monty wanted to come in. Switching off the light she went into the bathroom and eureka! there was a key. So, locking the door she sat down on a towel on the closed toilet lid. Suddenly she was overwhelmed. Things had been going so well, too bloody well and now, well now they were all falling down around her ears. She grabbed a hand towel and folding into four she buried her head in it and began to cry. This was her usual routine after all; but now it was getting to be something of a habit.

Meanwhile Mrs Shaw had joined her husband in the living room, surprised to see that Evie wasn't there. "Evie not been in, has she?"

"No I haven't seen her. Ben's just popped out to get something from the car, why?"

"Well I think I've put my foot in it rather."

Ben had just entered the hall and for some unknown reason he hovered outside the living room door and began to listen. He caught words like, "we were just chatting ... grandma... children...Ben big family......medical history...miscarriage...adoption.... IVF..... not at all possible...... accident."

Oh my God, he thought. What on earth had his mother said now, and where was Evie?

He checked the kitchen. Nothing. Then he took the stairs 3 at a time. Switching on the landing light he could see her bedroom door was open. Peering in he could see the bed was empty. Oh shit, had she packed and left already? Then he saw her wheelie case and exhaled; no she was still here. Finally he noticed a chink of light from underneath the en-suite door. Creeping up to it silently, he put his ear against the door – honestly, all he'd done since he'd got back was creep about and eavesdrop. He held his breath. He could hear Evie and it sounded like she was crying. It was muffled, but he'd place money on it that she was crying into a towel. His heart felt like it would break; they'd had such a great time away and just when it looked as if things between them were going to work out, this had happened. So the question was, what should he do now? Ben thought for a moment and remembered her telling him about a previous boyfriend who had been banging on a bathroom door whilst she'd been crying. He had to try a different approach. Creeping softly away he decided to let her cry and then go to bed. He'd leave it half an hour and then he'd come in and cuddle up to her; surely they could work through this? He went back downstairs, told his parents that Evie was tired and had gone to bed and that he was off to bed now too. It had been a long day etc. In reality he got ready for bed and then lay down to wait half an hour.

Chapter 63

Ben stretched out and looked at his clock. It was now after 1.00am and he'd fallen asleep. Jumping up he made his way across the landing to the guest room and seeing that the door was ajar he peered in. Evie's bed hadn't been slept in and the bathroom door was open and in darkness. His heart was literally in his boots. She'd gone, he could have stopped her and he hadn't. Not waiting to check if she'd packed, he made his way downstairs and looked out onto the drive; well her car was still there, so the question was where was Evie?

He checked the living room to find it empty and then opened the kitchen door. He saw her in the darkness curled up in an armchair asleep with Monty on her lap. She'd definitely been crying and he just wanted to hold her and tell her it would all be okay. He picked Monty up and off of her lap, setting the now grumpy cat onto the floor. Then he scooped Evie up into his arms. She was cold and he hugged her to him. Making his way back upstairs, she stirred and he just held her even tighter. Carefully putting her down onto her bed he tucked her in and then went round to the other side and joined her. She must have cried herself to sleep; God, how bloody awful! He wrapped his arms around her and she snuggled into them, seeking warmth and reassurance.

It was after 8.00am before Evie stirred. She stretched out, feeling all warm and cosy. Turning over she opened her eyes to find Ben looking right back at her. He smiled and stroked her hair. "Morning sweetheart, sleep well?"

"Mmmm lovely, thank you." For a split-second she'd forgotten the previous night's conversation and then it popped right back in her head. Now what was she going to do? Did he know anything about her conversation with his mother? Startled, she began to back away, but Ben simply moved closer put his arm around her and then she literally couldn't move at all.

"Hey, where are you going?" he smiled lazily at her. "I haven't had my morning kiss yet, or my morning massage or my morning… well you know…?"

"Oh." That's all she could manage, she had no idea, no bloody idea what to say or do; yet again she was like a rabbit caught in headlights.

He kissed her softly on the lips but she didn't respond, so he tried nuzzling her neck and stroking her back. Still nothing. She was freezing him out. Undeterred he continued his attempts to get her to respond to him. Where was the big bath and shower when he needed it? She would have responded then without a doubt. Finally he moved his hand to caress her breast whilst kissing her harder on the lips. He waited and then there was just the slightest movement from her and he pounced, pushing his tongue in her mouth and forcing her legs apart with his knee. Next thing he knew she was panicking and struggling to break free, pushing her hands onto his chest. "No, no I don't want this, Ben. Stop please." He stopped immediately; he'd gone too far, he thought if he made love to her everything would be okay but instead it was quite possibly the worst thing he could have done. Why didn't he just hold her and talk to her? Sex didn't solve everything.

Ben waited. He wasn't sure what to do next. Her big eyes seemed to bore right into him and he waited for her to say or do something, anything.

She was trying so hard not to cry, but she couldn't stop a tear from rolling down her cheek. Ben looked mortified and crushed her to him saying 'I'm sorry, I'm sorry', over and over. He held her, waiting for her panic to subside. Eventually she was quiet and they just continued to stare at one another, neither of them sure what to say or do. Ben took a deep breath. "I'm sorry I would never have forced you – you do know that, right? I just don't know what to do or what to say. I came to look for you last night and you weren't here and I panicked and thought you'd left; but I found you in the kitchen curled up asleep and I put you to bed. Please don't cry. I can't bear to see you unhappy, not after the last few days we've had together."

Evie took a deep breath. She really didn't want to have this conversation right now, but it looked as though she didn't have a choice. "Your mother and I had quite a chat last night."

Ben groaned. "Yes I know. I heard what she said to you, I'm so sorry."

"Believe me she discussed all the options and she told me that you want a big family… lots of kids… But you know… …you do know you can't have that with me don't you? I mean I have told you this ………the night we first met at Matthew's accident we sat up talking about, well about all kinds of stuff and I did tell you then……I haven't led you on or anything."

"No of course not, but you've been pregnant before; yes I know you miscarried, but surely we can work it out."

"I can't quite see how we're going to do that though, you want kids and I can't have them. It's a pretty big thing between couples." Ben started to speak but Evie held her hand up to stop him; "just let me finish please. Look I know this conversation is probably two years too early, but she does have a point. You need to think about this really carefully as although I love you I can't change my situation and maybe you'd be better off with someone who can give you what you want." There. She had said it. The ball was in his court now.

"So what are you saying, that you think we ought to break up over this even though we love each other?"

"Well it's not as if I can have babies and I'm saying I'll think about it or something, this is completely different. I don't want us to get two years down the line and then for you not to have changed your mind and begin to hate me," – Ben went to interrupt her; but again she stopped him. "It's like when you're on a diet and you can't have say chocolate – yes I know," she smiled, "you've probably never been on a diet in your life, but the more you know you can't have something then the more you actually want it until it becomes like an obsession – do you see what I mean?"

Ben couldn't believe they were even having this conversation, Things had got very serious very quickly. "So where do we go from here then?"

"Honestly I don't know." She relaxed and thought he was just as clueless as she was, neither of them wanting to be the one to call the whole thing off. Evie put her head on his chest and they just lay there together in silence. Eventually she started to kiss his chest and moved up to kiss him on the lips. He hesitated. "Are you sure?" She smiled back at him. "Yes very sure, please make love to me right now." He didn't need to be asked twice.

After showering and breakfast, Evie made her way downstairs with her bags. It was time to go. She said her goodbyes. Ben's mother said she was welcome any time; but Evie knew she wouldn't be coming back. With more hugs for Ben, finally they were on their way. It wasn't a very jolly journey home. The radio was on, but Evie had never felt less like singing along in her life. The tension returned and she was so glad when they pulled up in front of her home. Jumping out of the car Evie opened the boot and picked up her bags. Ben loaded his bags into his car and then they just stood there. Neither of them at all sure what to do next.

Staring at the ground Evie eventually spoke, "Look I'm no expert and this isn't easy for either of us, but I think you just need some time away from me." Ben went to interrupt her but she stopped him. "Some time for you to think things through. There's so much pressure these days and we've been together for such a short but really intense time…I think it's for the best."

Ben didn't know what to say. All he wanted to do was hold her and kiss her, but that wouldn't have solved anything and they'd be back to square one again. Sighing he said, "Okay, but don't think I'm giving up on us because I'm not, not for a second okay?"

"Okay… text me when you're safely back at camp… yes?"

"Yes of course."

Evie then just grabbed her bag and opened her front door. She couldn't stand there for one more second. Ben opened his car door and heard her crying loudly on the other side of her front door. He paused. He desperately wanted to go to her; but he knew it would solve nothing so he got in his car started the engine and drove away.

MUSIC: – ALL YOU HAD TO DO WAS STAY – TAYLOR SWIFT.

Chapter 64

Monday morning and looking in the mirror Evie didn't recognize that face peering back at her. Bloody hell she looked like crap, not like she'd just had a week's holiday. Perhaps she'd look better after a shower, yeah and pigs might fly, she thought. Standing under the hot water she had an epiphany. She'd tell a white lie and say she'd had food poisoning. Brilliant! That would explain why she looked so awful and then in a few days she'd be looking better, wouldn't she? This was the best plan she was going to come up with at such short notice and she needed to be at work before 9.00 so it would have to do. She planned to volunteer for any and every available class going over the next few weeks just to keep herself super busy. On Wednesday she was due in London and she would meet Alice and ask her advice. If Alice had a pound for every time Evie needed her advice she'd be a pretty rich woman by now, Evie smiled to herself. Come on; time to get ready.

Ben texted Evie when he'd arrived back at camp. He'd gone straight to his quarters and tried to get his head around everything. Yes, he'd known that Evie couldn't have kids, but she'd got pregnant once before. Okay she'd miscarried; but maybe that had more to do with the stress that her boyfriend had cheated on her before dumping her. Surely if she'd been pregnant once she could be again, maybe they needed to go to see a specialist together, get some new advice after all medical advances were made all the time and maybe there was something new they could try. Thinking back to the conversation he'd overheard it did sound as if Evie had already had a lot of specialist advice and had already explored all the options; but he couldn't just give up hope now, not at the first sign of things getting tough, that wasn't his style at all. Maybe he would text Evie and see if they could visit her doctor together. He'd text and ask her.

The week dragged by for both of them, even though Evie was busy with classes and Ben had more than enough to do at camp, neither of them really knew which way to turn. Evie had called in to see Fiona and had told her the gist of everything. Yes he was great, yes she loved him; the holiday had been amazing, but now it was all in jeopardy. He wanted the one thing she just couldn't give him. Fiona tried to reassure Evie; but the truth was Evie was right, some blokes really did want big families and if it was that important to him then really it was his decision to make, wasn't it? Alice responded in a similar fashion, firstly delighted that Evie had found such a good man after that last dickhead who had treated her in quite possibly the worst way possible; but what could she say? Evie had had all the tests and she knew it wasn't possible. Yes, she'd told Ben this from the outset and that wasn't going to change at any point further down the line.

Friday night and Ben decided to text Evie. He'd thought of nothing else for a whole week and felt quite sick at the thought of losing her.

Hey it's me, how are you? – SEND

Hi I'm okay, well that's a lie; I'm a bit rubbish really. – SEND

Yeah me too. Look I've been thinking. Can we go and see your doctor together and just see what he says? – SEND

Well my doctor is actually one of my closest friends. David and his wife Fiona know everything about me and I mean everything, so why don't I get him to call you and have chat? It would save you from travelling down here and give you time to think without me being there, you know less pressure – I'll tell him to be honest with you. – SEND

Um okay I suppose, I'd rather go and see him with you but if you think he'll talk to me then okay give him my mobile number. – SEND

Okay. His name is David Carter and I'll ring him now – SEND

Evie rang David and after explaining what she needed she passed on Ben's mobile number. She asked David to be honest about things, but not to go into detail about how she had been damaged., She didn't want to scare Ben witless.

Ben's mobile rang less than 10 minutes after he'd spoken to Evie and although the number flashed up as unrecognisable he knew who it was. David seemed very nice and they started off chatting about Evie and laughing at some of the scrapes she found herself in. Then predictably the conversation turned more serious and David was very through and explained as simply as he could that it was probably a million to one chance that Evie would get pregnant again. Even if she did there were no guarantees that she would then carry a baby full term. Yes, it had happened once before, but again no-one was exactly sure why and there weren't any definite answers as to why she'd miscarried. He stressed that if it was important to Ben to have children then he had to make a choice, as he was telling him in no uncertain terms that it wouldn't be with Evie.

The call over and Ben held his head in his hands. Why just when he'd found a great girl, no a bloody fantastic girl, did this have to happen? He knew she'd been honest from the start, but that was before he'd got to know her and they'd begun a serious relationship. He couldn't blame her she'd done nothing wrong and had only been kindness itself in telling him that if she couldn't give him what he wanted then he needed to find someone else who would. She now knew that having a family was really important to him and that he was unlikely to change his mind and she didn't want him to hate her. So the question was what to do now. He sighed; well right now he was going out to get drunk, raging drunk and then he'd make a decision.

David called Evie back once he'd ended his call to Ben. He explained what he'd said and advised her to leave him be to think about things for a bit. Fiona was concerned, but thought she already knew what the outcome was going to be. Whilst Fiona was pregnant she would make sure Evie was looked after, as yet again she was going to need her friends around her. Bloody hell why couldn't her friend catch a break, just one? She'd done nothing to deserve any of this crap and yet it was still haunting her 5 years on.

Chapter 65

A week had passed and there'd been no word from Ben. Evie didn't want to push things as she didn't know if he was on exercise and couldn't text or whether he was just struggling with the whole scenario. Have her and no kids, or leave her and have kids, either way she knew it wasn't going to end well for her and she'd already begun to prepare herself to move on yet again.

Ben had deliberately not called Evie, he was waiting for the right time. Problem was there didn't seem to be one and he knew he would need to talk to her soon. He had a regimental dinner coming up in a couple of weeks, maybe he would invite her to come with him? Then he'd see if he could cope with the thought of never seeing her again or if he needed her too much and the family thing would have to be over for him.

Evie's phone beeped. She had a message. It was from Ben.

Hi it's me. Sorry I haven't been in touch; things have been a bit hectic here. I'll get to the point. I have a regimental dinner the week after next and I'd like you to come with me, what do you think? –SEND

Oh blimey. She'd been thrilled to see who the message was from, but was this really a good idea?
Hi, um are you sure you want to see me? It sounds like a very formal do. Wouldn't you rather invite someone else? – SEND

No I need to see you again, please say yes. – SEND

Evie didn't know what to do; but she would love to see him too, nothing had changed, so maybe they ought to see if they could both handle being together?
Okay I'll come, text me the details. – SEND

Two weeks later and Evie pulled up outside a very nice looking hotel. Ben had booked them a room and a taxi to and from the dinner. After checking in Evie felt nervous. This was beginning to seem like the worst idea in the world now, but she couldn't just bale on him that would be embarrassing for him. After all she'd already resigned herself to know how it was going to end, as end it surely would have to. She had a shower, got dressed, applied her make – up and waited for Ben to arrive. He was cutting it fine as the taxi would be there at 6.45 and it was nearly 6.30 now.

Sure enough Ben came bowling through the door with ten minutes to spare and they just stood there for a moment staring at each other. Suddenly he was right in front of her, breathing fast and before she could move he wrapped his arms around her and kissed her. It felt so good and so right. Quite how long it lasted she couldn't say, but when they finally broke apart both of them were smiling.

"Sorry couldn't help myself. You look beautiful tonight."

Evie blushed. "Oh his old thing, here come on let me help you get ready or we're going to be the last ones to show up."

She helped him dress. It was a bit complicated with regimental dress, but finally he was all set and ready to go. Evie had chosen to wear her favourite skirt, the same one she'd worn to cook for Jamie and his friends, but had bought a new blouse in a striking shade of blue which made her eyes sparkle even more. In the taxi they held hands, relieved to be together again and after introductions were made they sat down to dinner. All the men looked incredibly smart. This was a unique experience for Evie so she sat back and let it wash over her.

Evie was cross. Where the heck was Ben? She hadn't seen him now for nearly two hours and she was tired and wanted to leave. Spying Lofty she walked over and asked him if he'd seen Ben. He admitted he hadn't but promised to go and look for him. Fifteen minutes later Ben was found clinging onto Lofty's neck completely plastered. So that's where he'd been, getting drunk to avoid her. Well it had been a mistake to come with him and now she had to get him back to the hotel. Lofty helped her get him into the taxi and finally they were on their way back. Ben was slurring his words and being rude to the driver. Evie could only apologise and wished the ground would swallow her up. She wasn't used to being embarrassed like this.

Arriving at the hotel and it was clear it was going to be some task to get Ben up the hotel steps and inside. Luckily Kieron, the night porter, saw them arrive and immediately ran out to help. Evie was one side and Kieron was the other. She apologized again to the taxi driver who told he not to worry, he'd seen it all before. The three of them only made it to the bottom of the steps when it became clear they would need more assistance. Andrew walked round the corner and spotting a girl with a drunken man and the porter decided to lend a hand.

"Here let me help, he's too heavy for you." And that had been it. Between Kieron and this stranger they managed to get Ben into Evie's room and sat him on the bed. Evie thanked Kieron and gave him a big tip. Turning to the man who had helped she was just about to thank him too when Ben tried to stand up and then promptly fell over back onto the bed. Evie was quite frankly relieved as she really didn't think she could take anymore tonight.

"Thank you for your help tonight, I'm sorry I don't even know your name."

"It's no problem, I'm Andrew. Here, let me help you get his jacket off, I'm not sure he should sleep in that." The two of them managed to get Ben's jacket off and then Evie knelt down to take off his shoes. Ben stirred and kicked out, his shoe kicking Evie on the arm. Taking her by surprise, this caused her to fall backwards and then she shook herself. Okay so this was how it was going to be. Andrew was full of concern for her, but she assured him she was fine it was just an accident. So shoes, socks, jacket, belt off and shirt loosened she wrapped the duvet around him and stared, How had it come to this? She'd never seen him like this before and it wasn't nice, no not nice at all.

She didn't want to sleep in the same bed so opened the wardrobe to get some extra pillows and blankets as it looked as if she would be using the sofa tonight.

"Here let me help you with those." Andrew was a lot taller than her and made light work of getting the extra bedding down for her. "I think these sofas convert if you just give me a second." And with that the sofa was turned into a bed and Evie thought it had never looked more inviting.

"Thank you so much for helping me tonight, I don't know how we'd have managed without you."

"It's fine, now are you sure your arm is okay?" Holding her arm Andrew inspected it, "I think you're going to have a hell of a bruise, but luckily that's it. Look I know this is none of my business, but are you sure you're going to be safe here with him?" Andrew nodded over to where Ben was now fast asleep.

"Yes, yes I'll be just fine. I've never seen him like this before, but he's out for the count now. I do however owe you a drink, a very large one at that."

"Um there's no need, umm sorry I don't know your name."

"Gosh how rude of me. It's Evelyn, Evelyn Wallace."

"Well Evelyn, if you're sure you've got this all under control I'll say goodnight. I'm not happy about leaving you like this so if you need anything I'm in room 19, just in case okay?"

"Evie smiled. "Thank you but I'll be fine, I think the drama is all over for one night," and with that she thanked him again and showed him out.

Sighing Evie undressed and made her way to the bathroom. She couldn't have predicted all that. She'd thought it would be a mistake for them to meet and this had turned out to be the case, but for all the wrong reasons. There was no chance to talk their situation through and heaven knows what time Ben would surface in the morning. Turing off the light she made her way over to the sofa; it looked all right but these things were never as comfy as you hoped they would be. She lay down and pulled blanket over her. Maybe tomorrow things would look different?

Chapter 66

Evie stirred. She didn't know what the time was but she was getting up now anyway. The sofa bed was quite uncomfortable and her back was sore. She hadn't slept at all well and now had dark shadows underneath her eyes as well as a beautiful bruise on her arm to match. On her way to the bathroom she noticed that Ben was in exactly the same position as last night. He was going to have one hell of a hangover when he finally woke up. Uncharitably she thought she didn't really want to be there when that happened and closed the door so that she could shower in peace.

Her arm was already changing into a delightful bluish tinge and she would have to cover it up before going down to breakfast. It was now 10.25 and she practically ran down the stairs and into the restaurant. Breakfast was only served until 10.30 and she prayed they would get her something to eat and drink before it was too late. Luckily they were very kind and showed her to a table in the corner. She was glad she could sink back into the shadows and pretend it wasn't her drunken boyfriend who had woken half the hotel last night singing and shouting at the top of his voice. She'd never been so embarrassed, well apart from when Jonathan had to look after her for a whole week, but that was a completely different thing. She ordered some juice and tea with lemon before asking if she was too late to order scrambled eggs. The waiter smiled; no it would be fine, she looked as if she needed some food and wondered why she was on her own as most weekends they were full of couples. Still, it was none of his business and he went into the kitchen to place her order.

Having eaten Evie went slowly back upstairs. She was planning on going for a walk and needed her jacket. Praying that Ben would still be asleep she opened their bedroom door. He was still comatose, snoring slightly and looked as if he would be there for the best part of the day. She opened the wardrobe and took out her jacket, but as she did so she noticed Ben's phone on the floor. It must have fallen out when they were trying to get his jacket off last night. Picking it up, she nearly jumped out of her skin when it beeped. A message had just flashed across the screen; it was a text from Charlotte.

Evie was breathing faster now, she held the phone in her hand, it was almost burning her skin she was so shaken. She had no idea they were back in touch. She stumbled over to a chair and plonked herself down. Now what was she going to do? She desperately wanted to read the message, but she knew it was wrong. Still, she reasoned, maybe it would explain why it had taken Ben so long to get in touch with her after David's call.

This was one of those agonising decisions. She'd be dammed if she did and dammed if she didn't. Staring at Ben on the bed she knew she would regret it if she didn't look, so taking a deep breath she scrolled down and began to read.

Minutes later she felt sick. Those eggs would be back up in record time if she wasn't careful so she rushed to get herself a drink of water. Trying to remain calm she looked at the messages again. There were quite a lot stemming from a couple of weeks ago. Charlotte was on holiday so couldn't make it to the regimental dinner after all. So that was the real reason he'd invited her, not because he wanted to see her again; but because he had no choice if he didn't want to show up on his own. As she scrolled back suddenly she felt faint for she saw that the very night he'd spoken to David he'd gone out and met up with Charlotte. So they were back on, the same Charlotte he'd professed to be a giant pain in the arse – her head became clear. Of course, of course, she'd been such a fool. Charlotte could probably have children so he'd made his decision after all and just hadn't told Evie about it. Stunned she then bolted into the bathroom; her breakfast came up and as well as being sick she felt numb and bloody cross.

Whilst she was brushing her teeth she wondered why hadn't he been honest with her? She'd told him it was his decision, she couldn't change things and so now he was in the bedroom sleeping off a major drinking session and she had questions for him; but they would wait she needed some fresh air.

Once outside she took some deep breaths. She felt a bit queasy, but whether that was the result of being sick or what she'd read, who knew? She grabbed her wellies and her sunnies out of her car and made her way down to the lake. The hotel had lovely grounds and she just needed to clear her head before she had 'that' conversation with Ben.

Andrew was staying at the hotel with his twin sister Christina and her children, twins called James and Juliet. He'd been very disappointed not to see Evelyn at breakfast and kept looking round until finally Christina asked him what was going on. He explained briefly about helping Evelyn the previous night and confessed he was a bit worried about her.

"Andrew I'm sure she's fine; you can't wade in where you're not wanted. Now look, I have a spa treatment booked for 11.00 so can you take the twins into the garden for me? They have an early lunch at 12.30 and then pony riding at 2.30. Can you manage?"

"Yes of course, off you go enjoy your day. That's why I'm here after all."

Christina left. Her brother what would she do with him. Yes he'd done a good thing last night and was obviously concerned about this girl; but it really was none of his business; in her experience he should just stay out of it. Andrew took the twins down to the lake, holding on to their hands. He didn't want any more incidents this weekend. He thought back to what his sister had said. She was probably right; Evelyn would be fine; but he couldn't help but wonder why girls like her ended up with blokes like that, it didn't make any sense to him. Rounding the corner there she was. He was sure it was her, same build, hair tied up dressed in wellies and sunglasses, but no sign of her boyfriend; not surprising really, he was probably still sleeping it off.

"Hello there. I thought it was you. Did you manage to get some sleep after all?"

"Oh hello, yes a bit. Those sofa beds are not the most comfortable things. Who do we have here?" She bent down and Andrew introduced her to James and Juliet. It was obvious they were twins and she shook their hands in turn. They were quite delightful.

"Would you like to join us? We're just having a walk before they have their early lunch. They've got pony riding this afternoon."

"That's very kind of you, but I'm not sure your wife would be very happy about this."

Andrew laughed. "No you don't understand, I'm here with my sister. These are her children, I'm just helping out with the baby sitting duties whilst Christina relaxes and gets some spa treatments. I'm not married."

"Oh I see, sorry, well then yes I'll walk with you."

Chapter 67

The four of them walked round the edge of the lake. She helped to swing Juliet between them and Andrew held tightly onto James. Chatting nineteen to the dozen about knights, pyjamas, spacemen, everything jumbled all together it was the perfect distraction from all the drama. Juliet was transfixed by Evie's hood which had the softest faux fur around the edge, so much so that Evie ended up carrying the little girl on her hip just so she could stroke the fur. They decided to walk over to the pony area where the twins would be having a riding lesson later and they sat them on the fence holding a child each so that they could see the ponies. Andrew glanced at Evelyn. She seemed remarkably calm after the drama of last night and he wondered if this was normal behaviour for her boyfriend? Maybe when the twins were having their special kiddies' lunch he would ask her some questions.

Next they wandered over to the activity centre and the twins were in luck: there were spaces for them to join in with the painting class. Andrew left them with the staff who would take them straight to lunch; he would just need to collect them before their pony lesson. Evelyn said her goodbyes to the twins and then the two of them walked back the way they had come.

"Thank you again for helping me last night, I didn't realise that Kieron and I wouldn't be able to manage."

"It was fine, no problem at all... but tell me something. Does this happen a lot... you know your boyfriend getting drunk ?"

Evie laughed. "No he's never been like this before, it was as much a shock to me as it was to Kieron I think."

"What are you doing for lunch, would you like to have something with me?"

"Um that's very kind, I'm quite hungry as it happens, but aren't you meeting your sister?"

"Yes, but the more the merrier. You'll like Christina. I'll introduce you, it's no bother." Andrew thought, no it's no bother, definitely no bother at all.

They arranged to meet at 12.45 in the hotel bar and Evie made her excuses to leave and check on Ben. Realistically she knew he wouldn't be awake so she set off on a different path glad of some air and space to think before she had to face Ben again. And with that she was gone, striding out back towards the hotel. Andrew watched her leave. He'd been single for a few months now and she seemed really nice, no better than nice; he wondered if he would see her again before they left tomorrow.

The hotel bar was fairly full but Evelyn spotted Andrew and a girl who she assumed was his sister and went over to them. Andrew jumped up. So she'd come to lunch after all; he hadn't been sure if she would show up. He introduced her to Christina and offered to get her a drink.

"That's very kind, but I think I owe you a drink for last night, so what'll it be?"

"No, no. I'm in the chair, I insist." Evie asked for an orange juice; she didn't want alcohol as she had no idea when she'd be leaving and wanted to be able to drive.

The three of them chatted before being seated for lunch. Christina was very nice and explained that she was currently separated from Charles, the twins' father and that Andrew had been roped in to help with the twins this weekend so that she could have some much needed time away. Evie and Christina got on like a house on fire and Andrew was more than happy to sit back and listen to their conversation. Lunch was over and Evie swopped mobile numbers with Christina and promised she would be in touch to meet up for a shopping day in the next few weeks. This had been unexpected, but Evie really liked her and thought it never hurt to have more friends. Thanking Andrew again, she left and made her way upstairs dreading to think what she would find back in her room.

Once back in her room she heard Ben in the shower. She decided to leave him alone for a bit. Evie made herself a cup of fruit tea, dreading the conversation she was about to have.

"Oh hi, you're up then?"

Ben was rubbing his hair with a towel. "Yes. Where were you, I was getting worried?"

"I went for a walk. I didn't know how long you'd be asleep."

Ben touched her arm. "Hey did you have an accident or something?"

"No, no I just fell, that's all, "She didn't want to tell him he had caused her bruise, no that felt all wrong. Evie paused. She had to ask him but she didn't want to. "Last night your phone fell out of your pocket and I saw a message from Charlotte. I take it you're back together?"

"You went through my phone messages?" Ben sounded mad as hell.

"No I didn't, I picked it up off the floor and a message flashed across the screen, that's all I saw. When were you going to tell me that you and her were back on?"

"It's really none of your business who I see, is it?"

"Ben why are you being like this? I haven't see you like this before ... so hurtful... I thought I was doing you a favour coming to this dinner ? I told you before it was your decision to make about...about us." Evie's voice broke; she should never have come, this was a huge mistake.

There was a knock at the door. Ben had ordered some room service, just for himself of course. After the waiter had left, Ben started on the minibar whilst Evie looked on. She thought that this wasn't a good sign of things to come and that maybe she should leave.

"Why don't I just leave, it's obvious you don't want me here? I was hoping to talk to you and I just can't seem to say the right thing." Her voice was quiet and she was close to tears. Maybe he was being deliberately mean just to force her to go.

There was silence. Eventually Ben spoke. "Look. I'm sorry I got so drunk last night, I've been very confused and I thought if I saw you again that things would become clearer but they haven't. I'm going out tonight with some lads from the dinner last night, they're collecting me at six so you don't have to leave on my account. I'm not really sure what else there is to say to be honest."

Evie took a deep breath. "Okay, at least I know now. I don't know why you're being so mean and callous to me. It was your decision to make, so when you get back tonight I won't be here and I won't bother you again."

There was silence and she excused herself from their room. She needed to get away; she'd wait until he'd gone out and then leave. So that was that, another relationship had bitten the dust and she was devastated. Yes, she probably knew all along that he would choose to be with someone who could give him a family, but that didn't make it any easier to hear. She'd drive over to her mother's tonight and spend the night there before going home as planned.

Chapter 68

Evie killed time by walking round the grounds, desperately trying not to burst into tears. She phoned her mother who was only too delighted to be seeing her, but quickly realized that her daughter was the victim of yet another failed relationship and her heart nearly broke-again. Just what did her daughter have to do to get some happiness? Was it too much to ask for there to be one man, just one man who would step up and make her happy? Evie then hid in the hotel lounge eking out a fruit tea until it was 6.15 and she was sure Ben would have gone. Sighing, she went back to her room and packed her things.

On checking out she looked at the bill. It didn't seem quite right to her. "Um excuse me, but I don't think this is quite right."

The receptionist was apologetic, "Oh I'm sorry Madam. What seems to be the problem?"

Why did they insist on calling women madam? It made her feel about 106! Evie explained that she was paying for the room, not the room service or the mini bar, but that her lunch from today wasn't listed.

"Oh let me just check that for you. It seems that your lunch was paid for by room 19."

She thought for a moment. Room 19, that was Andrew's room; no she couldn't let him pay for her lunch, rather she owed him a favour. She paused. "Okay can you do something for me? Could you send up a bottle of champagne to room 19 on my bill please and if you could pass me some paper I'll write a note to go with it." That done, she paid and left, relieved to be getting into her car and going home to her mother's.

Ten minutes later there was a knock on Andrew's door. On opening it he saw the waiter had a bottle of champagne in an ice bucket and he brought it into the room with a flourish. "I think there's been some mistake, I didn't order anything."

"No sir, there's no mistake, there's a note to go with the champagne," and with that the waiter left. Andrew tore open the note and began to read.

Dear Andrew,

I'm checking out now and I didn't want to leave without saying thank you again for helping me last night. I've just discovered that you paid for my lunch today which wasn't part of the deal as I am the one owing you a favour, so please accept this bottle of champagne with my good wishes.

Kind Regards,

Evelyn.

Andrew raced down to reception. Maybe he could catch her before she left. Spying Kieron, he asked if he'd seen Evelyn. "Yes, but sorry sir she left a good ten minutes ago. Is there anything I can help you with?"

"Um no, no thank you," and he walked back up to his room, annoyed he hadn't got the chance to speak to her. He didn't know where she lived or anything about her. Then it dawned on him; of course, Christina and Evelyn had swopped mobile numbers. They were going to meet up so he would see her again; he'd make sure of it somehow.

Evie drove straight to her mother's stopping only for fuel. She was close to tears; but as she well knew from previous experience she couldn't cry and drive at the same time, so she sniffed a lot and concentrated on arriving safely. Her mother opened the door and Evie fell into her arms. Her heart was broken again and this time she just needed to cry it all out.

"I told him mum, I told him – he knew I couldn't have a baby, he knew." Then she sobbed until she had nothing left. That night she drank plenty of water and took two tablets before going to bed. She knew that sleep would be the last thing on her mind but she had to try. Tomorrow she'd be home, home to Henry. She had to be ready for work on Monday and back into her old routine. She would text Fiona and see when they could meet and as it was the first Wednesday of the month she would be going to London and seeing Peter, Alice and Ian which was exactly what she needed right now.

That same evening in the hotel restaurant Andrew seemed a bit down. "Hey brother of mine, what's up with you tonight?" Christina was worried about him as this was quite out of character.

"Well to be honest, I'm worried about Evelyn. She just upped and left, sent me some champagne and a note, but it seemed very sudden. Could you text her tomorrow and check that she's okay?"

"Of course I will, but I'm sure she's fine. Probably just had a row with her boyfriend or something. Come on let's eat; I'll say something though, she made quite an impression with the twins. Juliet keeps going on and on about

Evie's fur hood, I'll have to ask Evelyn what that's all about when we meet up."

"So you're definitely going to meet up then?" Andrew was suddenly elated; this could all work out? Tomorrow he'd find out why she'd left so early and hopefully what was going on with that drunk boyfriend of hers too.

So a new week; but a familiar routine for Evie, get up/shower/eat two mouthfuls/work/shower/home/ try not to cry/stare at her plate-like groundhog day over and over until she thought she might scream. This was just the same after Jonathan had dumped her. The only diversion was her trip to London which was such a relief. Peter and Evie discussed various business proposals. Peter thought she looked a bit grim; and then lunch with Alice. Her friend had been married for a short while and carefully told Evie she was expecting her first baby. Alice knew this would be difficult news for Evie to hear, but she wanted to tell her in person and there was no reason to keep it from her, not with everything the two of them had been through together. Evie was thrilled for her friend, but to be honest it seemed so ironic that her own relationship with Ben had broken up over the same thing, namely her lack of being able to have a baby. Still, that wasn't Alice's fault. Alice's brother Angus wanted to know if she would like to go out on a date with him; but Evie declined, saying she was so on the rebound it wasn't funny and that Angus deserved better.

"Oh come on Evie, you like Angus, he likes you. What do you say? Just meet him the next time you're in London, just for a drink; pleeease do it for me, please Evie?"

Evie laughed, "Oh okay, okay, give him my mobile number and ask him to text me; but tell him I'm on the rebound. I don't want to lead him on or anything."

Alice laughed. "Great, he'll be thrilled. You never know, you could be my sister –in –law!" They hugged and went their separate ways. Evie was annoyed with herself. She never should have said yes to Angus. Oh well, maybe he wouldn't call at all?

Ian, well Ian was always the same. He'd seen Evie get through a lot worse than this, but even he was concerned at this repetitive pattern and where it was all going to end. On the train home Evie got to thinking, maybe she was being too fussy about men? She'd meet Angus if he called; but maybe she just ought to settle for some nice bloke, someone who maybe didn't set her heart on fire or make her go weak at the knees, because in truth she was fast running out of options.

Chapter 69

Two weeks later and Evie was her way to meet up with Christina. She'd been very sweet texting her the day after she'd left the hotel, checking that she was okay. Evie was looking forward to seeing her again. There was nothing quite like a day spent mooching round the shops looking at clothes/shoes/bags and make up whilst having a nice lunch too. Christina was good fun and despite her messy situation with her husband Charles, she seemed glad to be meeting up.

Lunch was at a very nice bistro where Evie found, to her delight, there was a good choice for her on the menu, which made a change. "So tell me to mind my own business but what's happening with that boyfriend of yours? Are you two still together?"

"No we're not. Not because of that night though. He had to make a big decision about us and he decided to walk away. To be perfectly honest I was half expecting it so it's back to the dating game for me although I'm not in any hurry to repeat that experience, I can tell you." Evie laughed. There, she had said it and funnily enough it hadn't been as bad as she thought. But Christina didn't know about her disastrous dating history or her issues. They could wait until they knew each other a lot better.

"Andrew says hello by the way, as do Juliet and James. Honestly Evie all I've heard about is fur hoods from Juliet and Knights of the Round Table from James. They certainly took to you. Any time you want to baby sit is fine with me."

"Your children were such a delight, you're very lucky to have them. So tell me: what's new with you?"

They agreed to meet up again in 10 days' time when Evie had a free Sunday and she would go over to Christina's for Sunday lunch. Evie explained she couldn't eat wheat, but Christina didn't bat an eyelid. There would be a group of them. As well as her and the twins, Andrew and some friends would be there too. She asked if she could give Andrew her mobile number as it would be easier if Evie parked at his house and they went together as there would be too many cars and not enough space on the driveway otherwise. They said their goodbyes and Evie realised she was looking forward to lunch. It would make a nice change and she would get to see the twins again too. She might even take then a little gift each; that would be a nice thing to do.

Rowan was quite concerned about Evie this time. She was putting a brave face on it ; but she just wasn't the same. It was just like her breakup with Jonathan and it had taken so long for Evie to get over that and now here she was again back to square one. Still this new friend Christina sounded very nice and maybe Evie needed to be around some different people for a change, people who didn't know all about her, but just took her for who she was and didn't ask a lot of questions.

Sunday came around and Evie was on her way to lunch at Christina's. Andrew had texted her his address and she'd agreed to arrive at noon to allow plenty of time for them to get to his sisters and have a chat first. Evie wasn't quite sure what to wear, but eventually settled on smart jeans, suede boots and a soft blue top, nothing fancy, but enough to say she had made a bit of an effort too. She'd bought Christina some flowers and chocolates as well as a book for James and a floral hairband for Juliet.

Arriving at Andrew's, he was out of his front door as soon as she pulled up. He had a very pretty cottage, but then as she'd learnt afterwards he was an architect so it should be nice, she reasoned. Andrew opened her car door and helped her out with her bags. There seemed to be a lot of bags for just lunch but he didn't mind. They would drive over in his car and he ushered her inside and offered her a cup of tea.

"No thank you I'm fine, but a glass of water would be nice."

"Coming right up. Sit down and make yourself at home." Andrew busied himself with her water and thought to himself how pretty she was looking today.

"So how have you been? I was a bit worried about you at the hotel to be honest."

"Oh that's very sweet of you, but I was fine, just fine. Did you get my note and the champagne?"

"Yes I did and that wasn't necessary, you know. I was happy to help."

Evie changed the subject. "So who else is coming to lunch today?"

At Christina's Evie and Andrew were the first to arrive, but no sooner was she through the front door and had given Christina her gifts, she was dragged away to the playroom by the twins who wanted to know if she'd brought them a present. Evie smiled; children were so predictable at this age. She duly gave them their gifts, which meant happy twins and a happy mother as they were quiet and entertained for a while. She sat with them in the playroom putting on Juliet's hairband and then reading James' new book. Andrew was watching the three of them through the kitchen door and thought how at ease she was. Perhaps he would ask her out on a date soon and keep his fingers crossed she would say yes.

Lunch was a convivial affair and there was a lot of noise and banter between the friends. Evie was happy to sit back. She was sandwiched between the twins at their request, much to Andrew's annoyance, so she had her hands full talking to the two of them as well as trying to eat. All too soon it was time to go and she thanked Christina for a lovely lunch and promised to text her again about meeting up again soon. Andrew drove her back to his and was disappointed that she declined coming in for tea and left straight away. Still he'd had plenty of time during lunch to sit and watch her and he was definitely going to ask her out to the cinema soon. He needed to search online for somewhere they could meet half way, but he thought that would be easy enough. Question was, how long should he leave it? He pondered on this and thought about a week or maybe ten days should be fine. He didn't want to look too keen but that sounded about right.

Chapter 70

Jonathan Dempsey was being driven back to his hotel. The evening function had been as dull as ditch water and he was glad it was over. Sighing he looked out of the car window and nearly had heart failure. On the pavement a young couple were walking together hand in hand. Jonathan knew the guy he was Angus Hunter, Alice's brother and the girl, he was sure it was Evie... His Evie. He turned his head round as the car passed. Quickly he asked his driver Alan to go round the block; he wanted to see her again. Once the car was back on the same road Jonathan saw they were standing outside of a hotel. Angus was smiling and laughing and Evie... His Evie was smiling back looking a bit embarrassed. Jonathan asked Alan to park up as he wanted to see how this was going to play out.

The two of them were talking. Angus stroked her hair. Jonathan watched and clenched his fists. Evie shook her head, kissed Angus on the cheek and went inside the hotel. Angus watched her go and ran his hand through his hair. If Jonathan had to guess he'd say that Angus was very disappointed to be stood outside. Angus continued to stare after her, he looked frustrated and then started to walk away. Jonathan was stunned. Was Evie dating Angus Hunter? Would she be ready to date Jonathan again if he asked her? Grabbing his mobile he sent her a text, just two words and waited. Nothing, no reply; he was really annoyed now and asked Alan to take him back to his apartment. He'd seen her, he'd finally seen her. Evie his Evie. She looked so pretty, just the same as he'd remembered; her smile, her laugh, everything really; closing his eyes he couldn't believe it, she was there literally five steps away from him and he'd done nothing – again! Perhaps she would text him back later just like the good old days?

THE MAN watched HER enter the hotel and looked down at his mobile. So the tracking devices on their mobiles were working well. Dempsey was in his car watching HER and she was inside oblivious to both of them. Still it was a lot easier if they were in the same place at the same time he supposed.

Arriving at the cinema it was clear to Evie that Andrew was used to having his own way. The film they'd planned to see was full and they couldn't agree on which other film to watch. Eventually she decided to just give in and let him chose and thought maybe they wouldn't be doing this again any time soon. It wasn't the best date in the world, but it was okay. She sounded ungrateful even to herself and shook herself; come on, come on! it's just a trip to the cinema, no big deal. Andrew didn't try to hold her hand or kiss her and for this she was thankful. She wasn't really sure why she'd said yes. Maybe this was how her dates were going to be from now on, no fireworks just slow and steady.

Over the next few weeks Evie and Andrew texted/emailed and facetimed although sometimes it was quite tricky with her shifts. He visited her for the day one Saturday. She'd had her usual morning classes so he showed up for lunch. Henry took an instant dislike to him and wouldn't even stay in the same room. They chatted easily enough, but Evie thought after he'd gone that there just wasn't any spark between them; but then chastised herself for being too mean; maybe they just needed to spend some more time together. Christina rang her and asked her over to stay with her this time. Charles had the twins for the weekend and if Evie wasn't working it would give them a chance to catch up properly. She jumped at the chance. Her new friend was like a breath of fresh air and also she thought she might ask her some questions about her brother.

Arriving at Christina's late on Friday night, Evie was glad she'd made the effort to come and visit her. Supper was in the oven and the two girls laughed, talked and drank wine until it was the next day. Evie discovered that Christina had met Charles through her solicitor and it had been pretty much love at first sight. They were soon engaged and married and then started to try for a baby. It took them quite a while before they realised that they may need some extra help, so decided that IVF would be their next option. Eventually Christina did get pregnant with the twins, but it had taken a heavy toll on their relationship and once the twins were born there just never seemed to be any time left for the two of them. Charles had had an affair and she had kicked him out. So currently they were separated but not divorced.

The next day Andrew had invited himself over for dinner and the three of them had a very pleasant evening. Lying in bed that night Evie started to think about events during the past year. It almost seemed unreal to her that so much had happened, plus maybe this time things with Andrew would work out? He'd made it very clear whilst his sister was busy in the kitchen last night that he wanted to see more of her and Evie had thought, well why not? She had nothing to lose, it could hardly be any worse than the previous year. She'd told him that she would like to see more of him too.

Sunday afternoon and the twins arrived home. Evie didn't get to meet Charles, but Juliet and James were soon demanding a story with voices and actions, the whole works and she was happy to keep them entertained before she had to leave to drive home. They didn't get to meet up again until her next free weekend. Andrew had a big project on at work and was flat out and of course Evie was also busy. Christina had mentioned she was having her bedroom revamped and that Andrew was looking after the twins at his house and would she mind if Evie helped out too? He had a guest room and she just needed them out from under her feet as well as the decorators too.

Andrew had reassured Evie it would be fine and she was looking forward to it even though it meant leaving Henry to be fed by her neighbour yet again. Maybe Andrew would visit her next time? Pulling up on the driveway on Friday afternoon she could see Andrew in the kitchen with the twins. They were laughing at something and although it was a happy scene it instantly made Evie sad, sad that she wouldn't be having the same scenes with her own children. Shaking herself she got her bags out of the car and knocked on the door. She could hear voices and squealing, then the door was open and the twins came bowling out grabbing onto her legs all talking together. Laughing she made it indoors only for James to launch himself at her, so she ended up flat on the floor with the twins crawling all over her. Smiling she looked up at Andrew. "Well hello; looks like I arrived in the nick of time."

They spent the rest of Friday painting, watching cartoons, playing in the garden and eating. She was worn out by supper time and was almost relieved when it was time to put the twins to bed and read them a story. That done, Evie and Andrew shared a meal and she felt more at ease with him this time. Maybe that was all it needed, a bit of time; after all it couldn't be fireworks and being swept off your feet by that first look all the time now, could it? Andrew had decided to pay it cool, but was definitely going to kiss her before the end of the weekend; he was just picking his moment. They said their goodnights and kissed each other on the cheek and Evie went to bed. Really what did she expect? He was hardly going to throw her over his shoulder and cart her off into his bedroom and have mad, passionate sex with her, well not in front of the twins anyway.

Very early Saturday morning and Juliet was out of bed. She wandered into Evie's room, scrambled under the duvet and snuggled down. Evie just moved over and put her arm around the little one. It was too early to be up and about, so they stayed put for another hour or so. Andrew looked in on her and was surprised to see Evie and Juliet cuddled up together; still Evie was very easy to like and he would have his moment with her later that morning hopefully.

Breakfast was a noisy affair and they'd run out of milk. Evie volunteered to go to the local garage shop and pick up supplies. Whilst she was gone, Andrew began to wash the breakfast things, Juliet was looking out of the window waiting for Evie's car to return, when all of a sudden she announced to no-one in particular, "Oh look! they're kissing." Andrew nearly dropped a plate and rushed over to see what was going on – just who was kissing who? Had he missed his chance already – no she didn't know anyone locally. He asked Juliet, "Sweetheart, who's kissing?"

"Look! your car and Evie's car: they're kissing see?"

Andrew had never been so relieved; their cars' bumpers were nearly touching; that's what Juliet had meant, not that Evie was actually kissing someone. Crisis averted, he went back to washing the plates and realised he'd been holding his breath. Once the twins had been collected in about an hour he'd make his move; yes, that's what he was going to do.

Evie breezed back in with the milk and then it was pandemonium again with requests for cartoons and books to be read. Andrew could hardly hear his own voice, but he did hear his mobile ringing and left to answer it. He came back into the living room looking none too pleased; it had been Christina on the phone. The decorators had overrun and she needed to leave the twins with him for another night. Well what could he say? He could hardly say: 'no, I was planning on kissing Evie his afternoon' now, could he? He just couldn't seem to have any luck with Evie lately. They decided to go to the park and spent at least twenty minutes just getting ready. Evie was glad to be going out into the fresh air, but to be honest they were wearing her out.

The afternoon flew by and in no time they were back at Andrew's trying to sort out something for the twin's supper. Eventually they decided on fish fingers, mash and peas. Then it was time for Andrew to give them their bath whilst Evie cleared away the dishes and started their own supper. Whilst a casserole was in the oven they wanted bedtime stories, complete with voices, actions the whole works. Finally they'd dozed off and Evie padded downstairs exhausted from the effort of looking after the twins. No wonder Christina needed a break from time to time, still at least they could just eat their supper in peace. They took their wine into the living room, Evie was just glad to be sat down quietly in front of the fire. Andrew was used to looking after the twins for an afternoon, but even he was weary from today's activities. He asked Evie a question, but got no response. Looking at her he realised she had fallen asleep on the sofa. He put a blanket over her and thought to himself, nope I just can't catch a break with this girl. He woke her at eleven and she stumbled off to the guest room, with no time for goodnight kisses.

In the morning, they'd all eaten breakfast and the twins' bags were packed and ready by the front door. Christina breezed in at 10.30 and decided to stay for a coffee and chat with Evie. Andrew was in charge of entertaining his niece and nephew again. It was good for his sister to have a new friend to chat to, he couldn't begrudge her that, not with all that she was going through right now. They all said their goodbyes at 12.30; now finally Andrew was ready. He found Evie in the living room and went over to her. "Alone at last," he smiled, "there's been something I wanted to…," At that instant doorbell rang and he ignored it. "Where was I? Oh yes, there's been something I."…ding dong! ding dong!. He looked infuriated.

"Maybe you ought to just see who it is?"

Grumpily he made his way to the hall and opened the door, leaning on the porch was his good friend Tim, "Are you coming to the pub, everyone's going to be there. Don't mind if I come in, do you? It's a bit nippy out there." He spied Evie. "Ah, so who do we have here, aren't you going to introduce me?" In his head Andrew thought: no, I'm bloody not, but outwardly he said, "Tim this is Evie, Evie this is my good friend Tim," Pleased to meet you Evie." She asked them to give her five minutes and true to her word she was back downstairs and ready to go bang on time. The three of them walked to the pub and Tim took this opportunity to ask her some questions. "So how long have you two known each other then?"

"Oh quite a few months now. I'm friends with his sister actually."

"Oh I see, well you'll like our crowd. There's quite a few of us but we're a friendly bunch."

Chapter 71

Introductions were made in the pub. There was Tim's girlfriend Naomi, Duncan, Mark and Amanda, Lucy and Steve and finally Aiden. Tim was right; they were a nice crowd and they all moved round so that everyone could sit together.

Drinks were brought over and Evie was happy to sit back and relax. No more babysitting for a while; she was exhausted. Andrew took hold of her hand underneath the table and she didn't pull it away. That was a sweet thing to do, she thought; but of course there would be more serious conversations to be had if they took their relationship further, same as always. It was decided that the boys would play darts whilst the girls chatted, but as soon as Andrew left, Aiden scooted round to sit next to Evie. "So come on, do tell, where did you meet? how long have you been going out? I want all the details," and he continued to monopolize Evie for the next hour. He showed her a photo of his boyfriend Troy. They'd met at an IT conference and it had been love at first sight. Evie laughed. "He looks very handsome, like a modern day Adonis."

"OOH I am going to text him right now and tell him what you said, he'll be thrilled." That done he proceeded to tell her about Andrew's past girlfriends, well the last three anyway. "The last one was Emily; not all there if you know what I mean, anyway she left to go and teach homeopathy at some retreat." Aiden rolled his eyes, "Yes we thought that too," then laughed uproariously. "Before that there was Susan. No-one got on with her and I mean no-one. She thought she was in love with Andrew after only a week, but she was so annoying that didn't last long; and before her there was Fleur. My, oh my, yes; Fleur. She was very highly strung." Lucy interrupted, "and high maintenance too."

Aiden continued. "She's an interior designer. They shared the same client I think, anyway – interior designer my arse!" Evie laughed. She liked Aiden, she liked him a lot. "Her idea of cutting edge design was to install a glossy white kitchen and stick a pillar box red sofa shaped like a pair of lips plonked at the other end of the room as a bloody focal point. I mean really, REALLY? One thing's certain, Kelly Hoppen she isn't. Also we think she thought she was onto a nice little gravy train with Andrew having his own architect's practice, she obviously wanted to be a lady of leisure whilst picking and choosing from Andrew's clients. When all she really did was fuck up their homes – what a nightmare. What she didn't realise was that Andrew and his business partner Richard have only been in business for 18 months and it's bloody hard work. He's talented of course, but I think she thought he was Norman Foster or something."

Tim came back briefly to the table and said, "I hope you're telling him to mind his own business if he gets too personal?"

"Don't worry it's fine. I'm enjoying our little chat," which was true; she hadn't had this much fun in ages. Aiden said, "Oh bugger off back to darts. I want to talk about elbows." Tim left them to it. They swopped mobile numbers with promises to text. she liked Aiden a lot; he was such good fun.

Aiden proceeded to feel Evie's elbows to see if he could guess her age, followed by him trying to guess her perfume. Honestly he was a scream thought Evie, I need more friends like him in my life. Tim went back to the lads at the dartboard and told Andrew, "You'd better rescue your girlfriend, Aiden has got the full am dram performance going on there. You know what he's like, he'll scare her off – in fact she's probably got her coat on and is legging it out of the door as we speak."

Wow, Tim had said 'his girlfriend', he smiled to himself then jolted back to the present as Andrew asked, "Why what's he saying?"

"Oh not much unless you count the gory details of about your three past relationships; now he's doing something to her elbows."

"Oh for fucks sake." He gave Tim his darts and told him to take his turn.

Andrew returned to the table. "Hey he's not too much is he?" nodding at Aiden.

"No he's fine," Evie laughed.

Aiden butted in, "We're getting along famously thank you until we were rudely interrupted." He rolled his eyes dramatically. "So seriously, how did you meet Andrew?"

"I met him at a hotel. I was there with my ex and he was there with his sister and the twins. He helped me get my boyfriend up the stairs and onto the bed because he was so drunk I couldn't manage him."

"No seriously, is that it or is there more?" Aiden was transfixed this was very juicy gossip indeed.

Evie laughed. "Well there's a bit more. My ex was being a right pain and as I was taking off his shoes he lashed out and I got kicked on the arm-it was an accident but I spent that night on the sofa-bed. So in a fantastic five-star hotel with a practically comatose boyfriend, sleeping on the sofa –then he dumped me the next day so a great time was had by all," she said sarcastically.

There was more banter as the subject changed swiftly to the five aside practice for this week. Evie asked Aiden if he played. Aiden reacted with fake horror, clutching his face, "What with these cheekbones? You cannot be serious." They decided to order lunch; the menu was quite tricky for Evie who insisted on ordering and paying. It was easier that way as she would have to explain what she would like and hope they could accommodate her. Lucy showed her where the ladies' cloakroom was, "So Evie, what do you think of Andrew then-is this serious or what?"

Gosh they were a nosey bunch, likable but nosey. She wasn't going to give too much away especially as she hadn't even kissed him yet. "Um well we're just getting to know one another really. It's a bit difficult as I work shifts and live a couple of hours away too." There perhaps that would be enough? Lucy seemed satisfied and when they returned to their table, some of the group were getting ready to leave. The weather was closing in and looked as if it was only going to get worse.

Goodbyes said and a hug for Aiden and then it was just the four of them. Tim and Naomi had been a couple for a few years and Evie thought they were adorable together-to herself she thought, that's what I need, a good man, honest, straightforward, someone who adores me and who I feel that same about too. Dave the barman brought their food over; he'd added on a bowl of sweet potato wedges for Evie. Apparently his sister in – law couldn't eat wheat either so they always had something in their own freezer in case she called in unannounced.

"Oh thank you it's very kind of you to go to all this trouble. Now what do I owe you for these?"

"On the house."

Tim spluttered into his beer. "Bloody hell Dave! We've been coming here for years and we've never had any free food."

"Well firstly it's my pub so what I say goes and secondly Evie's a very nice lady and I'm helping her out."

Evie thanked him again and then he left them to eat. Andrew was surprised. His friends all really liked her, especially Aiden who was a tricky so and so at the best of times; but she seemed to have him eating out of the palm of her hand; then Dave giving her free food, well that was definitely a first. Evie would be an asset to him and his work, make the prospective clients feel at ease, get them laughing and hopefully agreeing to be a client – yes this could work out very well, very well indeed.

The four of them left the pub together until it was just Andrew and Evie walking back. Andrew suddenly stopped and turned to Evie. "So, I have been dying to do this all weekend," and kissed her. It was an okay kiss, nothing dramatic, but okay all the same. Evie smiled at him. "Well we have had our hands full; but now it's just us," and they kissed again. Maybe she had been too hasty, spending a bit of time together even with the twins was just what they had needed. Back at his and Evie decided to leave, the weather was getting worse and she had a two-hour drive in front of her before it got dark. Andrew was disappointed and tried to persuade her to stay; but she had to be at work nice and early first thing tomorrow so she packed her things and loaded them into her car. They kissed again and she promised to text him when she was home.

Chapter 72

The next day on her way home from the gym Evie called round to see Fiona. She needed a chat, or rather some advice and Fiona knew her better than anyone. Sat at her kitchen table, mugs of tea in hand, Evie started to tell her about Andrew. "He seems very nice, I like his sister and his friends too. We've kissed and... well it was nice enough I suppose... only, well..."

"You don't seem very sure about this guy."

"You know me better than anyone and my last two relationships have been kind of intense –you know, good or rather great kissing and better than great...um ...IT... you know, in bed."

Fiona laughed. "Oh Evie you are funny."

"Yes I know, I'm a funny girl," she grinned back at Fi. "But well here's the thing, yes I know before you say it there's always a thing with me isn't there? I miss the flirty texting and other stuff too. There doesn't seem to be that, you know, that spark between us. With Jonathan and with Ben too we couldn't keep our hands off of each other; but this just isn't like that. Yes I know they both didn't work out in quite spectacular fashion and maybe this will be better, sort of quieter and more ... um normal?" She sighed, "Oh I don't know am I crazy to be trying again? I don't know how many times I can put myself through all this –maybe it's just not meant to be? I don't suppose David knows of anyone brave enough to take me on, does he?"

They giggled together. "I think you need a bit more time with this one, you know. There's no rush, just wait and see . Don't be in too much of a hurry to tell him everything about you; you know, just wait a bit and see how you feel in say a month."

"A month –gosh that's a long time."

"Okay well a couple of weeks then, whatever you're comfortable with."

"Yes, yes you're probably right. Um did I tell you I had a text from Jonathan a month or so ago?"

Fiona was suddenly on her guard, "No you didn't. What did he want?"

"I don't really know. I was on a date with Alice's brother, you know Angus and then suddenly there it was. It was very short and I didn't reply."

Fiona watched her friend. This was dangerous, she really didn't want Evie to go back down that particular road again, not after everything that had happened. "So are you going to reply?" Fiona was holding her breath.

"No I'm not. He hurt me so badly, I mean you saw how I was afterwards; I was a complete mess and I can't put myself through all that again, I just can't."

Sat in bed later the same night, Evie thought about what Fiona had said. She was right. There was no hurry; maybe she would invite Andrew out to dinner somewhere nice nearby? He could stay the night, guest room probably and see if she could figure out her feelings. Yes that's what she'd do, she'd call him tomorrow at his office and ask him. As for Jonathan's text, well she hadn't told Fiona, but Evie had been so tempted to reply. She'd actually sent a three-word reply and it had spelt out her true feelings; but she'd been tempted to text more all right. Yes, really tempted. She turned out the light and snuggled under the duvet. Suddenly she felt quite alone and sadness washed over her. She didn't want to be spending all her nights alone anymore; the truth was, she was fed up with the whole damn thing.

Arriving at work Evie noticed a poster advertising a charity fundraiser dinner/dance. Perhaps she would invite Andrew to go with her, it sounded like fun. After showering she called Andrew's office. Listening to the phone ring and ring, she was just going to hang up when a flustered voice answered.

"Hello, Signum Architect Practice."

"Hello. Could I speak to Andrew please?"

"I'm sorry he's in unavailable at the moment. Can I take a message?"

"Yes please, could you tell him that Evie called?"

"Of course. Would you like him to return your call?"

"Yes, if he has a spare few minutes."

And that was that, Evie was expecting him to call her back at some point the same day; but she heard nothing. After her evening shift had finished she debated whether to call him again; but decided against it. She'd call him again tomorrow. If they were going to the dance then she needed to buy the tickets. The next afternoon she still hadn't heard from him so she called his office again, left another message with someone called Sally – who in Evie's mind had a bad attitude, a bit shirty – kind of a 'well he's very important and so is his job – he's much too busy to talk to you' kind of attitude. Evie ended the call and thought if he didn't get back to her then maybe he was trying to tell her something. Andrew called her that evening, apologised for not ringing her sooner; important client, new commission, flat out, blah blah. Evie thought this was actually a bit rude on his part; but decided to let it go, perhaps her expectations were too high? She gave him the benefit of the doubt and ordered two tickets for the fundraiser. They'd have some fun, some drinks, get him in a good mood, then who knew?

Two days before the dinner dance and Andrew called her. "Hey it's me, sorry but I have some bad news."

Evie sat down. Was he going to dump her before he'd given their relationship a chance? "I'm going to have to cry off the dance thing, something important's come up, sorry and all that. I'll make it up to you I promise."

Oh so he wasn't dumping her, just decided he had better things to do with his time than spend it with her. She said she was disappointed and ended the call fairly quickly. Now what was she going to do with the tickets? There was no way she was going to the dance by herself, she'd have to give them away – she'd see if Fiona and David would like them, she'd offer to babysit and then the tickets wouldn't be wasted. She called Fiona straight away, who was only too happy to take the tickets off her hands plus with free babysitting thrown in she thought it was the best offer she'd had in ages.

Hanging up the phone Fiona turned to her husband. "Well we've got free tickets to a dinner/dance and Evie is going to babysit for us; but I'm a bit worried about her actually." She continued to voice her concerns to David, who whilst he agreed with his wife said there wasn't a lot they could do; although he'd like to meet this Andrew chap to suss him out for himself.

Evie had a great time at Fiona's, reading to the children settling them for bed, mooching about eating supper, drinking tea and watching TV., Maybe this was a better night than she would have had at the fundraiser, who knew? Andrew rang her the next night full of apologies again. Christina was throwing a dinner party the following Saturday night and would she like to go with him? Evie checked her schedule and said yes. She liked Christina and as for Andrew, well he had some serious making up to do so she'd give him a chance to do just that.

Chapter 73

Evie drove over to Andrew's; she was looking forward to a night out. She was going to stay the night so she'd wait and see if she was in the guest room or his room, make him decide where this was going –not her. She wore some navy trousers and a chiffon top in pale pink. She thought she looked pretty. She wasn't a stunning looking girl, she knew that; but when she made the effort she scrubbed up pretty well, even if she did think so herself.

Andrew looked pleased to see her and helped her inside with her bag, kissed her, hugged her, apologising again for having to cancel on her. At Christina's the twins had been put to bed and Evie helped herself to a glass of wine. There were some people she didn't know, but she chatted easily to them. Aiden and Troy arrived and Evie was soon sharing in their latest escapades. Andrew watched her from the kitchen. She was so full of life and energy, they would make a great team. Perhaps tonight back at his he'd step things up. If the meal went well, a few glasses of wine, then yes maybe tonight he'd make his move.

Tim and Naomi were the last to arrive. Evie was glad to see two more familiar faces and went over to chat to them. Christina was a great cook and the meal was fabulous. There was music in the background and lots of noise, chatter and laughing. Once the coffee had appeared on the table Tim announced it was time for a game. There were groans all round, but he persuaded them it would be fun, and nothing too taxing; all that was needed was pens, paper and bowls. Evie was intrigued but happy to play along.

Tim asked ten seemingly random questions and they had to write down their answer anonymously, fold up the paper and pop it into a bowl – they had to be really honest, but as there were no names then no-one would know who's answer was being read out. Aiden asked if he could ask one of the questions and Tim agreed.

Okay so question one – Name one thing you've never done but would like to try. There was general sniggering all round. Evie wrote Karaoke.

Question two – Name your secret TV guilty pleasure.
Evie wrote down the name of a reality show

Question three – write down your worst habit.
Over thinking things

Question four – Name one thing you've only done once.
Played pub darts.

Question five – Aiden's question was, 'What's the thread count of your bed linen?'
800-1000.

Question six – name the worst day of the year.
Valentine's Day

Question seven – if you were an animal what would you be?
Cat.

Question eight – your favourite food.
Cherries.

Question nine – Name your dream dinner date.
My father.

Question ten – if you could change one thing about yourself what would it be.
Be able to have a baby

All their answers went into ten bowls and then Tim dipped in and started to read out the answers. There were quite a lot of rude ones and funny ones too. Most of the girls put chocolate as their favourite food and the boys put either cheese or beer – no surprises there then. No-one was supposed to own up to what they'd written and it was fun guessing who'd written what. Evie owned up to Valentines' day being the worst day of the year, until someone piped up: just you wait until you have to spend Christmas with your mother-in-law! then Valentine's day will seem like the best day you've ever had. Aiden's question had obviously thrown some of the guys as they didn't even know what thread count meant. Troy and Aiden were extremely impressed by Evie's 800 to 1000 and practically invited themselves to stay at hers there and then.

They were all laughing, the wine was flowing and it was fun. It was over all too soon until the bowl to question ten was all that remained. Evie regretted writing what she had now; but it was too late. She'd have to brazen it out and they would either guess or not. Tim started to read out the answers, they included: have more hair, be able to dance, be thinner, so far no surprises, then he picked the next one out and looked stunned; he quickly recovered and, laughing, said: "Well, even I'm not reading that one out." Everyone laughed, thinking it had been obscene, probably from Aiden and Tim kept the paper in his hand before reading the next one. Evie's reply wasn't read out, she guessed that had been the one Tim put in his pocket when he thought no-one was looking and for that she was thankful. It would have been too much to divulge to people she hardly knew. She wondered if he'd guessed who'd written it, but he showed no signs of giving anyone a knowing look. Coffee and game over they spilled out into the kitchen and turned up the music, not too loud to wake the children, but just loud enough to jolly everyone along.

After midnight and people began to leave. Soon there was just the three of them and Evie and Andrew finally left Christina in peace. Walking back to his house, they held hands, didn't talk much, just the usual stuff. That was good fun; yes I enjoyed it, and so forth. Back at his, he leaned in and kissed her in the hallway; what was it with kissing in the hallway? she wondered, thinking back to when Jonathan and her had got way too excited in her hallway with her against the front door. This was hardly in the same league, but maybe she was being ungrateful?

Andrew left her to get ready for bed and then knocked on the guest room door. Evie was sat on the bed in her pyjamas. He came in and took her hand. "Come on, share with me tonight." And that had been that, it had started out fairly promising but he'd kept her pyjama top on and although he'd climaxed she didn't orgasm – he held her in his arms afterwards and seemed very happy. Evie lay there with her eyes shut, thoughts running through her head all jumbling on top of one another – so this was what sex with Andrew was like: over quickly, dull and no excitement or orgasm either. She must have done something really bad in a previous life for this to be her penance. She'd never failed to orgasm before, in fact Rowan and Evie had been discussing this topic only the other day. About some letter in a newspaper article stating some amazing (in their eyes) statistic about women who had never experienced an orgasm – well what was the point of sex then? they had wondered out loud.

    Maybe it would get better, she tried to convince herself; you know the first time with someone new it was never good was it? Although with Ben it had been, well the best she'd ever had and Jonathan was skilled in the bedroom too. Perhaps she'd been spoiled by those two experiences and she was being unfair? Sighing she moved away from Andrew's grip and once she'd made sure he was asleep she went downstairs to get a glass of water. Tonight had been fun, well up until half an hour ago. She slumped into a kitchen chair. She needed to think. She'd written she always over thought things, but this time she just didn't know.

Chapter 74

Back at work bright and early on Monday, Evie finished showering and called Fiona to see if she was at home. She pulled up on her driveway less than 15 minutes later and went inside.

"So tell me all about this dinner. Did you have a good time, did he ...well did you and he, you know?" Fiona was laughing, trying to jolly Evie along; but Evie didn't look very jolly at all.

"The dinner was great. I liked the people, we played a fun after dinner game and then back at his... well yes, we went to bed together."

Fiona was desperate to hear all about it. "So... how was it then? You know?"

"Um... To be honest...well here's the thing. It wasn't great, in fact it wasn't good... actually it was pretty awful."

Fiona looked shocked. "Oh my goodness, really? Well of course the first time isn't always that good is it, you know it can take a while to get into sync together." She didn't really know what else to say. "How did he take your news about the accident and scars and things – was he okay about them?"

"Um I never told him. Put it this way, my pyjama top stayed on so there really wasn't any point in raking all that up again was there – not so soon anyway."

Fiona was concerned, no worried was closer to the truth. Evie was normally so happy and always laughing; to see her like this, it just wasn't like her friend at all.

Evie deliberately kept herself busy at work, met up with her friends at their local pub for a good gossip and told them she wasn't sure about this chap, things weren't going too well. Rowan was quick to ask her what it was she wanted.

"Well to be honest, here's the thing: I'm so confused, the two relationships I wanted to work didn't and now this one is so different from them that I don't know if this is it. I mean, is this how it's going to be for me ?"

Rowan glanced at Claire and Viv. "Maybe it's too soon to say. Why not go away together, a weekend away at a hotel might put things into perspective? No work – just relaxing, just the two of you. What do you think?"

"Maybe." Evie didn't know, she didn't seem to know much about anything lately.

Christina had invited Evie over for lunch on her Wednesday off. The twins were going to be picked up by Charles that afternoon so he could take them to the park – the usual absent father activity. There'd been a shocking report on the news about two children being abducted and the two of them talked about it in low voices so James and Juliet wouldn't hear them. Christina was a great mum and Evie wondered if it really was all over between her and Charles, still it was none of her business really. The doorbell rang and Christina shouted down for Evie to get it as she was struggling to get the twins ready.

Evie left the safety chain on and opened the door. A man stood there, he was wearing a suit and looked weary.

"Hello I've come to collect the children. Are they ready?"

"Um no, not quite. Who are you?"

He laughed, "I'm Charles their father."

Evie was unsure what to do. Given what had been on the news this morning plus she'd never even seen or met Christina's husband, she decided to play it safe. "Right, can I see some ID please?"

Charles looked stunned. "You're kidding right? Is my wife at home? Who are you anyway?"

"Look Christina is trying to get the twins ready and with what's been on the news today I'm not taking any chances. You could be anyone."

He thought for a bit. Maybe this was the nanny, okay he'd play along for now. "Here's my business card." He passed her his card through the gap in the door. Evie took the card and looked at it.

"Sorry. This could belong to anyone. Do you have anything with a photo on it like a driving licence?"

He was incredulous. "Really, photo ID?"

"Yes afraid so, or you can sit and wait outside until Christina is downstairs; it's your choice."

Well she wasn't backing down now. The guy looked cross; but he took a deep breath, reached into his jacket for his wallet and handed over his driving licence. "Here you are and surely it's not Christina – it's Mrs Dunbar to you!"

Evie took it and looked at the photo and then looked up at him. "Very well, I'll open the door." She let Charles into the house, returned his ID and offered him a cup of tea or coffee.

He followed her into the kitchen. He didn't know Christina had hired a nanny, still he was admiring Evie's bum as she walked in front of him. Maybe if his wife had hired a nanny before, he wouldn't have had to go so far to look for someone to have an affair with.

He sat at the kitchen table. "So you never told me who you were – seems only fair." He smiled lazily at her.

"I'm Evelyn. Would you like a cup of tea of coffee?"

"Tea please, milk no sugar." He watched her fill the kettle and reach for the cups. She certainly knew her way around his kitchen. He wondered if she knew her way around other things as well. He was just about to ask her another question when the twins and Christiana bowled into the room.

"Oh there you are, Charles. Is Evie looking after you?"

"Yes; when she eventually let me through my own front door."

Evie glanced at Christina. "I didn't want to take any chances – you know not today with everything.." She trailed off, conscious that the twins were there too.

"No no, quite right too." The twins were sent into the playroom for five minutes whilst Charles drank his tea. Evie joined the children and left Charles and his wife to chat.

Once her husband had left with the twins, Evie decide to make her way home. It was very nice to spend time with them all; but all this driving to and fro was tiring and she wanted to get home to see Henry. Christina tried to persuade her to stay even trying the old 'Well Andrew will be sorry he missed you' routine. Evie wasn't too sure he would miss her at all and made her excuses and left.

Unbeknown to her, Charles was asking his children about their new nanny. "So has your nanny been with you long?" James answered: "Oh you are silly daddy, we don't have a nanny."

"Well who's Evelyn or Evie then?" He was intrigued, if she wasn't the nanny then who was she?

Juliet giggled. "Evie is Uncle Andrew's girlfriend. We like her, she's lovely, she reads us stories with voices and everything."

Charles pondered on this; so she wasn't the nanny, but his brother-in laws – girlfriend. Well if that was true then Andrew was punching way above his weight with that girl. How come blokes like Andrew got girls like Evie? – it was a mystery to him.

Andrew tried calling Evie but kept missing her. She was always working shifts with such funny hours, wasn't it about time she started to make him a priority? His thoughts drifted to Sally his P.A., now she was very efficient, went out to get his lunch every day, made sure he was the number one priority. Now if Evie was with him she could make his lunch and look after him full time whilst he devoted his time to building up his business. The sooner he persuaded Evie to give up that silly little job of hers the better. His sister had left him an e-mail saying she'd seen Evie for lunch and didn't he think it would be a good idea for the two of them to go away for the weekend, you know spend some quality time together? She told him the story about Charles thinking she was the nanny; the twins thought this was so funny. Andrew thought to himself, yes a weekend away might be a very good idea. He could suss out whether she would give up her job and rent a flat nearby or move in with him full time – yes he'd think about that.

Chapter 75

A few weeks later, arriving at the hotel Evie was pleasantly surprised. It looked delightful.. They were shown to their room and although it wasn't as large as she was hoping for nonetheless it was still very pretty. Disappointingly the shower cubicle and the bath would be a tight squeeze for two; still if this weekend went well, then maybe next time they would splash out on something bigger. The studio at the gym was being re-furbished this weekend so she had four days off; although it had meant her working flat out beforehand she hoped it would be worth it. Her thoughts flashed back to the hotel where Ben and her had stayed, that was, well that had been amazing on every level. They unpacked and had some tea. Their room phone rang and on answering it Evie discovered that Christina had booked them a couple's massage at 6.00pm as a surprise treat.

Andrew didn't seem too keen, but Evie was glad to have some relaxation as she was starting to feel tense and they'd only just arrived. The two female masseuse set up their tables and Evie asked if they could use some frangipani oil she'd brought with her as she loved the scent and so they began to work their magic.

"Oh my goodness, what's that awful smell?"

"That's the frangipani oil; doesn't it smell heavenly?"

"No, it does not, you're not to use that on me."

Andrew sounded very cross; why couldn't he just let go and enjoy the experience? He refused to let them use it on him and after the two girls had left he asked Evie to take a shower and wash it off.

"No, I love the smell. It's all exotic and sexy."

"Well I think it smells like a tart's boudoir, so if you won't wash it off we'll have room service tonight and give the hotel restaurant a miss. It'll put everyone off their food."

Boy he was miserable all of a sudden, maybe he was hungry? Evie didn't want to appear uncharitable; but he was seriously starting to piss her off.

They ordered room service. It just wasn't worth having a fight, not on their first night. Andrew ordered steak and Evie had chicken. It arrived fairly quickly and Evie asked if she could have two chips from Andrew's bowl.

"Why didn't you order your own if you wanted chips? Why do girls always do this?"

"Because I only want two and I seriously didn't think it was going to be a big deal; but now I can see that it is so just keep them." Evie was getting mad, in two seconds she'd be packing up her things and leaving, sod the bloody chips.

"Sorry, sorry I'm just a bit overtired. Work, you know; it's been pretty full on. Sorry, have some if you like." Andrew sounded sorry; but Evie was in no mood to forgive; if he was going to be moody over two chips then where was it going to end? They ate their meal in semi silence and Evie was relieved when he put the TV on and started to watch the news. She went into the bathroom and got ready for bed. This wasn't quite how she'd imagined their first night to pan out. Maybe he was tired; but she worked too, physical work at that. Switching off the light she was almost relieved to find that he had fallen asleep in front of the TV, so she climbed into bed and snuggled down. Things would look better in the morning, they always did – didn't they?

The next morning the alarm clock said 7.15 and unable to get back to sleep, Evie decided to go down to the hotel gym. Andrew was fast asleep so she changed into her gym gear in the bathroom and wrote him a note. She needed to work off some aggression. Last night had been a bit of an eye opener and she needed some distance to think. On entering the gym, the young trainer Joe perked up. He didn't normally see anyone this early on a weekend and after chatting with Evie they started a rigorous PT session together.

Back in their room Andrew stirred. He noticed the bed was empty next to him; so now where was she and what was she up to? He strolled over to the desk and picked up the note. She'd gone to the gym, suggesting he go for a swim and then they'd breakfast together. While he wasn't overkeen to swim he quickly realised he could keep an eye on her at the same time and decided to go down to the pool in ten minutes. The pool was separated from the gym by a huge glass wall so everyone could see each other. Andrew dangled his legs in the water; he had the pool to himself which was a luxury and he glanced over to the gym to watch Evie. It looked as if she had the gym to herself and the trainer lad who looked about 16 was giving her his full attention. She was laughing at something he'd said. Was she deliberately trying to make him jealous? He wondered if she did this with all the guys at the gym. He'd have to keep a closer eye on her once they were home, maybe he'd try to get her to give up her work and then she could look after him full time? Why did she have to constantly flirt with people, didn't she realise it looked cheap? Sighing he dropped into the water and began his laps. He'd call in and collect her in half an hour then they'd go down to breakfast.

Walking into the gym, Andrew watched the trainer make Evie do some weird looking tummy exercise. He thought he'd probably chosen this particular exercise deliberately as the only place she could look was straight up at the trainers' crotch.

"Hello sir, I'll be with you in just a minute." Once he'd released Evie's legs she'd flopped down.

"Oh my goodness, I'm worn out." She laughed. "Oh! there you are, Andrew, let me introduce you to Joe. He's the trainer here. Did you enjoy your swim?"

"Um yes, it was very thought provoking."

"I've just got to stretch out and then I'll be with you."

"I'll only be 5 minutes or so sir and then she's all yours." Joe grinned at Andrew

He wasn't going to let Joe manhandle his girlfriend right in front of him so he decided to wait. "I'll just wait for you over here then."

Walking back to their room Evie told Andrew about her gym session. "Yes he was really very good, he kept making me laugh though. When I was on the rower he insisted on saying 'we've got this, we've got this' until I pointed out to him that 'um no; we didn't have anything; but I had this' – it was so funny." Andrew didn't really get the joke but let her chatter on. Back in their room, Andrew made straight for the shower. "Hey make room for me?" Evie started to soap his back but Andrew shrugged her off.

"I'm surprised you have the energy for anything else."

Evie was taken aback; where had that come from? She left him to shower alone and wrapped herself in a towel to wait her turn. Now he was sulking and they hadn't even had breakfast yet – why did she have a bad feeling about this weekend and why was this relationship such hard work?

After a quiet breakfast they got wellies and her sunnies from the car and went for a walk.

"What's up, you're very quiet this morning?"

"Do you have to flirt with all the gym guys at the hotel?"

"I wasn't, it's a friendly business, it's all about people skills and interaction."

Andrew sneered, "Oh yeah right, interaction – is that what it's called these days?"

"Hey what's gotten into you? Are you overtired, is it work or is it me or rather us, because I'd really like to know"!

"Sorry, I think it's just being overtired, work is full on right now, let's just enjoy the day." He leant over and kissed her. It didn't exactly set the world on fire, but it was better than fighting.

The rest of the day passed off peacefully enough. They had a quiet lunch and read the papers. Once back in their room, Andrew promptly fell asleep and Evie read her book. Thinking uncharitable thoughts Evie was quite relieved so she caught up with her friends by text and e-mail. She really wanted to call her mother for a chat, but was worried about disturbing him so she didn't. Evie took a shower and got ready for dinner, giving Andrew a shake just after 6.30.

They went down to dinner and ordered drinks at the bar. After looking at the menu Evie decided to try to jolly Andrew out of his mood.

"Hey do you want some oysters tonight? You know, give you some energy for later?"

The waiter arrived back at their table at that very moment. "Will you behave?" he whispered to her. "I expect he heard that?"

They ordered their food, pate and lamb for him and goats' cheese followed by chicken with sweet potato for her.

"Well I expect he's heard worse, don't you?"

The atmosphere was quite tense; but it was fairly quiet in the bar. Perhaps once he'd had a drink he'd relax a bit, Evie was nothing if not hopeful on this score. They were shown to a nice corner table, again Evie sat facing the room she liked to see what was going on. The starters arrived. "Oh thank you that looks lovely," she beamed at the waiter.

"Please Evie can you just give it a rest just for tonight. You must say 'lovely' a thousand times a day, it's really starting to get on my nerves."

"Well it's better than saying 'you know' or these teenagers that say 'like' every two seconds." She was seriously pissed off at him now; he was doing his best to ruin the weekend – never mind settling for this type of relationship, it was a bloody nightmare.

Their plates were removed and Evie decided to have some fun. It was turning into the night from hell and she'd had enough. Kicking off one of her shoes, she began to press her foot on Andrew's ankle. He jumped a mile in the air, banged his knee on the table and she had to steady their glasses. The waiter rushed over. "Is everything alright here?"

"Oh yes we're fine, thank you, "Evie smiled at him.

"Andrew took a gulp of wine. "It's not funny you know."

"Oh lighten up will you?" Evie laughed. "It was only your ankle… good job my foot wasn't a lot higher"!

Andrew spluttered and choked on his wine.

"Oh darling, you must get that cough seen to when we get back."

Evie glanced around the restaurant; some couples were hardly talking to each other and it instantly made her feel sad. For the first time she thought: God, is that what I've got to look forward to?

"Isn't it sad the way that some couples run out of things to say to each other?"

"Well maybe they've just heard it all before."

One couple looked very tense; there wasn't much being said, but the woman looked upset and left the table.

Evie decided to follow her just to make sure she was okay. "I'm just nipping to the ladies' room, back in a minute."

On entering the ladies' cloakroom, Evie saw that the lady was indeed very upset. She passed her a tissue and made her sit down. After talking quietly together for a few minutes, Evie made her excuses and returned to her table. Poor thing; she was obviously having a horrid time, she grimaced to herself, yes there's a lot of it about this evening.

"Where have you been? Was it really necessary to leave me here by myself for so long?"

"Well you're a grown up, you can take care of yourself for five minutes can't you? Anyway I was worried about her."

"It's none of our business."

"I know, but she looked miserable and I wanted to help.." Evie trailed off. She had lost her appetite now

The waiter had to delay bringing out the main courses, but seeing Evie was back he produced their food with a flourish.

Evie grinned. "Oh thank you this looks lovely." Once he had left Andrew chipped in. "I think we need to have a bet when we get back, you can't seem to go a whole day without saying something is 'lovely.' It's driving me mad."

Evie said nothing but thought 'well sunshine, you're driving me mad too', so decided to wind him up just for the hell of it. Putting her cutlery down she slipped off her kimono jacket to leave the top part of her jumpsuit on display.

"What are you doing?" he hissed at her. "For God's sake everyone is looking."

"No they're not – they're looking at you behaving badly. You're being paranoid, anyway I was getting hot. I expect it's the wine."

"Well drink a bit less then."

Evie took a large gulp of wine just to spite him.

"Oh grow up will you?"

"Me? I'm not the one acting like a sulky 5 year old. I'm actually trying to have a nice time here but you're deliberately trying to spoil things; I don't know why, have I done something to upset you?"

Andrew leant back in his chair. "Oh very good. You've only just figured it out? "

"Well maybe you could enlighten me?" She picked idly at her food having lost her appetite.

"So you can't think of any reason today that I might feel like this?"

"Um no."

"Okay then let me fill you in – what about that trainer this morning; Joe, wasn't it?" He sneered, "you seemed to be very cosy with him?"

"Are you kidding me?" she said raising her voice slightly.

The waiter returned to clear away the plates. "Was everything alright for you both?" he asked

"Yes it was lovely thank you," and she grinned at Andrew just to make a point.

"So are you having another 'session' with Joe in the morning?" he asked sarcastically. She'd already decided not to, but was having second thoughts. He was seriously pissing her off and she would definitely need to work out some aggression if he kept this up.

"Probably yes, he's a very good trainer."

Andrew looked really cross. "And what if I asked you not to?"

"Well you could ask but I'd probably say no." He looked even angrier.

Evie sighed, "Look I don't want to fight, it's supposed to be a romantic weekend away for both of us." Andrew interrupted her. "Well stop deliberately making me angry and jealous."

"I don't understand what's got into you, everything was fine yesterday and today it's turning into a nightmare."

"Well if that's how you feel I'll leave you to dessert and see you back in the room." And he strode out of the restaurant leaving Evie on her own. She thought she'd give him some time to cool off. Blimey this was all starting to go horribly wrong, very, very quickly. Evie went to wait in the lounge and after half an hour made her way over to the lift. When the doors opened a young couple sprang apart. Evie smiled at them; she thought: well, at least some of the guests here were having a good time.

Back in their room, Andrew was already in bed reading a book. She undressed and used the bathroom. Getting into bed, neither of them were in the mood for a chat or sex, thank goodness. She leant over and kissed him goodnight on the cheek, but there was no response. Oh bloody marvellous, She thought maybe he would have realised he was being a complete and utter dick by the morning, but wasn't too convinced.. But at least she was allowed to sleep in the bed and didn't have to make do with the sofa this time; that would definitely have been a step too far even for her. She lay there with her eyes closed. Maybe this was it: she would have to settle for this, whatever this was? In the morning she woke and rolled over and kissed his cheek hoping for a cuddle at the very least; God, she thought, what does a girl have to do around here? There was still no response from him so she sighed and decided: right if that's how it's going to be – she hated people who sulked it drove her crazy, so she got up and put on some fresh work out gear and five minutes later she was at the hotel gym. Joe seemed very surprised to see her that morning. She asked if they might do some boxing as she needed to get rid of some aggression before she went back upstairs. On entering the room Andrew was out of bed and in the bathroom. She knocked. "Can I come in?"

"Sure of course." He didn't look at her.

"Did you sleep well?

"Yes think I was overtired, work has been pretty full on these past few weeks."

Evie hoped things would get back on track after all? He kissed her on the cheek. He just had to make her see that she was behaving badly. If she was his wife he'd have to put his foot down. There wouldn't be any more workouts at the gym for starters; she'd have to toe the line and realise that he was her number one priority.

Chapter 76

After a late breakfast they read the Sunday papers in the lounge with tea and coffee. "What do you want to do today?"

"Don't mind really I would like some fresh air though."

Andrew went to see the concierge. "There's a local rugby match kicks off at 2.00, Dan from the desk could take us at 1.15 and drop us back he's going with this son?"

"Yes okay that could be good fun. Let's do that then."

They got to the match in plenty of time. Evie was just relieved to be out in the fresh air with a crowd of people, less chance of there being a scene with her boyfriend. It wasn't exactly Twickenham, but it was pretty good fun. Andrew still wouldn't hold her hand so she looped her arm through his trying to jolly him along and out of his bad mood. She wore her black padded jacket, the one with the hood trimmed in softest brown faux fur and it was without doubt her favourite thing in her wardrobe. With a few minutes to go until half time, Dan went off with his son Nick to get some juice and coffees. The referee blew the half time whistle and people were making a move towards the burger stand.

For some reason Evie turned round to look at the pitch. One of the rugby players was lying motionless on the ground and no-one seemed to be making any attempt to see if he was alright. Removing her arm from Andrew's she said, "Back in a jiffy," and jogged over to where the player lay.

Straight away she could see he wasn't moving and her first instincts were that it must be concussion or a bang on the head. She took one of his hands in hers and after checking for his pulse she placed the palm of her other hand against his cheek. "Hello, can you hear me? Hello, you need to wake up now." A small crowd had gathered round, someone said his name was Gavin, so she continued: "Hey Gavin can you hear me, you need to wake up now? Gavin, Gavin I'm Evie, can you open your eyes just for me please?" Still nothing; finally one of the team ran over with a sponge and a bucket. "I think you need to call for an ambulance or a paramedic," she explained. He helped her put Gavin into the recovery position which wasn't easy as he was a big bloke. She continued to talk to him, "Hey Gavin it's Evie, come on now I'm getting worried you need to wake up now." There was still no response.

"Where are your first aiders?"

"Um they're dealing with an injured child, I think, near the burger stand."

"Okay can you get a blanket or something to cover him and tell the coach he'll need to substitute him for the second half." The guy with the sponge just stood there. "Look, sponge bob! just get a bloody move on will you? He needs medical attention now and where's that blanket?" She was shouting a bit now, well honestly he had to get a move on.

Finally the sponge man spoke, Well you've got a coat, won't that do?" Evie looked incredulously at him. "My coat won't even cover his arm. Now go and get a blanket. Substitute him. Call for a medic. Go on!," she was shouting at him now. Under her breath she said 'just bloody do as you're told. You're not Jonny bloody Wilkinson. Go and cut up some oranges or something.'

A man came panting though the crowd. "Um do you need some help? I'm a doctor. Evie took one look at him and thought yes, and I'm a nun. "What type of doctor?"

"Um what do you mean?"

"Well are you a doctor of history, phycology or medicine?"

"Oh medicine."

"Right you are then. Gavin there's a doctor here. He's going to take a look at you. I'm not leaving you okay, I'm right here. Gavin, come on wake up now."

Gavin stirred just as the doctor touched his face. He tried to sit up, opened his eyes, looked at Evie, went very pale and promptly vomited on her wellies and moaned at the same time. Evie pulled a bottle of water out of her coat pocket, let go of his hand and washed her wellies off, dampened a tissue and wiped Gavin's mouth. Then she gave him the bottle to rinse his mouth. Gavin couldn't stop staring at her. "Hello are you the new sponge girl?" he asked.

Evie laughed. "Um no not exactly."

He couldn't stop staring at her. She was quite small with huge brown eyes, long brown hair tied back into a pony tail. She wore a black padded jacket with a hood trimmed with fur and when she put the hood back up she looked just like a baby bear.

They got him to his feet and he staggered over to a bench beside the clubhouse. Evie went too, then the paramedic turned up and began to examine him. Gavin spoke to another man who asked Evie to complete some questions for insurance purposes. She filled it in as quickly as she could before asking

Gavin if he felt okay. He stared back at her and asked her name. "I'm Evie. You gave me a bit of a shock there sunshine," and she smiled at him.

She left the paramedic with Gavin and went back to Andrew to watch the second half. Putting her sunnies back on she could tell that Andrew's mood hadn't improved; in fact if anything it looked a lot worse than 20 minutes ago. She put her arm through his, but he wasn't responsive at all.

Gavin was watching her from the bench. He'd seen the back view of her now and she had a bum to die for; what he wouldn't give to squeeze that right now. Gavin couldn't see her eyes anymore as she had her sunglasses on and her hood was up. He watched her talk to a man with a young boy before putting her arm thorough the other chap's arm. So not her son then? She must be with that miserable looking boyfriend of hers. Gavin didn't take his eyes off her for a second and when the referee blew the whistle for the end of the match he watched as she jogged back over to where he was sat.

Pushing her sunglasses on top of her head, Evie said, "Hi. We're off now, I just wanted to make sure you were okay?"

"Um yes thank you feeling a lot better. Thanks for looking after me."

She laughed. "Oh it was nothing really. I was a bit worried that's all, can't be too careful can you. You'll have to take it easy for the next few weeks. I don't think you're allowed to play for 2 maybe 3 matches though. Look I've got to go. Bye." And she was gone. Gavin asked his dad if he'd got all her details and Neil nodded and passed the piece of paper over to his son. Gavin read it and grinned, okay once he was home he needed a plan.

Andrew was impatient to leave to return to the hotel. They ordered hot chocolate from room service and as Evie felt cold she ran a hot bath and had a lovely soak. Meanwhile Andrew switched on the TV and watched some football. It wasn't quite the romantic bath she was hoping for! Lying in the hot water Evie thought she ought to try to smooth things over before they spiralled even more out of control. Wrapping herself in a fluffy robe she padded out into the bedroom.

"Hey, would you like a hot shower or bath? It was pretty cold stood out there this afternoon"

Andrew ignored her question about the bath and shower and sulkily responded: "I don't know why you have to get involved all the time?"

"What do you mean?"

"Well that woman yesterday at dinner and now this rugby chap, neither thing was anything to do with you."

Evie bristled. "Firstly she was upset and it seemed like the right thing to do and secondly he could have been seriously injured. How would you feel if you keeled over in the street and everyone just ignored you and stepped over you?"

"Oh now you're being ridiculous."

They had a very quiet dinner in the hotel restaurant. Evie thought they already looked as if they had run out of things to say to each other. She tried to lighten his mood, but there was nothing, no meeting her half way just sulky silence. Secretly she couldn't wait to check out in the morning and go home, at least Henry would be glad to see her.

Just before lunch Andrew dropped her home and Evie went into the house to feed Henry. Andrew was still angry with her. "Honestly," he said, "sometimes I think you think more of your cat than you do of me."

"Now you're being ridiculous," she replied but secretly she thought 'well, most of the time yes, I probably do – as at least he knows how to behave himself!' They said their goodbyes and she was relieved to be on her own. It was over, her romantic weekend was finally over – what a bloody nightmare. Could she really settle for this? Surely this wasn't it for her, it couldn't be unless someone up there was playing some kind of huge practical joke.

Chapter 77

The evening before the studio re-launch at the gym Evie received a call from Andrew.

"Hey it's me, wondered how you were? Look I know the hotel trip wasn't a great success, but I have another offer for you, one which I think you might like."

Evie was so glad he couldn't see her face. She wasn't sure about going anywhere with him ever again. Instead she said. "Go on I'm listening."

"Well my business partner Richard has done his back in and he was all set to attend this conference this weekend in London, so I'm going instead and wondered if you'd come with me. It's a five star hotel, all expenses paid; you never know it could be fun, what do you think?"

She thought: un – bloody believable, didn't he realise what she was doing this weekend? "Have you forgotten it's the studio re-launch at the gym this weekend? and I'm working solidly Friday through to Sunday night."

"Surely you can skip it? This conference is important to me and my business; can't you get out of it and come along?"

"No sorry, I can't." The truth was she wasn't sorry at all. He sounded really sulky again and obviously still thought that his job was way more important than hers. "My job is just as important to me as yours is to you, so no I can't just drop everything and go to London with you."

Sounding very pissed off Andrew responded. "Well I suppose I'll have to go on my own then. Other girls would love to go to a free conference at a luxury hotel with me."

"Look, you know I can't go and I'm not other girls – maybe you should take one of them away with you instead."!

"Well I might just do that." And with that he hung up and was gone.

Evie was so cross; who the hell did he think he was, expecting her to drop everything for him? If he'd been listening to her at all he'd have known full well what she was doing this weekend. It was too much, just too bloody much.

Evie arrived at the gym on Saturday morning, all ready to go and full of energy. Sod Andrew. He didn't deserve her. She had better things to do with her time than worry about him. Last night she'd been very busy so hopefully the weekend would be the same. She took two ½ hour aerobics taster classes before midday and was upstairs in the main gym when she got called down to reception. Making her way down the stairs she was surprised to see the rugby chap Gavin and another chap who looked vaguely familiar waiting for her.

"Hello, this is a nice surprise. What are you doing here?"

"Well I brought you some flowers to say thank you for looking after me the other week. Oh, you don't know my dad do you, Evie? This is Neil. Dad, this is Evie." Introductions done they sat in the gym coffee bar and ordered some drinks.

"You didn't have to buy me flowers you know, I was happy to help. But thank you, they are lovely. How did you track me down?"

"Yes I did have to buy you flowers. No-one else was looking after me and we had all your details, remember? I looked online and saw that the re-launch was on this weekend and figured out you'd be here for sure."

She laughed. "Oh you're quite the detective aren't you?"

Gavin just grinned at her. "So when do you get a lunch break?"

"Not until 2.00pm I'm afraid, but you're both welcome to stay. You can use the pool or the gym if you like, it's all free this weekend."

"Okay we'll stay, Dad will probably have a swim but what's on at 12.30 for me?"

"If you hang on here a sec I'll go and check."

Whilst she was gone, Gavin spoke to his dad. "See. I told you this was a good idea didn't I? There's no sign of her boyfriend and she's pleased to see us." Neil replied: "Just don't go getting your hopes up okay? For all you know she's madly in love with her boyfriend. Maybe he just doesn't like rugby?"

'Well then he's more of a dick than I thought"!

Evie came back. "It looks as if 12.30 is going to be me doing a spin class taster session for 30 minutes as Josh hasn't turned up again, so if you fancy that you can met me upstairs in 10 minutes and I'll put you to work."

Neil decided to use the pool and Gavin got changed for a spin class, whatever the fuck that was. He'd have a go anyway.

Up on the gym floor at 12.30, the spin class was full and she asked for people to just join in with the music if they wanted to whilst on the crosstrainers, bikes and treadmills. Gavin was enjoying the class. He was pretty fit and trained twice a week with the rugby team, as well as working out regularly too; but nothing like this spin thing. After the session Evie was tired but happy; she chatted to prospective new members then got a break to talk to Gavin. "Did you enjoy that then?" she laughed.

"Um yes it was interesting," and he smiled at her. "So where are we going for lunch?"

"How about I meet you and your dad by reception just before 2.00 and we'll go out and grab a quick bite to eat, okay?"

At the coffee shop, they chatted about Gavin's rugby team and the fact that Evie went on regular refresher courses for first aid. It turned out that Neil had been a rugby player too. Evie kidded them both it was a genetic thing.

"Oh by the way how is your man, sponge bob?"

Gavin laughed. "Well to be honest he's still a bit miffed with you, showing him up like that and everything. Are you sure you don't want to be our new sponge girl as I think we could swing it pretty easily?"

"Thanks but no thanks, I've already got a job and it's a bit of a commute. You do know you could have had the flowers delivered don't you? They do have such things as delivery vans; you didn't have to come all this way just for that?"

"Yes I know; but it was important to me well to us to thank you properly, I didn't get much of a chance once the medic turned up."

They ordered lunch and chatted about this and that. Suddenly Gavin asked, "So is your boyfriend coming over to see you in action this weekend?"

"Um no he's at a conference in London, last minute thing." She didn't tell them that Andrew hadn't even bothered to send her a text message wishing her luck for the re-launch.

Gavin excused himself and Evie chatted to Neil. It turned out that Gavin's mum walked out when he was little and Neil brought up Gavin and his sister Bethan. He got Gavin to focus on rugby to stop him from going off the rails. Evie thought, 'way to go dad'.

All too soon Evie was due back at the gym. They said their goodbyes and hugged. What a nice family, she thought.

Driving back home, Gavin thought it had been a bloody brilliant idea to bring her flowers to the gym and also to bring his dad too, so as not to scare her off. She was good at her job and fit too which he liked, in fact she looked very fit indeed in her Lycra work out gear and Gavin wondered how any guys got anything done at all if she was in the gym.

After a long day Evie was glad to be home and soaking in a hot bath. The day had gone really well, better than she expected. After eating her supper she sent a quick text to Andrew. She wasn't really sure why she was bothering; but she'd been brought up properly with nice manners so a quick text wouldn't do any harm.

Later that night Evie's mobile rang., It was Andrew and she was surprised but optimistic he was ringing her. Her optimism didn't last long though because as soon as she picked up it was clear to her that he'd had quite a lot to drink.

She told him about her day, how things had gone really well and mentioned that Gavin and his dad had turned up out of the blue with some flowers for her and wasn't that a lovely thing to do? Andrew was immediately very jealous and told Evie in no uncertain terms that she'd been encouraging him.

"Oh Andrew for heaven's sake, it was a nice gesture. I didn't know he was going to turn up did I? He even brought his dad with him for crying out loud."

"This is so typical of you; you encourage them all the time, if it's not complete strangers, it's gym trainers or rugby players –where's it going to end?"

"You're being totally unreasonable. Nothing's going on with anyone, it was a lovely thing to do. He's too young for me anyway."

"Well you hear about these older women throwing themselves at younger men, cougars I think the word is."

"Now you're being ridiculous. Stop being so childish, what's gotten into you?"

"But why did he come? I don't understand. You must have been encouraging him?"

Evie was exasperated; this conversation was unreal.

Andrew continued, "How do I know you haven't been texting him since the rugby match?"

"Because I haven't, I don't even have his mobile number. For heaven's sake grow up. I don't want to fight with you, I'm with you aren't I?"

There was silence from Andrew. Evie was fed up, "It sounds as if you want to break up with me?"

After a long pause, Andrew finally spoke. "Well maybe I do, you never put me first. You wouldn't come here to this conference with me, you're always flirting with everyone."

"I'm not; it's a sociable industry, I've already explained all this." There was silence. Finally Evie said, "Well I don't think there's anything more to say, I'll leave you to your conference." She hung up. What the fuck had just happened? She stared at her phone before turning it off. Lying in bed, she felt cross, bloody cross, numb and too tired to cry. Why didn't he send her a good luck text message himself, or turn up at the gym and surprise her? He only had himself to blame, all this jealous nonsense and sulking – it was ridiculous, completely ridiculous.

Andrew went back inside to the conference hall where a colleague asked, "How was the missus?" Andrew replied: "I think we just broke up. "

Chapter 78

The following Saturday Andrew decided to go to the pub for a night out. Aiden asked after Evie and Andrew told him they'd broken up. Troy and Aiden whipped their heads round, surely he was joking.

"You're kidding right?" said Aiden.

"Um no I don't think so." Aiden sent a text to Evie straight away.

Tim chipped in, "Jesus what happened?" Andrew didn't answer and left the pub pretty much straight away and stumbled home. He spent a terrible night tossing and turning. In the morning he sat at the kitchen table eating a piece of dry toast he didn't really want.

Andrew was hungover, felt terrible and still needed to get showered and changed; but both very slowly as his hangover wasn't going to disappear any time soon. He arrived at Christina's door for Sunday lunch. She opened the front door took one look at him and said: "God you look rough."

"Gee thanks Sis; how about: Andrew! how lovely to see you – do come in," he said sarcastically. He was in a bad mood, which sleep had done nothing to improve. His head was thumping and going to lunch was a bad idea.

"Where are the twins?"

"In the playroom watching a cartoon. Why?"

"I need to talk to you; but first what do you have for a hangover?"

Christina sighed dramatically and ordered him to sit down. She fetched a glass of water and put in two fizzy vitamin c tablets plus another glass with a rehydration sachet in it plus two Paracetamol. She banged them all down hard on the table.

"Oh go easy my head is pounding."

"I trust it's your own fault?"

"Pretty much."

"So go on what's up?"

He told her all that he could remember. When he'd finished talking and drunk the hangover remedies his sister began to talk.

"Well do you want to know what I think?"

He looked at her. "Do I have a choice?"

"No you bloody well don't." But at that point the twins rushed in dragging him off to watch a cartoon about a magic monkey. He got up slowly from the table. "Sorry sis; gotta go."

Christina whispered: "This conversation isn't over not by a long way."

They all ate lunch and then the twins were persuaded to do some colouring in the playroom. Andrew did his best to explain what he thought had happened.

"Okay so what's the verdict?"

"First things first. Is this all you can remember?"

"Yes."

"And you're pretty sure you broke up?"

"Umm yes."

"Have you tried to call her today?"

"Umm no."

"Okay, this is how it's going to be." God he hated her when she was this bossy, but his head felt so bad he couldn't think and as he couldn't get up from the table in any kind of a hurry he just sat there.

"I'm going to speak and you're just going to listen. No interruptions, okay?"

"Okay," he nodded slowly.

"As I see it you've been a complete arse,."

Andrew started to protest, "Steady on."

"No interruptions I said, okay? You get drunk, no doubt egged on by some of your colleagues, some of whom are great and some need a kick in the balls. So they all go home to their wives/girlfriends and you're the saddo who's just ruined everything. You call her and get insanely jealous about some boy you both met at the rugby last week 'cos he turns up to give her flowers and thank her for helping him; oh and he brings his dad – just what the fuck (he hated it when she swore but she was super mad at him) did you think was going to happen in a gym with hundreds of other people about?"

He chipped in. "They went for lunch."

"Yes to a coffee shop with other people! She never asked him to turn up did she, even though you accused her of inviting him? She didn't want to fight and you decide it would be a good time to break up with the best girl that you have ever met – EVER – ON THE PHONE WHILST YOU'RE DRUNK!"

"Yes that's about right. You, Aiden and Troy are certainly telling me loud and clear what a mess this all is."

"So they agree with me that you've been an idiot and God knows if she'll take you back after this little stunt. Why haven't you called her? Do you want to get back together? Just tell me." She sighed.

"I don't even know what to say if I call"

"So text her instead, something like: we need to talk, and see what she replies? Okay? Secondly she's my friend too and now I can't call her as she'll know you've been round here telling me everything, so now I'll have to wait until the middle of the week and call her casually – fan bloody-tastic – it's not all about you, you know! Text her now, right now this bloody minute."

"She'll be at work."

"Well she'll pick up the message as soon as she's done won't she? So she should be home by 7.00pm."

"Alright. What do I say?"

"Well you could start by saying you're sorry, you were completely drunk, you don't remember everything but you're sorry and will she give you another chance?"

He brightened up – "Do you think she will?"

"Text her Andrew, just bloody do it now or I'll do it for you."

He got out his phone and typed, 'Hey we need to talk –I'm sorry, text me when you can.' He pressed send but his message didn't go anywhere. Maybe her phone was switched off at work; he'd keep trying. Finally he decided to leave a voice mail message.

Hey it's me. I keep texting you but it's not delivering the message. I'm sorry I was drunk, I don't remember everything; but I'm sorry and we need to talk okay, call me when you can? –SEND

Christina sighed dramatically, "You'll be bloody lucky if she ever calls you."

Lunch was well and truly over so he made his excuses and left. Once home Andrew decided to take yet another shower and more paracetamol. Then to take his mind off things he opened up the Williams file. Best to be very prepared for a tricky meeting on Tuesday with clients; but hopefully Sally would have everything under control as always, she really was becoming indispensable.

Chapter 79

Evie's mobile had been switched off for days now. She just couldn't face it anymore, she was worn out and he'd worn her down. She'd rather be on her own then stuck in a relationship like that! Never again, it was all very well to tell yourself you'd settle for less but when the less in question was with someone like Andrew, well her answer was a big fat no – not even if you paid me.

Now it was late on Wednesday afternoon and Evie was sat at home. It was her day off today, She didn't feel sad but more angry than anything, so she decided to go for a run. After showering she couldn't put it off any longer and switched her laptop back on. There were the usual emails from companies trying to sell you things you didn't want or need, a reminder about her hair cut and nothing from Andrew or Christina; maybe that was another friend who was going to bale on her too?

She breathed in hard. 'Okay phone, do your worst;' and switched it back on. The icons showed there were 10 missed messages and three voicemails. She clicked open the messages first. There were four from Andrew before he gave up all saying the same thing, 'we need to talk;' one from the dentist reminding her of her appointment on Friday, and some rubbish from her phone company. There was a text from Aiden asking her if she was okay; that was sweet of him she thought, she'd reply later. The voicemails consisted of one from Andrew and two from Gavin. She hit that one first – it was from Gavin. He'd been trying to contact her, was getting a bit worried now-her phone seemed to be permanently off, was he somehow in the doghouse, hoped not can she call him please? She thought why not? anything to put off texting her now ex – boyfriend. She pressed call and waited.

"Hi Gavin, what's up?"

He replied straight away – "Oh hello this is a nice surprise. Are you okay? I've been trying to call you and I was getting worried"

"Yes fine; my phone's not been working," –she sighed. "No wait, that's a lie and I hate lying. I've had it switched off since Sunday night. Sorry."

"Why was your phone off?"

"It's complicated."

"Sounds like this is going to be a long conversation; do you want to facetime?"

"Um okay, just a sec."

Minutes later they were looking at each other on the screens. He was at home in the kitchen by the look of things, she was sat at her kitchen table having hastily pulled on a hoodie as she realised she was in her pj's with no bra – not exactly the image she wanted to convey.

"Hi there." He was so glad to see her. "So your phone's been off for days; what's going on?"

Evie started to tell him briefly about Saturday night. Then she said: "Hold on a minute, can you just give me a sec?"

"Yes sure." – She disappeared from view but he heard her saying, ' I know, I know I've been out all day and you're feeling neglected, how about I give you a cuddle whilst I chat to Gavin and you can say hello too –yes – well okay then?".

Gavin began to panic. Who was she talking to? It didn't sound like her boyfriend; maybe she had a child? Then she was back in front of him holding a big ginger cat who was cuddling into her chest. He realised he'd been holding his breath, thank God it was only a cat, he grinned, feeling very relieved; although he wouldn't have minded swopping places with the cat right then.

"Sorry about that – this is Henry."

"Hi Henry you're a handsome fella aren't you?"

"Yes he is, isn't he?"

"Why Henry?"

"Well he's ginger as you can see, so I called him after Henry 8th."

Gavin laughed. "Oh. Right you are then."

"Now where was I, oh yes," Evie carried on trying to keep it brief about Saturday night.

He looked shocked – "Jesus. I never would have predicted that."

"No me neither." She looked and sounded sad. Gavin would have given anything to hold her in his arms right then and tell her it was going to be okay but he continued, "Anyway the reason I've been kind of stalking you – in a good way that is."

"Is there a good way then?" She kissed the top of Henry's head and tickled his ears whilst she listened

That's so distracting, Gavin thought. I wouldn't mind a bit of that attention.

Gavin laughed, "Okay well – we as in the rugby club have got a fundraising dinner next week and I wanted to know if you would like to come as me and my dad's guest?"

"Oh that's really kind of you, but I'm not great company at the moment."

"Okay I get that, but hear me out. First it's not a date, it's a night out with lots of other people. There'll be lots of music and dancing which I thought you'd love. You get to see my dance moves which will make you laugh if nothing else and my dad will be there so no funny business I promise. All the more reason to come out with us. My dad doesn't get out much and he's just broken it off with Julie, the woman I was telling you about so he needs cheering up too. I was going to invite your boyfriend too; but maybe that's not a good idea?" That had just popped into his head – good timing or what? as it didn't sound like she would want to bring that arsehole with her – not now anyway.

"Oh great. All the lost souls together getting drunk asking where it all went wrong? Sorry. I'm joking."

"It really will be fun, lots of music and dancing. I thought you'd love it and it sounds like just what you need? It's a good crowd, me and dad will look after you scouts honour"!

"Oh were you a boy scout?"

"Umm no not exactly," he laughed.

"I don't know I'm not very good company right now." Gavin looked so disappointed that it made Evie feel bad.

"Okay if I decide to go I need some info."

His face broke out into a big grin, "I knew you'd come, I told dad she'll come through don't worry."

She laughed, "I haven't said yes yet? Okay so details when and where and dress code, is there a hotel nearby where I can stay?"

He filled her in, "7.30 for 8, carriages at 3.30am."

"3.30 am! You can tell you're all rugby boys"!

"I could get offended at that," he pretended, "but I won't. Dress code is black tie and there's a budget hotel chain around the corner, not grand but clean and cheap and 5 minutes' walk away."

"I don't know."

"Oh go on. You never know, you might even enjoy yourself. Please Evie, it'll be fun."

"Okay okay I give in, I'll come."

He grinned, "Fantastic. I knew you would."

"I'll sort out my classes and travel up in the afternoon. Let me check availability at the hotel and I'll text you back."

"Okay text me as soon as you know."

"How much are the tickets?"

"On the house."

"No really; how much are they?"

"Seriously it's fine, you can buy us some drinks and some raffle tickets if you like – we just both wanted you to be there, you know to say thanks and seriously now I think you need a night out to take your mind off of things."

"You're not wrong there," she sighed.

They chatted for another 5 minutes or so and then signed off. She checked the hotel online and booked a room at a bargain price of only £25. She would need some fuel and check that Mrs Harris next door would feed Henry and she was all set.

Now what was she going to wear? Not the dress she wore with Ben, not the jumpsuit she wore with Andrew – but she didn't want to buy anything new that she would end up wearing just the once with all the bad associations that went with it, so she ran upstairs to look in her wardrobe for some inspiration. Maybe this would be just what she needed. She loved her girlfriends; but after a while it was all the same talk how rubbish their boyfriends were, picking over the bones – she shuddered. What an awful expression that was; and she just needed not to talk about any of that at the moment she just couldn't cope with it. Plus it was music and dancing, which she loved and she would hardly know anyone there which was a good thing right now. Away from the gym she realised she was actually looking forward to it. Now back to more serious stuff – what to wear?

Chapter 80

She still hadn't called Andrew. She was making him wait, he deserved little else from her really. Maybe she would call him after her rugby trip away and see if he said anything she wanted to listen to.

Andrew was still smarting from the fact she hadn't called him. He was going to have to make Christina call her by the end of the week. So on Friday night he invited himself round to Christina's and asked her outright to call her. Christina needed little persuading and agreed to call her once the twins were in bed; to be honest she was a little surprised Evie hadn't called her brother by now. Maybe there was more to this than met the eye? Perhaps her dear brother had been economical with the truth? Anyway whatever the reason she had to get to the bottom of it. She would banish him upstairs whilst she called – it was bad enough that he was here at all and she didn't want him watching her whilst she chatted.

So once the twins were asleep she poured herself a small glass of wine and picked up her mobile. She sent Andrew upstairs; but he only went as far up the stairs so as to be out of sight, he wasn't missing a word of this make no mistake.

Evie's phone rang, she picked up as she could see it was Christina. "Hey you; just wondering how you are, I've been thinking of going shopping over the next few weeks if you fancy it?"

"That sounds great, but I'll need to check my shifts first."

"Okay let me know which days you're free and we'll meet up."

Andrew was going nuts sat on the stairs; come on! come on! talk about me not shopping, he thought.

Christina couldn't put if off any longer, " So what is new with you?"

"Well you know the same old stuff –work – my horrid boss – oh and your brother dumped me; but then I guess you know that already? "She regretted sounding so mean and apologised straight away.

"Sorry, sorry; not your fault that last one, just not sure what happened that's all?"

"Has your phone been off?"

"No; had a problem with it," she lied. She hated lying to Christina; but she wasn't sure if Andrew was listening in so was being a bit careful – "all sorted now."

"Okay, look I know things are tricky right now but can I ask you a question?"

She thought about when Ben had asked exactly the same thing and she replied: "Yes you can ask but I may choose not to answer."

Crikey! thought Christina, this was going to be a lot trickier than she thought. "Okay I'll ask anyway – why haven't you called my brother, it's been nearly two weeks?" There was silence. "Are you still there?"

"Yes, yes I'm here." Unbeknown to her Andrew was holding his breath on the stairs; although he had been moving down one stair at a time as he wanted to hear everything.

"It's –well – I don't know – everything was going okay; but here's the thing: as soon as we went on that weekend away he got so strange and jealous and then all that nonsense with the conference – he knew I couldn't go, it's as if my job is not important at all. Yes it's a small salary, but I love doing it. Anyway, go back to daily life and then boom! out of nowhere he calls me and accuses me of all sorts of mad things – you do know it's all rubbish, don't you?"

"Yes, yes of course," she murmured. She could see Andrew was now sat at the bottom of the stairs hanging onto her every word. This had been a mistake to call her when he was still here. Never mind, she was on the phone now and could hardly just end the call without it looking suspicious.

"But you do miss him don't you?"

Evie thought about it; no, not as much as she ought to, was the honest answer but instead she replied, "I don't know."

"Do you still love him?"

There was a big pause. Evie wondered if she ever had loved him, then she said, "Sorry I can't do this now" – surprisingly she started to cry quietly. "Sorry just can't. I've really got to go, say hi to the twins for me and I'll text you about that shopping day. I promise. I just can't talk about this now." She hung up.

Christina stared at the phone.

Andrew grabbed the phone, "It's me: hello? hello?" He realised she'd hung up. He turned and looked at his sister, "So what did she say?"

"Well, she said it started to go wrong on your weekend away together."

"Okay then what?"

"I asked her if she still loved you."

"Yes," he said impatiently, "I heard all that and, and?"

"She started to cry and said she couldn't do this right now and hung up."

Andrew stared at his sister. "Crying."

"Yes very quietly though, like she was really hurting and didn't want anyone to know just how much."

He slumped into a kitchen chair – with his head in his hands. "It's really over. I never even, I mean it never even crossed my mind that we wouldn't get back together."

"Are you sure you didn't say anything else to her on the phone from the conference?"

He started to think. To start with it had been a blur but bits were coming back. "I remember asking her about the gym guy at the hotel and then why she felt she needed to get involved with everyone like that woman in the restaurant and Gavin" – he almost spat out the name. "But she said she hadn't heard from him at all after the rugby until he showed up at the gym. I think I said I didn't believe her."

Christina rolled her eyes, "Bloody marvellous. So you called her a liar and then what? Anything else?"

Suddenly Andrew said, "Well I think I accused her of encouraging Gavin and saying I was sure she was going to sleep with him that night or something like that?"

"What do you mean something like that? Think Andrew, think what did you say?"

"Something like, 'Well you may as well just get on with it and sleep with him if that's what you want. And other girls would love to come to a free conference with me .'"

Christina looked incredulously at Andrew, "You actually said that to her. So now she's a cheat and a liar – oh Andrew honestly what did you expect?"

"Umm it's a bit of a blur to be honest."

Evie hung up and stared out the window. She wiped her eyes and couldn't even be bothered to carry on crying; she was so over it, it was almost funny. This was never going to be easy; but maybe some time out would put things back into perspective. Andrew was never going to be the love of her life, that ship had sailed twice already and although she was sad, she was more annoyed than anything. She'd wasted her time on someone who didn't love her, not really love her deep down, not like Jonathan before he'd cheated or Ben before he'd left her to have his own family. She still had Henry, her cottage and her job, which apart from horrid Steve she really loved; and now she had agreed to go to some rugby dinner with Gavin and his dad. She hoped this wouldn't be another mistake. Still she couldn't back out now and later that evening she realised that actually she didn't want to. Maybe a night out dancing with people she didn't know that well and no baggage trailing around behind her would be fun? Maybe she was kidding herself but she'd already promised to go and decided to pick out what to wear once and for all. There was still a week until she had to drive up to the hotel so plenty of time for her to change her mind again.

Later that night she realised she hadn't missed Andrew as much as she thought she would. Perhaps they just weren't right for each other after all? She was all too aware of her own faults; but she'd seen another side to Andrew lately, one of jealousy and sulkiness which weren't very attractive qualities. He thought his job was way more important than hers and he never wanted to stay over so she always had to go to his house which meant leaving Henry yet again, which wasn't fair. Henry was the one constant thing in her life except for her family. Not a lot of give and take if you started to look at things from a distance; maybe that was what she needed, some distance or a different perspective?

She was rostered on the Sunday morning shift and was actually looking forward to it as her boss wouldn't be there and they could have some fun. Evie would switch the music up a little louder and work harder or what she really meant was work hard to try and forget what the last 10 days had been about. You had no time to dwell on anything once the class started other than what was coming next so perfect for zoning out of all life's problems.

Monday morning came and went. It was always good to get that class out of the way. Yesterday had been fine and she had really pushed her group hard.

She met up with her girlfriends in a pub after work and they had a good natter. Claire's boyfriend was being a twat again as usual so she managed to avoid the subject of her car crash love life pretty well. She decided to tell them about Andrew; but not to tell them about the rugby club dance. Some things she wanted kept private and she was sure they thought she'd been an idiot with Andrew even though his behaviour was bloody unbelievable. After they said their goodbyes she got into her car and drove home. She wasn't in the mood for music which was unlike her; but they'd talked nonstop for over 3 hours and although she loved hanging out with them what she wanted right now was some peace. At the same time she nearly missed her turning. Surprisingly she was looking forward to Tuesday night after all, sighing loudly she thought it couldn't be any worse than lately could it?

Chapter 81

Tuesday was fine and dry. She took two classes back to back in the morning and was home for a shower and some lunch. She checked there was enough food for Henry and called in to see her neighbour just to make sure she hadn't forgotten she was feeding her cat yet again. Evie locked the front door after kissing Henry and put her bag in the boot of her car, set the satnav and was off. The display told her she would arrive just after 4.30 which was perfect to have a soak in the bath first before getting dressed and doing her make up. In the end she had decided not to wear anything too fancy, but settled on some stretch satin dark grey patterned trousers with silver mules – her old favourites; gosh, if only they could speak the tales they could tell. She'd also put on a misty grey/blue halter top in chiffon which left her shoulders bare and to be honest she had forgotten she'd bought. It had never been worn and she had to cut the labels off before trying it on. She had packed her multi way bra – honestly, boys had no idea about the trials and tribulations girls had to go through.

She focused on the road and put on one of her favourite CD's. Less than two hours later she pulled into the hotel car park. It looked reasonable enough from the outside and as she checked in the girl was smiley and helpful. The hotel was bright and clean and her room had a large window overlooking the front where her car was parked.

After her bath she ate a snack she'd brought with her as she was never too sure quite what she would be able to eat at the dinner. Teeth cleaned and face cleansed, she put on her clothes and then did her makeup. There was plenty of time to spare, so she checked her e-mails and messages then put her phone on the dressing table; no need to lug that thing about tonight. Then she spent five minutes wrestling with the room key and finally managed to get the huge plastic hotel logo thing off the key so she could just take the small room key/ lipgloss/ money and a tissue in her bag. She put her patterned kimono jacket on. It was still too chilly not to wear a coat. All set, she suddenly realised that she felt nervous and put the evening news on to try to concentrate on something else. It was 7.25 so after using the bathroom she switched her phone off and went outside to see if Gavin and his dad were there.

Gavin was feeling nervous, which wasn't like him at all; but then this whole thing was unlike him too. Not for a second did he think she'd say yes to this dinner. He expected her to have brought her boyfriend too and was over the moon that she would be here on her own. He didn't want to blow this one chance to make a good impression; he had a lot riding on this night. His dad Neil was struggling to tie Gavin's bow tie. Neither of them were entirely sure why they were wearing them as they would probably be taken off and left on the table as soon as the meal and speeches were over. They agreed they passed muster and left at 7.15 to park the car at the rugby club before strolling over to the hotel. As they rounded the corner Gavin could see her sat on a bench outside swinging her feet. Even from this distance he could see she had made quite an effort and the closer he got the better everything was looking. They exchanged smiles and said all the usual things about looking nice before walking over to the club. Gavin looked down at her and was very happy that she'd dressed up; he thought she looked so pretty and he would tell her later when they were on their own.

He held the door open for her when they arrived and placed his hand on her back to guide her in – he didn't really want to move his hand but had to when the club boss rushed over to welcome them. It was already quite busy when they arrived and Evie could tell that a lot of the women had gone to town with their outfits. Still she felt at ease in her choice and didn't want to be the centre of attention tonight anyway. Gavin introduced her to quite a lot of people and got her a glass of wine. They chatted to a group of his friends and their girlfriends before finding their table and sitting down. Evie was relieved to find Gavin was on her right and Neil was on her left. She ate what she could and drank some wine, not too much wine, but quite a lot of water. Tables were cleared then there came the speeches. Fundraiser – blah blah – thank you all for coming, raffle – blah blah, then tables were moved away from the dancefloor as the DJ blasted out the first track. Ten minutes later the music started to get really good and lots of couples were already on the dance floor.

MUSIC: – SOMETHING KIND OF OOH – GIRLS ALOUD.

Gavin grabbed her hand. "Come on then, let's show them how it's done." Evie removed her jacket and he led her onto the dance floor. He didn't realise her top was a halter neck until she twirled round for him. Wow! you're full of surprises, he thought. Gavin was a surprisingly good dancer and they danced on and off for the next couple of hours and then she needed a time out and went to the ladies' room. She thought it was funny but they were always full and she waited in line until a cubicle was free, there was a lot of chatter and girls were swopping eyeshadow and laughing. The room went quiet and then a moment later the main door burst open. She could hear two voices chatting and giggling the only way that girls do in the ladies' toilet, one voice said, "This is turning into a good night after all, better than I thought – just hope Adam doesn't have too much to drink like last time, ruined my evening." The other voice said, "Yeah I know what you mean but my Dave's a good 'un really; never gets too legless," and they laughed together. She was just debating on whether to make it clear that she was there when voice number one said again, "Did you see Gav? Fit or what?" "Yes. Very," came the reply, then more giggling. "Mind you I don't know who he's with – not sure I've seen her before." "No, me neither – lucky cow," then more giggling; the main door opened and silence again.

Evie opened the cubicle door and washed her hands. It never ceased to amaze her the stuff you overheard in a ladies' loo. She waited another few minutes as she didn't want them to see her leave otherwise they would know she had been eavesdropping and that would look rude. When she got back she sat at the table, she could see Neil at the bar talking to the barmaid who she had learnt was called Sheila and they were obviously getting along very well. A tray of drinks was brought over by one of Gavin's team mates and she thanked him. She was quite thirsty now so drank half of the glass of fizzy water before she'd even realised. There was no sign of Gavin but she didn't mind, the room was noisy and she didn't have to do anything she didn't want to. Gavin reappeared at her table, "There you are."

"Yes still here. I haven't done a runner yet," she laughed

It was now past midnight and the music was really loud

"I didn't think you'd actually come tonight."

"Well I promised you and a promise is a promise."

"Are you having a good time?"

"Yes it's fun, and it's just what I needed."

"Good," – he held her hand –"Blimey! your hands are tiny"!

"Or it could just be that your hands are very big," she laughed

He put his palm against hers. "They're like baby hands; how do you hold things properly?" He winked at her, thinking about her hands running through his hair right that second.

"Oh us girls have our ways; thanks for the drinks by the way."

"I didn't buy any."

"Oh I think they were from your team mate over there," she pointed at a guy near the bar. A guy raised his glass to them as if to say cheers.

"Oh him. That's Spencer. You want to watch him."

Obviously no love lost there, she thought.

Just then the music changed and one of her favourite tracks was blasting out. Suddenly she felt full of energy and grabbed his hand. "Come on then. Let's dance."

MUSIC: – SO STRONG – MECK FEAT DINO.

He took her hands in his and on the dancefloor they started to move. It was a very fast song with a catchy rhythm and beat. She moved slowly and sexily in front of him. Wow, he thought; this is something else. He caught Spencer's eye who was still standing at the bar. He didn't know how Gavin Johnson did it, but he was regretting spiking her drink now as it looked as if they were having way more fun than him tonight – his girlfriend Sheridan had gone off to the ladies with her girlfriends and wasn't a big dancer so he was forced to watch Gavin and his new girlfriend get it on.

The song finished and a slower number was playing. Gavin held her in his arms, one hand was on the soft skin of her shoulders and he didn't want to remove it anytime soon. As they swayed together he thought that had been some dance. Soon after she felt a bit unsteady on her feet for some reason; she'd only had two glasses of wine and needed some fresh air.

"Can we get some air?"

"Sure." He took her hand in his and they went outside to sit on a bench.

"Oh that's better. I don't know what's wrong with me. I've only had two glasses of wine and the soft drink your friend sent over."

Gavin thought that Spencer had probably put vodka in the fizzy water – his idea of a joke. Well he would keep for another time.

"That's the effect I have on women." He smiled at her and really wanted to kiss her; but just then the door opened and a group of people all piled out talking and laughing. They were obviously going on somewhere and walked noisily and unsteadily out towards the main road.

"Would you mind if I left soon? I'm suddenly feeling quite tired."

"Nope, to be honest past one o'clock these things tend to die down a bit, we'll just duck in and tell dad okay?"

She nodded. They found Neil and she said her goodbyes. He really was a sweet man and he'd done a great job raising Gavin all by himself. Gosh she felt sleepy all of a sudden and definitely needed some air.

Gavin was back in a flash and held her hand, then moved his arm to around her waist. They navigated the parked cars and made for the roadside. All too soon they were stood outside the hotel.

"Well thank you for a lovely evening," she said, slurring her words slightly. "I had a lovely time, really, really lovely," she swayed a bit and he put his hand out to steady her.

"Easy there. Shall I walk you to your door?"

She giggled. "Why thank you, kind sir; you are a true gentleman," and she placed her hand on his chest to steady herself

If you knew what I was thinking, he mused, you'd run a bloody mile. He took the key out of her hand and helped her up the stairs.

They reached her door and he opened it, "In we go." She nearly tripped over her feet. "Steady there."

"Now if I ask you if you want coffee I really do mean coffee," she slurred.

"I think I'd better make the coffee!"

Evie sat on the sofa bed and kicked off her shoes, dumped her bag on the floor and watched him make coffee. "I need to use the bathroom back in a sec."

She was in there quite some time as she decided to brush her teeth, wipe off her make – up and when she stepped back into the room she found Gavin flat out fast asleep on the bed. Evie took his shoes off and undid his cufflinks and unbuttoned his shirt. She stood gawping at his torso. Bloody hell but these rugby boys were fit lads! She shook her head and wrapped him in the duvet. Then she opened the wardrobe and found spare pillows and a blanket so that she could get better acquainted with the sofa bed. This was turning into the story of her life, she thought as she stood with her back towards him and pulled on her pj's. Evie drank some water and then lay down. She was so tired that as soon as she closed her eyes she was asleep.

Sometime later she woke feeling thirsty and stumbled into the bathroom to get some water. When she came out she was still half asleep and without thinking she just got into bed and pulled the duvet over her and snuggled down. She was asleep in less than a minute. Gavin woke after 5.00 am feeling cold. He looked at the room. Where the fuck was he this time? He soon figured out he was in her hotel room when he saw the sofa bed and blankets. Standing up slowly he took off the rest of his clothes apart from his boxers, used the bathroom and got into, bed this time under the duvet. No wonder he was feeling cold lying on top of it like that.

Chapter 82

Evie stirred; but for some reason couldn't move to stretch out as there was a very heavy weight over her. She inched around bit by bit and came face to face with Gavin. She hadn't expected that. Evie stared at his face watching him sleep, his hair was sticking up at the front and she fought back an urge to flatten it down. She nearly jumped out of her skin when he suddenly said: "Morning," before opening his eyes and staring into hers.

"Um," she gulped, "Hello."

He grinned back. "Hello yourself, had a good sleep?"

"Not enough yet, it's still early-um I don't remember getting into bed."

"Mmm not sure what happened there; looks as if you started out on the sofa bed, but have to say this is a nice surprise."

She looked nervously at him and squeaked out: "Can I ask you a question?"

He propped himself up on his elbow. "Sure, go ahead."

"Umm the thing is, you see the thing is," She wished the floor would swallow her up and that his other arm would stop stroking her back as she found it really distracting and she was trying to concentrate. "The thing is: are you wearing anything under there?" She pointed vaguely at the duvet.

He grinned. "Why, are you worried we are naked here together?"

She swallowed hard. "Umm kind of yes."

He let out a huge laugh. "Well I'm sorry to disappoint you, but we both have something on."

"We do?"

"Yes we do. Shall we take a look together? I'll lift up the duvet and you can take a peek."

"Umm well, okay then." She glanced as quickly as she could.

He had boxers on and she was in her short pj set. Thank the Lord for that! she thought.

"Oh that's a relief. So we didn't......... we didn't?"

"No we didn't and I was thinking that it's a shame."

She went bright red. Oh no, how was she going to get out of this intact?

"Look it's... it's..."

"Do you know you have the most gorgeous eyes?"

Before she could stop herself she said, "Well your eyes are all soft and twinkly." Then she blushed like mad again and felt foolish.

"Well that's a start."

"Look. I had a lovely time last night, but …..but………..I'm a lot older than you and I only became single two weeks ago."

"How old?"

"Pardon?" His hand was still playing havoc with her brain connecting to her mouth and it was way too early to be having this conversation

"How old are you?"

"I'm going to be 28 the week after next."

"Cool!"

"Cool?"

"Yep no big deal is it?"

"Um isn't it?"

"Not really no."

"Oh how about you?"

"I'm 24."

Oh my God! she thought, much younger than her, practically a baby. His arm was now under her pj camisole and stroking her bare skin; this was torture but torture of the best kind.

"Yes this night out was always in the plan."

"Let me get this straight; you had a plan?"

"Yes. I was going to woo you slowly."

"Woo me?"

"Yep, woo."

"Woo me," she started to laugh. "Woo me, woo me, that's, well that's …" he joined in the laughter.

"Let me explain. Whilst I lay on the pitch all I could hear was your voice and I liked the fact you were worried about me and then I opened my eyes and I knew I was going to have to see you again."

"What did you actually hear?"

"Well just bits and bobs, you know; it's a bit vague. I just stood up too fast and fainted; but Alan told me you were being all unreasonable with him and the doctor."

"Who's Alan?"

"I think you called him sponge bob."

"Oh him."

"Point of reference here: but you do know that half time oranges are for football?"

"Yes," she smiled, "but I wanted him to go and get a blanket and he was just standing there."

"I don't remember the doctor showing up."

"Yes I'm afraid I gave him a bit of a grilling too."

"Then I threw up on your wellies and you just seemed so calm and unfazed and poured water on your boots to wash it off and then carried on as if nothing had happened – about that – I apologise by the way. I thought: wow! most girls would have made a huge song and dance. Then I opened my eyes properly and looked into these big deep dark eyes and kept thinking deep dark thoughts so it was an inevitable conclusion I would see you again."

"Oh," she didn't know what to say. "Can you stop doing that with your hand?" she asked

"Sorry. Don't you like it?"

"Um – yes – no – look it's early, I'm tired and I'm getting confused."

He said okay, but his hand stayed right where it was.

"So your only objection to us being an item is that you're older than me?"

"Well we don't know anything about each other and I don't live near here either."

"You're forgetting me and my dad have been to your gym. It's two hours by car not two days away you don't live in Australia." he said.

Funny; she thought that Andrew had only been to her house twice and always made out it was so much easier for her to go to his – lazy git.

"Hello where'd you go?"

"Sorry you were saying?"

"So when exactly is your birthday?"

"April 20th."

"What are you planning?"

"Um nothing actually because I thought I would have a shit enough time being on my own again this year, thank you."

"Well that's not going to happen now is it? Tell you what: I'll come over and cook for you."

"You can cook?"

"Oh Evie! you have no idea about my special talents do you? Yes I can cook although I may need a bit of help with stuff like no wheat etc."

"Oh …I don't know can I think about it?"

"Yep, sure."

"So what exactly are you looking for?" She asked him

"What do you mean?"

"Well I don't want to be rude, but are you wanting a one night or morning stand or what? I don't quite understand."

"No I don't want a one night stand. That's not my thing at all. I want us to be a couple in a proper relationship."

"Oh, my." He seemed very sure of himself which made her even more nervous.

"So this age gap does it really bother you that much as I'm just pointing out that if it was the other way around no-one would bat an eyelid would they?"

"Um no. I suppose not."

"Well there you go then. I can't change the age thing, but judging on your last boyfriend who was a similar age to you if I'm right, then that didn't work out too well so what do you have to lose? Secondly, once we have spent the day together today we will know a lot more about each other and we can figure the other stuff out together."

"We're spending the day together? "

"Well we need to swing by my place and collect some clean clothes, gym gear and stuff. Then breakfast and after that if it's still sunny then a walk in the park is always nice. Maybe a quick run if you're up for it, then back here to change and out to the pub for a meal tonight you can meet some more of my friends. It means staying here for an extra night but they don't look very busy to me."

Quietly she said, "Oh you seem to have it all figured out."

"If it's all too much then that's okay too; tell me: what you want to do?" Gavin was praying he hadn't gone too far.

"Umm I suppose I could stay another night here. It's quite nice really. I'd have to phone my neighbour to feed Henry."

"See not all 5 star fancy bollocky nonsense."

Suddenly she thought: how do you know I can stay another day? "Whoa hang on a minute, there! Sunshine." She put her hand on his chest. "How do you know I don't have to be back until tomorrow?"

"Cos I called the gym and asked them."

"You did what?" She was suddenly cross with him

"Well actually that's a lie and before you say it yes I know you hate lies, so I got my sister Bethan to call and ask when your next class was, as she really wanted to work out with you. They said Thursday at 6.00pm."

"Well this is all very well and good and I suppose you have today off as well?"

"Yep. All planned, you see." His hand had now moved under the waistband of her pj shorts and was slowly caressing her bum.

"Gavin you've got to stop this is madness," she whispered.

"Can I ask you a question now?" he asked, leaving his hand exactly where it had been for the last few minutes.

"Okay."

"How come you're still single? Yes, I know about your most recent bloke – who sounds like a right dick, by the way – and don't get me wrong I'm glad you were with him otherwise we never would have met; but there must have been other blokes before him. I can't understand why you're still single. I mean, I think its bloody brilliant luck on my part," he grinned, "but still."

"Well I could just say I haven't found the right one yet; but to be honest here's the thing – I'm just not very good at all this and I had a bad experience some time ago that put me off of guys for a long time. It's ....well......... I'm quite complicated and a lot for most guys to take on."

"What type of thing?"

"Can we leave that just for now... please?"

"Well okay, but only because right now I want to kiss you."

"I'm not sure that's a good idea."

He grinned. "Well I disagree and it's just occurred to me that even if the wooing plan was ticking along nicely there could be a big hiccup if I didn't enjoy kissing you and then I'd have to bail out pretty quickly."

She frowned. "I don't understand; what do you mean, not enjoy it?"

"Well as you are about to find out I am a fantastic kisser and I was hoping you would be too, but of course you may be terrible; so then I might need to forget the whole idea."

"That's just so bloody cheeky, you're very sure of yourself sunshine I..." Evie never finished her sentence.

He didn't wait and just lent over her and kissed on her lips.

Oh he was so good.

He moved over so he was practically on top of her and continued to kiss her gently whilst still stroking her thighs and her hair. Bloody hell her hair was so soft too.

She heard herself moan. This was ridiculous, insane; but so wonderful at the same time.

He stopped and looked at her. "Not bad; maybe a B minus."

She was getting cross, "Are you insane? a bloody B minus?"

"Language, language!" he laughed and kissed her again harder this time

Oh he was good; no doubt about that, she responded. She could feel him hardening beneath her thighs this was getting so out of control and had to stop.

Her hands were in his hair and he groaned. That felt just as good as he hoped it would. Moving slightly away from her, he held her eyes – "See. We are great together, definitely an A star that time." She nodded, not trusting herself to speak

"I wasn't expecting this to have moved so fast; although I'm pleased that it has and I want to ask you another question now. "

She nodded because for some reason she still couldn't speak.

"Promise to spend the day with me and then make up your mind. It's your decision. I know how I feel but if you need more time then that's okay with me."

"Really?"

"Yes really. You're a bit shy really aren't you?"

She nodded.

"Just so you know I'm going to kiss you again now okay?"

She nodded again.

"Wow your skin is so soft," he said. "Seriously if you want to stop then just say so okay?"

She nodded and they kissed again for what seemed like forever.

"Got to stop now," he said. "Or else I won't want to."

She giggled.

"You really do have tiny hands," he said gazing at them.

"You should see my feet they are tiny too," they lay side by side and pulled up the duvet to check. Evie squealed, "Oh my goodness look at the difference, you really are a big bloke."

He grinned. "Not just hands and feet." She blushed bright red. "Sorry, was that too much. You're actually blushing. I thought no girl did that these days."

"Ah I know, but I'm afraid I do and …I'm not most girls."

Chapter 83

Evie had been lying there for a few minutes when finally her brain leapt into action. What in God's name was she doing? Every time she'd been with someone it had gone wrong, mostly in quite a dramatic fashion; this was just way too much too soon. She was definitely on the rebound and they didn't know anything about each other.

She pulled back the duvet and got up.

"Hey! where are you off to?"

"Shower." she mumbled – maybe the water would bring her to her senses. She definitely couldn't think straight lying next to him like that. The water was running and she stepped into the bath using her shower foam which was soft and creamy and didn't take long to get the job done. Her thoughts were racing and tumbling all over on top of each other, her shoulders slumped. Had she been a complete idiot again? She finished and was grabbing a towel when suddenly Gavin appeared and stepped into the bath and under the shower.

"Save some hot water for me," he laughed. She shuffled out of his way, not wanting to look him in the eye and stepped out wrapping the towel around herself.

He peeked out from behind the shower curtain to see her standing on the tiled floor. He would have preferred them to have showered together, but maybe that was pushing things. He continued to wash and turning the water off, picked up a towel and rubbed it over his hair before wrapping it around his waist and pulling back the shower curtain.

Shit, she was still standing exactly in the same spot with her back towards him; but she had her hands over her face and she was eerily still.

"Hey," – no reply, fuck, FUCK! this was going very, very wrong, very quickly.

He stepped out of the bath and took two steps towards her and touched her lightly on the shoulder. She nearly jumped a mile in the air; but he didn't take his hand away. Gavin waited and there was still nothing, he'd gone way too far too fast this time; if he wasn't careful she'd be running out the door and he'd never see her again.

"Hey," he said quietly. "Come and sit for a minute." He looked round, where to sit, he certainly wasn't going to sit on the downturned loo seat so that only left the edge of the bath.

He gently took one of her hands away from her face and led her towards the bath. He sat down and motioned for her to sit on his thigh. "Come on; this will have to do."

Evie sat down and nestled her face into his shoulder. He wrapped his arms around her and waited for her to talk. He felt her tears on his skin; but she didn't seem to be crying anymore. He gently stroked her hair to let her talk in her own time.

It seemed like ages before she sighed and said quietly, "Sorry it's just a bit, well all a bit…"

"I know, I know. It's all been a bit much," he interjected and she nodded her head slightly

She continued. "I'm overtired and over emotional and to be honest overwhelmed too."

"Most of that is my fault; I'm like a steam train sometimes and people get railroaded and I'm sorry, okay?"

She nodded again.

"Look. I get it, I really do – just because I've been planning for us to have a relationship it might have been useful to actually tell you that to give you a bit of time to get used to the idea; but I was just so excited and know 100% that this is the right thing I guess I moved too fast."

She raised her face to look at him. "Oh so we're having a relationship are we?" she smiled softly

"Yep; better get used to it."

"Do I have a choice?"

"Nope not really; as I said before, why don't we just see how today goes?" He wiped her tears from her face. "Please don't cry."

She placed her hand on his skin. "Sorry I've made you all wet."

"I was wet already from the shower so a few tears won't hurt me; I'm sorry I caused them in the first place." He was desperate to kiss her again; but knew if he did it might be the last chance he got, so he kissed the top of her head instead. "Look we don't have to do any of the things I'd planned for us today if you don't want to. If you'd rather go home, then although I'll be very disappointed, I'll help you pack."

"You do know I'm on the rebound, don't you?" she whispered.

"No such thing in my book, you're either with someone or you're not – simple as – and I'm single and you're single so there's no problem okay?"

"Okay."

"How about you go back to bed?" She froze momentarily – "No not us – just you – just to sleep. It's still really early, you sleep and I'll make some tea and eat all your free biscuits."

"You're obsessed with food," she smiled at him.

"Well I haven't had my breakfast yet and I'm a growing chap."

Evie smiled. Jamie always said exactly the same thing. He'd like Gavin, she was sure of it.

"Can you just give me a minute to get my pyjamas on and I'll be right out?"

"Sure." Gavin strolled into the bedroom whilst Evie pulled on her shorts and cami, taking a deep breath she went back into the bedroom, padded over to the bed and climbed in.

She sat up, pulled the duvet up and under her arms and patted the top of the duvet next to her motioning for Gavin to come and sit down. Evie had had enough of going through the same palaver again and again. She would tell Gavin everything right from the start and then he could decide. It would be quicker this way if he wanted to leave as they barely knew one another anyway.

Gavin sat down and picked up one of her hands in his. He didn't like where this was going and was silently praying for a happy ending.

"So here's the thing: before I have my nap I thought I'd tell you some things, things which I don't normally mention until I'm actually having or nearly having a relationship with someone. This could save us both a lot of time and pain so if you could try not to interrupt I'll start."

Gavin just nodded and squeezed her hand.

"So here's the thing – warning: there's always a thing with me, just so you know. Where to begin? Four, no maybe five years ago something terrible happened to me. I mean it was bad, really bad and I was quite a mess for a long time. It messed me up medically, emotionally (she touched her head) and physically too. I had a lot of counselling, in fact I still have it once a month in London and I have a lot of scars on the front and back of my body. You may have seen some in the bathroom. They're not pretty, in fact they're pretty ugly," she laughed wryly, "and not everyone can cope to look at them." Gavin went to say something; but she squeezed his hand. "Please just let me finish. Because of what happened I can't have children so if you want a family then it won't be with me and, yes, I have seen every specialist under the sun before you ask. I still get anxiety dreams without warning and if... if you're here when it happens then you need to wake me up, all right? Also I have huge trust issues with blokes and unsurprisingly none of them have wanted to stick around when they find out all of this. So I'm telling you now so there are no secrets further down the line." She paused. Well, he hadn't grabbed his things and made a run for it just yet, so she continued.

"You should know that I don't normally even kiss a boyfriend on the mouth until after the 3rd or 4th date and I don't sleep with them until the 5th or 6th, so you see I'm complicated, very nervous with huge trust issues, that's me. So now I'll briefly fill you in on my past few relationships and you can judge for yourself if you still want to be with me."

Gavin nodded. This was serious stuff, but he wanted and needed to hear it all if they were to have any kind of future together.

"Okay, so I'll go back about 18 months or so. Before that I tried to have relationships, but they never worked out. Now where was I? First there was Jack, trainer at the gym. We kissed, it was okay I suppose; and then I found out he was kissing all the other girls at the gym too, so I kicked him into touch. Next came Jonathan, city boy; we met through friends, all we did was fight and then we stopped fighting and it was great, he was a good kisser and good in bed, things moved on. I went to London to stay with him and everything was fab, then I got hurt in a fight – I wasn't fighting, just wrong place wrong time kind of thing; so no, well you know, no umm funny business for quite a few weeks. I discovered I was pregnant – I know, I know; but this was a billion to one chance. I went to surprise him with the news and found him with another woman. So to sum up he said he loved me, got me pregnant, cheated on me, dumped me, he fled the country and then a few weeks later I lost the baby. I was a complete and utter mess yet again." Gavin grimaced; bloody hell, he sounded like a right bastard.

"Then I met Jason, who was a policeman. He kissed me once on the cheek, no sex, he helped me get through the worst and said he loved me, got promoted and wanted me to leave with him; but I didn't love him so off he went. Next was Ben, he was in the army, we met helping at a road accident. He was just a friend then he got deployed and I wrote to him. When he came home we got together and it was, well it was something else; he was a great kisser and the umm, well the umm sex, well, it was amazing. (Gavin squirmed at this point; she hadn't had sex with him yet so the jury was out as far as he was concerned.). Turned out he wanted a family, so he went back to his ex and that was that; although he knew from the outset I couldn't have a baby he buried his head in the sand until he had no choice but to make the decision.

And now we come onto Andrew, the guy you met or saw me with at the rugby. As far as kissing went it was only so-so and as for the sex well there wasn't very much of it and it wasn't good; in fact it was awful really and he always wanted me to keep my pyjama top on, so what does that tell you? Again we met as friends and it took me a while to think of him in a different way. I thought I could settle for him, but to cut a long story short he was quite jealous and controlling, accused me and, well, you as well of all sorts and so I ended that and the rest you know. I know it sounds like a lot of relationships, but really it isn't. She was embarrassed but Gavin just held her hand in his own even tighter.

"Oh apart from I now know I hate sleeping on sofa beds even in posh hotels they are so bloody uncomfortable – never ever again. I'd rather sleep in my car – just so you know. So now I'm going to have a nap and you can make tea or whatever and if you want to pack and go then we'll say no more."

Gavin swallowed hard, "Okay I get it, I really do, you're telling me all the bad stuff because you think I'll leave if you push me away hard enough. We've both had previous relationships so nothing new there. Yes we've kissed already and I suppose that technically this could be our second or third date and again waiting all those months for your previous boyfriend to get it on."

Evie interjected, "What a delightful expression!"

"Yeah well it didn't work out too good by the way now, did it?"

"Play nice Gavin; for all I know you could turn out to be a dick too and you said that last night wasn't a date!"

"Nope, that's another guy, but fair point I'll lay off him for now. And if I'd told you it was a date then you never would have come and that would have been a shame. But the thing is: I don't care about the scars, yes I hate how you came to have them in the first place but I've got scars too from rugby – yes I know you'd win that round easily enough but they don't bother me. I've seen the ones on your back, so that tactic isn't going to work. I'm glad you're having counselling because if it helps you then it'll help us too. As for the baby thing, well my sister Bethan wants at least 5 so I figure we'll babysit. I'll be their uncle and their godfather and then give them back at the end of the night and then it's more time for just you and me. If you get an anxiety dream then I promise to wake you up. And just so you know, sex with me is definitely going to be the best you've ever had." Evie laughed out loud. He was very sure of himself, maybe it was the confidence of youth but she'd have to wait and see. "So I'm grateful for you telling me everything but it won't work. That might be all the bad stuff, but I'm as sure that there's masses more good stuff and we're going to be just fine. I'd put money on it."

Gavin stood up and tucked the duvet around her, "Okay now get some sleep and see how you feel when you wake up." He kissed her on her forehead and turned away to fetch the kettle. Now for some tea and biscuits, and he needed to think about what to do next.

Chapter 84

Pouring water onto a tea bag, Gavin glanced over at Evie. She hadn't moved and if he had to guess he'd say that she was already fast asleep. Opening the first packet of biscuits he got his phone out of his jacket, he may as well catch up on some texts and emails whilst she slept. He thought he would have liked to know what had happened to her, it sounded truly awful. Scars, well that was nothing. Trust, he could build on that. As for the baby thing he wasn't bothered, it wasn't the be all and end all. If he wanted to be with her then he'd have to make sacrifices and so far he wanted to be with her more than anything he'd ever wanted before.

Nearly three hours later she stirred under the duvet and stretched out – "What time is it?" she asked

"Hello sleepy, it's nearly half past ten. Feeling better?"

"Yes thanks. You were right; it was just what I needed."

He sat down on the bed next to her and she shuffled over to make enough room then he took her hand in his. "So Gavin what are you thinking now? I see you're still here. But I need to know if I've put you off with the incident, the scars, the trust; oh, and the no babies thing too; but I haven't been involved in a wooing plan of action before."

"No I can see what you're doing, you're throwing all this negative stuff at me in the hope that it will put me off well no sorry it hasn't. If anything it's just made me more determined .So what about the rest of the day, do you want to stay or leave?" He hoped she'd stay, He'd be devastated if she left now.

"I'm going to stay but no promises, mind. We'll see how things go, fair enough?"

"Yep," he grinned, "Fair enough." On the inside he was punching the air. Crisis averted he'd got a break, a bloody big break. "Do you still want to book in for tonight?"

"Yes I think so. I need to call my neighbour; but then I can meet your friends. However, you do know there's no guarantee that you'll be staying here with me don't you? I don't want to lead you on."

"Alright, understood."

"Well let's get this day started properly shall we?"

God I'm so bloody lucky, he thought

"Now tell me is it a lovely day outside?"

"It certainly is a really lovely day."

"Now I've got you saying it too, sorry. I do say that word an awful lot but it just means I'm happy."

"Well you are quite lovely and it doesn't bother me in the slightest."

"If you're sure – it used to annoy Andrew a lot."

"Well you already know my opinion about him."

Evie giggled. "Gavin, play nicely."

"Well how ridiculous."

"Can you open the curtains whilst I finish in the bathroom?"

"Sure thing."

When he turned back the bed was empty and he could hear the taps running. He ran his hand through his hair; crikey, this was trickier than running the U.N or at least what he imagined it to be like running the U.N., that was.

Sometime later the door opened. "All done, do you need anything?"

"I'd like a shave, but I don't suppose you've got a spare razor?"

She went over to her travel wheelie and pulled up the telescopic handle and clipped on a folding sectioned wash kit to it. "Let me see. Yes you're in luck this one is new," she handed him a disposable razor and said, "Use the blue tube by the basin for shave cream and you should be fine."

"Blimey! never mind me being a boy scout you're a regular Bear Grylls you are – or maybe a baby Bear Grylls."

"Just get in the bathroom will you?" she laughed

"Okay okay, going right now baby bear," and he grabbed her, kissing her cheekily and squeezing her bum as he went by.

She left him to it whilst she put on her underwear. It was one of her favourite sets, in pale aqua lace, plunge bra with matching shorts it was fun and flirty and a bit sexy too. He came out of the bathroom. "Jesus, what are you trying to do to me?" she ducked away and opened the wardrobe door so he couldn't see her put her top on. Evie grabbed her jeans and started to wiggle into them they were stretch jeans and very comfortable but this was the best way to get them on.

"What are you doing behind there?" He asked

He closed the door and watched her wiggling into her jeans. He thought we'd better get going before we spend the whole day in here.

Five minutes later she'd called her neighbour, ensuring Henry would be fed tonight and tomorrow morning. Next she went down to reception where she extended her stay for another night and ordered two breakfasts, not for her, but she was sure Gavin would want something to eat if he ended up staying over. She wasn't sure about that yet, but if he was here then he would definitely be hungry before he left for work. He sat outside on a wooden bench in the sun waiting for her.

"All sorted?"

"Yes," She zapped her BMW 4x4, "Hop in but you may have to adjust the seat. Okay give me some directions to yours."

"I forget you don't know where you're going."

"That's why I have you," she smiled back at him whilst putting on her sunnies.

Ten minutes later she drew up outside a semi-detached house in a small cul de sac, "Is that your car?" she asked pointing to the Mitsubishi 4x4 parked on the drive.

"Yes. I use it for dad's business and it's got to be big enough for me to get in and out of." He explained

He opened the front door and said, "Okay let's get some clean clothes," and as headed up the stairs he called to her, "Are you coming up?"

She followed him up the stairs and he went into room at the front. "This is my domain," he grinned at her, "where all the magic happens."

"Yes I can imagine," she replied dryly

He started to take jeans out of drawers and shirts out of the wardrobe: socks, shoes, underwear and put them in a holdall. His gym kit was already packed and he went to the bathroom to get some toiletries.

"Shall I draw the curtains whilst you change? I don't want you giving the neighbours a thrill?"

"Okay if you like, mind you they've seen it all before." Two things popped into Evie's head; firstly, lucky old them and secondly when was she going to see it all? and she started to giggle. When she turned around he was stood there in some very sexy looking black stretchy boxer shorts

"Are they new?"

"Well I saw them on the telly and thought if they were good enough for that footballer then they'd be good enough for me; what do you think?"

She swallowed hard. "Umm very nice," she murmured. They looked amazing on his physique; it was getting hot in there all of a sudden.

"Can I ask you something?"

"More questions?" he said teasing her, "Go on then if you must."

"Why me? I mean you're a good looking guy, you could have your pick of the girls around here."

He laughed. "Well that's true enough and I do use that deodorant off the TV where the girls come flocking round and I have to swat them away all the time; it gets very tiring."

"Yes I'm sure it must," she said dryly. "Seriously I need to know what you're thinking."

"Well if we're being all serious and stuff, once I know what I want, then I focus on it until I get it."

"Are you never disappointed?"

"Sometimes, but probably because I haven't tried hard enough in the first place."

"This still doesn't answer my question."

"Because I think we'd be great together. No that's not it, actually. I think we'd be bloody fantastic together and I just need to convince you that I'm right, plus you haven't had the Gavin Johnson sex experience yet, have you?"

Evie felt her face go hot and red; what did she say to that?

She was a bit shy and that turned him on even more. Seeing she was uncomfortable he continued. "Call it a feeling it sounds bonkers I know but I knew as soon as I woke up on the pitch, well it was like all my Christmases had come at once."

"Are you sure it just wasn't concussion and you're still suffering the after effects of a bang on the head?" she laughed.

"Nope definitely not, just wait you'll see. I've just got to convince you that's all. We've done the kissing thing and you haven't run a mile yet."

"Yet!"

"So I reckon there's hope and we've got to take a chance."

"Of course you do realise that if you don't get on with Henry then that is a deal breaker? "

"Everyone loves me I'm sure he will too."

"We'll have to wait and see, he's a huge part of my life."

"Like me then."

She smiled. "Yes just like you."

"Okay doesn't sound too difficult to me. Like I said, everyone loves me." Suddenly he was right in front of her, "Yep. Even if they don't realise it straight off," and he stared into her eyes and then kissed her and kept on kissing her until they had to stop before things got way out of hand.

"Come on. I'm starving, time for breakfast," and they picked up the bags and went downstairs into the kitchen. "I'll just leave a note for my dad."

The front door banged open.

"Gav is that you?" a voice called out. "Some dickhead has parked right in front of the house again so I've had to park outside number 11. You know what Mrs Hawkins is like. She'll give me a right earful if she sees me....Oh hello."

Gavin had his arms around her, "Evie this is Bethan, my sister. Bethan this is Evie."

Evie held out her hand, "Pleased to meet you."

"Oh you too."

"Sorry about the car. We're just going so it'll be out of your way in a jiffy."

"No problem. Secretly I think Mrs Hawkins likes a bit of banter it's what keeps her going."

"Gavin was telling me you're desperate to join one of my fitness sessions."

"Um well," she hopped from one foot to the other looking at her brother to step in and say something.

"It's okay sis. I told her I made you ring up for me."

Evie smiled. "I'll let you off the hook, it is rather a long way to travel; although I may make your brother do a class instead."

"That's sounds like a much better idea, as long as you work him very, very hard," laughed Bethan.

"Oh you can count on it."

"Okay ladies I know how you girls love to chat but we're off to breakfast."

"Breakfast"! Bethan looked pointedly at the clock, "It's 11.15."

"Well brunch then, better late than never. Now say your goodbyes."

"It was lovely to meet you."

"Yes, you too."

Ten minutes later they walked into a large café holding hands and as soon as Gavin was through the door a female voice rang out. "Alright Gav. The usual, is it?"

"Hi Jackie, can we just grab a menu?"

"Ooh sorry I didn't realise you had company."

"Jackie this is Evie, Evie this is Jackie."

Evie held her hand out, "Pleased to meet you."

Jackie paused for just a split second then shook her hand. "Likewise," she said. "What can I get you tea /coffee.?"

"Um we'll have a look and let you know."

"Right you are. How about two orange juices to be going on with?"

"Yes okay that's fine."

They found a table and sat down, "So this is a regular haunt of yours is it?"

"Yep; best breakfast for 50 miles."

Evie looked at the menu. This could be tricky.

Jackie appeared at their table. "Two orange juices, there we go. So have you decided – usual for you Gav?"

"Yes please."

"How many rounds of toast today?"

"Better make it 5 I need lots of energy for tonight," and he winked at Evie across the table.

"Right you are. And for you?"

"Um, do you have soy or almond milk?"

Jackie's face went blank. "Um no, I don't think so."

"Okay no problem. Can I have a big jug of water and a cup of hot water with some lemon in it please?"

"Just hot water with lemon?"

"Yes like lemon tea but without the teabag."

"Oh okay no problem," she looked puzzled, "and to eat?"

"May I have tomatoes/mushrooms/bacon and one egg scrambled?"

"Just the one egg?" Jackie looked amazed, as if no one had ever asked for just one egg before.

"Please."

"Sausage/ toast?"

"Are they gluten free?"

Jackie looked confused, "Um I don't think so. I'll get Mick to check."

"I'm allergic to wheat, you see."

"Okay I could get some in for you next time if you like? Anything else?"

"Plain yoghurt and fruit would be good."

"Make that two." said Gav.

Julie looked relieved to be back on familiar territory – "Okay coming up."

Evie smiled at Gavin. "I think I nearly gave her a heart attack."

"Yes, not much call for soy and gluten free stuff around here – she looked like you'd asked for a pint of virgins' blood or something?"

They chatted until Gavin said, "So can I ask you a question now?"

"Sure."

"What's the story with the hotel sofa beds?"

"Oh that. Can I tell you when you're eating your whole toasted loaf of bread so there are no interruptions?"

"Okay fair enough." Just then Mick arrived at the table. "Okay tea for you Gav, jug of water, glasses, lemon tea without the tea for the lady and some yoghurt and fruit for two. Mains will be out soon. Sorry Gav hasn't introduced us. I'm Mick."

"Pleased to meet you Mick. I'm Evelyn."

"Sorry about the other stuff. There's not a lot of call for it round here you see, but if you're going to be a regular…?" he left the sentence hanging

"I could always bring some with me next time if that would help and if you wouldn't be offended?"

"No, no offence taken. So you known Gav long then, have you?"

"Bugger off Mick. Stop being so bloody nosy," Gavin laughed

"Okay, okay just making polite conversation," he grinned and went back to the counter."

"Yea right. They like you, you know."

"How can you tell?"

"They would throw out anyone else who brought their own food in here so you've already got special treatment."

They started to eat; the food was very good. Cooked breakfasts appeared soon after. Evie raised her eyebrows at the size of Gavin's meal.

"I'm a growing boy, got to keep my energy up for later." Then he winked at her.

Jackie came back to clear their plates. "More toast is on its way. Are you sure I can't get you anything else?"

"No no, we're fine really."

"Right you are then."

Toast and fresh tea arrived and Gavin said, "Okay, so sofa beds. I'm listening."

She started to explain about Ben and Gavin just listened; but when she got to the bit about it getting a bit rough, he said 'bloody hell'.

"I thought you weren't interrupting?"

"Sorry. Go on."

"So I didn't want to risk being accidentally," she stressed, "kicked again. I decided that the sofa bed would be the safest place. Romantic weekend away a night on the sofa bed at a five-star hotel, then he dumped me the next day– fantastic weekend."

"Sounds grim if you ask me"

"So last night it was me that was all over the place."

"Not your fault. I'll be having words with Spencer later. I think he spiked your water."

"Oh that would explain a lot. So you were fast asleep on the bed and I took your shoes off and wrapped you up in the duvet to keep you warm and took the sofa bed again. There are benefits to being small as it's plenty big enough for me, it just means a bit of a sore back in the morning; but it was beginning to look like déjà vu."

"I can rub your back better later if you like"

She smiled. "We'll see."

"Can I say something now?"

"Sure."

"I don't think these five-star hotels are all they're cracked up to be you know."

"How so?"

"Well just compare the last two romantic" – he used imaginary quotation marks – "weekends away you've just had, one with a drunk and one with an arse. But then compare that to last night and today in a budget hotel – nothing wrong with them, by the way, and you're having way more fun aren't you?"

"Hmm that's true I suppose. But just so you know: I love big rooms with big beds, soft duvets, big showers, huge baths, room service, movies in your jimmie jammies, if it's with the right person it can be wonderful. Plus I figure that if have these things at home then why wouldn't I have then when I stay away?"

"Questions now, why do you need a big bed and bath and shower, you're tiny?"

"Well I like to stretch out and sometimes the sheets get hot (Gavin thought you're not wrong there, desperately hoping to show her just how hot they could get later on that same day), and I can move along to a cool spot again and again, also I like to sleep diagonally if I want to just for the fun of it. As for big baths and showers well if you're at a five star hotel chances are you're not alone so they're really meant for two, aren't they?

Gavin thought about what she had just said, "Hang on a minute, what do you mean, you have these things at home?

"In my bedroom I have a superking-sized bed and in my en-suite I have a big bath and a walk in shower too."

"So all the time we've been sat here eating we could have been at yours trying all this stuff out?" He sounded incredulous.

"Well I think you might be getting a little bit ahead of yourself don't you?"

"Sorry maybe a bit……… but really… You have all that at yours? Cos it sounds fan-bloody-tastic." It sounded great to him, maybe the two of them would try it together soon?

Chapter 85

Gavin suggested a walk in the park, lots of fresh air and sunshine. Walk off all that food then maybe a quick run, back to the hotel and then dinner at the pub. They drove round to the park and she was beginning to realise that nothing was more than 10 minutes away from anywhere else.

"This looks lovely."

He laughed. "You would say that even if it was shit."

Evie blushed. "Well I told you my ex hated me saying 'lovely' all the time and he even bet me I couldn't go a whole day without saying it."

"I've already said he sounds like a dick – sorry – I think it's just very you, somehow."

"Yes I suppose so, and I am a glass half full sort of girl, in fact my glass is nearly always full apart from a teeny tiny space at the top."

"Yeah I'm beginning to realise that and it's another thing I love about you."

Bloody hell! she thought. Big words already.

He took her hand as they strolled in the sunshine idly chatting.

She stopped walking and said, "Shall we sit for a bit?" After a few moments she said, "Can I ask you about baggage?"

"What do you mean?"

"Well when you start a new relationship there's always some baggage that comes along, it's inevitable I suppose?"

"Yes makes sense," (fantastic, she said the relationship word. Gavin was so happy she was coming round to his way of thinking).

"So?"

"So?"

"Seriously Gavin, what baggage do you come with?"

"Can you give me some examples?"

Okay I'll just ask you outright shall I? He nodded. "Well do you have any ex – wives?"

He burst out laughing. "No definitely not."

"How about children?"

"Nope. None of them either."

"Gambling debts?"

"No I have a credit card but pay it off every month."

"Okay then."

"How about you?"

"Well no ex – wives or ex – husbands come to that, no children as you know, no debts, just me, my home and Henry."

"That's a relief!"

"So we're pretty much baggage free?"

"Yep. Looks like it."

She stood up. "Come on let's carry on walking."

They strolled on hand in hand. The park wasn't the most glamourous of locations, but she was beginning to realise that glamour was seriously overrated.

She stopped again. "One more thing I just need to say."

"Another thing?" He joked but she looked deadly serious. "Okay; should I be worried?"

"I don't know; but it's pretty much a deal breaker for me." She pushed her sunnies on to the top of her head and glanced up to look him straight in the eye, "IF we get together and IF I give this a go then if you ever, ever cheat on me then we're done – finished, no talking me round, no second chances, nothing, it's over."

He wrapped his arms around her, "You need to know that I... kiss... would... kiss... Never... Kiss... never ...kiss ...cheat... kiss ...on... kiss ...you," he kissed her passionately and squeezed her bum with his hands.

A lone jogger ran past, "Alright Gav – get a room."

"Piss off Gary. I'm busy," he smirked.

"Do you know everyone around here?"

"Pretty much."

They enjoyed the park and now the sun wasn't so warm – well it was early in the year.

"Come on, let's get changed for a run"

They drove back to the hotel and whilst they got into their gym gear she put some music to play on her phone. Evie changed in the bathroom and left Gavin to change in the bedroom, she needed to keep a clear head.

"So how am I doing so far?" he asked.

"You're doing okay."

He looked mock offended, "Just okay?"

She smiled, "Don't push your luck sunshine. It was nice to meet Jackie and Mick."

"Well you can meet some more friends tonight; although some of them would have been there at the rugby do."

"You do realise I can't actually remember any of their names, don't you?"

"No problem. They only have to remember yours so how hard can that be? Although I can think of other things I would rather be doing right now," he murmured.

"Yes I bet you can," she laughed. "But we're going for a run remember?"

"Oh okay then if we must." He sighed and pretended to look cross.

They crossed the hotel car park and started to jog back towards the park, her strides were quite small. Gavin was a big bloke with big strides and although he wasn't fast it was proving difficult to keep up with him. Once in the park they stopped by a bench. "Do you want to do some stretches?"

"Not really, but I'll watch you of you like" he was grinning now.

"Okay then," and she began her stretches.

Gavin bet her he would reach the bandstand first, winner got to choose their reward. Evie agreed; she was quite fast so maybe it would be close thing.

He said, "On your marks, get set…"

She didn't wait for go but took off. He jogged on behind her. He was going to win this one easily enough, but right now he was enjoying the view of her swinging ponytail and that bum, there should be a law against bums like that. He was desperately hoping he'd get a chance to squeeze it again sooner rather than later too.

Two minutes later he speeded up and passed her easily enough.

Oh bloody hell, she thought. I need some more energy to be able to beat him today.

He got there with time to spare and tapped his watch. "What kept you?"

"Very funny."

He stood behind her whilst she got her breath back bending forward with her hands on her knees.

"God, that's a great view!"

Evie looked up all she could see was an industrial estate in the distance, "Really?"

"Oh yes."

"Oh well. Whatever turns you on I suppose?"

Gavin put his arms around her and swung her round. They were laughing just like kids then he put her down and it was suddenly serious

"You are okay about all this aren't you?"

"You mean the wooing action plan?"

He nodded.

"Surprisingly – yes I think I might be."

"Come on then time to jog back – I'll take it slow just for you."

"Gee thanks; you're all heart. Have you decided on the winner's prize for the bet yet?"

"No. I'm still thinking about that."

They reached the entrance to the hotel car park and slowed to a walk. "Okay then yes, I have decided on your forfeit."

Warily she asked. "What's it to be then?"

"Hang on," he said, "what's that over there?" pointing to something to her right.

She turned round. "What am I looking for?"

"This," he said and without warning he picked her up threw her over his shoulder into a fireman's lift and started to jog towards the reception.

"Gavin put me down," she hissed.

"Nope. I won the bet fair and square."

"I didn't realise this was the deal."

"Stop fidgeting up there, baby bear," he playfully slapped her bum.

"I mean it Gavin. Put me down this minute or so help me I'll I'll…"

"Or you'll what little miss feisty knickers?"

"You'll regret it."

"Don't think so somehow," he murmured. She continued to ask him to put her down just as he continued to ignore it.

He opened the reception door. "Oh hiya, Shaz. How are things?"

"Oh hi Gav. You know, same old same old, you've got your hands full I see?"

"Yep. Never a dull moment with this one I can tell you, a whole heap of trouble."

"I am still here you know – you can see me? I can hear you talking." Evie spoke but no-one answered.

He ignored her. "Say, is your Darren still at that T-shirt place?"

"Yeah why?"

"I got a small job for him that's all I'll call him next week?"

"Fair enough."

"I'm still here." Evie said to no one in particular.

"Calm down. I'm just having a nice chat to Shazzer here. We go way back, I was at school with her brother, you know."

"Fascinating," she hissed.

"Oh," he said. "Where are my manners?" He turned around so she was facing Sharon.

"Evelyn this is Shaz, Shaz this is Evelyn."

"Nice to meet you Sharon," said Evie.

"Yeah you too." Sharon giggled.

Just then the reception door opened and a chap in a suit was standing there with his suitcase. Sharon said, "Checking in sir? I won't keep you a moment."

"Umm yes." He said looking at the scene in front of him.

Evie's face was well and truly red by now and not just from the run. Maybe if she closed her eyes, when she opened them again he would be gone. She tried it but no such luck; he was still standing there. She smiled and politely said hello.

Gavin said. "Right. Can't stand here all day, things to do you know how it is?"

"Bye Shaz."

"See you Gav."

"Say your goodbyes now ladies."

As he walked past. Evelyn smiled at Sharon. "Bye then."

Sharon felt all flustered and turned back to the man in reception. "Now then sir, just the one night was it?" She'd put him in a ground floor room as she suspected there might be some noise from a certain room upstairs that night.

Later on she was idly fanning herself with the company's latest brochure, wondering whether she would make her Darren's favourite for supper, just to see if any of that fireman stuff could rub off on him.

Gavin walked up the stairs and opened the room door. He kicked the door shut and she started to wriggle a lot.

"Okay baby bear. Hold still, I'm putting you down now." He placed her feet on the floor and took a few steps back. She looked really mad and very feisty; it was such a turn on.

"I am so mad," she said. "I don't even know where to begin!"

"Oh I could give you a few pointers," he said smiling at her.

"Don't play smart with me Gavin Johnson! you're in big trouble."

"Yes I was hoping I would be," and he ducked as she threw her hairbrush at him. "Come on little Miss Feisty," he said. "We're all sweaty, time for a shower."

"Don't you little Miss Feisty me." Then she threw one of her trainers at him which he managed to duck away from too, then the other shoe quickly followed.

"You need to do some work on your overarm throw, your aim is terrible," he smirked. He grabbed her hand before she could throw anything else at him and led her into the bathroom she was still all fired up. "Time for a shower to cool off."

"Okay out you go then," she motioned towards the door.

"Really I can't stay?"

"Nope, not after that little stunt you just pulled. Give me ten minutes."

He could hear her muttering out loud. "So annoying, bloody big ego, who does he think he is…so frustrating…how embarrassing….?"

Five minutes later and Gavin couldn't wait any longer. He opened the door, went in, dropped his boxers and pulled back the shower curtain.

"Come on, time's up."

"Are you kidding?" She stood with her back towards him not wanting to turn round.

"Here. Give me the shower stuff and I'll do your back." She passed it behind her and then he began to soap her shoulders and back, his hands moved lower and began to massage her bum. She groaned inwardly; he'd have to stop that soon or she'd be in big trouble. His hands were so big that it was done in no time. "How about the front?"

"No," she squeaked. "I've done that."

"Okay then you can do me," and she shuffled round him letting him stand under the water. She started on his shoulders she could only just about reach and then worked her way methodically down his back.

God, he thought they'd be there all day at this rate and he had plans for the two of them. She carried on down his back over his bum and down his legs, she deliberately skimmed lightly over his inner thigh.

"Okay all done here."

"Good job I've done the front isn't it?"

She stepped out and wrapped herself in a big towel. Gavin followed suit wrapping a towel around his waist and rubbing his hair with a smaller one.

"Now you can help dry me, might as well make yourself useful." She began to dry his back. So far so good; again skimming his inner thigh He dried the front but said, "Oh can you just do my tummy?" Evie stretched her arms around him from the back and began to dry his tummy, going lower past his belly button then stopped.

"Hey you no cutting corners. I think you've missed a bit," so she thought: okay mister, hold on tight; and began to slowly rub his penis with tiny patting motions and then between his legs. She heard him inhale and respond to her touch, but she kept it light and then said, "All done now."

Wrapping the towel around his waist he turned to her. "Okay, your turn now," and began to dry her back. He could see the scars; truth was he'd already seen her back last night when she had been getting ready for bed and she thought he was asleep; although they were unexpected it didn't matter a jot. Carefully he dried her bum and then her legs she kept the towel over her front whilst he did this. Then his arms came round and started to rub gently on top of the towel to dry her shoulders and tummy and her legs. Stretching up he moved closer and gently patted between her legs, she stiffened: oh, so it wasn't just him reacting to her; she felt it too. He moved his hands back up to her breasts and gently eased her hands away and began to massage her breasts through the towel. Suddenly he couldn't wait any longer and pulled her back against him letting her know he was very turned on. She could feel his erection pushing against her bum and she closed her eyes. This was way too soon, but if he didn't stop then ...she swallowed hard. "What are we doing?"

"We're doing what thousands of people do every day," he whispered.

"Yes but I doubt they've only known each other a nanosecond."

Gavin turned her round and put his arms around her and began to kiss her. Evie slid her arms around his neck and he lifted her up against his body. She wrapped her legs around him and then there was just her bath towel between them now as Gavin's towel had been on the floor for some time.

She moaned softly and he took this as permission to use his tongue to explore her mouth with a lot more determination.

Eventually he broke off breathing rapidly now, "Well I think you know what I'd like to do next, but only if you want too?

Evie opened her eyes. "Okay but not in here." With that he carried her out into the bedroom and laid her on the bed. She dived under the duvet leaving the towel on the floor.

"Just so you know, we're going to need a condom," she whispered.

"All taken care of," he said as he began to make love to her. "This is all for you, I'm going to make love to you now okay?"

Evie nodded. Her power of speech had well and truly deserted her. Gavin kissed her all over, her neck, her shoulders, between her breasts, behind her knees her inner elbow absolutely everywhere. When she'd tried to do the same to him he had said, "No this is all for you," and continued where he'd left off. His hands went everywhere, touching every part of her body until neither of them could wait a second longer.

Quite some time later Evie was snuggled into him. That had been lots of things: he was very, very skilled, gentle, passionate and sooo good she smiled to herself; yes, he definitely knew what he was doing in the bedroom department. Gavin had his arms around her. This afternoon had gone much better than he could ever have dreamt it would. Making love to her she'd been shy at first, but they both really wanted it and as she'd reached orgasm he'd been surprised at how noisy she was. That was such a turn on all by itself, he'd come straight afterwards and now they were tangled together enjoying the moment. He was wondering whether to push his luck for round two when she wriggled around and stared at him.

"Thank you."

"What for?"

"You know. For being so unselfish with me, it was lovely." He kissed her again.

"So tell me more about these big beds, big showers and big baths."

Evie moved so she was lying on top of him and whispered. "Well at home I have a very big bed... just for me ...and in my en-suite I have a huge bath ...and walk in shower big enough for two, but.." she looked at Gavin, "I'm not sure now if you're going to fit!"

"There's only one way to find out, so when I come round to cook for you on your birthday will I be using all these things?" He bloody hoped so.

"Maybe, plus you definitely won't fit in the other bathroom."

"So why aren't I at yours with you right now, trying these things?" Gavin sounded very miffed.

"Well I didn't know how this was going to pan out now, did I? Plus it'll give you something to look forward to, now stop talking and kiss me again."

"You're so demanding," Gavin obliged and then wouldn't stop, so he made love to her all over again.

"Come on. Let's get ready to go out."

"Do we have to? we could just stay here you know."

"Nice try Gavin, but going out was actually your idea in the first place so come on let's get a move on." Groaning Gavin got up and Evie put on her underwear. She was in her aqua lace underwear again.

"Do you have a lot of stuff like that?" he asked pointing at her lingerie.

"I certainly do. Why, do you want a private viewing Mr Johnson?"

"You bet your life I do, the sooner the better."

She wriggled into her jeans

"Jesus. Can you please stop doing that?" he said.

"It's the only way to get them on," Evie giggled.

"Yeah right, sure it is."

They dressed for the pub, there was no time for a nap. "Now are we ready to go?" he asked.

"Just got to put on some make up, I'll be 5 minutes."

"Oh that's another ½ hour then."

"No. I told you 5 minutes."

"Look I know you girls you're all the same, Bethan says five minutes and it's more like 25."

Looking at him quizzically Evie asked: "Does your watch have a stopwatch on it?"

"Yes of course."

"Okay well time me, then."

"What's the prize for the winner?" he asked, thinking this is in the bag!

"Anything you like.." She left the sentence hanging and sure enough he took the bait; boys they were so predictable sometimes.

"Anything?" Yes, this was definitely in the bag!

"Yes absolutely anything…"

"Okay then I'll count you in, 3 2 1 go."

She sauntered over to where he was standing. "Excuse me," picked up her hairbrush and brushed her hair before tying it up then put her shoes on.

"This all counts toward the five minutes," he told her.

"I know, I know. I'll keep the bathroom door open so you see there's no cheating going on."

She got out her makeup bag and started applying concealer, eyeshadow, mascara, 2 minutes, brow gel, powder to cream foundation with a big brush, 3 minutes, blusher and then lip-gloss.

She came out, put her jacket on, zipped it up and put the fur trimmed hood up and then picked up her bag. "Ready to go then?"

He'd been had. "You've done that before," he accused her.

"Well yes of course I have." She laughed.

"Okay then so what's the penalty?" he hated losing and was regretting taking the bet in the first place now. But right now she looked exactly like the first time he'd ever seen her when he'd woken up on the pitch and looked into her big brown eyes – his baby bear

"Bend down and I'll whisper it."

"No funny business."

"No. No funny business, I promise."

He bent down and true enough she whispered in his ear. This really was Christmas come early

He grabbed her hand. "Better get going now – sooner we go sooner we're back!"

They arrived at the pub at 6.00. It was quiet this early in the evening, but would get livelier as Wednesday evening went on.

Gavin took her over to where a large group of people were standing chatting. "Hey." They made room for them in the group.

"Everyone, this is Evie. Evie this is everyone."

She smiled back. "Hi everyone."

TEAM EVIE.

Sophia Wallace

Thomas Wallace

David Carter

Fiona Carter

Alice Hunter

Peter Stoddard

Ian Greene

H. C.